the echelon
vendetta

the echelon
vendetta

david stone

G. P. PUTNAM'S SONS | NEW YORK

G. P. PUTNAM'S SONS
Publishers Since 1838
Published by the Penguin Group
Penguin Group (USA) Inc., 375 Hudson Street, New York, New York 10014, U.S.A. •
Penguin Group (Canada), 90 Eglinton Avenue East, Suite 700, Toronto, Ontario M4P 2Y3,
Canada (a division of Pearson Penguin Canada Inc.) • Penguin Books Ltd, 80 Strand, London
WC2R 0RL, England • Penguin Ireland, 25 St Stephen's Green, Dublin 2, Ireland (a division of
Penguin Books Ltd) • Penguin Group (Australia), 250 Camberwell Road, Camberwell, Victoria
3124, Australia (a division of Pearson Australia Group Pty Ltd) • Penguin Books India Pvt Ltd,
11 Community Centre, Panchsheel Park, New Delhi–110 017, India • Penguin Group (NZ),
67 Apollo Drive, Mairangi Bay, Auckland 1310, New Zealand (a division of Pearson New
Zealand Ltd) • Penguin Books (South Africa) (Pty) Ltd, 24 Sturdee Avenue, Rosebank,
Johannesburg 2196, South Africa

Penguin Books Ltd, Registered Offices: 80 Strand, London WC2R 0RL, England

Library of Congress Cataloging-in-Publication Data

Stone, David, date.
    The Echelon vendetta / David Stone.
        p.   cm.
    ISBN-13:   978-0-399-15408-9
    ISBN-10:   0-399-15408-6
  1. Intelligence officers—Crimes against—Fiction.   I. Title.
    PR9199.3.S833E35   2007   2006027013
    813'.54—dc22

Printed in the United States of America
10 9 8 7 6 5 4 3 2 1

Book design by Paula Russell Szafranski

This is a work of fiction. Names, characters, places, and incidents either are the product of the author's imagination or are used fictitiously, and any resemblance to actual persons, living or dead,
businesses, companies, events, or locales is entirely coincidental.
    While the author has made every effort to provide accurate telephone numbers and Internet
addresses at the time of publication, neither the publisher nor the author assumes any responsibility
for errors, or for changes that occur after publication. Further, the publisher does not have any control
over and does not assume any responsibility for author or third-party websites or their content.

for catherine

God created the world,
But it is the Devil who keeps it going.

—TRISTAN BERNARD

the echelon
vendetta

1
friday, august 31
two moon trailer camp
mountain home, idaho
11:59 local time.

at six minutes after midnight everything *changed:* Runciman
sensed it, even in his drunken sleep. He was not alone. There
was a *thing* in the room with him, and an unfamiliar scent drifting
on the stale air, mingling with the tang of cut pine and the rancid
reek of grease from the Arby's across the highway—a sharp biting
scent almost but not quite like eucalyptus. Runciman, his heart
pounding against his rib cage like a boxer working the heavy bag,
snapped fully awake, lying on his back in the damp tangle of his
sheets, staring up at the bars of blue light that rode upon the ceiling
of his trailer, listening so hard to the breathing silence in his room that
his skull began to ache.

He looked carefully to his right and saw a dim manlike figure,
wrapped in a formless darkness. It appeared to be standing in the
middle of the long narrow room. Runciman slid a hand under the
pillow, got his fingers around the grip of an old blue-steel Smith &

Wesson, and rolled off his bed into a crouch on the side away from the shape, the revolver aimed out into the darkness.

The shape in the center of the room did not move.

"You want to die doing this," Runciman said, his harsh voice oddly loud in the silence of the trailer, "you've come to the right place." Out in the humid night an eighteen-wheeler chuffed its air brakes and ground its gears down the falling grade that led into Mountain Home. The shadow in the room did not react to him in any way—if it *was* a shape and not a trick of the light. It seemed to Runciman that whatever *it* was, its attention was elsewhere.

Keeping the muzzle on the center of the dark mass, Runciman fumbled for the bedside lamp and flicked it on. The warm yellow light spilled out into the room, picking out the shabby sofa, the yard-sale furniture, the card table littered with empty beer cans, and the remains of Runciman's takeout Chinese. There was nothing there.

No shape. No shadow. No . . . thing.

He lowered the gun and wiped his sweating face with a shaking hand, steadied himself on the cot, and stood upright, weaving slightly, old joints cracking, head pounding, lips and mouth dry.

He sighed, wiped a hand across his lips, and turned to stumble down the narrow hall into the tiny stainless-steel bathroom, where he set the Smith down on the toilet tank and ran the water into the rusted cistern until the cold made his fingers ache.

He scrubbed his face hard with a threadbare towel that smelled of mildew and spilt beer, braced his hands on the edge of the cistern, and stared into the mirror, seeing the remnants of a once-hard man whose features were now sagging into pouches and lines and seams, like a wax mask melting. He dried his hands on the curtain over the window, sighed, and stepped back out into the hall.

Where a big man stood very close. A tall shadowy shape, a skull with black pits for eyes. The skull-man lifted his open palm up to his lips and blew a cloud of fine pinkish powder into Runciman's face. Runciman caught a fleeting scent of eucalyptus—not *quite* like eucalyptus—before his world cracked wide open.

A pale-green corpse-light poured up through the grates beneath his bare feet and the tin ceiling of his trailer peeled back to reveal a vast cobalt sky marbled with pale glowing mist. Runciman rose up and drifted through this limitless universe, disembodied, pierced through with starlight, his skin burned with the heat of violet suns. He watched, detached, as the thread that held his mind to his body stretched out into a thin golden wire that hummed like a plucked string.

AFTER A LONG, nameless time he came back to this world and was not surprised to find that he was naked and taped to a wooden chair under a bare bulb. In his heart he knew what was about to happen. He had seen this many times before. The only thing new to him was that this time *he* was the naked man taped to the chair, surrounded by darkness.

Just within the small circle of light containing him he saw the silver-tipped toe of a cowboy boot made of some sort of reptile hide, greenish-black, the frayed cuff of black jeans, a long leg rising to a patched knee, a crossed leg on the knee, a leathery hand holding a thin stiletto with a narrow tapering tip. A quicksilver light shimmered along the edge of the blade. A voice, a hoarse whisper, spoke to him from out of the dark:

"You know where you are?"

Runciman, sighing softly, considered the man's question.

"Sure. It's my karma. What goes around comes around."

"And you know what happens next."

"I do. The way you took me, you're no hack. You're a pro. You're street. I figure you're maybe from the Agency, but you might be off the reservation. Maybe not. Somebody's nervous back East, or somebody wants to know something you think I know, or wants to find out if I don't know something I *should* know, or maybe you're just a freelancer come to make me pay for some evil-ass shit you think I did to you or somebody you loved and you're gonna fuck me up so bad I'll be happy to die."

Here Runciman paused, squinting into the glare.

"And you know what, pal? You know what the bulletin is? I really don't give a shit. This night's been coming all my life. I've got spots on my lungs the size of silver dollars, my liver's as hard as a stone crab, and I piss nine times nightly. So I really don't give a rusty fuck about your whiny little beef with me, your sorry-ass problems, whatever they are, however long you been packing them around in your hip pocket like they added up to something real. I got enough of my own. So fuck you. Now, tell me, what was that *fine* shit you blew in my face? That shit was deeply righteous."

"You are in the presence of Goyathlay."

"Goy-AT-lay? Who the hell is he? And who the fuck are *you*, pal? I know you? I think maybe I know you."

"You know me."

Runciman blinked into the light.

"You do sound sorta familiar. I can't quite place the voice."

"You know my name. You know who I used to be."

"Jolly. We're old pals. Hugs all 'round. What can I do for you?"

"Who was the man in the long blue coat?"

"What the fuck does *that* mean?"

"Who was the man in the long blue coat?"

"No idea. Your turn. Where are the snows of yesteryear?"

"Who was the man in the long blue coat?"

"Pal, I really don't know what the *fuck* you're talking about."

"Who was the man in the long blue coat?"

"You're boring me here, man. You gotta narrow it down."

"Trinidad. Nineteen ninety-seven."

"Last year at Marienbad. Next year in Jerusalem."

"Who was the man in the long blue coat?"

"The man in the long blue coat . . . Is that you, Milo? It's not Milo. Man, is that you?"

"Yes. It's Milo."

"Is it? You don't sound like Milo. Tell me something only Milo would know?"

"Huey Longbourne sends his best."

"Huey Longbourne?"

"Talk to me about Trinidad."

"If you're really Milo, you don't need me to tell you about Trinidad. Milo was *there*. Is it really you, Milo? We all thought you were dead. Dead in that freaking storm. We *looked* for you, man. We all did. If this is about *that*, then fucking undo me man, this is all a joke. Where you *been* all this time? Were you in Tularosa? Willard always said you'd be holed up in Tularosa. Milo, is it you? Is it really?

"Who was the man in the long blue coat?"

"Ah Jeez. Hey. Fuck you. You're not really Milo. How you know about Huey Longbourne I have no idea. I guess you hadda cut it outta Milo before you got to me. If you were really Milo, then you'd know. There's nothing I could tell Milo about Trinidad that Milo didn't already know. None of us knew who the man in the long blue coat was. Not Willard. Not Pete or Crucio. Not even Moot. Maybe Bob Cole knew."

"Bob Cole called him Cicero."

"Cicero. *That's* what we called him. His name was Cicero."

"Bob Cole called him Cicero. What was his *real* name?"

"We were never told. And Bob Cole's dead. We *all* called him Cicero. Remember? That's how it works. That's fieldcraft. Nobody knows the cleaner's name on a thing like Trinidad. Everybody has a legend, other names—we *all* did, you skanky freak. That's the way it's always done. Know what, man? I'm through talking to you. You wanna know what happened at Trinidad, go ask somebody else. Ask Barbra Goldhawk, why don't you? See what you get outta that old bucket of grits. I don't like you, pal—I don't like how you do business, I don't like your fancy-ass Hollywood boots with the little silver toe tips like you're some kind of pansy fucking homo-on-the-range fairy, and I'm not telling you shit. So it's howdy-go-bye-bye time, Hop along. Let's get her done. Either unass my AO or start in cutting."

"Who was the man in the long blue coat?"

"Even if I knew I wouldn't tell a Jody like you. Lock and load."

The man stood and stepped into the light. Runciman looked at him, at the man's face, at what was in it, and he knew that he had come to the final hours of his life. The first cuts were not the deepest.

2

sunday, october 7
via berrettini, cortona, tuscany
7:30 a.m. local time

d uring the night a heavy fog had gathered around the ruined
Medici fortress on the crest of Cortona and spread itself down
through the ancient city. By early morning the squares and towers
and narrow medieval streets were shrouded in mist, and a cold slanting rain was beating against the shuttered houses along the Via Berrettini. Beyond the shoulder of the young policeman in front of
him Dalton could just make out the image of another man in a
trench coat, looking down the narrow lane at them as they made
their way up the hill. The man, his face partially hidden under a wide-
brimmed black fedora, was standing by the iron gate that led into
the stone-walled courtyard of the ancient Roman chapel of San
Nicolò. Dalton got the impression of an angular jaw, a large gray
mustache like an inverted crescent, lined and haggard cheeks. A cigarillo drooped from the corner of his mouth and his hands were

shoved into the pockets of his coat, his collar turned up against the rain and the wind.

The column of men escorting Dalton up the hill passed an open laneway, and glancing to his right, Dalton saw through a curtain of dripping laundry the stone parapet that ran beside Via Santa Margherita: beyond the parapet he could see the faint outline of Lake Trasimeno. A memory came to him of a summer afternoon and the sunlit terrace off the Piazza Garibaldi, where he and Laura had once sat watching the cloud shadows drift across the olive groves far below them, the lake in the distance glimmering in a pure southern light. They had talked of Hannibal and Rome and the Etruscans while they shared a bottle of chilled pinot grigio, well pleased with the day, with Tuscany, with each other.

The memory had only half-formed when he shut his mind against it, concentrating instead on the rain beading up on the navy blue tunic of the carabiniere in front of him, on the rounded old stones beneath his shoes, on the graveyard reek of the running gutters, the damp-wool smell of the rain itself. In a few more minutes they reached the chapel gates. The senior carabiniere—a dark-skinned man with craggy Sicilian features whose difficult name Dalton had heard but not retained—snapped out a tight salute, to which the trench-coated man returned an ironic bow.

"*Ecco 'inglese, Commendatore. Il Signor Dalton.*"

"*Sì.* Mr. Micah Dalton," said the man in the trench coat, stepping toward Dalton, his right hand out. He shook Dalton's hand once, twice, a firm dry grip, strong lean fingers. His regard was direct, penetrating, but not unfriendly. He had the air of a man who was willing to be favorably impressed. His smile was wide and revealed strong yellowish teeth. He had a gap between his upper middle incisors, and deep brown eyes with a clear light in them. Dalton, whose trade required him to make rapid assessments of everyone he met, put him down as smart, professional, experienced, and therefore dangerous. The man's voice was a baritone purr, and he had a cold.

"I am Major Alessio Brancati. I am the chief of the Carabinieri criminal division for Cortona. We thank you for coming."

"Good morning, Major Brancati," said Dalton, trying not to look beyond the major's left shoulder, where he could see that a black nylon crime scene tent had been set up against the doors of the chapel.

Brancati's lined and weathered face broke into a wry smile.

"This morning is not so good. Rain, and this wet wind from the north. It sinks into your lungs. This fog. A terrible morning. I offer you a cigar?"

He held out a crumpled packet of Toscanos. Dalton saw there were only two left. The major pulled his shoulders up in a very Italian way and grinned fiercely at him. "Take! You will help me to quit."

Dalton took one and the major held out a very worn and apparently solid-gold lighter with the crest of the Carabinieri engraved on its face. Dalton drew the smoke in deep. The major seemed to approve of his obvious pleasure in this. Dalton looked past the man at the crime-scene tent. Rain drops beaded on the slick surface and pooled in the sagging folds. Two glum-looking boys in sodden police uniforms stood on either side of the tent, which had been zippered shut against the rain. A blue-and-red police tape with the words *Polizia non passar—Polizia non passare* had been stretched across the heavy wooden doors of the chapel. On a bench by the chapel gates an old man in an ill-cut tweed jacket and brown corduroy slacks sat limply, staring into nowhere, fingering a green-glass rosary, his eyes as dull as quartz. A tall athletic-looking young man in a black suit and a clerical collar stood next to him, staring at Dalton with a fixed intensity. The priest, if that was what he was, had a sharp-featured, almost brutal face.

"May I ask," said Dalton, looking away from the priest's disconcerting glare and exhaling a blue cloud of smoke, "who that man is? The priest."

"That is Father Jacopo. He is the pastor of this chapel."

"He looks like an assassin. What's his problem with me?"

Brancati shrugged and pulled the edges of his mouth into an exaggerated downward curve, making him look briefly like a Venetian mask.

"He has some belief about you. It is of no importance. Superstition may be found even among the educated. I thank you for coming all the way to Cortona."

"I was grateful for the call. I do wonder why the identification could not be done at the hospital."

Brancati lit his last cigarillo and dismissed the Sicilian carabiniere with a nod while he considered Dalton's question. The other men drifted away and began to talk in low tones, their voices lost in the sighing of the wind.

"This is true. Normally we do not let civilians into the crime scene, but the formal identity must be made soon and Father Jacopo"—here he inclined his head in the direction of the tall man in the black suit, who returned his look without warmth—"wishes the body not to be moved until he can give a kind of blessing. *Il vecchio* with him, that is Paolo. The verger. He is the one who found the body. You are Catholic?"

The question—unexpected, and for Dalton a very pointed and painful one—made him flinch visibly.

"No. I was once. Not any more."

Brancati smiled apologetically. "I am sorry. A personal question. But you are like me. We are the *new* Holy Roman Church. The not-any-more Catholics. *Allora*, Father Jacopo is here for the chapel. Paolo wishes him to say some prayers for the release of spirits from this place. Before he will open up San Nicolò to the people again. Paolo is very superstitious."

"Spirits?"

Brancati sighed, raised his palms. "Myself, I am from Sansepolcro, a town famous for death. But these Cortona people. They are not like the rest of Tuscany. Cortona folk believe that ghosts fly around the mountaintop like clouds of swifts. They think the old *fortezza* is crowded with spirits that clutch at you as you pass, hissing spells and curses in your ears. Three thousand years they make here a cult of the dead. The whole mountain is a tomb. The Etruscans built it. The Carthaginians besieged it. Then came the Romans. Then the Medici. One cannot resist the weight, the force of such ancient customs. We do not try. Paolo believes the people need the priest to release the chapel. So the priest will say some words. Paolo will be happy. The parishioners will be happy. No harm is done. Tell me, Mister Dalton, how do you come to know the victim?"

"I'm not sure I do know him. I haven't seen him yet."

Brancati pulled an English passport out of his breast pocket. He handed it to Dalton. Dalton flipped it open, looked at the photo.

"This was with him?"

"No. It was in his room."

"He was staying at a hotel here?"

Brancati's expression grew more guarded. His reply was short.

"No. In a student hostel. The Strega. On Via Janelli. Down by the Palazzo Comunale."

Dalton handed the passport back to Brancati. "That's Porter Naumann's passport, anyway."

"And how do you know Mr. Naumann, Signor Dalton?"

"We are both employees of the same company."

"And that is . . ."

"Burke and Single."

"The British bank?"

"Yes."

"So you are in Italy on business?"

It begins.

"No. I was in Berlin on business. My company called me because I was closest to Italy. Actually, we were looking for Mr. Naumann ourselves. He had not been in touch with his office for hours. He had missed an important client meeting yesterday. We were making inquiries. Then you found him. They sent me. I flew in a few hours ago."

"Flew in on what?"

"Burke and Single operate a small fleet of Gulfstream jets."

"How pleasant to be rich. And this Gulfstream jet landed where?"

"Florence."

Brancati smiled at him. Dalton did not return the smile. Nor did he fill the silence with elaborations on the theme. The truth was he had spent two hours last night going through Porter Naumann's hotel suite in Venice before taking the company chopper down to Florence, but the wonderful thing about private jets and private helicopters was that you didn't have to file detailed flight plans. You could touch and go and most of the time, especially in Italy, the records would be inaccurate. And it was true that the company jet *had* landed in Florence a few hours ago; Dalton hadn't been on it. It offended his sense of professionalism to tell this paper-thin excuse for a lie, but there hadn't been enough time to prepare a more substantial one. Brancati let the silence play out enough to become obvious. That didn't mean he knew Dalton was lying. It was a device that Dalton knew well, since he often used it himself. Guilty people hated empty silences and tended to fill them up with self-defeating babble.

"And do you know what brought Mr. Naumann to Italy?"

"The bank has been building a funding infrastructure for a Chinese trading syndicate seeking a branch in Venice. Naumann is a specialist in international trade. Last time I saw him was two weeks ago. He and I had dinner at a café on the Riva degli Schiavoni. We talked business."

"Burke and Single is a British bank. You are American, I think."

Another flinch, but this time he managed to suppress it. The line *"a hit, a palpable hit"* rose in the back of his mind, and for a moment he wondered how much Brancati actually knew about him.

Nothing, he decided.

"I was born in Boston. I'm not an American citizen any more. I'm a British subject. I haven't been an American citizen for several years."

"But you are from Boston? Good. I approve of Boston. In Boston the streets make Italian sense. A perfect assassin's tangle, just like in Florence. You know what Vespa means in Italian? It means 'wasp.' Florence is a stone hive buzzing with wasps. It is made for love affairs. Have you ever tried to follow someone in Florence? In Naples, even, or in Venice? It cannot be done. This is deliberate. This is the Italian way. I was also in Washington—"

"Where the streets do not make Italian sense?"

"A Frenchman did them. It's the only thing they can do well. They make straight streets. Perhaps the French are afraid of being followed. God knows why. They never go anywhere interesting and they make love with their faces. They are a crazy people. Napoleon made them crazy. Which café?"

"I beg your pardon?"

"On the Riva degli Schiavoni. Where you had dinner with your friend two weeks ago. What was it called?"

"Carovita."

"I know this café. Wonderful risotto. The owners, not so nice. But the food—*perfetto*. And you stayed . . . how long?"

"Until the bell in the campanile rang at midnight. Porter wanted to walk. He liked Venice best late at night. I went back to our hotel."

"The Savoia, yes?"

"Yes. Burke and Single keeps a suite there."

"Why not at the Danieli? It's right next door."

"Have you ever stayed there?"

"Yes. Very tired. Although once a beauty."

"Yes. That's why."

"And Mr. Naumann?"

"The same hotel. Savoia e Jolanda. The company suite. It belongs to Mr. Naumann. Occasionally I stay there, if I'm in town."

"How long was Mr. Naumann assigned to Venice?"

"As long as it took. He's been there since August."

"Has he a family?"

"Yes. In London. A wife. Two teenaged daughters. They have a town house in Belgravia."

"You have spoken to them? Your firm?"

"Not yet. We wanted to . . . know more."

There was a silence. Dalton thought about Porter Naumann's wife and kids. The teenagers were a pair of hard-eyed foulmouthed club girls, pale-skinned, blue-lipped, with crystal meth sizzling through their veins. It wouldn't have surprised Dalton to find out they slept hanging upside down in a belfry. Joanne Naumann, once a Wellesley stunner, cordially loathed the little thugs and passed her days getting herself gracefully outside Baccarat flutes of Cristal. Brancati, who had been quietly turning the problem of Micah Dalton over in his mind, seemed finally to arrive at a decision.

"*Allora,* Signor Dalton. I tell you what we have learned. We have made our inquiries, as the English say. Mr. Naumann liked this Carovita café, because his credit card says he had dinner there again the night before last. The owner says he dined alone. He did not go back to his room at the Savoia e Jolanda that night. So after his dinner at Carovita, Mr. Naumann disappears. Yesterday morning he pays cash for a room in the Strega hostel on Via Janelli and does not identify himself. Now the puzzle. Something terrible takes place. What, we do not yet know. The verger finds him here."

Dalton said nothing.

Brancati's smile became a centimeter less warm.

"Maybe you can think of some useful observations?"

"I have nothing to suggest."

"Anything would be welcome. Please. Try."

Dalton pretended to try. He had no intention of saying anything useful about Porter Naumann's life and times. That wasn't his job.

"I'm sorry. Nothing in Porter's life explains any of this. Have you looked at his room in this hostel?"

"We have."

"And?"

"And it reveals little. Mr. Naumann bought a bottle of Chianti and some cigarillos. He smoked the cigarillos and drank the Chianti and slept on top of the bed. At one point he smashed an old pot filled with morning glories, and then he made a fire in the wastepaper basket—"

"He started a fire?"

"Yes. It set off the smoke alarm. The clerk went up. Mr. Naumann did not open the door. He said it was only a cigarette. He was very apologetic. The clerk went away."

"He broke a flowerpot?"

"Yes. It was full of morning glories. My wife, Luna, calls them moonflowers. She loves them because they are nocturnal, as she is. They flower only at night. They were in one of those tall round *cilindri*, like you put would put white wine bottles into. Terra-cotta. To keep them cool."

"Was anybody with him?"

"As I said, Mr. Naumann did not open the door, so the clerk

could not see. Mr. Naumann made no calls and received no calls. The girls in the next room heard some talking. The walls are very thin. They heard two people, a man's voice, very low, and another. A conversation. Not angry. The second person they said had a strange voice. They cannot recall what time."

"Strange? What does that mean?"

Brancati made a face, drew on his cigarillo.

"They said it was droning, like a bee. But very loud. Neither male nor female. More . . . *come si dice*? Like a bear growls?"

"Guttural?"

"Guttural? What an ugly word. But that is what they said."

"But it means someone was in the room with Porter?"

"According to the clerk, who guards the door all night, no one came in to see him. The hostel has many young girls there and they keep order because of it. Guests are always observed and announced. No one came for him. Therefore we must assume that Mr. Naumann was alone."

"What? Talking to himself?"

Brancati shrugged.

"Unless it was someone who was already in the hostel."

"The guests have been interviewed. Mr. Naumann would have had nothing to say to any of them. They are all these traveling *blatte*. These cockroaches. Americans. Canadians. Swedes. These *backpackers*." Brancati made the phrase sound like a risky sexual deviance.

"Did this desk clerk see Porter leave?"

"He says he did not."

"I don't believe him."

"He is a reliable man, a cousin to one of my men. It is a puzzle."

"Damn straight it's a puzzle. Somebody's lying to you. On what floor was Porter's room?"

"The third."

"Was there a fire escape? Outside stairs?"

"Fire escape? The buildings on Via Janelli are the oldest in Cortona. From the twelfth century. They do not have these 'fire escapes.'"

"Then how did he get out?"

Brancati shrugged again, palms raised as if in divine supplication. "We do not know."

"On the face of it, if I were you, I'd take that desk clerk apart and I'd talk to everyone who was in that hostel. Somebody is lying."

Brancati studied Dalton's face for a time. Young, late thirties, perhaps as old as forty; tall, slightly tanned, with long white-blond hair swept back from his forehead like a Renaissance princeling. He had the scarred face of a gentleman boxer, with strong nose knocked slightly out of true and flattened at the bridge; a hard, fit frame under his blue cashmere topcoat and his dark gray pinstripe, his pristine collar and the gold bar under his pearl-gray silk tie.

His pale, almost colorless eyes were wide-set. There was something in his face that was not quite right, as if it had been badly damaged, perhaps in an accident, and then expensively repaired by someone who was an artist at the work. Dalton waited out the appraisal in an uneasy silence.

"You interest me, Signor Dalton. Were you ever in the military?"

"Never."

"*Polizia,* maybe? Or the government?"

Dalton shook his head.

"I would not take you for a banker. Maybe a fencer. Do you fence, Signor Dalton? In the army, I was a fencing instructor. You have the eye."

"No. I box a little. I don't fence."

"You ask good police questions, Signor Dalton. For a banker."

"Thank you."

"You think well. You ask clear questions, like a policeman would.

You are observant and intelligent. You are his friend, his colleague. You meet for drinks and dinner. You know his family. And yet you tell me you have no idea why he would leave his suite at the hotel, leave all his clothes, even his shaving things, all his papers save his passport, and drive down to Cortona to hide himself in a student hostel on the Via Janelli? Then to come up here and die in this outrageous way in the courtyard of San Nicolò? Do you not even wonder about such things?"

"Of course I do. So what? I have no standing. These are your problems. We'll let you handle them. Naturally we'll provide whatever assistance you require. But our policy in situations such as this is to leave the inquiries to the professionals."

"Burke and Single has a policy about employees who die like this?"

"No. It's a policy about not interfering with official investigations."

Brancati looked as if he had more to say and then decided not to say it.

"Okay. *Basta*. Time is running. Come with me. We will do this."

A rising wind was whipping the material of the tent and a cold rain lashed at their faces as they crossed the gravel courtyard. Father Jacopo stepped into their path as they walked, gently brushing aside Brancati's intervening arm, his dark face fixed on Dalton.

"You are Micah Dalton?"

"I am."

"You must forgive me. I have something to say to you. I do not mean to offend. It may sound ridiculous. *Ma* . . . It *is* ridiculous. But Paolo has begged me to speak to you. You will permit?"

"Please, Father."

"Paolo says you stand in darkness, Signor Dalton. Paolo says a man calls for you along the Via Margherita. Paolo wants me to say that if you see this man or hear him call out to you, you should turn away. He says this man is a ghost, a spirit, and he has been standing there for almost a full year now. Paolo says the ghost has been calling out a name. The name of an *inglese*. The name Paolo heard was Micah. I know this is absurd. But when Paolo heard your name from the police, heard that you were coming here, he came to me and told me. I said this is godless. Mere superstition. But Paolo was determined. So I felt I should say something. And this I have done. Forgive my intrusion. You are going into the tent now. To see your dead friend. May I give you the blessing of Our Lady?"

Dalton glanced at Brancati, whose face was unreadable. "I would be grateful, Father."

The priest made the sign of the cross in the air between them, uttered a few unintelligible words in low but sacred tones, and then held out his hand, his face solemn, his dark eyes intense.

"I wish you grace, Signor Dalton. If you wish to confess later, I will open the *chiesa* and hear you. Good bye, now. God be with you."

The priest withdrew, and after a long silence—puzzled and vaguely uneasy on Dalton's part, simply exasperated for Brancati—the major reached out, unzipped the closure, and pulled the flap back. Then he stood aside and opened it to Dalton.

Dalton stepped into the tent, and Brancati followed him inside, moving around what was on the ground in front of them until he could watch Dalton's face. Dalton looked at the figure on the ground, its back up against the heavy wooden doors of the chapel; it took a while to make sense of what he was seeing. When he finally put it together with the smell of fresh blood and intestinal fluids, a rush of hot acid flowed up into the back of his throat and a chilly sweat came out on his cheeks. He swallowed with difficulty and opened his mouth to take in shallow breaths so the smell wouldn't overpower him. He swallowed twice more and shoved his hands into the pockets of his Burberry coat. Brancati said nothing for a time and then crouched down beside the body, pulling on a pair of latex gloves.

"This person has been very badly damaged. As you see. So it is very hard to make the identity. I regret asking this, but you must try."

Brancati pulled out a Streamlight and shone the beam directly onto what remained of the face. Dalton had to make himself concentrate on seeing any remnant of an old and familiar friend in shredded flesh and torn muscle, in a face that was no longer being ruled by the mind and the emotions that had made it live. Even a death mask has a shadow of the living spirit in it; this was barely human.

"Yes," he said, after a minute. "That's him."

"You must name him, Signor Dalton. For the record."

"That's Porter Naumann."

"You're sure."

"I think so. Yes. I'm sure. What . . . ?"

"What happened to him? We think he came up here wearing only what you see, the bottom of his . . ." Brancati hunted the word.

"Pajamas."

"Yes. Pajamas. And barefoot. Look here." He indicated the soles of the corpse's feet, where the flesh was torn and bruised. "He ran all the way from the hostel, it seems. People on the Via Berrettini say they heard a man running last night. Around midnight. They heard him saying something. But not screaming. More like a prayer, or simply talking out loud. But it was raining very hard. No one went to the balcony to look. Bits of the gravel outside we find also in the skin of his feet. See, here, he fell once at least. You see the gashes on the palms. He fell hard onto the gravel. He gets up, stumbles, finally he reaches the doors of the *cappella*."

Brancati aimed the light at the wooden doors of the chapel.

"See here the marks. His palms were bloody and he struck the doors. Several times, from the smears here . . . and here . . . struck them hard."

"No one heard?"

"Paolo lives two streets away. And the wind was high all night.

The rain washed a lot of things away. Anyway, so far, no one has come to us."

"Do they know? The people around?"

Brancati gave him a disdainful look. "The whole of Cortona knows. Cortona is not Napoli."

"What happened to his belly?"

Brancati sighed. "It is speculation only. But we think maybe the dogs."

"Dogs? Dogs chased him up here and killed him? Jesus Christ. What kind of dogs do you have in Cortona? Werewolves?"

"All dogs are carnivores."

"His guts have been torn completely out. No poodle did that."

"No. But the town dogs—many are half-wild. They breed in the *fortezza* above the town. They would have smelled this in the wind."

"So the dogs killed him? Is that it?"

"No. That is not possible. He was dead before the dogs found him."

"How do you know?"

"The wounds. Men don't bleed after death. If you look at the way he sits, his back against the doors, his ankles crossed so, his knees spread, this is not the position of a man fighting off dogs. And when dogs kill they do it at the throat, at the head, and at the tendons in the legs. The belly they open afterward. After he was dead. It is natural. The scent would bring them."

Dalton felt the acid rising again. His vision blurred and he swallowed it down again with difficulty. Brancati's sympathetic look was unconvincing.

"You wish to go now, Mr. Dalton?"

"Is there anything else?"

"Yes. There is. If you are all right?"

"I am."

"You tell me Mr. Naumann was a banker, yes?"

"A lawyer, actually. His brief was international trade."

"Never a soldier?"

"No."

"You're sure?"

"I've known him for eight years. Ever since I came to work at Burke and Single. He was one of my first trainers. He would have mentioned it."

"Trainers? Bankers have trainers?"

"Instructors. A mentor."

"A mentor. I see."

Brancati pointed the flashlight to an irregular row of coin-shaped lesions across Naumann's right hip. "Okay. These are bullet wounds. Not recent. But not that old either. Not many years. And this . . ." He indicated Naumann's left shoulder. "This is a scar like one gets from a knife. A big knife. It is quite recent. No more than a year old. And he was a very active man. Very strong. See the musculature of the chest and the arms. Here on his left pectoral he once had a small tattoo. It has been partially removed with a laser, but you can see it was once in the shape of a helicopter with spread wings behind it. Do you know it?"

Dalton shook his head and internally damned the Agency medics. Brancati waited for something more, realized that nothing was immediately forthcoming, shrugged, and continued.

"Well, I may know this tattoo. We are military, we Carabinieri. Many years ago, when I was a young man, we took part in a military exercise with some American forces. The tattoo of a helicopter with wings signifies Air Assault training in the U.S. Army. Look at his hands. He has the kind of calluses on his hands that you also have. I have seen these before. I recognize them. They come from a long practice of the martial arts. So, very strange for a banker whose entry visa says he is fifty-two years old. Bullet holes. Tattoos. Knife scars. Mr. Dalton, are your office parties so dangerous? Do the ambulances stand by?"

Dalton didn't laugh. "I can't tell what those wounds are. They could be cigarette burns. I have no idea how he came by a knife scar. About the tattoo, many men come to regret the tattoos they get when they're young and stupid."

"Like you? A banker only. Never a soldier?"

Dalton shook his head.

Brancati got to his feet, groaning with the effort.

"I don't think you will say yes if I ask you to take off your shirt?"

"No. I won't."

Brancati raised his hands, smiled again. "A joke. Otherwise it is all too dark, too *sfumato*."

"A joke. Great. But somebody killed him? Right?"

Brancati's face altered again, hardened. "Possibly. Possibly not."

"But you said he was running from someone."

"I said he was running. I did not say that he was being chased."

"For Christ's sake, Brancati. Look at him."

"I have."

"What killed him? If not the dogs, then what?"

"Look at his hands, Mr. Dalton."

Dalton leaned down. Brancati shone the narrow beam of the Streamlight onto Naumann's lap, where his hands lay palms-up in the bubble-and-squeak of his opened belly. The tips of his fingers were shredded and pulpy.

"Someone has pulled out his fingernails."

"No. They are just full of blood and flesh. Only two are gone. We found them. In the muscles of his face and in his throat."

It took Dalton a while to get the picture.

"You're saying he committed suicide by . . ."

"Tearing at himself?"

"Do you believe it?"

"I do not *wish* to believe it. I am too fond of my sleep."

"But do you?"

"I believe that he has been hurt by his own hands. Whether or not this means he committed suicide is another question. He may have been under the influence of some delusion. Temporary insanity. Perhaps a drug."

"Porter didn't do drugs."

Brancati performed an ironic bow, his face impassive. "Maybe. Maybe not. We will do the blood work. Perhaps he was in the grip of a psychotic event. What they sometimes call a 'fugue.' Or there is some lesion of the brain. Such facial disfigurement is not unknown. Several years ago a young girl of Cortona who was suffering from paranoid schizophrenia used poultry scissors to slice off her nose, her cheeks, her ears . . ."

"A man would have to be insane to do something like that."

"And was Mr. Naumann insane? Did he have psychological problems? Was he seeing a therapist, or on any kind of medication?"

"No. At least . . . No. If he had a problem, someone at the bank would have known about it."

"What kind of man was he, Mr. Dalton?"

"Competent. Skilled. A professional. He had a hell of a sense of humor. He liked to eat and drink. Liked the women. He was a gentleman. He danced. Badly, but with joy. Played the trumpet. Played it well. As good as Harry James, when he had enough scotch in him. He used to do 'Cherry Pink and'—"

Looking at Brancati's slightly alarmed expression, Dalton realized he was getting a little emotional. He had liked Porter Naumann very much in a professional sort of way, and the manner of his dying was going to sink in deep and stay there for a long time. Brancati sensed the strong emotion in Dalton and said nothing. There was tight silence in the tent. In a moment, Dalton spoke again.

"So your theory is that he killed himself with his own hands?"

Brancati shook his head slowly, looking doubtful. "He tore at himself, yes. But his heart killed him."

"Loss of blood? Shock? Catastrophic pressure drop?"

Brancati shrugged.

"Shock perhaps. He still has much of his blood inside him. The work of his hands may have only taken a few seconds. No damage was done to the carotids, the heart, the lungs. The belly, I cannot say. But even if the dogs came before he was dead . . . Men die from being disemboweled, but it takes a very long time. That is why it was so popular with the Inquisition. Many men have survived even such wounds. It can take hours for a man with wounds such as these to die. But Mr. Naumann died almost at once. I am no specialist, but I believe something stopped his heart."

"Like what?"

Brancati shrugged. "For a man to tear at himself this way, and for his heart to stop . . . It seems possible that he was in a state of great fear. Perhaps a hallucination. That is the only answer I can think of. Some kind of drug. A powerful psychotropic drug. In rare cases, this is the kind of thing you see when things go very bad. A terrible hallucination could make a man tear at himself, and some people have been known to die from fear. Not often. But it is known."

"I've told you. Porter Naumann didn't take drugs. Nor was he insane."

"As far as you know. There may be much about Mr. Naumann that you do not know. For instance, whether or not he had been a soldier."

"You're saying this was a suicide? Is that it?"

"Technically, no. I do not believe it was suicide. Under our laws, for it to be self-murder, the man must have been in his right mind. Clearly Mr. Naumann was not. When one dies as a result of a drug overdose—"

"He didn't—"

"—do drugs. As you keep reminding me. But if, and I say only if, drugs played a part here, or even a passing madness, then there is no intent. No culpability. It is a death by misadventure. By accident. You understand? Was Mr. Naumann a Christian man?"

"Christian? Yes, he was. At least, he was an Episcopalian. That may not be the same thing as being a Christian."

"And what is this 'Episcopalian' faith?"

"Like an Anglican. High Anglican. Church of England."

Brancati smiled, savoring the new word. "An Episcopalian. Still, a Christian. So here is the important point. If we can say he was not a suicide, then it is still possible for Mr. Naumann to be buried in consecrated ground. To go to his Episcopalian heaven. Otherwise . . ."

Brancati made a vee of his joined hands and pointed to the ground.

To hell.

"Is that where this case is going?"

Brancati made a broad gesture, taking in the ruined corpse, the wooden gates with the bloody palm smears, the wind-rippled tent walls.

"What brings a sane man to this terrible end? There is no sign of any other party involved—"

"What about the second voice? The droning voice like a bear? The girls in the hostel heard two voices. Someone was with him."

Brancati shook his head slowly, his expression sympathetic. "The clerk at the Strega is certain no one came in. And I have told you already that he is a reliable man, and known to us. The hostel has many pretty young college girls, tourists, travelers. The management intends that nothing bad shall happen to these silly children while they are staying at the Strega. You have to buzz at the barred gate to get in. Also there is a camera, which we are told showed nothing unusual. The testimony of the clerk is clear. Other than a nursing sister who went to see one of the girls, nobody went in or out. Mr. Naumann had no visitors. He was alone in his room."

"This clerk, he never left his post? Not once?"

"There is a small privy off the reception area. He of course made use of this from time to time. He admits this. But he insists that he saw no stranger arrive, no one he did not recognize. He is a reliable man."

"Someone who was already inside the hostel, then."

"We've discussed that. In these matters, I am sorry to say, it is often true that the most simple explanation is also the correct one. I believe Mr. Naumann died in the middle of some kind of psychotic episode. Perhaps triggered by a powerful drug. How else could a man come to this?"

Dalton could think of no other answer. A sudden blast of wind rattled the tent walls and rain pattered against the roof. Brancati pulled his collar up around his neck.

"Enough, Mr. Dalton. We will interrogate the hostel clerk, as you suggest. We will interview the residents again. We will be vigorous. *Allegro vigoroso*. On Mr. Naumann, blood tests will be done. Eventually we will get our answers and we will both have to live with them. Let us come away. We will get the blood off our shoes and the stink of this place out of our noses. And maybe we will sit in a nice warm café and talk a little more about Porter Naumann."

"I would like to come along. Observe."

"I thought your policy was to let the officials conduct the investigations? Now you want to . . . observe?"

"I put it badly. I'm asking permission to come along and do whatever I can to help in the investigation. I'd like to see his room at the hostel. I know this is irregular—"

"It is ridiculous. And you tell me you are only a banker."

"But if you come across something anomalous—"

"*Come? Non capisco.*"

"Something that doesn't fit with Porter's life. I'll know it."

Brancati's face showed a stony kind of amusement.

"Anomalous? Perhaps. But when you know it, will you tell *me*?"

"You have my word on it."

"The word of a banker is not the word of a soldier."

Brancati's hard eyes were on him, but Dalton had nothing to say.

3

monday, october 8
riva degli schiavoni, venice
11:00 a.m. local time

dalton was sitting at the sunlit café outside the Savoia & Jolanda, his coat pulled tight against a biting wind off the Adriatic, a glass of *vino bianco* at his left hand and a Toscano cigarillo in his right, watching a long-legged, tight-skirted, black-haired young tour guide striding briskly east along the stone quay of the Riva. The girl was holding aloft a large plastic daisy taped to the end of a pool cue. She had a gaggle of elderly Hindu tourists waddling along behind her and absolutely mystical thighs. Dalton, who hadn't had sex in years, watched her passing with cool clinical detachment. No doubt they were headed for the Piazza San Marco, where they would pose with verminous pigeons on their heads and more verminous pigeons on their outstretched arms. Beyond the shuffling column of tourists the great basin of Saint Mark was busy with droning work boats and burbling mahogany cruisers. A lemon-yellow sun glittered on the churning surface of the green water, filling the basin with a clean, pure light. Across the basin the Palladian façade of San Giorgio Maggiore glowed with the pale pastel tints of fall in Venice. Rain was gathering in the east. Winter was coming in low out of the rising sun; he could feel its breath on the side of his neck. The tour guide was using a bullhorn to bellow something brightly misinformative about the Bridge of Sighs when the cell phone on the linen-covered tabletop shrilled at him.

"Micah Dalton."

"Micah. Stallworth. What did you get?"

Jack Stallworth, the section chief of Dalton's Cleaners Unit out of Langley. Stallworth was a great intelligence tactician, but he was also a short, sharp, bullet-headed hard-nosed razorback hog with all the languid charm of a quick knee to the jaw.

"Jack. *Lovely* to hear from you. How *are* you?"

"Forget that butterscotch bullshit, Micah. How bad is it?"

"I went through his rooms before they got there."

"I know that. And . . . ?"

"And we're okay. I sent you a memo."

"I got the memo. I need reassurances. No company stuff? No records, papers—nothing that caught your attention?"

"You have something specific in mind, Jack?"

"No. *Specific?* Hell no. Specific! Why ask me that?"

"No reason. You sound worried. Anything I should know?"

"No. Not a thing. But you're sure he's clean. You didn't miss anything? You went through it all and nothing stood out?"

"Naumann was a pro, Jack."

"Yeah. He was. And you went in low? If they figure out you went through his room before his body was found? That's heat, Micah. Heavy heat."

"You mean serious. Or major. Not heavy."

"Serious what? Major what?"

"You can't have heavy heat."

"Don't jerk me around, Micah, I'm not in the mood."

"If I'd been made, Brancati wouldn't have let me leave Cortona."

"What about this hostel Naumann stayed in? In Cortona? The Strega?"

"I tried to get a look at it again last night. They've got two cops on the entrance. I can't get anywhere near it until they release it."

"And when will that be?"

"Tomorrow, I think."

"You in Venice now?"

"Yes."

"Why not wait in Cortona?"

"Brancati. The cop. He wanted me to go. I went."

"Why did he want you to get out of Cortona?"

"I made the mistake of asking him if I could help out."

There was plenty of dead air in his earpiece now, so he managed a quick pull at his wineglass. He even had time to light another cigarette.

"You did *what*?"

"Yeah. I know. Thing is, he's going to lay this down as a drug-related accidental death. I think partly so Naumann can get into Heaven."

"You're kidding."

"No. He asked me if Naumann was a Christian."

"He was an Episcopalian. They don't believe in God. If it wasn't a suicide, then what are they calling it?"

"Death by misadventure. An accidental overdose or some sort of psychotic episode. They're going to look for a brain lesion too."

"They're doing an autopsy, they're gonna see those old bullet holes in Naumann. And I hear he got marked up pretty good last year in Syria."

"Brancati's already seen that stuff. Naumann was pretty much naked at the scene. Brancati was military too. He even made Naumann's Air Assault tattoo. So all in all we're lucky he's playing it for a simple OD."

"Okay. No murder. Drug overdose. What's wrong with that?"

"Naumann didn't do drugs," said Dalton with a resigned sigh.

"As far as you know. Anyway, what do you care? Your job is to clean up after our field guys. Not figure out what the hell happened to make them go out on the high side. We lose field guys to drugs or suicide all the time, and when we do, we send in a cleaner. We've *already* looked into the backstory and nobody here thinks that anybody in our game had a reason to kill him. Turn him, maybe. Or pay him off. But taking him out in the way you saw? No, it wasn't company business. You stick to cleaning, Micah. That's what you do. Field operators lead complicated lives. Now and then they lose it and take themselves out. Naumann's domestic life was a swamp. I've heard all about his zombie-bitch daughters. And you knew he had prostate surgery two years ago?"

"Prostate surgery! The guy was fifty-two!"

"Didn't tell you *that*, did he? Welcome to *my* world. It was real invasive. You know what that means. Guy like Naumann, no sex. He'd hate living like that."

"I thought it was some kind of kidney thing."

"Well it wasn't. Only way I knew was Personnel sent me his medical claim for a signature. It's not the kind of thing guys bring up over a beer. So he's maybe looking at wearing a diaper for the rest of his life and his dick might as well be a sock full of sand for all the good it's gonna do him. Plus his marriage was in the tank. I'd say he had some reasons for taking himself out. You know, Micah, sometimes a thing can be true even if I think it. I have the tiniest feeling one of my people died from enemy action, I'll send in the metal-meets-the-meat boys. That's why you're a cleaner. *That's* your job."

"Don't you want to know *why* it happened?"

"Repeat after me: 'I'm a cleaner. That's my job.'"

"Where were you all this time? I called in sixteen hours ago."

"On the Hill having a séance with some PUNTS. People of Utterly No Tactical Significance. They're not at all amused about Naumann. So how the hell *did* he die?"

"You want it in the clear?"

"Just draw me some pictures in the air."

While Dalton was giving Jack Stallworth the gruesome essentials, a red-cheeked waiter-boy in a fur-lined jacket arrived radiating sulk. Dalton lifted his glass and winked at the boy, who stalked away to get another bottle, trailing sotto voce imprecations like willow leaves in autumn.

"You drinking again, Micah? It's eleven o'clock where you are."

"What time is it where you are?"

"That's not the point. Are you drinking again?"

"*Again* implies that at some point I stopped. And I sure as hell would be if you'd quit asking me questions. Every time I get the glass up to my lips you ask me something else. The crux is, what you should be asking is, *why* am I drinking. You didn't see him. I did."

"Toughen up. You were in the Horn."

"That was a straight-up interdiction. This was different."

"Are you saying Naumann committed suicide by ripping his own throat out with his bare hands?"

"No. I'm not. Brancati thinks he died from a heart attack."

"And what are *you* saying?"

Fur Boy swept in, plunked the bottle down hard. Dalton handed him a fifty-euro tip and waved off a newborn Fur Boy with a gladsome eye and birdsong in his shriveled black heart while he thought about his answer.

"I think it's possible that some kind of drug was a *minor* factor."

"You mean like one was slipped to him?"

"Yes. No. I don't know."

"This is what I like to hear from my cleaners. 'Yes. No. I don't know.' It gives me a warm glow." Stallworth paused here.

Dalton, who knew his man well, wasn't surprised to hear what came next.

"I tell you kid, if some kind of drug *was* a factor in this, and I'm not saying it was, but *if,* and it was something freaky enough to derail a seasoned pro like Porter Naumann, man, I'd *love* to know what it was. I mean, the company could *use* something like that."

"You asking me to find out?"

More hissing dead air from the cell phone. Maybe Stallworth's heavy breathing in the background. Office noises in the distance.

Finally . . .

"*If* I let you poke around in this a little more—and I mean if—I want your word you're not going to take it any further than finding out whether or not Naumann had any kind of unknown psychotropic drug in his system."

"Then all I have to do is wait; Brancati will tell me that as soon as he knows. Was Naumann doing anything for us that would make somebody want to see him dead?"

"We looked into it. I mean really looked. He and Mandy Pownall were keeping an eye on investment patterns, looking for indications of insider trading, money laundering that might be connected to al Qaeda operations, or the people who fund them. Hard work? Yes. Boring? Massively. Lethal? No."

"You're sure?"

"Damn sure. Whatever happened to Porter, I'm morally certain that it wasn't connected to what he was doing at Burke and Single. Sometimes things *are* as simple as they look."

"Okay then. On your head, if you're wrong."

"I'm not. What next?"

"Well, the Carabinieri will do the toxicology. I'll get the report from Brancati. I was wondering, while I'm waiting around, let me at least do a workup on his room at the Strega. Walk his last walk. See if something stands out. What harm can it do?"

More pensive silence from Stallworth's end of the line. He came back in a petulant mood. "With you I never know until it blows my ears off. Somebody has to go to London and hold hands with Joanne. It ought to be you."

"Has anyone talked to her lately?"

"Sally says she's been pretty silent. Not a call for four days, and she's not answering her voice mail. My take is she figures Naumann's gone off on a bit of a bender. He's done it before."

"She's going to call in soon. What are we going to tell her?"

"The truth. He had a heart attack."

"Joanne's got money and muscle. What if she digs in a little? Asks for another autopsy, for example?"

"You're the cleaner. Make sure she doesn't."

"What if she wants an open casket?"

"Can't he be prettied up a bit?"

"Jack, you buy him a steel casket and weld the lid shut unless you want to see the funeral guests puking into the flowerpots. Haven't we got anybody in London Center who could do this up right?"

"Mandy Pownall. She knows the family pretty well. I guess we could send her."

"She'll need a case of Cristal and some major meds."

"She'll have them."

"And a couple of handlers for the girls. They're a treat."

"I've never met them."

"Good decision. Now, how about it?"

While Stallworth was working out the many ways in which he could come to bitterly regret saying yes, Dalton poured some more wine into the glass and watched the tour guide girl coming back along the Riva. Her thighs remained wonderfully mystical and now her hapless Hindu tourists were liberally dappled with variegated tones of pigeon shit. She had the kind of look on her strong young face that said *My work here is through.*

"All right. I admit I'd like to know what kind of drug could make a pro like Naumann go batshit. We'd have a tactical interest in something like that. Go to Cortona. Toss his room at the Strega. And make sure you get a clean copy of the toxicology report. Not just a verbal description. And see to it that they don't lose the tissue and blood samples. If you can, have them handed over to you before you leave. Tell Brancati that Naumann's insurance policy requires an independent medical exam before they can release any funds to the family. And Micah, hear me on this—"

"I live to serve, Jack."

"Whatever you get—anything at all that looks weird to you, anything that catches your eye—it comes straight to me. Person to person. No *messages.* No *e-mail. Verbal* report to me direct. Got that?"

"What about Sally?"

"Not even her. No reflection. But that's the way it is. Got that?"

"How could I miss it?"

"I know it sounds hinky. But this comes from the Vicar himself."

"A policy thing?"

"He *said* it was. If Deacon Cather farts, farting becomes policy."

"Is Cather *personally* interested in Naumann?"

"No. It's a general order. Cleaners talk only to their handlers."

"Has he asked about Naumann?"

"Yes. He'll see the synopsis once you file your report. He sits on the Losses board. But we're losing a lot of field guys these days, thanks to our lovely little War on Terror. Just do what you can. Make sure there's nothing I have to worry about. File it direct to me, every detail you get, no matter how pointless. Send it by diplomatic courier, sealed, paper only, no copies, and my eyes only."

"This directive from the Vicar too?"

"Like I said. It's policy. Then go back to London and take it easy for a while. You follow?"

"About the hostel, I can't get into it until tomorrow."

"So do it tomorrow. Tonight, stay out of trouble."

"I'm in Venice. It's an island. What can I do on an island?"

"Cuba was an island too, and look what you did there. Gotta go."

"Jack . . . ask Mandy Pownall to be gentle with Joanne. She was once something to write your mommy about."

"My mommy died in a knife fight. They buried her in an oil drum."

"I was speaking metaphorically."

"Well don't."

THAT EVENING, against Stallworth's better judgment, Dalton went for a stroll. Venice was cool but not cold, with a few early stars glittering in a cobalt sky, and the canals were, mercifully, reeking only a little. Dalton wandered aimlessly along the ins and outs of the Riva with the eventual goal of a dinner at Ristorante Carovita. He smoked a couple of Toscanos on the way to sharpen his appetite, idly harassed a mime who was pretending to be a white marble statue, and bought a little ruby-colored Murano glass heart to send to Laura. It was their tenth anniversary next week. Maybe she'd remember who he was if she got a ruby glass heart from Italy. Probably not, and the bitter awareness of this hopeless delusion burned him a little as he crossed the canal bridge and came down to the little lantern-lit courtyard café under the awning, where he elected to dine alone in a tiny corner table at the back. He ordered a bottle of Bollinger in honor of Porter Naumann, wherever he was and however he may have gotten there. Now cracks a noble heart, and flights of angels sing him to his rest.

Dalton's mood, which had been dark and oppressed during the late afternoon, brightened somewhat, as it always did after the sun went down, a transformation not unrelated to his third glass of Bolly. He even tried for happy. Not that he got there. He never did these days. Happy was for FNGs, what the company called Fucking New Guys.

But he realized that he was looking forward to going back to Cortona and doing something useful, even if only as a diversion. Another round of Bolly and the image of Naumann in death that had been floating in front of his eyes for the last thirty-six hours began to recede. Easing back in his chair, he took a more active interest in his surroundings.

There were very few other people in the room, and the place had the look of a dinner party after the hosts have cleaned the ashtrays and put the cat out and are now standing at the wide-open front door in their pajamas and slippers, looking grumpy. Venice was winding down like a clockwork circus, and Dalton watched the six other diners scattered around the room with his usual level of semi-professional interest: two slender Italian girls in cashmere twin sets and flowered skirts leaning in close to whisper over their *vongole* with their hair falling down around their silky cheeks and their ankles demurely crossed; an elderly man in a well-cut suit that had fit him perfectly thirty years ago, having a plate of sole and staring mournfully across his table at an empty chair that looked as if it should have been filled with a loving wife but wasn't. An American couple who had the love-stuffed look of newlyweds on a six-city budget tour.

And a big broad-shouldered stiff-backed man with shoulder-length, silky-gray hair sitting at a table-for-one with his back to the room, smoking a Toscano cigarillo; it seemed that everyone in Venice was smoking Toscanos this season. His strong-looking leathery hands were laid out on either side of an open book. The man had his head down, and seemed to be reading it intently. Something in the look and carriage of this man reminded Dalton of Father Jacopo.

The man's silvery hair was hanging down his cheek, hiding his face, but the skin on the man's hands was dark, tanned almost a mahogany color, veined and ridged and gnarled, the hands of a man who had spent his long life using them to hammer, bend, and break. He wore a heavy turquoise-and-silver bracelet on his left wrist and a solid silver ring on the middle finger of his right hand.

An American, thought Dalton. From the Southwest, or California. Maybe a rancher or a cattleman. There was as well some other quality in his upright frame that suggested strength, vigor—even menace. Dalton made a point of marking the man down—shiny dark-green lizard-skin boots, tipped with silver, black jeans, a long black trench coat that looked pricey. He wore it the way Venetians do, over the shoulders like a cloak. One ear was poking through the man's long silver hair, a smallish ear, pasted flat to the skull, like a seal's ear. Piercing the lobe was a silver earring in the shape of a crescent floating above an iron cross, an oddly Islamic crescent moon for a man who looked so much like an American cowboy. Or perhaps an Indian? Navajo? Lakota?

He realized he was intrigued by the guy and waited patiently for the man's waiter to arrive, which would require the man to look up so Dalton could see his face. This never happened.

No one in the restaurant paid the slightest attention to the man in all the time that Dalton was there—no waiter approached, no guest smiled at him on her way to the washroom—so when Dalton stood up and walked carefully to the little hallway at the front of the café to pay for his *vitello al limone* and the two bottles of Bollinger that he had somehow managed to consume, he made it a point to leave his pack of Toscanos and his gold Zippo on the table so he could go back for them and try to get a better look.

While he was dealing with the bill and the doe-eyed heavy-breasted but mathematically challenged young girl behind the counter, he realized that not only had the old man not moved once during the last hour, he had not turned a page of the book on the table in front of him. Dalton handed a sheaf of euros to the girl and said, *"Mi scusi, signorina.* I forgot my cigarettes."

But when he got back to the main room the man was gone. His table was a blank, the plates taken away, as if no one had ever been there. All that remained on the table was a pack of Toscano cigarillos. Dalton picked them up, flipped the lid. The pack was still half-full. He closed the lid, dropped it on the table, and walked down the rear hallway, where he found an open door that led out into an alleyway, and from there to a walkway that ran into darkness far along the canal.

In the distance he heard the sound of boots on stones echoing down the twisted lanes. He stood and listened until the striding sound of steel-capped cowboy boots faded away and then he went back into the café, picked his own Toscanos and his Zippo off his table, and considered the pack the man had left behind for a moment, finally picking it up as well and putting it in his suit coat pocket. He returned to the till, where the girl was still holding his change, her soft brown eyes troubled.

"Mi perdoni, signorina."

She looked at him, her full lips open, her expression blank. *"Sì, signore."*

"L'uomo in nero—"

"I speak English bad, sir. Sorry."

"The man in black? With the long gray hair?"

Her face changed. She shook her head. *"Mi dispiace, signore. Non capisco."*

Dalton held up his pack of Toscano cigarillos.

"He was smoking these. An old gray man. Do you know him?"

She put the glass shell with his change down in front of him, shook her head, and stepped back away from the till, folding her arms.

"*Non parlo* . . ."

"The man in black who was sitting alone. At the back—"

She looked toward the rear of the café, and then back at Dalton. "There is no one there."

"The man who *was* there. We all saw him. Do you know him?"

"No. I do not."

"Would the owner . . . ?"

"He is gone."

"The owner?"

"Yes. The owner is gone too."

"Is the man a regular? The man in black?"

She was through talking; that was clear from her face. The gates were closing as he watched her. She tightened her lips, made a slight bow, and said, "There is no one there, sir. *Mi scusi. Buonanotte.*"

DALTON WALKED BACK ALONG the Riva degli Schiavoni—the quay of the slaves—pausing in front of his hotel to briefly consider and happily reject the idea of doing what Stallworth had specifically ordered him to do: go home and stay there.

The hotel café was closed, all the tables stacked up under the green awning. Out in the basin an empty vaporetto was chugging slowly into the distance, an oblong of yellow light far out on the water. The black gondolas along the Danieli docks were shrouded in blue and chained to their poles, where they bobbed and bumped in the wavelets that ran in ripples across the face of the quay. In the distance he heard the hollow echo of music: violins and the mellow snake-charm piping of a clarinet. He crushed his cigarillo into the stones and turned away from the hotel.

It was too early, and far too depressing, to go to bed.

A glass of port, or two, at Florian's in the piazza, if there were seats available, just to balance the champagne, and then a stroll around the campo to clear his head, until the bells rang in the campanile at midnight. He would do what Naumann had liked to do on an evening just like this. What he *would* have done if he weren't busy lying buck-naked on an autopsy table somewhere in Cortona.

He crossed the bridge canal and stopped to look at the Bridge of Sighs, the covered stone arch that linked the Palazzo Ducale with the old *bargello* where the Doge's thugs liked to take their political enemies apart with heated tongs—this was why the bridge was called the Bridge of Sighs. He leaned against the railing, looking out at the basin and the lights playing on the church of San Giorgio Maggiore across the water, and spent a few moments idly wondering about the counter girl's reluctance to talk about the guy in the black coat.

Probably a cultural thing. Venetians protected their own. For that matter, so did New Yorkers and Bostonians. It was possible that the man was a family friend, an uncle or a cousin, or perhaps a public figure whose privacy needed protecting. The guy did have a vaguely religious aura. He could have been a local bishop.

If the local bishops wore Southwestern jewelry and had hands like an open-pit miner. Dalton raised the old man's cigar pack to throw it into the canal, changed his mind, put it back in his pocket, and walked on past the Moorish walls of the palazzo Ducale. He turned right into the *piazzetta* that led to the Basilica of Saint Mark. There were dark shapes under the cloistered archway that ran along the palazzo walls; the smell of marijuana and the tinny buzz of Middle Eastern music snaked outward from the shadowy dark.

A girl called to him from out of the crowd of kids crowded together in the dark, drunkenly, with a petulant edge, demanding a *fucking* cigarette, *man*. He ignored them and walked on through the piazzetta. The slender red-brick tower of the campanile rose three hundred feet into the Venetian night beside him. Beyond it the heartbreaking sweep of the Piazza San Marco opened up before him, possibly the most beautiful open space in the world: a huge three-sided cloistered square of oddly Moorish design, with the bizarre monstrosity of the basilica holding down the open end.

The piazza was filled with music and light. Florian's was still open, as it had been since the late 1700s: he walked across the cobbles toward the old café tucked in under the portico on the southern side of the square. In spite of the cool, damp evening a little quartet was playing Ravel's "Bolero" under a pink silk marquee set up in front of the restaurant. Dalton took a chair to one side of the marquee and waved to an alert waiter who quickly brought him a half bottle of *vino bianco de la casa* (the hell with port). He lit up another one of his cigarillos and sat back to listen.

It was his view that there were few moments in a man's life, and lately this included sex, that could equal an evening at Florian's, listening to a spirited and skillful quartet play "Bolero," and he dedicated his pleasure in it to the memory of Porter Naumann.

"Bolero" came to its fiery conclusion, followed in its turn by "The Moonlight Sonata," an étude of Liszt's, and then one of Chopin's piano sonatas. Through it all Dalton sat alone and watched the crowds swell and peak and dwindle away while the stars turned in the sky above the luminous walls of the square. As the time passed, so did much of his bitterness and anger.

One of the many marvelous gifts of *vino bianco* was the perspective and detachment it could provide: Naumann was dead, a bad death, and something would have to be done about it. If Naumann had been killed, then whoever did it was going to die in a memorable and instructive way, because that was how their game was played. But Stallworth was right. Company business *was* inherently risky, and many of the field operatives suffered from acute stress. Although most of the Agency's field work was little more than skilled forensic accounting in the service of the War on Terror, some of the people doing it cracked in truly spectacular ways.

It was in the nature of their game.

But the curiosity remained, undimmed by the wine. Dalton was still possessed by an intense desire to know what *exactly* had happened to his friend in the last hours of his life, what unknown forces drove him to his terrible death in the courtyard of San Nicolò. At midnight an immense bronze bell sounded once, its deep vibrating tone echoing from the walls and rooftops all around the piazza. The violins ceased, the people stopped moving, and all the pale white faces turned toward the campanile like a field of flowers bending in a wind. The huge bronze bell began to ring the twelve tones of midnight, as it had for over six hundred years. The waiters started to pick up the chairs and collect their bills. The people in the square began to melt away into the alleyways and shadows as the great bell tolled and the echoes rang and reverberated across the rooftops of Venice. Soon the square was almost empty. The soft lights inside Florian's flicked off one by one. Dalton got to his feet, gathered up his cigarillos, left a generous stack of euros, drained his glass, stretched, and walked, a little unsteadily, through the piazzetta, in and out of the shadows that lay all around the old Ducal Palace.

He opened the old man's pack of Toscanos, gently turned the slender brown tube with the gold tip between the thumb and index finger of his right hand for a few seconds. What the hell, he decided, lighting it up with his Zippo. He drew the smoke in deep, let it out in a luxurious cloud, snapped the lid shut, and shoved the pack it into the pocket of his trench coat.

Wrapped in a blissful cloud of wine and smoke, Chopin playing sweetly in his memory, Dalton strolled idly along the covered cloister that ran down the Florian side of the piazza. The cigarillo was a perfect coda to an evening of such sublime beauty. He stopped for a time, one shoulder up against a pillar, and looked out at the plaza, admiring the way the moonlight bathed the farther wall and how it played with the stonework and the shadows. He found himself *seeing* it as he had never seen it before. Above the three-tiered windowed wall the night sky pulsed with light and he felt himself drawn upward into it, as if he were suddenly weightless.

He finished the cigarillo, stubbed the butt out on the pillar, and put it in his pocket. He turned, with regret, away from the perfection of the plaza at night, crossed over to the covered archways of the Palazzo Ducale, and walked in a strangely swelling sensory daze through its dark cloistered walkway, heading, perhaps a bit vaguely, in the general direction of his hotel.

As he reached the turning of the cloister, he became aware of two large figures standing in the shadows. They stepped forward as he approached, blocking his path, two black shapes silhouetted against the amber lights on the churning water of Saint Mark's Basin.

"*Scusi*, marigold," said one. "You have smokes?"

The man's accent was mainly gutter Croatian with a touch of Trieste in it. His partner, who was moving to block Dalton's path to the open courtyard, said nothing, but he said it in a way that implied he was fully on board with the evening's program. He had something long and sharp-looking in his right hand, which he was holding slightly away from his body. The bitter stink of strong Moroccan dope came off the men like heat from a radiator. *Mugged*, thought Dalton, suddenly earthbound and sobering fast.

How embarrassing.

Mugged like Patsy from Peoria, Stallworth would say.

Dalton looked at the two men, both now moving to block him in, and deep inside his brain a scaled green thing turned over in the primeval muck of his subconscious and opened one slitted yellow eye. He backed deeper inside the covered archway and got his shoulders up against the damp stone walls. The two men stepped into a shaft of moonlight under the Moorish arch. The silent one raised his long thin blade, turning it in the moon glow.

"You speak English, marigold?" said the other. "Give us cigarettes. I smell them on you. Give."

In the moonlight coming over the big man's shoulder Dalton could see the side of his face. Little beads of sweat glittered on an unshaven and sunken cheek. His eyes were two black holes and he had his right hand in the pocket of a puffy down jacket. Both men were wearing jeans and heavy boots. Shit-kicker boots, Stallworth would have called them. Jack liked those hard-boiled forties names.

Dalton looked briefly to his left and saw piles of clothes and backpacks stacked up under the arch, and several shadowy figures slouching against the Doges' walls. Tiny red sparks glowed in the darkness, and grass smoke rose up and curled in the shaft of moonlight, along with more of that tinny nasal whining that passes for pop music in the modern world.

Dalton's self-contained silence was either puzzling or irritating the two men in front of him. They still hadn't quite decided what to do with him. Ordinarily he would have tried to talk his way out of something like this, because choosing the other method of dealing with this sort of thing always made his life more complicated, and he wasn't in the mood for that.

Actually, he was in an uncharacteristically *peaceful* place, and he *liked* being there. He liked being there so much that he found himself getting angry with these two assholes for breaking his mood. It had been a *fine* mood. And now, just like that, it was gone.

"No," said Dalton, his anger rising up. "I don't speak English. And I don't smoke. So how about you two just fuck right off?"

"Hey, Milan! Don't let the faggot punk you out," said a girl, her voice slurred and languorous. "Make him give us some cigarettes."

"You are faggot?" asked Milan, in a tone of polite inquiry.

Dalton was wondering what to do with these two guys. They

weren't kids, that was certain; Milan was perhaps in his mid-twenties. His partner was in the shadows but he looked big and solid enough to be a grown man. Dalton had a vision of the kind of lives these two were leading as clearly as if it were a film being shown on the inside of his skull: they stole, they beat people, they screwed the girls. They lived like hyenas. How many people had they terrified in just this way? How many young gay men had they kicked to a bloody ruin just for fun? These two were like stones—

No, like turds. Huge hairy balls of steaming fresh dung, dropped by the careless frigate bird of fate into the sparkling pool of life, and whenever they hurt someone, the ripples of everlasting grief would run outward to infinity.

Dalton, sighing, knew these men for what they were. This is what they did. They had done this all last year and for all the years before that. They would do this sort of thing next year, and the year after that. If Dalton let them.

Stallworth's voice replayed in his mind. *No trouble, Micah.*

"Answer, boy," said Milan, his temper flaring. "You are faggot?"

"We prefer *gay*," drawled Dalton. "This your toy boy?"

Milan glanced at the other man and snorted.

"Hey, Gavro. Queer boy here, I think he like you."

As far as Dalton could make it out, Gavro told Milan, in idiomatic Serbo-Croatian, to engage in reciprocal oral congress with a ruminant quadruped of the goat persuasion, by their standards such an Oscar Wildean quip that Milan put his head back to let out a braying hoot. Dalton took this opportunity to kick Milan solidly in the nuts in the approved manner, which requires you to visualize your upper arch—*not* the tip of your shoe (which hurts like hell, by the way) but the *flat* of the upper arch, the way dropkickers do, to *visualize* your foot passing completely *through* the recipient's crotch to an imaginary point a foot above and beyond it. This follow-through method allows the full kinetic energy of the kicker's blow to be passed efficiently to the meatier parts of the kickee's crotch, with truly gratifying—at least to the impartial observer—results.

In this particular case Milan rose upward off the ground a couple of feet and balanced for a moment like an Olympic gymnast on Dalton's outstretched leg while he emitted a kind of teakettle squeal through his clenched teeth before tumbling off Dalton's foot and forming himself into the skewered-shrimp position that one traditionally assumes after one has been forcefully booted in the nuts.

Gavro, unfazed, came in silent and fast with his knife in a sweeping throat-level sideways slash from left to right that would have opened up Dalton's neck like the lid of a Pez dispenser if Dalton had not stepped inside the arc of the attack, catching Gavro's knife arm with his left hand while using the butt of his right hand and the full force of his body from the toes up to deliver a sharp rising blow to Gavro's upper lip and nose that, if executed properly, shatters the bone and cartilage of the nose with sufficient force to drive the whole detached mass of bone chips, splinters, and cartilage right through the nares and pharynx and deep into the brain. The blow is designed to be fatal, and Dalton *meant* it to be fatal.

Gavro went reeling backward, his limp body hitting the Doge's cobblestones like a burlap sack full of fresh guts. Dalton stepped lightly around Gavro's limp body, stooping to pick up the weapon Gavro had been carrying, which turned out to be a very expensive Serbian switchblade with a wonderfully carved ivory hilt, which he slipped into the pocket of his trench coat. He walked over and stared down at Milan's white sweating face and his wide blinking eyes gleaming in the moonlight, fully aware of the profound silence that was coming from the huddled masses under the cloister. He crouched down beside Milan and asked Milan in a kind of whispering purr what his favorite show tune was.

Milan, distracted by some pressing internal issues, stared up at him. Dalton asked the question again, this time in his best Alan Rickman drawl: "What's your *favorite* show tune, Milan? We marigolds just *love* show tunes. Come *on,* bunnykins. Won't you tell me yours?"

"Fuck . . . you . . . faggot."

" 'Fuck You, Faggot'? Don't know it. Now *I* really like 'People.' You know, from *Hello, Dolly*? Barbra sings it. It goes something like this."

Dalton straightened up, set himself.

"People"—he slammed a vicious boot into Milan's sagging belly—*"People* who need *people."* With each *people* Milan got another brutal kick in the guts, Dalton moving around the man writhing on the ground like a dancer, singing the chorus aloud, puffing hard with each blow, "are the luckiest *people* in the world—"

"Hey, man," a slightly strangled male voice called from out of the darkened cloister. "Leave 'im alone, okay? He's fuckin' done!"

Dalton stopped, looked down at Milan, who was curled up in a ball and chuffing like a cow about to calve. Tears were running down his cheeks and his mouth was full of blood.

"Are you 'fuckin' done,' Milan? Or do you have a comment?"

Milan seemed to be struggling to find one of those Noël Coward lines that would bring the house down but in the end he had to settle for a throat-clearing gargle followed by an attempt to spit in Dalton's face that ended up with a bloody gob of it running down his own cheek. Dalton waited for a polite interval to see if Milan had anything illuminating to add.

"Okay," he said, straightening up. "Let me get that for you."

Dalton gauged his angle and then kicked Milan very hard in the center of his face, getting a wonderful follow-through that snapped Milan's head back on his neck with a meaty crack. Where it stuck, still and fixed, its skull-to-shoulder angle now slightly *wrong.* Something inside Milan came flowing out in a rushing gush.

Dalton stepped daintily back, surveyed the scene with the air of a satisfied choreographer, and, turning to address the stunned kids in the cloister, bowed deeply:

"If we shadows have offended, think but this, and all is mended. That you have but slumbered here, while these visions did appear . . ."

He paused, searching his memory for the line, and then, the Shakespearean spirit coming back in a sudden flow, he continued in a stronger voice that echoed around the piazza: "And so good night unto you all. Give me your hands, if we be friends, and Robin shall restore amends."

No response from the audience. Everybody's a critic these days. He bowed again, straightened, pivoted neatly on his right heel, his long coat flaring out, and strode with quiet dignity, stage left, out of the piazzetta, his heels striking hard and his footsteps echoing around the square. Silence, nothing but silence, followed him all the way back to his hotel along the quay.

Reaction set in fast and he was weaving and a little breathless and trying not to throw up by the time he reached the brassbound doors of his hotel. He stopped there, leaning against the entrance, his breath coming in short painful gasps. Beyond the edge of the quay the basin of Saint Mark was a black bowl marked here and there with a flickering sliver of light. Far across the bay, floodlights illuminated the impassive façade of San Giorgio Maggiore. From the eaves of the hotel next door a gargoyle with the face of a lizard stared down at him, cold and unblinking.

AFTER HIS WORLD STOPPED spinning and he got his breathing under control, he pushed his way into the hotel lobby, raised a hand to the old bellman slumped behind the rosewood desk, and rode up in the narrow mirrored elevator to the top floor. He fumbled at the lock and eventually unlocked the door into what had been Naumann's company suite, a lush and well-appointed room with a wide and inviting carved wooden bed, an antique desk with a Venetian candelabrum on it, and sliding glass doors that led out to a small balcony overlooking the basin. The room had been cleaned and dressed, and Naumann's luggage was still there at the side of his bed. Dalton figured the maid had been in, because there were fresh flowers in a tall clay cylinder standing on the dresser, a towering viny tangle with several huge white flowers, all of them as tightly closed as butterfly cocoons.

Dalton, for whom the land of plants was an undiscovered bourne, ignored them while he poured himself a glass of wine and passed on through to the balcony, where he pulled a wrought-iron stool up to the ledge and sat down on it with his back against the wall, looking out across the basin.

He pulled the pack of cigarillos out of his pocket and, with a hand that trembled only a little, held the case up to the pale light of the balcony lantern. He flipped the lid and pulled out one of the few remaining cigarillos. It looked and felt and smelled in every way wonderful. He put it to his lips, lit it with his Zippo.

The smoke poured down into his lungs and spread a comforting warmth through his body. He leaned on the flower basket—gardenias? lupins? rutabagas?—and looked down at the almost-deserted quay.

A single white-robed figure was wandering past the equestrian statue of Garibaldi. Not a ghost; the mime he had teased earlier in the day, on his way home now, heading for the vaporetto station in front of the hotel. Dalton looked up and saw the stars of the Milky Way like a shell-pink veil waving in a sea breeze blowing in from an infinite black ocean. The city smelled of sea salt and garlic and sewage and damp stone: human corruption and the bittersweet joy of still being alive. It was a night that Porter would have savored: the superb little orchestra at Florian's, the *vino bianco,* the cigarillos, but it was too damn late for all that and too damn bad. Porter Naumann was dead now and would never see another evening in Venice.

He sighed, saw his glass was empty, and went back into the room to get some more wine, brushing past the floral display on the dresser;

he was a little disconcerted when he saw that the large white flowers were now in the process of spreading their petals wide open.

Moonflowers.

The name came up from somewhere in his memory. *Moonflowers.* He had heard that name before, recently, it seemed; they were a kind of morning glory, weren't they? Jack Stallworth was a fanatical plant guy. Maybe Jack had talked about moonflowers at some point. Dalton brushed by them and plucked another bottle of *prosecco* out of the minibar beside the dresser, popped the cork, and went back out to the balcony.

He sat back down on the stool and breathed in the night air, pulling it down deep, smelling something new in the breeze, a sharp tangy scent a little bit like eucalyptus. There was a stirring tickle on the back of his left hand. He looked down to see a large emerald green spider resting there.

He jerked his hand reflexively and as he did so he felt the spider bite him, like a spike being driven *deep* into the back of his hand.

Stricken with mindless horror, he dropped the pack and stumbled backward across the balcony, slapping at his clothes and wiping his forearms vigorously, his breath coming in short sharp rasps and his heart pounding. The stinging pain in his left hand was building into a fire that seemed to blaze upward through the veins in his left forearm. He stumbled into the bathroom of the suite and ripped his shirtsleeve up to his biceps. Under the blue-white light over the sink he watched as a thin red network of inflamed veins slowly spread upward toward his elbow. The flesh of his wrist was getting puffy. He turned his hand over and saw a large red welt about the size of a silver dollar on the back of his left hand. In the center of this welt there were two tiny dots of red blood welling up.

He fumbled at his waist, pulling his thin leather belt out of the loops. He wrapped the belt around his left arm just above the elbow joint and pulled the belt as tight as he could. He watched as the thin red lines grew upward on the underside of his forearm. The pain, a hot flooding rush that burned him down to the bone, was now replaced by an icy chill. He realized he was gasping for air.

He tried to calm himself, thought about antidotes: he had been trained in jungle survival. What kind of spider was emerald green and had a bite this powerful? What kind of venom had this rapid effect? Would he go into anaphylactic shock?

Realizing that hyperventilating would only speed the poison, if that's what it was, he tried to calm himself, tried to think clearly. He looked up and saw his face in the mirror, wet with sweat, his skin blue-white in the fluorescent light, his pale-blue eyes staring back at him; the face of a fool who might die if he didn't do something very effective right now. He opened the door to the cabinet above the sink and fumbled through the toiletries, found a pair of stainless-steel scissors that glittered in the cold light.

He put his left hand down on the edge of the sink and sliced into the blackened welt on the back of his hand, ripping at the wound until he had it flayed opened like a red flower that gushed out bluish blood. He could see the pink cords of the exposed tendons in his hand and the blood drained from his head. He swayed at the sink, his knees shaking.

He threw the bloody scissors clattering into the sink and fumbled through the bottles and cans in the cabinet until he found a spray bottle of lime-scented cologne. He doused the open wound again and again with the cool liquid, ignoring the pain that spread through his hand.

Extending his arm, he watched the red lines spreading, a delicate tracery of spreading poison. His fingertips had already gone numb but the pain that had been crawling up his arm eased. Panic began to recede and his heart stopped trying to hammer a hole in his sternum. He picked up the scissors and ran the blades under steaming hot water for a full minute. Then he sprayed the length of his forearm with the cologne, braced his left hand on the edge of the sink, pulled the tip of the belt tight with his teeth, and began to slice into the skin of his forearm, cutting a series of diagonal wounds across the thin red traceries, concentrating on nothing but the shining steel tip of the scissors as they carved a bright bloody path through his flesh. He flexed his fingers and cut too deep. A sudden leaping gout of red blood from a large vein sprayed itself across the sink and the bathroom mirror, a spouting burst that he could feel in his upper arm. He let the tip of the belt drop from his teeth, easing the tourniquet. Blood ran down his forearm in a widening river that glistened in the light like red satin.

He rested his forehead against the mirror and watched the blood swirling and roiling down the drain. Steam from the hot running water rose up and floated around him, reeking of copper and limes. A sudden cold sweat broke out across his cheeks, his neck, his back and shoulders. A vein in his neck started to pound slowly. A white light filled the bathroom and a great calm rose up from his chest and spread itself out across his upper body, rising like a flood into his mind. He felt his fear leaving him, replaced by a kind of blissful acceptance, a lack of caring.

His forehead began to slip down the mirror, leaving a streak of bright red as it moved through the blood spray on the glass. The sink below him looked like a pool filled with white light. It had a bright red center that looked like a setting sun. Comforting warmth and the scent of fresh limes rose up from it and he began to let himself fall gently downward.

"Christ, Micah! What the *hell* have you done to your arm?"

The voice was behind him, strong, deep, familiar. He jerked his head up, reeling as he did so, and saw Porter Naumann's reflection in the mirror, standing behind him. Naumann's mottled skin was pale blue. He was dressed, absurdly, in a pair of what looked to be emerald-green silk pajamas. His facial wounds had been sewn back together, badly, by someone with neither skill nor art, but it was still the old Naumann visage, piratical and wild.

His pajama top was open and Dalton could see that a vivid yellow-lipped scar ran down his naked body from the point of his chin to his flat belly, sewn shut with thick black thread. Dalton turned around and stared at Naumann, who grinned, showing bloodstained teeth in pale-gray gums.

"Why the *hell* were you hacking away at your arm like that?"

Dalton looked down at the slashes and cuts on his forearm.

"A spider . . . it bit me. Now the poison is spreading up—"

"And so you're hacking your arm to ribbons? Where'd you get that notion? 'Hints from Heloise'? Put some pressure on that."

Dalton looked down at his arm. Blood was running off it and spattering onto the floor. The belt slipped off his arm and fell onto the tiles at their feet.

"Use the Kleenex," said Naumann.

Dalton picked up a box of tissues from the toilet top, ripped off a wad of them, and pressed them into the wound. Naumann bent down, picked up Dalton's leather belt, and handed it to him.

"Use this to tie it off."

Dalton took the belt. He noticed that Naumann's fingers had been swabbed clean. His strong hands looked as they had looked when he was alive, but of course the color was wrong. His feet were naked, the toes splayed and purple-looking. Naumann, for his part, gave Dalton a worried appraisal in return.

"Don't you pass out on me, kid. Cinch up good and tight with that belt there, or you'll pass out."

Dalton tied off the tissue pack, twisted the belt tip in under the band, and jerked it in tight. Naumann shook his head.

"Not that tight. You'll kill tissue. Back it off a bit."

Dalton loosened the belt a notch. Underneath the wad of Kleenex the blood was welling up, but more slowly, seeping into the compress. Dalton swayed as he looked down at it, and closed his eyes. When he opened them again, Naumann was gone.

He sat down heavily on the toilet, shaking violently. At his feet the bathroom floor was covered in blood, smeared rectangles of bloody red tile. His suit pants were dappled with it and his shoes were stained almost black. The bathroom mirror looked like a Jackson Pollock painting. He leaned against the tank and let his head roll backward. The soft white light came back again, growing brighter, and his blood began to sing in his ears. His lids grew heavy again and he let them slowly close.

A brassy bellow from the other room snapped him upright, Naumann's baritone vibrato, full of striding jovial life:

"Micah! Wake up. Where the hell's your booze?"

He got to his feet, swayed, steadied himself on the tank, stepped around the blood pooling in squares across the tiled floor, and went back into the main room. Naumann was standing in front of the dresser. He had the top drawer pulled open and was riffling through Dalton's shirts. He looked up when Dalton came into the room.

"The minibar's empty, you drunken sot. You always have something in reserve."

"I think I finished it all."

Naumann waved that off with a sideways flick of his hand.

"Not you. How much have you had today, by the way?"

Dalton tried to give the question some thought while Naumann watched him. Was he really going to have a chat with this hallucination? Dalton decided that in reality he was passed out on the bathroom floor right now and that this was all a dream, the kind of out-of-body experience he had always heard about but never actually believed in.

What the hell.

When in Wonderland, talk to the Cheshire Cat.

"I started this morning. I believe I never stopped."

Naumann leaned an elbow against the top of the dresser and shook his head slowly at Dalton. "Man, I have to tell you, Micah. You look like death."

"I look like death? *I* look like death?"

Dalton sat heavily down on the bed, cradling his bloody left arm, and watched in a detached but vaguely appreciative way as Naumann went through the rest of the dresser drawers, rapidly and efficiently, as if he were tossing a crib for an entry unit.

Finding nothing, Naumann turned and pointed down to a place beside Dalton's feet.

"How about your briefcase?"

Dalton reached under the bed and pulled out a travel-worn leather case with solid gold fittings. He threw it on the bed beside him. Naumann came over to the bed. He ran his hands over the top and then down the sides, stopping at the left-hand hinge plate. Sitting this close to him, Dalton caught an autopsy-room smell of disinfectant and dried blood coming off Naumann.

He managed to give every appearance of not being sickened by this. Naumann was an old friend and, although dead, deserved some consideration for what he had just been through.

Naumann found the release and pressed it and the case popped open. He stood up and shook his head slowly. "Same trigger you've always had. You should change it."

"I'm on it. If I live through the night, I'll make it a priority."

"You think you're dying?"

Dalton let out a slightly self-pitying sigh. "I think so. I think I've passed out from loss of blood."

"What about the spider bite?"

"Or that, yeah—from the spider bite."

"And now you're . . . where? Lying on the bathroom floor having an out-of-body experience? Don't go into the light, Carol Ann?"

"Yes. Something like that."

"Melodrama. Your generation drives me nuts."

Cursing softly to himself, Naumann leaned down and fumbled around in the papers, picked up Dalton's Agency-issue Beretta, thumbed the magazine release, letting the magazine plop onto the bedspread. Then he racked the slide once, deftly caught the flying brass round as it popped out of the ejection port, and tossed the unloaded Beretta onto the bed beside it. He handed the round to Dalton, patting his cheek with a raspy palm as he did so.

"Don't take it personal. I don't trust you around loaded guns when you're all maudlin and pitiful."

He gave Dalton a fatherly smile and fished a silver flask full of Napoleon brandy out of Dalton's case, unscrewed the top, and took two long gulping swallows. Dalton thought about going back into the washroom to see if his dying body was still spread-eagled out on the floor in there, and decided against it. If he was really having an out-of-body experience, one of the advantages of it was that his left arm wasn't hurting like hell right now.

Naumann pulled the flask away from his lips, exhaled noisily, and handed the flask to Dalton with a satisfied smile. The light from the street glimmered on his teeth and put a sickly wet sheen along his right cheek. It reminded Dalton of Milan and Gavro, Gavro's mean leer in the moonlight, Milan about to get himself kicked to death.

"Go on," said Naumann. "I left some for you."

Dalton put the flask up to his lips and then hesitated, displaying a reluctance that made Naumann laugh, in itself an unsettling sound.

"You're talking to a dead man while dying from a spider's bite, but sharing a flask of cognac is where Micah Dalton draws the line?"

Naumann had a point, even if he was dead. Dalton put his head back and let the cognac sear its way down his throat. He screwed the top back on while Naumann pulled a chair over and sat down by the bed. Naumann leaned forward and took the flask from Dalton, unscrewed the cap again with a wry look, put it to his lips, and gulped a mouthful down with obvious enjoyment.

The light from the street flared around Naumann's silhouette, giving him a pale aura in the darkened room. The cold blue glow from the open bathroom door lay in a luminous wedge across Naumann's feet and ankles. Naumann wiggled his toes in the shaft of light, stretched out his legs, and leaned back into the chair with the silver flask cradled in his hands. Dalton leaned forward and plucked it back, giving Naumann a significant look. Bogarting a flask of Napoleon, Dalton recalled, was a typical Naumann trait. Naumann shrugged, smiled, and spoke out of the dark.

"I suppose you're wondering why I called this meeting?"

"Not really. You're a hallucination, that's all. A figment."

The room seemed to ripple and the aura around Naumann brightened. Dalton's vision was suddenly flooded with white light. He blinked several times and shook his head hard, squeezing his eyes shut. When he opened his eyes the room was back to normal, but Naumann was still there.

"You are, however, a damn persistent figment," he said, with some resentment. He needed to either wake up or finish dying. Naumann watched him drinking from the flask with amusement, took the flask back and had another sip, set it down. Dalton woozily considered another drink and realized how little he needed more of *anything* alcoholic right now.

Naumann seemed to be of much the same mind.

"Man, we need to ease up on this stuff before we're *both* tanked. I never knew you could still get drunk after you're dead."

"So you actually *know* you're dead?"

Naumann gave him a look. "It's kinda hard to overlook being dead, Micah. It's the sort of thing that jumps out at you whenever you look in a mirror."

"Do you know anything about how you died?"

Naumann shook his head. "No idea. All a blur. Maybe there are rules about this sort of thing. Maybe I've got amnesia."

"You can't have amnesia when you're dead."

"I'm the only dead guy in this room. So far. I've even been autopsied. I'm certifiably and reliably dead. I think that gives me a measure of credibility."

"Stallworth thinks you committed suicide. So do the cops."

"Suicide? Not my style. I had too much to live for."

"Stallworth didn't think so."

Naumann cocked his head to the side.

"Yeah? Why not?"

"He said you had a prostate operation. Lost your will to live."

Naumann snorted. "He knew that, huh? That surgeon of mine couldn't keep a secret if it was hammered up his colon and sutured shut. Sure I had a prostate operation. And it screwed up my courting tackle. So what? I could still play the trumpet, enjoy a scotch. Life was sweet. Come to think of it, I wish I'd paid more attention to being alive when I was still alive."

"This is a real Hallmark moment for me, I'm sure. I'm touched beyond words. *La douceur de la vie* and all that. But I have to figure out what happened to you."

"Look, kid, I haven't got much time—" Naumann made a move as if to check his wristwatch, realized he didn't have one anymore, and sighed heavily, his mood darkening.

"Damn. That was a Chopard. I wonder who got it."

"It'll be in your effects, Porter. I'll get them tomorrow."

"Make sure you do. It was an anniversary gift from Joanne. However, back to my point, as much as I've enjoyed seeing you one more time, and I admit that I have thoroughly loved freaking the living Jesus out of you, I'm actually here to give you some advice."

Dalton emitted a pained groan and put his head in his hands. "Please. Not Marley's ghost."

"What? You don't think you need some advice?"

"Not from a ghost."

"Ghost? I thought I was just a figment? How about we ask Milan and Gavro if you need any advice?"

This brought Dalton's head up. Far too quickly. The room reeled, steadied, and somewhere inside his skull a vein pulsed in time to the gentle heaving of his stomach. "You saw that?"

"Saw it? Christ, Micah. It was hard to miss. You sang 'People' while you kicked Milan around the plaza. Where did *that* ugly shit come from?"

"I gave those assholes a wake-up call. That's all."

"You really think Gavro's gonna wake up?"

"I actually don't give a flying bat-fart. No offense."

"He's in a coma. And Milan's gonna spend the rest of his life in a wheelchair down by the seashore, wearing a diaper and drooling at the nurses."

"You don't think the world's a better place without those mutts?"

"Yeah. I probably do. But you're gonna get some serious grief for it. Believe it or not, Gavro had family. A nasty vengeful family. So like they say in those legal notice letters, govern yourself accordingly. But that's not why I'm here. I mean, watching you do it was diverting as hell and I can hardly wait to tell the guys back in the station all about it. But I was gonna drop by for a talk anyway."

"Lucky me."

"Yes. Lucky you. You're going to wake up tomorrow morning and convince yourself this was all some kind of fever dream. Then you'll go on about your business for Stallworth and the Agency. You shouldn't. None of that shit really matters."

"No. And precisely what shit *does* matter?"

"You need to go see Laura."

"Laura? *That's* why you're here? Jesus. You banged on that tin drum way too much while you were still alive. Give it a rest."

"No. Laura is what this is all about. You have to make amends."

"Amends? Since when did you start using words like 'amends'? There must be a thesaurus in Hell."

"I always tailored my vocabulary for my listeners. With you I had to stick with words of one syllable or less. We were talking about Laura. You need to make things right with her while you're still alive. Which, by the way, means you've got maybe three weeks. Max."

"Three weeks! I'm going to die in three weeks?"

"Don't whine, Micah. It makes your face go all pouty. Everybody dies. Even whiskey-soaked little fruitcakes like you."

"I'm going to die? How am I going to die?"

Naumann took another long pull at the cognac flask and then stared off into the middle distance. Dalton found the wait quite trying. Finally, Naumann leaned forward, handed the flask back to Dalton.

"I'm not really sure. It's kind of a Magic Eight Ball thing. Reply hazy—ask again later. I'm getting the idea I'm not allowed to affect outcomes. We're not licensed to do fate. How about you just consider me . . . Man, what's the word?"

"An omen?"

"Yes! An omen. I'm an omen!"

"An omen? Of what?"

"I'm an omen of you needing to change your fucked-up life before some massive cosmic doom gets all biblical on your ass."

"The details, Porter. The details!"

"There you go. The devil is in the details. Who said that?"

"Goethe. And I think it was God who was in the details. We were talking about how I'm going to die in three weeks."

"That's beside the point."

"Very few people would consider their impending doom beside the point, Porter."

"It's not all about *you*, kid. Laura's in a bad place. Go see her."

"Forgive me, my friend, but she's in a very *nice* place, as a matter of fact. Maintained at great personal expense, by the way. And unlike you, I am not richer than Agamemnon's broker. Anyway, I would think being newly dead would take up a lot of your attention, Porter. Why this obsession with somebody else's wife?"

Naumann stood up and walked toward the doors that led out to the balcony. Dalton could see the streetlight shining through Naumann's body. Naumann turned at the doors and looked back over his shoulder at Dalton. He looked like an image painted on fog.

"To get the answer, you must survive the question."

"Oh, Christ, Porter. To-get-the-answer-you-must-survive-the-question. Don't go all Yoda on me now. What answer? What question?"

Naumann shook his head slowly, fading away as he did.

"Wait, Porter. Wait. What do we tell Joanne? Your kids?"

"Thanks, kid, but no one can help my family now."

Then there was nothing but the wind off the sea flowing through the curtains and in the distance the soft tolling of a cathedral bell ringing in the new day. Micah cradled his arm and put his head back on the pillow and . . .

. . . A LEMON-COLORED LIGHT glaring through his closed lids woke him up several hours, possibly *years,* later. He raised himself onto an elbow, his head pounding dully, his throat parched. He looked blearily around, trying to piece himself back together after what he dimly recalled was, even by his own exacting standards, a truly Olympian binge. He was relieved to find that he was lying, fully clothed, heart dutifully beating, lungs right on the job, still very much alive, on his bed in Naumann's old suite at the Savoia & Jolanda.

The sun, a pale wintry one, was shining in through the billowing curtains next to the open balcony doors. He raised his hands to shade his eyes from the glare and stopped as the memories of the night before came back in force, and along with them a very pressing question: Where was that emerald-green spider?

He rolled quickly off the bed and got to his feet, staggered into the center of the room, and stared wildly around, his flesh crawling. Where was it? Under the dresser? In the bed?

Sweet Jesus, not in the bed.

He reached down to tear off the coverlet and stopped, gaping at his left hand. It was a mass of dried blood and crisscross wounds. There was a large gaping wound on the back of his hand, crusted with blood. He looked down at the bed where he had been lying. Blood was smeared all over the Italian linen. His shirtsleeve was ripped all the way to the shoulder and caked in blood. His briefcase was lying open at the bottom of the bed, his silver flask beside it. And next to that his service Beretta, with the slide locked back and the magazine safely removed. Beside the magazine a single brass nine-mil round lay glinting in the sunlight. Which meant that last night he'd been playing with a loaded gun while stoned out of his mind.

Oh, yeah. Wait one. There was more. Much more.

Last night, dear Micah, you either killed or seriously damaged two Serbo-Croatian thugs in the Piazza San Marco. And that image brought back the hallucination of Porter Naumann, sitting in that chair—the chair that was still right where Naumann had put it, next to Dalton's bed so he and Naumann could have a drink and a fatherly chat. A drink and a fatherly chat with the mutilated *corpse* of Porter Naumann, if he wanted to press a tiresome point.

He shoved these grim realizations aside for later consideration—which meant hopefully never—and went back to the critical issue here. The last time he'd seen the spider—if there really *was* a spider—it had been out on the balcony.

He stepped around the chair, giving it a wide berth, and crossed the carpet to the balcony. The cigarillo pack was lying where he had thrown it in a panic last night, on the stone floor of the balcony, up against the flower stand, next to a burned-down stub of cigar. The lid of the Toscano pack was half-open. To Dalton it loomed as wide and terrible as the gates of Mordor. Some cloudy recollection from a film on the Discovery channel surfaced then.

Spider's *nest*, don't they?

He went back into the suite and picked up a copy of *Venezia* magazine, rolled it into a tube, and stepped lightly back out onto the balcony. Standing motionless next to the door, his head aching brutally and his mouth painfully dry, he stared out across the busy lagoon for a moment and decided it was time to get the hell out of Venice before it killed him.

He looked around the narrow space, checking all the cracks and nooks and corners with painstaking care, then he knelt down in front of the half-open pack of Toscanos. He reached out and tapped the lid lightly and then drew quickly back, the tube raised, ready to turn whatever the hell came scuttling out of it into a dark-green inkblot. Silence. Nothing stirred. He looked around the floor of the balcony again. If the spider was hiding anywhere in the crevices, he was doing a stand-up Seal Team job of it. The Toscano pack lay there in the weak fall sunlight, surrounded by what seemed to Dalton an unnatural stillness and an unreal glow.

With the rolled-up magazine in his left hand, he gently pushed the cigarillo pack up against the balcony wall, fixed it there, and pressed the lid tightly shut. Holding his breath, he reached out, picked the pack up in his right hand, and stepped backward out of the balcony, carrying the packet as if it were a block of plastique. He set it upright on top of the little neoclassical escritoire next to the plasma-screen television, pulled what he was still thinking of as Naumann's chair over, and sat down in front of it.

Holding the pack in his damaged left hand, he pulled out his

Zippo, flipped it on, and held it over the top of the pack as he thumbed the lid back. Skin rippling, holding his breath, he leaned forward and stared down into the container. Black shadows played around the six remaining cigars as he moved the lighter around. When the glow of the flame caught a shimmer of emerald fur in one corner of the pack, and then two tiny red glitters sparkling at the bottom of the pack, he jumped a yard and let out a castrato's shriek. The spider raised two of its legs and waggled them defensively in the light of the flame, and then scuttled backward into the shelter of the cigarillos.

It was *real*.

And it was right there.

He snapped the lid shut and kept his right hand on the lid while he fumbled around with his left in the desk drawer until he found some elastics. He wrapped the box around and around with them until it looked like a shredded baseball, rattled the box viciously several times just for some payback, and set the pack down hard on the desktop. He leaned back into the chair, blew out a long ragged breath, and closed his eyes. Sixty silent seconds passed and then a shrill metallic howl like a dental drill shot up from somewhere in the room and struck him right between the eyes, lodging itself in his brain like a crossbow bolt. He staggered across the room. The awful skull-cracking whine was coming from somewhere around the bed.

No. Under it.

He dropped to his knees beside the bed and fumbled around blindly until he got his hands on his cell phone, which he scooped up, punching the Send key savagely.

"Yes! Hello! For Chrissake hello!"

"Mr. Dalton?" An Italian voice, a woodwind baritone.

"Major Brancati?"

"Yes. I catch you at a wrong time maybe?"

"No. Not at all. Absolutely great."

He lowered the cell phone to check the time. It was a little after one in the afternoon. He'd been asleep for . . . he had no idea. Hours.

"I did not wake you, Mr. Dalton?"

"No. I just got out of the shower, that's all."

"Good. You are well, I hope?"

"Yes. Yes I am. I'm absolutely fine."

He managed to shut himself up before he said "peachy" or "top-hole." He wasn't at all fine, but that was his own fault. He pulled himself together and shoved the nightmare of the past several hours back into the darker recesses of his mind, where it had no doubt come from in the first place. He sat down on the bed and shook the flask, a little reassured by the gurgle of leftover cognac.

"Good," said Brancati. "I was worried about you."

"About me? Why?"

"There was trouble in the Piazza San Marco last night."

Dalton's hangover went away in a buzzing of wasp wings. His mind was painfully clear at this moment. He tried not to show it.

"What kind of trouble?"

"You did not see it? Hear the police boats?"

"I was in bed. Sound asleep. What happened?"

"Two men were badly injured. In some kind of fight."

Dalton could not repress the next question. "How badly injured?"

"One is in a coma. They think he will come out one day. His face has been greatly disfigured and he will need much plastic surgery. The other one lives too but has no feeling in his body. His spine has been broken. Near the neck. He will not walk anymore."

"I'm sorry to hear it."

Brancati laughed, not persuasively. "Do not be. They were garbage. Serbs and Croats, from Trieste."

"How did it happen?"

"Well, that is why I was worried about you. Because this fight was just around the corner from your hotel there. Also because the witnesses—"

Dalton's recollection of the evening came into sharper focus.

"If we shadows have offended, think but this, and all is mended. That you have but slumbered here, while these visions did appear."

"—there were several of them. *Turisti.* Backpackers. They describe the man who did this thing. The girls they lie a great deal but the Venice police think that these two Croats, they tried to—how do you say?"

Never finish a cop's sentence. It's a trick.

Dalton finished it anyway.

"Mug?"

"Yes! To *mug* this man, and he resisted them."

Brancati's tone contained an element that Dalton finally pinned down. *Satisfaction.*

"Was he hurt?"

"We do not know. But the girls, they give a description. And the description is of a man very much like you. Tall. Strong. Long blond hair. Well dressed. He was a good fighter, they say."

"That's every Italian man in Venice."

"They say he had an American accent. And he sang and danced while he did this. He sang 'People.' You know this tune?"

"I know it. I hate it."

"I too hate this song. Once it gets into your head, it flies around and around. You cannot get it out. Now it is in my head. Right now. Like a wasp."

"I know. Now it's in *mine.* Thanks for that."

That made Brancati laugh. "Ha! Now you know! We share this, eh? Anyway, this ugly thing, this very terrible fight, so close to you. I worry about you."

"Well, I appreciate that. But it wasn't me. I'm fine."

"But you *were* in the piazza last night."

It wasn't a question. Had he paid cash or used his AmEx card? He couldn't recall. Too much wine. He recalled Naumann's warning, from a company field-training session in Munich many years ago.

Tell as much of the truth as you can get away with, kid.

"Yes. I had a drink at Florian's."

"Of course. I remember your friend loved to do that. I thought you would go, as a remembrance. A drink for your old friend. And you stayed until the tocsin rang? From the Campanile?"

"No. I left early. I was still pretty shaken up."

"About Mr. Naumann?"

"Yes. Do you have any news about him?"

"And you are okay? You had no *avventura* last night?"

"No. Just a drink and then to bed."

"Really? Good. Because, you know, I am a little worried for this man who did this thing. To defend oneself is a man's right. To dance and sing 'People' while kicking a man so hard he becomes a cripple is different. A man who could do such a thing, perhaps he has some sickness. In his heart."

"Couldn't agree more. But I didn't see a thing. Sorry not to help."

"Also, there is the family of these men."

Family?

This was nuts. Guys like that didn't have families. They multiplied on the underside of toilet tanks in flophouse latrines.

"Family? I don't understand."

"You would not think it, but it seems that the one in the coma, his name was Gavro Princip. He is the youngest son of a large Serbian crime family. Very famous. Do you remember the name Gavrilo Princip, perhaps?"

He did. It rang a distant chime. But he couldn't—

"His great-great-uncle was the man who shot the Archduke Ferdinand. In Sarajevo. They say he started the First World War. It is a matter of much pride, so I am told, in parts of Serbia. Even to-day, he is seen as a hero. Anyway, his family, the Princips, they are now part of a crime organization run by a very bad man named Branco Gospic, who lives in Split, and the Branco Gospic organization, they make money in mysterious ways and are well known to the police, as the saying goes. So although Gavro Princip is a thief, still he is connected to the Branco Gospic family, and it is very likely that Branco Gospic will take what has happened to Gavro as an af-front, an insult. As a matter for vendetta. Such things are taken very seriously in Serbia and Croatia. Look at the Bosnian War. The *lex talionis*, you know this?"

Peachy.

Isn't that just peachy.

Brancati let this wonderfully eloquent silence run for a while.

"So, no matter. *You* are not involved. And these two, they were *rifiuti della società*! I am happy they are so much punished. Venice is a better place. Italy is better. Of course, should the man who did this thing let himself do it again, then perhaps the police will not think it such a fine thing. But if he does *not* do it again, at least not in Italy, then I think, if the Venice police find this man, they will buy him a big dinner. Maybe at Carovita, eh?"

That was a polite Italian warning, Micah. Hear it.

"Yes. I hope this man would take that advice to heart."

"You do?"

"I know I would, if I were in his shoes."

"*D'accordo?* And this song, 'People,' it is still in your head?"

"I'll put something else in it."

Maybe a bullet.

"You know this musical?"

"*Hello, Dolly?* Never saw it."

"That's what this man said also. Last night. That it was from *Hello, Dolly.* But my wife tells me it is from a play called *Funny Girl.*"

Dalton managed not to groan out loud. Barely.

"Is it? Well there you go."

"Yes. There we go. Well, about Mr. Naumann we do have news. You sure you are okay to talk. You are well?"

"Yes. Peachy. I'm peachy. What is it?"

He'd actually said "peachy" out loud.

Twice.

"Coroner? Is that your word? The coroner?"

"Yes."

"His report is in. The preliminary. No blood work. The brain was very inflamed. It seems there had been some sort of *colpo apoplettico*—I do not know the English words—"

"A stroke, you mean?"

"Yes. A stroke. But the doctor says that such a stroke as this could have had the effect of creating a very strong derangement of the senses. The doctor is telling us that Mr. Naumann died as a result of this stroke."

"Directly, you mean?"

Brancati said nothing for a moment. Dalton got the impression that he had put his hand over the phone and was talking to someone else in the room.

"No. Not directly. He also examined the heart, which was not in good shape. Mr. Naumann had signs of previous minor heart attacks and some of the atrial walls had atrophied. He was not a healthy man. So the stress of—how to say—the brain attack, this placed a fatal strain on his heart."

"So he did die of a heart attack? After all?"

"Yes. I hope this puts your mind at ease."

"What about the . . . the damage he did? To himself?"

Brancati sighed. In his mind Dalton could see him shrugging.

"We can never know. In his last moments he was in a terrible place and his death was horrible. I wish never to die as he did. But we may at least say that he did not commit suicide. This death was not a murder either. So there we have it. Natural causes. A tragedy, but sadly, also a part of life. You will come to Cortona? We can release the body to you."

Dalton picked up the flask and unscrewed the lid, but he did not drink. He sat there thinking about the man in black and his emerald-green spider and what Naumann had said—about Laura.

But none of that was real.

It was all a nightmare, born of too much booze. And of course the side effects of a bite from some sort of poisonous spider. Maybe even from the soul sickness that comes on you after you've let your red dog run and serious damage has been done because of it.

But it was over now.

This was another day. The spider *hadn't* killed him. The ghost of Porter Naumann had *not* appeared in his room. When he thought it over in the cold light of day, everything that Naumann's ghost had told him was something he either already knew or already suspected. And that would certainly include the warning about Laura.

Except the bit about Gavro's vengeful family. And even that could have come up from somewhere deep in his own guilty mind.

"Yes," he said, watching the afternoon sunlight play on the tall tangled vines of the moonflower plant, its large blue-white flowers closed tight again, huge white cocoons that seemed to glow with a ghostly interior fire. "I'll be in Cortona tonight."

IT TOOK DALTON two hours to clean up the suite: the bathroom looked as if he'd staged a cockfight in it, and the Italian linen bedspread was a total loss. He took some more time to clean himself up well enough that when he walked out the door he wouldn't frighten the horses.

He put the ominous little cigarillo pack, still bound up with several elastics, into the breast pocket of his dress shirt. Everything else, the ivory-handled switchblade he'd taken from Gavro, the silver flask, the bloody towels, and his Beretta, went into his briefcase. He closed the lid and locked it with superstitious care. Naumann's bags—including everything Dalton had been wearing the day before, which, in view of Brancati's deeply implausible insouciance about the Milan and Gavro affair, were better out of the forensic reach of the local authorities—were standing by the door, tagged for Dalton's London address and due to be FedEx'd by the hotel bellman later this afternoon.

His own luggage consisted of his briefcase and one battered alligator-skin suitcase. He did one last walk-through of the company suite, including the balcony, looking for any remaining sign of the previous night's excesses. Other than the bloody bedspread, in reparation for which he peeled off another three hundred euros and dropped them in a soap dish beside the daily twenty-euro tip for the maid, the room looked pretty much as it should.

He stood in the middle of the living room and spent a moment thinking about last night's dream and what Naumann's ghost had said about Laura. In his mind's eye he saw Laura sitting on a blue wooden chair in a white room bathed in golden light. She was wearing a pastel pink dress belted at the waist. Barefoot, her short red hair carefully combed, her pale face scrubbed, without makeup, she stared fixedly into emptiness. Cradled in her upturned hands was a small rounded form wrapped in an emerald green blanket. Overhead a ceiling fan with huge palm fronds for blades whisked through the salt-scented air and a sea wind stirred the white linen curtains.

He held the image for as long as he could and then shut it down and locked it away in an iron cage at the back of his skull. There was nothing he could do for Laura. She had left him long ago, had traveled as far away from him as it was possible to go. He picked up his luggage and his briefcase and turned his back on the room and on everything that had happened in it last night.

On his way out he stopped in front of the long mirror by the door and examined himself—navy pinstripe over a crisp white shirt, a pale gold silk tie knotted over a gold collar pin, a long blue cashmere coat and shiny black wingtips. Black leather gloves to hide the wound on the back of his left hand. Shaved, scented, combed, and pressed. He looked like death. He slipped on a pair of tortoiseshell gold-trimmed sunglasses and considered his reflection. A verse ran through his mind, an old Dorothy Parker rhyme:

> Life is a glorious cycle of song,
> A medley of extemporanea;
> And love is a thing that can never go wrong;
> And I am Marie of Romania.

His bags were in check and he was ready for a five o'clock water taxi ride to the Piazzale Roma, where his rented Alfa waited for him. Dalton stepped a tad warily out the doors of the Savoia & Jolanda and into the pale afternoon sun, expecting a shriek of recognition from a chorus of traumatized backpackers. No one even looked his way.

It was business as usual for the quay of the slaves, and he saw the same black-haired mystical-thighed tour guide striding past, this time trailing a litter of Chinese tourists slated for today's Ordeal by Pigeon over in the piazza. He flipped his collar up, straightened his sunglasses, turned hard left, and headed briskly away from the San Marco, on his way to Ristorante Carovita.

To satisfy his curiosity.

Nothing more.

A little side trip to look into the small matter of an emerald green spider, perhaps to discuss the events of the night with the spider's careless owner. Maybe even to *return* the spider. Then on to Cortona to pick up the threads of what had been beginning to feel like his *former* life for a while there last night.

The café was open when he got there, with a few tourists and regulars sitting out under the awning and a damp salt wind blowing in from the distant palm-fringed line of the Lido beaches. The doe-eyed girl was nowhere around. Seated behind the counter inside, barricaded behind a heap of linen napkins waiting to be folded, was a parrot-faced old crone with evil black eyes, her fingers and hands bent and twisted into talons. She glanced up from her work as he came into the café and a look passed swiftly across her face, an unmistakable flicker of wary recognition. She looked like a sable basilisk and he was for a time torn between using his boyish charm, of which he had far less than he imagined, or calling in an exorcist.

Dalton opted for charm.

"Buongiorno, zia! Come sta?"

"I speak English."

"What a happy coincidence, my dear lady. So do I."

This brought a noncommittal grunt and she went back to her folding. Dalton looked at the thin greasy gray hair plastered across her skull for a while and decided that boyish charm was not this old bat's weak point. He looked around the café and saw that all of today's business was out under the awning. They were more or less alone. He leaned forward, placing his hands on her laundry. She stopped folding and looked up at him, her flat black eyes cold.

"Zia, I am looking for a customer who comes here."

She said nothing but now a light was in her eyes, an acquisitive glitter rather like a gold coin in a shallow pond of black water. Dalton pulled out his wallet and extracted a sheaf of euros. She focused on them for a moment and then looked up at him again, her face closing like a fist.

"Who do you want?"

"He's an older man, very big, very strong. He has long silver-gray hair—down to here," said Dalton, touching his left shoulder. "He wears a black coat like a cape and the long boots of an American cowboy—"

Her hard eyes narrowed at this. Dalton searched for the Italian. *"Come vaccaro. Capisce?"*

"Pellerossa," she said, her voice harsh and rustling in her throat like dead leaves in a gutter. It wasn't a question.

"Yes. Mr. Pellerossa. Do you know where he lives?"

Her black eyes flickered to the entrance and followed a young woman who looked as though she could be the doe-eyed girl's sister as she walked through the café toward the kitchen. When she was gone the old woman's eyes moved back to Dalton and stayed there, as full of low cunning and evil intentions as the eyes of a gull.

"His name is not Pellerossa. *Pellerossa* is what he *is*. Why do you want him?"

"I have something of his. I wish to return it."

"Is it money? You can leave it here. He will come back."

"When?"

A shrug, her leathery neck contracting, her tendons bulging out. "I do not know. Soon."

"I have to leave. I wish to see him before I go."

Her eyes settled on the euros in Dalton's gloved hand. Rested there. Dalton stripped off two twenties. She did not look up but the signal was clear. He peeled off two more. The fifth one did the trick. She showed him her tooth—a fine sharp tooth and it would have looked even more fetching if it had not been all alone in her blood-red gums. Her tongue moved inside her open mouth, a blind white snake-head. She held her hand out, and Dalton placed the euros in her upturned palm. Her fingers folded over the crisp new bills like the valves of a Venus flytrap, and with a papery crackle the money disappeared. She stuffed it into the innards of her black dress and looked up at him again.

"How do you know him?"

"I don't."

This answer amused her. She bared her tooth at him again and touched it with her white snakelike tongue. Dalton had the idea she was tasting his scent. It was an unsettling concept.

"He is not Italian. He is from America. This is between you."

"Thanks for the advice. Do you know where he is now?"

She reached under the counter and pulled out a large cloth-bound book. It was the *Missa Solemnis,* tattered and ancient, with the leaves falling out. She laid it down on the folded napkins and opened it up.

Her talonlike finger moved down the open page until she reached a passage. She turned the book around so that Dalton could read it, keeping her blackened nail on the spot. It was the ordinary for the Giorno dei Morti, the Feast of all Souls.

She tapped it twice, staring up at him. Dalton looked at it for a while, trying to understand. She seemed unwilling to speak the words. Finally she sighed and frowned at him and then she spoke in an impatient whisper.

"In the Dorsoduro. Near this church. In the Calle dei Morti. *Numero quindici.* Number fifteen."

She pulled the book away, closed it slowly, and went back to her folding. The thing was done, her manner said.

Dalton was almost at the door when he heard her calling to him. He turned around. She raised a clawed hand and tapped the side of her skull with a blackened nail.

"Il Pellerossa. Ha dei grilli per il capo. Capisce? Guardatevi dal vecchio, scolaro."

Dalton understood some of it. She was telling him to be . . . careful? Gentle? To be gentle with the old man? And she was calling Dalton *scolaro,* a schoolboy. The rest was gibberish to him.

He bowed his thanks to her and walked back out into the sunlight. He was halfway through the Campo San Stefano and headed for the bridge over the Grand Canal that led into the residential district of the Dorsoduro when he finally worked out the translation of *grilli per il capo.* She was telling him that the old man named Pellerossa had maggots in his head. And *guardatevi dal vecchio* didn't mean be *gentle* with guy. It meant *beware* of him.

THE DORSODURO NEIGHBORHOOD was a warren of narrow lanes and back alleys on the far side of the Grand Canal. The workers and waiters and laborers and gondoliers, the people who kept the Grand Guignol theatrics of Venezia up and running for the tourists, lived down here in this maze of ancient stone alleys, along with the students and backpackers and eco-vagrants who could not afford the grand hotels along the canal or the villas behind San Marco.

The Calle dei Morti was at the far eastern end of the Dorsoduro. It was a tiny medieval laneway off the broad boardwalk. The waterway was used by freighters and cruise ships that docked along the Giudecca across the bay. The boardwalk was essentially deserted. The temperature had dropped in the hour it had taken Dalton to reach the turning of the alleyway, and a wind with a knife edge to it was blowing scraps of paper up the lane as he walked slowly along the street, looking for number fifteen.

He found it at the corner, where the *calle* turned into a wider canyonlike lane. He stopped in front of a battered ironbound wooden door set deep into a stucco-covered three-story house no wider than ten feet. Three narrow slitted windows with rusted iron bars rose upward above the door, one above the other. The eaves hung over the street, supported by old hand-hewn beams. In the middle of the door was a heavy lion's-head knocker.

Dalton lifted it up and struck the wooden door twice. On the second blow the door popped open about an inch. The door was unlocked. He pushed it open slowly, revealing a narrow flight of worn stone stairs rising into a gloomy darkness. Motes of dust floated in the cold sunlight. There was a scent in the air.

Something familiar. Cigarillos. Toscanos.

Not fresh, but present, drifting in the dead air like a miasma. Under the tobacco scent was the smell of unwashed clothes and dried sweat. Dalton leaned in to look up the stairwell. Beyond it there was only shadow.

Inside the door there was a dented bronze mailbox with three compartments. Two of them had names scrawled in pencil on scraps of paper: Alessandra Vasari had Numero Zero, and someone named Domenico Zitti had Numero Due.

The third compartment, Numero Tre, had no name card at all.

Dalton looked through the bronze grillwork and saw a thick sheaf of letters for Alessandra Vasari, many of them with American stamps. It appeared that no one was writing to the entity known as Domenico Zitti, at least not this week.

The third one, the unmarked one, was empty as well.

He gave up on the mail and went slowly up the narrow stairs, painfully aware of what a vulnerable position he was in as he climbed them, trapped by the pressing stone walls on either side, nowhere to go if somebody appeared at the top of the stairs with ugly intentions.

He reached the landing and saw that the stairs made a one-eighty-degree turn and continued to the second floor. There was light at the top of the second landing, a narrow bar of pale sunlight coming through the first of the slit windows. On this landing there was no light, only a hallway that ran about fifteen feet, ending in blackness.

He felt along the edge of the wall and found an old light switch. He twisted it and a dim glow appeared at the far end of the hall, coming from a light fixture set into the wall by the door to what Dalton assumed was Appartamento Tre. The floorboards creaked as he came down the hall, and the scent of Toscano cigarillos grew stronger. For reasons he could neither explain nor overcome, the skin on his belly and across his back tightened as he got to the door.

Standing in front of the heavy nail-studded barrier, he listened for a while. Although the door was thick and well set into a stone jamb, some sort of sound was coming through the planks. He put an ear up against the wood. It smelled of old paint and turpentine and cedar. What was coming through the thick planks was a low droning. No, a low muttering sound, rhythmic and oddly musical, but not quite music.

It was a sound that suggested speech, a kind of language, in that it had intonations and pauses, callings and responses, almost like a prayer or a chant.

But it was neither a voice nor an instrument; it was a sound unlike anything Dalton had ever heard. He stepped back, breaking contact with the door, put a hand up on the wood, and felt the beat of the sound like a muffled drum.

Maggots, the old lady said.

The man had maggots in his head.

He made a fist of his hand and pounded on the door four times, hard enough to shake dust out of the frame around the door. It silted down like fine sand and drifted in the glow of the pale light on the wall. Nothing. He pounded again, harder, leaving his fist on the door at the end of the last stroke. While he was standing there he remembered what Brancati had told him, about other guests in the Strega hostel and the strange moaning they had heard coming from Naumann's room. Was this the same sound? Dalton gave the latch a wrenching turn. The door was locked tight.

He pounded on the door again, his anger rising up. "Open the door! It's the police. Open up the door!"

Nothing.

He put his ear against the door and the sound came vibrating through the wooden planks. He jerked his head away, feeling suddenly dizzy and slightly nauseous, as if the floor had begun to rise up under his feet.

"Excuse me. Can I help you?"

He wheeled around, his balance a little off, and steadied himself on the wall. A woman was standing at the far end of the hallway, surrounded by a pale glow, her face in darkness but a shining aura of light in her hair.

"No, I'm sorry. I'm—"

"Are you the police? I heard you calling."

Dalton gathered himself together and came down the narrow hallway toward the woman, pasting a cardboard smile on his face.

"Not exactly. I'm with the American consulate."

"I heard you say you were police."

There was intelligence in her voice, and suspicion. Her accent was aristocratic Roman, her diction precise and careful.

"Yes. I did say that. I'm in a semiofficial position. I guess saying 'police' helps with the language barrier. I'm more of an investigator."

He reached the end of the hall and the woman backed away into the light flowing up the stairwell from the street door he had left open. She was tall, almost as tall as he, with long black hair in a severe cut, prominent cheekbones, and full scarlet lips. She was wearing a pale green cashmere top under a matching long-sleeved cardigan. Short black leather skirt; fine long, well-turned legs; and expensive Italian shoes, the stiletto type, in no way intended for walking.

She was full-figured (the word "luscious" came to him) and she smelled of single-malt scotch, a fine peaty scent. Also of cigarettes, and under these spicy aromas a familiar perfume that he dimly recalled but could not place. She was looking at him, directly and without emotion, a closed and guarded look.

"Do you have some identification?"

"Yes. Of course."

Dalton reached into his coat and extracted a slim blue leather folio with the seal of the United States on the cover. He flipped it open so that she could read it in the light. Next to an embossed holographic seal of the U.S. State Department there was a picture of him taken a few years ago, when he still had an Army haircut, and beside that his name and station: Micah Dalton/Consular Security Division.

She read it carefully and took her time comparing the photo with the man standing in front of her. Dalton let her take all the time she needed. If she didn't like this ID, he had four others just as impressive in his briefcase.

Finally she snapped the folio shut, handed it back to him.

"There is no one in that room. He left a day ago."

"I'm sorry. I don't know your name."

She looked sharply at him, and then smiled. "I am Alessandra Vasari. I own the building."

Her voice was low, with a rich vibrato, and it had the husky undertones of a smoker. Dalton made her age at forty, perhaps younger. She had no rings on her fingers. No jewelry of any kind, for that matter. But to Dalton's experienced eye she had that indefinable aura of very old money.

In spite of his dislike (face it, his envy) of old money, not to mention his throbbing headache and a general feeling that he had spent the last forty-eight hours poisoning himself with licorice-flavored cough syrup, he felt a mild resurgence of his long-extinct libido.

If Signora Vasari reciprocated any of this animal emotion, she was concealing it beautifully.

"May I ask who *was* living here?"

Wrong question.

He saw the suspicion flaring up in her hazel-brown eyes.

"Don't you know?"

Time to get official.

He altered his tone, hardened it.

"Ma'am, this inquiry has to do with matters of state. I'm following up on a request from an agency in Washington, D.C. We have an interest in the man who was living in this room. Under what name was he registered?"

That backed her off a bit.

"We do not 'register' guests. I rent out the rooms to people who seem reliable and honest. On a monthly basis. I have been told this man's name was Mr. Sweetwater. I believe he was an American Indian. What name were you looking for?"

"Pellerossa?"

She smiled thinly at that. "*Pellerossa* just means 'red skin' in Italian. Or, I suppose, Red Indian. I wish to know why are you interested in Mr. Sweetwater?"

She placed a slight ironic emphasis on the word "interested." Signora Vasari didn't approve of him. Either she didn't like authority figures or she didn't like Americans. Probably both, he decided. And seeing her dislike of him so manifestly apparent made Dalton think a little more carefully about this . . . *escapade* would be how Stallworth would put it, and not with a loving heart. This "innocent little side trip" to the Dorsoduro.

He had already used a solid State Department jacket with this stunningly delicious but intimidating woman, and if she got curious and followed up with the Consulate, the word would get back to Stallworth faster than a French soldier could throw away his rifle. The resulting cell-phone séance with Stallworth would go roughly as follows:

Jack: You used what?
Dalton: My consular ID, but—
Jack: So you could find some fucking Indian?
Dalton: Yes, but—
Jack: And this was company business how?
Dalton: The guy had this spider in his cigarette case and—
Jack: A spider?
Dalton: Right, a huge honking emerald green spider—
Jack: I asked you how this connects with Naumann!
Dalton: Well this Indian, he was eating at the same restaurant—
Jack: What restaurant?
Dalton: The restaurant where Porter used to eat. Carovita—
Jack: Hold the line for a moment, will ya? Don't go away now.

Three minutes later there'd be a knock on the door of his hotel room, and when he opened it there'd be these two no-neck ex-Marines from the company's Meat Hook Squad reaching for him, and then everything would go black. This was what he was risking right now and the burning question was . . . *Why?*

All of this flashed through Dalton's rather banged-up brain in a heartbeat. She was still waiting for an answer, an answer he didn't have.

"What do you do for a living, Miss Vasari?"

"Scusi?"

"Your work? May I ask what it is?"

Got her back on her heels now. Good.

"I . . . I am—*dottoressa.*"

Great.

Rattled her enough to bounce her back into Italian.

"Really? How nice for you. A doctor? In what field?"

"Psicologia. A Firenze."

"*Psicologia?* Psychology, you mean?"

"Yes."

A shrink. She was a shrink. *Run for your life, my friend.*

"Sounds fascinating. Want to know what I do?"

"What you do . . . ?"

"Yes. What I do is I *find* people. Sometimes I do this with the help of the Carabinieri. Is it necessary that I go and get the Carabinieri so that you will do me the great honor and courtesy of allowing me to have an interest in Mr. Sweetwater even though you do not approve of me?"

"Do not approve . . . ?"

Dalton held up a hand, palm out, and gave her a wry smile.

"I know. I am an instrument of the global Yankee Imperium and you despise me and all my works. When the revolution comes the proletariat will rise up and I—and all of my parasite kind—will be nailed to the doors of the basilica."

She stepped back and folded her arms across her breasts.

"You are—*tu sei pazzo!*"

"You called me '*tu.*' Does this mean we're friends?"

She started to smile, struggled against it, and then let out a short, sharp full-throated laugh that he could feel in his lower belly.

"You are very wrong, Signor Dalton, if you think I am one with the proletariat. My mother's family can be traced back for a thousand years. For much of that time they collected taxes for the Doge. Often this required the application of heated irons. When the revolution comes, I will be right up there beside you, also nailed to the doors of the basilica."

"It's a date, then?"

She gave him the cool professional appraisal of a full-grown Italian woman, an experience not to be missed. When it was over he felt like sharing some espresso and a biscotti with her in a tangle of scented sheets.

"*D'accordo.* And you do not have to tell me why you are interested in Mr. Sweetwater. *Allora,* you want to see his room?"

Yes. Then yours.

"I would love to."

Alessandra Vasari was wearing what Dalton had assumed was a gold link belt around her waist. It turned out to be what Laura would have called a "chatelaine," a chain with keys attached, the keys to the manor. In this case, the keys, among others, to the massive wooden door to Apartment Three. She led Dalton down the darkened hallway—Dalton would have followed her down any darkened hallway in the world at that point—her keys a-jangle and trailing her scotch-and-cigarettes scent behind her like a shimmering train of sparkling fairy dust. With deep appreciation Dalton watched the muscles across her shoulders working as she wrestled with the lock.

There was a snap and a rumbling as of tumbrels and the door rolled slowly backward, filling the darkened hallway with autumnal sunlight. In the glow from the opened room, she gave Dalton a theatrical bow and waved him through in front of her.

Dalton, who knew very well that old Italian families never advertised their wealth and that some of the best villas in Venice had entranceways that looked like the door to a toolshed, should have expected that Numero Quindici was a lot more than it had appeared to be from street level. It was as if they had stepped back into the Renaissance.

Five large wood-framed windows, each one eight feet high and two feet wide, ran along one whitewashed stone wall, the glass in them so old it had thickened along the lower part of the frames. Through the glass and over a sea of terra-cotta roof tiles the spire of the Church of All Saints rose up into the afternoon sky, a cloud of swifts swirling around it. On the end wall of the one-room flat was a massive stone fireplace with a great curved stone mantel. Above the mantel was the lion of the Medicis and over that two medieval lances forming a cross.

A rudimentary kitchen—added later, perhaps in the seventeenth century—consisted of a brick oven and a grill and a chimney above it. The floor was made of inlaid wooden marquetry, deeply worn but shining and smooth. A single bed, stripped, with the sheets and a brocaded coverlet neatly folded on the mattress, had been placed under the window wall. Two heavy green leather club chairs were positioned in front of the fireplace, in which was set a small pyre of cedar over a mound of torn paper. The room smelled of Toscano cigarillos, boot polish, and stale coffee.

Dalton took this all in with one glance while Alessandra Vasari stood behind him in the open door. None of it held him long. His attention was drawn to a tall terra-cotta cylinder, hanging by a leather thong in the center of the room. The cylinder was spinning slowly on what looked like a length of thick twisted sinew, the tube weighted enough to wrap and rewrap the sinew as it spun down and rewound, keeping the pressure on the cord, making the cylinder hum in the strong wind from the open windows. A strange murmuring buzz was coming from this cylinder, rising and falling, stopping and starting again, almost like a rhythmic chant.

He reached up to the spinning cylinder.

"Be careful, Signor Dalton. I think it has bees in it."

Incisions—slices—had been carved into the wall of the cylinder. They ran in wavelike forms all around the circumference. Standing close to it, watching it turning in the wind, Dalton could feel the sound waves swirling around it, rising out of its mouth. He reached up for it with both hands, hesitated.

And then he closed his hands around it.

The music ceased at once, and silence settled into the room. He raised the cylinder enough to slip the thong off the ceiling hook, and turned around to say something to Miss Vasari.

As he turned the motion disturbed a small round leather pouch balanced on a ledge inside the cylinder. It plopped to the floor at his feet, a swollen little leather balloon. Cocaine, he thought, kneeling down to touch it with a fingertip.

As soon as he touched it the neck of the bag burst open with a puffy little pop and a cloud of palepinkish smoke; the scent was almost exactly but not quite like eucalyptus, and it rose upward and covered his face. He fell back, dropping the cylinder onto the marquetry floor, where it shattered into pieces.

His head was pounding.

He could not draw a breath.

He was dimly aware of Alessandra Vasari's voice, but it was coming from a great distance. Incapable of either speech or motion, he watched as each shard of the terra-cotta cylinder changed into a scuttling spiderlike creature. They began to close in around him. The whole room turned a soft pale blue and then flashed into a blinding bright white—

—AND HE IS in the basement of their decrepit old federal town house in Quincy standing at his paint-stained workbench with a broken alabaster lamp base in his left hand and a tube of porcelain glue in his right but not really thinking just watching the snow fly sideways across the frost-glazed window and beyond the falling snow the slope of their lawn now mounded six feet deep with snow and past that to the churning sweep of Quincy Bay and Long Peddocks harbor; this would be his last happy memory of Boston Bay. He hears the front door open and then Laura's voice calling. No, not calling.

Crying his name, and the urgency of her tone is so electric that he drops the alabaster vase onto the workbench and runs up the staircase toward the half-open kitchen door, through the door, sliding on the braided rug; yes Laura is everything okay?

She is still screaming his name as he rounds the final turn down the front hall. Laura is standing in the open door with the blizzard swirling around her and her blond hair flying. At her feet is a paper sack of groceries spilling out its contents like a cornucopia of baby food and Handi Wipes. What chills him is the look on her face, as if she has been bled white and flash-frozen: the only color is in her wide open deep blue eyes and they are filled with horror. Past her, just out on the front porch, is the antique emerald green baby carriage with the gold trim and the golden springs, and now Laura is whispering his name and her face is as white as the snow that is whirling around her; she turns to point at the emerald green carriage, he rushes past her, she reaches out for him but he breaks through her grasp and blunders out into that wind-driven swirling white cloud of powdery snow. He looks down into the mounded green blankets and he sees—

—AN UNKNOWN WOMAN LEANING over him, an aura of light surrounding her, and under his back he's aware of a hard wooden floor and now he recognizes her scent, whiskey and cigarettes and the *name* of that perfume. It was Eau de Sud by Annick Goutal, Laura's favorite, drifting around him. The woman is leaning close, and as he focuses on her he sees that her strong, handsome face is full of worry and her voice is low, urgent, and frightened. He also notes, dimly at first but with increasing interest, that she is holding a large hypodermic needle in her left hand. And she's wearing surgical gloves.

"Signor Dalton? Are you all right? Are you okay?"

Dalton tried to raise his head. The room started to go white again and he let his head fall back against the tiles. He looked up at—

What was her name?

"I . . . I think I passed out."

"Yes. You did. *Sta prendendo medicine?* Do you take any medicines? Are you allergic to anything? Are you sick with anything?"

Dalton blinked at the ceiling for a minute, trying to get the room to stay still and not fill up with the disturbing white light again. For a moment he seemed to be caught between two worlds: Boston; Quincy, Mass.; the snow swirling around the window, his broken alabaster lamp, the baby carriage with its terrible little pink-wrapped package.

He shut those pictures down and by sheer force of will brought his unsteady focus back to Miss Vasari's strong Italian face and to the frightened expression in those amazing eyes.

"No. No medicine. Not sick. Just lost my balance."

She pursed her lips and shook her head.

"You did not lose your balance. You have been drugged by this powder. You were hallucinating. I have given you some Narcan and some Adrenalin to counter it. I have wiped the powder off your face. Can you stand up?"

Narcan? Adrenalin?

"I don't know."

"Perhaps I should call the Consulate?"

Please, don't, he thought to himself.

"No. No, I'll be fine."

He raised a hand to rub his eyes and saw that he wasn't wearing his black leather gloves. She must have pulled them off. He looked around him. His topcoat was lying in a heap beside him, next to his tie and his suit jacket, and his right shirtsleeve was pushed up to expose the vein in his arm. He closed his eyes and managed to sit up.

The room stayed mostly in Italy, and with her help he managed to get to his feet. She moved in close and put her arm around his waist, supporting him. Her body heat came through his shirt and her perfume—Laura's perfume—filled his head.

"You should sit. Here, on the chair."

She half-carried him—God she was strong—across to one of the two green leather club chairs in front of the big fireplace. Shards of pottery cracked under their feet as they crossed the floor.

Pottery.

Not spiders.

She got him into the chair and knelt down in front of him, the tanned skin on her fine knees dimpling white, her black leather skirt creaking.

"Would you like some water?"

"Water? Dear God. No water."

She smiled up at him. Some of the tension went out of her face.

"A scotch, then?"

"Yes. That would be wonderful."

She got up, peeled off her latex gloves with practiced skill, picked up what looked like a leather-bound medical kit, and considered him warily.

"You will be here when I get back?"

"I'll do my best. No . . . wait."

She stopped, an impatient look on her face.

"What did you stick me with?"

She glanced at the leather-bound kit, and shrugged.

"Narcan. And Adrenalin. It's an antidote for most narcotics."

"How did you know what to give me?"

"I'm a doctor."

"You're not a medical doctor."

Another shrug, which reminded him of Major Brancati.

"È vero. You wish to sue me?"

"No. God no. I'm sorry. Thank you."

Her broad smile reached all the way into her deep brown eyes.

"Un momento. Aspetta. I'll be right back."

Dalton watched her leave the room and thought in a pale lemon yellow kind of haze how nice it would be to watch her leave a room the way she left rooms for the rest of the long Venetian winter.

This of course he could not do, because in the deepest places of his heart, and, he realized, in a sudden crystalline clarity of thought that was probably the direct result of the Narcan, he knew that he had been well and truly *played*. Set up and baited and waltzed straight to this room by a calculating mind three steps ahead of him.

He knew that if he went back to Carovita to ask that old dragon some hard questions, he would find out that she had been paid to tell Dalton exactly what this strange old man had wanted him to know. And of course he came running, and got himself a faceful of hallucinogen for his trouble. Whatever the powder in that pouch was, and he assumed from its sudden and overwhelming effects that it was a psychoactive drug of some unknown kind, it had a kick like a Valparaiso jackass.

Stallworth's words came floating back to him:

"I tell you, kid, I'd love to know what it was. I mean, the company could use something like that."

Dalton looked down at his hands and saw, in his Narcan-induced acuity, that his left hand carried *no* bite mark at all.

He flexed it and saw the tendons rising like cables out of his clear skin. There was no blackened wound where he had ripped at the flesh with his scissors. No tiny red pinpricks where the green spider had supposedly bitten him.

He lifted the sleeve of his shirt enough to bare a length of his left forearm. It too was unmarked. No crisscross network of gouges and scratches. He patted his shirt pocket and pulled out the elastic-wrapped packet of Toscanos.

He shook it once.

Twice. Then, gathering his nerve, he ripped the elastics off and popped the lid. Six cigarillos lay in the box. He tipped the packet out over the floor, letting the cigarillos tumble out. The box was empty. There was no emerald green spider.

He had *never* been bitten.

None of that had ever happened. It had all been a hallucination—and a very deep and long-lasting hallucination, with much of its power remaining in effect even by the following morning. But the essence of the thing was plain: he had been drugged, set up in Naumann's room and drugged.

But how?

The cigarillos? Had the man left them on the table, knowing that Dalton would pick them up and smoke them?

That was leaving a lot up to chance, wasn't it?

Moonflowers.

Now he remembered where he had heard about moonflowers. Not from Jack Stallworth. Brancati had mentioned moonflowers when he was talking about Naumann's hotel room in Cortona. The cops had found a broken vase full of morning glories in Naumann's room. Brancati had told him that morning glories were nocturnal. That meant that they opened up their petals in the night. Last night there were moonflowers in Dalton's room at the hotel.

Right on the dresser. Near the minibar.

And his . . . attack . . . hadn't it come on shortly after the flowers opened? Opened up to release . . . what?

What had he been exposed to?

The persistence of the illusion seemed to imply . . . what?

Long-term residual effects?

Flashbacks?

Irreversible organic damage?

And even the grim possibility of ever-increasing impairment—leading to what? Insanity. Madness? Confined for life to some high-security institution. The question chilled him to his core.

As if to underscore his panic, the room began to grow pale again. He concentrated on his breathing and fought the rising panic. Gradually his vision stabilized; the colors of normal life came seeping back into the room while he considered the shattered terra-cotta cylinder and the small fan of pinkish powder lying on the parquet flooring.

If the idea had been to drug him for some unknown purpose, a vase full of doctored morning glories seemed like a damned uncertain way to accomplish that. But it had sure as hell worked, hadn't it?

Is that how Naumann got taken?

Taken by whom, Micah?

Who were *they*?

And why had *they* come after Dalton next?

If the idea had been to incapacitate him, or to confront him later in his room, or even to kill him, why had no one followed through? Why go to all the trouble to plant a vase full of doctored flowers in his room and then just walk away?

Unless they had assumed that drugging him was all they had to do, that the drug itself would have killed him, or driven him to kill himself. His reaction to being bitten by the imaginary spider was to take an imaginary blade to his left arm.

But it need not have been imaginary at all. In that state, out of control, hallucinating, a desperate life-threatening act was not only possible but very damn likely.

If he had taken a real blade to his arm, he would have bled to death in the bathroom. If the drug had persuaded him that he could fly, he would have stepped right off the balcony.

These things happened all the time; they were in the news every day. The verdict would have been suicide, or death by a suicidal misadventure, brought on by too much drink and by some unidentified narcotic. Just like Porter Naumann.

Brancati had already decided that Naumann's death, although possibly drug-related, was just one of those tragic outcomes that happen so often in the world of recreational drug use. In a way, the hallucination of Naumann's ghost may have saved Dalton's life, because he spent the rest of the evening chatting with a delusion instead of taking a flier off the balcony. Even if there had been no intent to kill him with this drug, there certainly was a criminal lack of concern with the outcome, which meant that the idea may have been simply to take him out of the picture.

He needed to get all of this stuff to a company lab as soon as possible. Dalton looked around the room for something to put the powder and the shards into and saw a wicker basket by the old woodstove. He got to his feet and staggered over to the oven. The basket was filled with torn scraps of paper, a crumpled grocery sack, a section of knotted raffia cord with a burned end, and the brittle remains of some kind of flat bread.

He rooted around in the basket and found a section of newspaper. He was kneeling on the floor carefully sweeping up the remains of the white powder with a gloved hand when he heard Miss Vasari's footsteps in the hall, and the sound of ice clinking in silver. To his drug-heightened perceptions, the sounds were amazingly distinct, each silvery bong of the ice as pure and crystalline as a temple bell. He closed his eyes and *saw* the notes, tiny ruby-colored fireflies floating through a deep-blue cloud. It was beautiful, but scary. Please God, don't let this be permanent.

"Signor Dalton, I am sorry. I have only Chivas. I hope—"

He opened his eyes as she came into the room, carrying a silver tray with a decanter, a silver ice bucket, and two scotch glasses, and saw him kneeling on the floor.

"What are you doing?"

"Still hallucinating, I think. How are you?"

She set the tray down on the kitchen counter and came over to kneel down beside him. She moved in a cloud of scent and her body was painfully *present* when she got this close.

As much as Dalton wanted to attribute this alarming return of his sex drive to sheer youthful resilience, he had the feeling that, despite the Narcan injection, whatever drug had been used on him was still sizzling away in his cortex.

Alessandra looked down at the powder. "You should not touch that. Not even with a glove on. And not without a mask. It is poison. You must see a doctor."

"I know," he said, still sweeping up the powder. "I can feel it. It's still in my head. But I need to get this stuff into a container. We can't let it blow around the room. Whatever it is."

Sighing, keeping her mouth closed tight, Alessandra helped him to sweep up as much of the powder as they could, keeping it off their skin. The powder went into a folded scrap of paper that Alessandra had retrieved from the wastebasket by the grill. The shards of pottery she put in a paper bag with the name *Mercato Via Gesa* on the side. Afterward she helped him sit down and knelt down in front of him, biting her lower lip as she studied his face.

"What is it like? Tell me. You are seeing things?"

"I don't know. Drugs aren't my usual sport. It's as if I had no skin and my hearing is abnormally acute—I can hear your skirt creaking and I can hear your breath in your throat. Visually? I can see that your eyes are not just hazel but a kind of auburn with tiny flecks of gold and green and silver around the iris. I can hear birds rustling out on the eaves and there are children playing with a jump rope down the street."

She lifted her head and looked to the window. Dalton studied the way the satiny white skin on her long graceful neck tightened as she did this. A large artery under her left ear was pulsing gently. He stared at it and found that he could *hear* her heart pumping under the swelling curves of her breasts, keeping perfect time with the push and release of that pale blue artery under her ear.

She looked back at him, and as her head moved it left afterimages of her face streaking across his mind's eye. When she spoke, her voice was like an organ in a cathedral. Her scent was extraordinary and he inhaled it with inner delight as she spoke.

"Yes, I can hear them. Your pupils are very large. The light must hurt. And you are flushed. Your breathing is shallow and rapid."

She reached out and placed two fingers of her right hand against the muscle of his neck at a point just under his jawline. Her fingers seemed to melt right through his skin. He found that he *adored* her. He reached for her. She caught his hand neatly as it came up to cup her left breast and held it firmly in the air, smiling a little to herself as she did this, but she kept her fingers under his jaw and she was counting to herself in Italian, a throaty whisper: *diciassette— diciotto—diciannove.*

When she finally spoke her tone was all business.

"Your heartbeat is febrile. I will call a doctor."

"No. I'm sorry. I can't see a doctor."

"You must. You have been poisoned."

He closed his eyes and shook his head. In his skull ruby red fireflies bounced off the curve of his mind and skittered away over a green velvet horizon. He opened his eyes again and she filled up his sky like a planet.

"I'm stoned. It will go away. I cannot see a doctor. And you're going to have to back away or I will probably kiss you."

She smiled again, and stood up, looking down at him. In his mind she was like a tall cypress swaying in a sea wind.

"That is the drug. It has aroused you sexually. But are you always like this? I think maybe no. You are far too dissipated for sex. Whatever it is you do for a living, it is very hard on you. If you go on doing it, it will probably kill you. You are not having a good life and there is in your heart some ugly thing. Although you are a young man, or at least not yet very old, already you have the outward marks of *tor-*

menti di spirito. I wonder how long since you have had a woman. With any real pleasure in it. Any joy. Or even with any kind of true libido. *Allora,* this drug may be an aphrodisiac. Perhaps it is ecstasy mixed with something like psilocybin. The effects are very pronounced."

"Damn right they are," said Dalton, trying to conceal his obvious physical response to her. "How about that scotch?"

"Can you stand up?"

"I can get up, I think."

He tried.

The room started to disintegrate, the walls opened onto galaxies.

"But . . . I think I better not."

She walked away and Dalton heard the delicate tinkling of silver bells as she dropped three ice cubes into a glass. The sound of the scotch pouring was like river rapids hissing through his head.

When she came back her footsteps echoed and reechoed around the bare walls of the room. She sat down in the chair opposite him and crossed her legs. Dalton found himself delighted that she had and he sincerely hoped that she would do it again.

"Who is Laura?"

"I talked about her?"

"Not clearly. Is she someone important to you?"

Psicologia.

"What else did I say? While I was under."

"Something about the snow. And, I think . . . *ghiacciolo?*"

Icicle.

The word lanced right through his skull.

He closed his eyes. He heard the creak of leather and the tinkle of the ice in her drink as she leaned forward and placed a warm hand on his knee. He opened his eyes and saw the concern in her strong, handsome face.

"This is something you do not want to talk about."

"No. I don't."

"You should. With someone. The drug has brought it out, but it was always there. May I call you Micah?"

"Please. May I call you Alessandra?"

"No. My friends call me Cora."

The suggestion of growing intimacy implicit in her use of the word "friends" warmed him for a moment, a feeling that was shattered completely when the ghost of Porter Naumann materialized a few feet behind Cora Vasari's shoulder. His looks had not appreciably improved in the daylight. He was still wearing those green pajamas.

"I ask you to go help Laura, I find you flirting with a babe."

Dalton shot him a hunted look, feeling a crawling tingle of sheer panic slithering up his spine. Irreversible brain damage. A lifetime of mental impairment. Delusions. Madness. He shook his head, trying to drive the illusion out of his mind. But when he opened them again, Naumann was still there, looking mildly offended.

Cora seemed unaware of the existence of a six-foot-tall ghost in green pajamas leaning on the mantel of her fireplace, supported by an artful elbow, a half smile on his mutilated face as he took in the large medieval room with evident appreciation.

"So," she said, "I have a question. You will be honest?"

"Of course. A little. Sort of. It depends."

"This is nuts," said Naumann, shaking his head. "If you're looking to boink this babe—and I admit she is eminently boinkable—then find another method. Sympathy fucks are pitiful."

Dalton kept his focus fixed on Cora's eyes as if they were the only doors out of Hell.

Cora touched his hand. "You look terrible. What is happening here?"

"I wish I knew. I really do."

She frowned. "I too am involved. The man stayed in *my* home. I could have touched that . . . thing . . . myself. I was here. I saved your life. You are . . . *come si dice* . . . *obbligato*?"

"I *am* grateful, Cora. I am. But I really have to go."

She lifted her glass to him in an ironic *salute*.

"*D'accordo.* No problem. *Ciao!* I will watch."

From over Cora's shoulder, Naumann watched with evident amusement as Dalton got halfway to his feet before the blue-white tide came roaring back, this time rising up from the floor. He felt the chair creak under him as he fell heavily back into it. She regarded him with a sly smile over the top of her glass.

"So. *Aspetta.*"

"I've got to sleep this off."

"No sleep for you. You are drugged. *Incapacitato.* Talk."

For a time, Dalton said nothing. She waited in a self-contained calm. Naumann watched Dalton's face with wary intensity, shaking his head slowly.

"I can tell you some of it. I do owe you that."

"*Oh, please,*" said Naumann.

Dalton looked down at his hand, and then took a sip of Chivas.

"I was in Italy to look into the death of a friend of mine. His name was Porter Naumann—"

Naumann threw his hands up in frustration and walked away shaking his head. Dalton forced himself to look only at Cora.

"He was a good friend. He died of a heart attack the day before yesterday. In Cortona. His death was unexpected. The company—"

"What company?"

"Naumann worked for an English bank called Burke and Single."

"I do not know this bank."

"They're not well known. Anyway, when his body was found—"

"Where?"

"In the courtyard of the Cappella San Nicolò."

"Oh yes. I know it. A sad little church. Very old. Your friend died there? Of a heart attack? Was he old?"

"No. Fifty-two. And in good health. Or so I thought."

"You are not telling me everything about this death, are you?"

"Let's just say it was ugly."

"In what way?"

What the hell? She was a grown-up. He laid it all out for her, the rain in Cortona, the crime scene tent, Major Brancati. The ruined body of Porter Naumann. The injuries he suffered.

He said nothing about the green spider and stayed far away from any mention of what had taken place in the piazza. Cora took the narrative in without a flicker, and when he finished she was quiet for a while. Dalton found that he could stand up and went to pour two more scotches. Naumann came over to meet him by the drinks tray.

"This is very nasty territory, Micah," he said, in a stage whisper, as if Cora could hear him. "Don't drag her into it."

Dalton mixed the drinks without looking at or in any other way acknowledging Naumann's warning. When he handed Cora her scotch, she took it without much attention, her professional self now fully engaged.

"To me this sounds like your friend had some kind of psychotic break. People undergoing such a psychotic break have done terrible things. To others. To themselves. This may be consistent with what has happened to your friend. Sometimes the . . . the trigger? . . . of such an episode has been drugs. Psilocybin. Peyote and its hydrates. Mescaline. LSD. Occasionally you will find organic causes. This Brancati has told you that he thinks Mr. Naumann had *un colpo apoplettico,* yes?"

"Yes."

"But there was no time for all the blood work to be done?"

"No. I'm going to Cortona tonight, as a matter of fact. To take charge of his body. And his insurance firm will want to do their own toxicology tests."

"Don't forget my Chopard," put in Naumann. Dalton glanced up at him, and then forced his attention back to Cora.

"Of course," she went on, "I do not have much regard for the pathologists who work for the Carabinieri. They are *buffoni*. Clowns. You tell me this policeman says the forensic autopsy suggests stroke. I have seen cases where psychotic episodes have caused *un colpo*. There may have been a physiological flaw, such as an undetected aneurysm. Your friend was fifty-two? His age makes a stroke very plausible. Was he . . . indulgent? A drinker? Given to excess?"

"Hey! I was in damn good shape, lady," said Naumann.

"He was in excellent shape."

"There you go, kid. Thanks."

"Except for his prostate."

"Schmuck."

"Well, at his age, a prostate problem is very usual."

"My age? I was *fifty-two*, for Christ's sake."

"*Allora*, what I do not understand is what any of this has to do with the old Indian man and his spinning pots."

"Not a damn thing, sweetheart," said Naumann, coming across the room and dipping his index finger into Dalton's scotch, stirring the cubes around. The tinkling sound drew Cora's attention again to the glass, so Dalton snatched it up and took a sip, watching in mute horror as Naumann stuck his index finger into his mouth and sucked the scotch off it. Dalton found the action impossible to ignore.

"Why do you *do* that? You can't taste anything?"

"What?" said Cora, staring at him, but he was looking up at Naumann and did not hear her speaking. Naumann took his finger out and stared down at it with a thoughtful expression.

"Like hell I can't," he said, licking his fingertip.

"Who are you talking to?" asked Cora, in a soft voice.

"Sorry. Sorry, Cora, I guess I was thinking out loud."

"No. You were *talking* to . . . someone else."

"It's the drug, I think. Last night I had a terrible time with it."

"*More* drugs? What drug did you take last night?"

"I mean, I had a dream, a nightmare. Last night."

"What kind of nightmare?"

"Nothing. I meant today. I meant to say today. That thing—whatever was in that pouch—it made me see things."

"For a CIA guy you are one lousy liar," said Naumann.

"Yes. But you *knew* them?" Cora persisted. "The images were familiar?"

Dalton instinctively shied away from the question, but his face was answer enough for her. She was alarmingly bright.

"Yes. They were . . . familiar."

"From your past?"

"Yes," said Dalton, and only because any attempt at a lie would have been detected at once. She looked as if she wanted to press for more, but then she let it pass.

"I see. And did your Mr. Naumann also have bad memories?"

"If you answer that," said Naumann, "you're a total putz."

"I don't know."

"You do not know *anything* about your friend's personal life?"

"She's shrinking you, buddy," said Naumann. "Just shut up."

"Not much."

"His past?"

"Nothing comes to mind."

"You lie easily, but not well. You shut me out. There it is. I do not care. But you should try to find out. Perhaps he was seeing a therapist. Psychological issues. There might be official records."

"Tell the little bitch to mind her own damn business."

Shocked, offended, Dalton sent Naumann a black look.

"Watch your mouth, Porter."

Cora was silent for a time, studying Dalton's face while he tried to force his expression into what ended up as a twisted parody of innocence. She took his hand in hers, leaned forward.

"Porter? You are talking now to your dead friend Porter?"

"No."

"Your dead friend Porter is talking to *you*?"

"No. Yes. Maybe. I think he *thinks* he is."

Cora blinked, sighed. "He is in *this* room? Now?"

Naumann shook his head vigorously, holding his hands up. "Leave me out of this."

"He's behind you," said Dalton. "He's leaning on the fireplace."

Cora turned and of course saw nothing at all. When she looked back at Dalton, her expression had softened and there was a worried look in her eyes.

"You *must* let me take you to the clinic, Micah. I know the best people there. We need to make some tests. You might have some neurological damage. Truly, Micah. This is very dangerous for you. These . . . these visions, they could come again. Without warning."

She spoke with such unshakable confidence, such searing professional certitude, that her words cut deep. He had a fleeting vision of Laura in her white room by the sea, the salt wind billowing the curtains as she stared dead-eyed into eternity.

"Now you're *getting* it," said Naumann, his tone gentle. "I said this situation was dangerous. This is exactly what I meant."

Dalton took Cora's hand. It was warm and strong.

"Thank you, Cora. I promise that when I get back to London—"

"I thought you were stationed *here*? At the Consulate?"

"My base is in London," he said, glad that this at least was true.

"Then you must go back tonight. I will go with you!"

"I will go. Not tonight. But as soon as I can find out what happened to Porter."

She withdrew her hand, her expression closing. "You're an idiot," said Cora. "I'm sorry. But it is true."

"Yes. I am."

She sat back and glared at him, her face reddening. "Fine. *Basta*. I don't care. Who are you to me? I don't even *know* you. It is ridiculous to care. I do *not* care."

She turned and looked behind her: by chance, she happened to be glaring right at Naumann, who stiffened, his ironic detachment vanishing.

"And the same for you, *Signor Spettro Cancrenato, mostra che divora i cadaveri, chi si diletta di orrori. Io ti caccio via! Ciao!*"

Here a vulgar but classic Italian gesture—done with snap and fire—and then she rounded again on Dalton, her face flushed and her dark eyes glittering.

"So. *Dove conduce questa strada?* Back to business. You are pleased to imagine that if this man, he wants to harm your friend, that he will do this by giving him this . . . this drug?"

"It's a theory," said Dalton, rattled by the intensity of her concern, and even more so by her unshakable conviction that profoundly ugly things awaited him in the medical line if he didn't get to a hospital right now. "The catch is, there's nothing to connect Porter directly to . . . to this man. Other than a restaurant."

She hesitated. Dalton could see she was holding something back. He waited it out, saying nothing to distract her.

"Yes. There is," she said, at last, with a resigned sigh.

"What is it?"

"If I understand you, it is possible that this Mr. Sweetwater—this Indian man—was in Cortona. When your friend died."

"How do you know that?"

She reached down and lifted up the paper bag with Mercato Via Gesa printed on the side.

"This. It was in the refuse bin."

"A shopping bag?"

"It is not mine. The rooms are cleaned every day and all the garbage goes out. Every day. But today my woman was not able to come. So this bag was left by Mr. Sweetwater himself. And it is not old. A very new bag."

"I don't understand."

"Mercato Via Gesa is a grocery store."

"Yes?"

"It is a grocery store in Cortona."

Dalton's cell phone rang, a high-pitched shriek that made them all jerk. An expression of fleeting resentment flashed across her face as she stood up and walked away to the windows, passing right through Naumann's ghost on the way, her back stiffening reflexively as she did so and a tremble rippling down the length of her body. She stood at the open window and looked out at the spire of the Ognissanti basilica, her strong arms folded across her breasts and her expression closed, shuttered, cold.

Dalton fumbled through his coat pockets, found his phone:

"Hello. Yes?"

"It's Mandy. Where are you? I hope you're still in Venice."

"Last chance to bail, Micah," said Naumann. "From here on in, it's all running with scissors."

"Mandy? Yes, I'm still in Venice. What's the matter?"

"Get to Marco Polo Airport. The company jet is waiting. You have to come back to London. You have to come back *right now*."

"Why? What the hell's the problem, Mandy?"

"You want it in the clear?"

Naumann's ghost was standing near to Cora as she stood by the window, her back to the room, staring out at the red-tiled rooftops and the spire of the Church of All Saints, at the clouds of swifts that swirled around the spire, crying and wheeling, rising in the wind. Naumann was looking at Dalton and the expression on his face was closed, unreadable. After a moment, he shook his head slowly and turned away.

"Yes, Mandy, I want it in the clear."

"Okay. It's Joanne. And the girls."

"Yes. What?"

"They're dead."

"Dead?"

"Butchered, Micah. Slaughtered. It's awful. They're saying Porter did it. They're saying *he* killed them. You have to come home."

monday, october 8
the bighorn mountains
eastern wyoming
8 p.m. local time

the shadow of the Bighorns had stretched out across the rolling
brown hills of the Powder River country as far east as Ranchester
and a deep cobalt night was rising up out of Kansas when Pete Kearney came out to call for his dogs. Pete was tall and hard-looking,
with a weathered mahogany face and deep-set black eyes. He stood
on the porch of his cabin, his Winchester 94 in his left hand, and
waited for a while in the twilight, watching the light changing on
the plains far below the limestone outcrop on which he had built his
home. In the stand of lodgepole pine beside the square-cut log
cabin, a horde of crows had settled into the trees for the night, and
the sound they made reminded Pete of dry corn husks rattling together. He pulled in a breath and whistled for the dogs again—three
clear high-pitched tones, descending. The echoes of the whistle
bounced off the limestone cliffs behind him and faded into the forest all around.

Nothing.

The dogs did not come.

Pete frowned and stood a while in quiet consideration.

This was not like Cisco, the wizened old blue tick, who in their sixteen years together had never missed the dinner bell, but it was like Brutus, the young piebald bull terrier who had come ambling out of the brush only six months back, black eyes full of fun, tongue hanging out, grinning like a crocodile, trailing a snapped leather leash. His paws were bruised and bloody and his muscular shoulders had withered from hunger. His ribs showed like barrel staves along his flanks. It had taken Cisco a while to warm to the young pit bull, but Pete had taken to the stray right off. Nobody had ever called to ask about a missing pit bull, and Pete never put it out that he had one, and in the eastern Bighorns people kept to themselves, so the time passed and it was just Pete and his dogs and the day-to-day of living in the half-wild.

Until tonight.

"Cisco! Brutus! Come on, boys! Dinner's up."

The crows began to caw in the lodgepole stand, and a few flew up in a rattle of black feathers, settling again after a few wheeling turns. A dry wind stirred the pine needles and set up a dust devil in the clearing in front of the porch. A feeling got started in Pete Kearney's belly. It slithered around his hips and started to crawl up his backbone and he lifted the Winchester, levered a 30-30 round into the chamber, and stepped down off the porch.

His boots made a dry, scraping sound as he crossed the clearing and walked to the drop-off fifty yards ahead. He stood there for a while, looking out over the sweeping valley floor a thousand feet below, listening to the woods around him. The Winchester was heavy in his hand, and a cutting chill was in the wind off the eastern plains.

He did not call for the dogs again. He walked to his left, moving as quietly as he could, keeping the ledge beside him, heading for the turn in the drive. As he moved he looked at every bush and tree, looked down at his feet and up into the treetops, their branches swirling in the rising wind. The leaves began to hiss and bristle and rust-colored pine needles skittered across the stony ground. Pete reached the curve of the gravel drive and looked down the tree-branch tunnel as the road curved around and bent itself out of sight. Shadows grew along the edge of the road, and darkness welled up as if from out of the ground, like black water. Pete lifted the carbine and stared down the iron sights, traversing the road and the woods along its edges. It was the only way in here, and if someone was coming for him, this is where he would have to come from. This narrow gravel track was the only way in.

Where were the dogs?

His back was twisted tight and his belly muscles jumped as he stared out at the surrounding darkness with a flat wary look on his battered face. His cabin was hard to get to—built right at the base of a cliff that rose up another five hundred feet, sheer as a rock face.

The outcrop was shaped like a big scythe, a flat crescent of yellow limestone that projected out over a cliff that fell away a thousand feet to the floor of the valley. The road was the only way in, and the dogs would have told him if anyone was coming.

And *nothing* gets past the dogs.

Ever. So . . . where were the dogs?

Pete moved into the brush on the cliff side of the road and walked slowly down through the grade, the carbine up and out. He was like a soldier walking point on hostile ground. About twenty feet down through the brush a scent came to him, and a sound like a clock ticking—a steady tick . . . tick . . . tick . . . the scent grew stronger.

Something flashed down, a tiny red spark in what was left of the light: it hit a soft bed of pine needles about six feet in front of him, making a sharp ticking sound when it struck.

Pete looked up into the lodgepole pine and saw a tawny blunt shape in the twilight, about forty feet up the trunk. Brutus was hanging there, his stomach ripped open and his ropy guts looping down from his slit belly. He had a bright silver wire around his neck—it had cut almost through; his head was almost off. The other end of the wire was looped over a branch, from which it ran backward and down into a stand of trees about fifteen feet away, a thin silvery thread ending in a blackberry bush. The ground below Brutus was thick with blood. As he watched, another drop separated from a loop of the dog's guts and fell down onto the nest of pine needles.

Tick.

Tick.

Pete moved past the hanging dog, his mind quite still, his breathing steady, his senses fully awake. He felt no particular fear, and he was not angry in any use of the word that would mean something to a civilian. He was *set.*

Focused on the outcome.

Whoever did this was good, and clever, and artful in the woods, none of which would help him one damn bit, because he was going to die anyway. Pete was going to kill him. He'd killed many a man in the woods or in the jungles and later in the dry brown hills of Afghanistan.

A few yards more and a much stronger smell of death—of sewage and fresh blood—was very close: he found Cisco dead in a tangle of pine boughs and ivy, his head twisted almost all the way around on his neck, his bowels having emptied as his spine snapped. His eyes were wide and the white showed all around. His pink tongue was out, and someone had sliced three inches off the tip with a very sharp knife.

For amusement, it seemed.

Pete looked around him and moved back into a stand of tall pine. He settled his back up against the rough bark of an old jack pine a few yards away from Cisco's body, placed the carbine across his knees, and stared out into the gathering darkness, breathing through his slightly open mouth, his breath curling in a blue frost in front of him.

He had the cliff on his left and the tree at his back and the road in front of him and there was no way whoever was out there could get to him, unless he came straight in.

Pete looked upward and saw through the black pine boughs far above him an arc of indigo sky with a few early stars glittering. The night wind was now rising off the Great Plains, and the deeper mountain cold was coming down. In the rolling valley far below him the lights of Ranchester glimmered in the darkness, and over the mounded shapes of the faraway hills he could see the yellow glow of Sheridan. The heavy barrel of the Winchester was cold in his hands.

He looked out into the night, into the black forest all around him, the tall pines rising up, felt the soft carpet of needles under him. He wished Cisco and Brutus an easy run to green fields under a rolling sky with snow-peaked mountains in the far blue distance, and then he emptied his mind of all thought. His heart was beating slowly, his breathing was calm and steady, and when he exhaled he did it silently. The Winchester carbine had a big hollow-point round in the chamber and the hammer was cocked and the magazine held six rounds and he had ten more in his jacket pocket. Pete Kearney was ready.

tuesday, october 9
london, england
11 p.m. local time

ondon in the great all-surrounding English dark, a gleaming galaxy
of city lights rising up at him through the cloud-rack and the
fumes of the sprawling city, the pearl-string of lamps that ran along
the banks of the wide curving Thames, the Gothic façade of the
Parliament reflected in the broad run of the river by Westminster
Bridge, the glittering disk of the Millennium Wheel slowly turning
on the pier by the Jubilee Gardens as the shuddering Bell bore south
for the Westland Heliport in Battersea, where a company driver—a
woman named Serena Morgenstern, who looked to be about eleven—
was waiting for him, leaning on a big blue Benz, her long black hair
fluttering in the downdraft from the clattering machine, scraps of
paper swirling into the cool weed-scented air, the lights of Chelsea
across the river glimmering on the broad black waters of the Thames.

"Sir," said Miss Morgenstern, bowing, giving him a meaningful
look as she held the back door open for him. Dalton—groaning only

a little—melted into the plush black leather. She closed the door with a solid Teutonic *whump*, rocking the machine on its springs hard enough to rouse Dalton from his confusion. He ruefully contemplated the back of her head as his driver slipped in behind the wheel, and eventually recalled with horror that *she* had been the girl who, after the last Christmas bun-fight, he had taken back to his flat on Wilton Row, where he had then failed quite dramatically to follow through on the agenda so clearly laid out in the protocols for these encounters.

As they rolled out onto Lombard heading for the Battersea Bridge, she confirmed his worst fears by giving him a raised eyebrow and an impish grin, which he found it possible—barely—to overcome thanks to a brutal hangover and the lingering effects of Cora's Narcan shot. He put his head back into the rest and said, more to himself than to his driver, although she heard it anyway, and smiled when she did, "Nymph, in thy orisons be all my sins remembered."

"Beg pardon, sir?"

Dalton closed his eyes; his bones turned to lead and his blood to sand. Under the wheels the Battersea Bridge boomed with a deep metallic roar as Chelsea filled up the windshield. "Serena, got any coffee, at all?"

"Hot and hot, Mr. Dalton. In the cooler. There's some dough-nuts if you want them. And some crisps."

Dalton, who knew what vile threats the English intended by the word "doughnut," settled for a tall cup of strong black coffee poured straight from the pot. He leaned back again and watched the late-night strollers walking along the shops and pubs of King's Road. He observed them with a detached out-of-body feeling, as if what was going on out there beyond the glass of the Benz was a hand-tinted film of a time long gone, all the people in it dead and their old bones burned.

Cup listing perilously in his lap, he was asleep by the time Serena pulled the limousine to a halt in front of Porter Naumann's London town house at 28 Wilton Place in Belgravia, a four-story neoclassical town house with a white stone lower façade, a black spear-tipped wrought-iron fence surrounding a garden with two very large urns holding tall spiked dracaena, a black lacquered door between stained-glass lights, a polished brass plaque and three bricked upper floors, and tall sash windows neatly ordered row upon row, and all around the white-stone façades floated the settled comfortable air of compound interest and dependable stocks.

All the lights were on—on every floor—and the interior of the house seemed to glow with rose and the half-seen reflections of polished brass and antique silver. The heavy wooden door opened before Dalton could touch the gilt handle and one of the station heavies— a black man in civvies whose name he could never recall and who looked in silhouette like an industrial freezer—snapped out a Marine Corps salute, which Dalton returned so crisply that the neck wrench brought his headache right back.

"They're all upstairs, sir," he whispered, as Dalton came into the center hall and stood under the glow of a Tiffany chandelier. He looked up at it and remembered all the fine times that he had been a part of in the years that the Naumann family had lived here. Porter had brought the Tiffany chandelier back for Joanne in the third year of their marriage. The interior of the town house was frigid, as if the air-conditioning had been turned on to Full and left that way for days.

"Thanks, Barney," said Dalton, the name coming to him from some recess of his brain where such things were imperfectly stored. He dropped his briefcase on the black-and-white marbled floor and threw his topcoat over the Duncan Phyfe chair that he had once tripped over while backing away from one of Naumann's predatory daughters during a New Year's party. That seemed like a century ago. He went up the curving staircase into a breathing silence, aware of Barney's placid equine stare on the back of his neck.

Mandy Pownall, one of the Agency's Vestal Virgins—one of those frighteningly efficient female staffers without whom there would be no Agency at all—was waiting for him outside the master bedroom. Mandy, a long-necked, fine-boned, and aristocratic-looking woman with a slim but nicely rounded shape, was wearing a gray pinstripe jacket-and-skirt affair, black ballet flats, and, intriguingly, charcoal-tinted 1940s-era silk stockings with seams.

She glided forward to him as he walked down the hall and took him into her body, wrapping her arms around him and burying her face in his neck. He held her there for a moment, breathing her in, aware that she had been into the gin but not recklessly and that her perfume, though floral, was not cloying.

Her unsteady breathing slowed in a while and she pushed him back, holding him by the upper arms as she gave him a look-over, her eyes a little black around the lower edges and her lipstick slightly smeared.

"Jesus, Micah. Are you all right?"

"No. Not in the slightest. How are you?"

"Ghastly. What happened to Porter? Do we know?"

"Not yet," he said, glancing at the closed bedroom door. "They're all in there?"

Mandy shuddered—a whole-body tremble—and sighed.

"All three of them. Joanna. The girls."

"Who's seen them?"

"Only our medics."

"What about the police?"

"So far we've managed to paper it over. There were only eight messages on Joanne's voice mail, three of them from Jack Stallworth's assistant, Sally Fordyce. The last one is only six hours old."

"What about the girls?"

"No voice mail. We've gone over their computers. We broke their passwords and sent out a general e-mail to everyone listed in their books, saying that they were all going away for a while and hinting obliquely at a detox issue, which I'm sure all their friends would find totally convincing."

"What about the neighbors?"

"This is Belgravia. The *last* thing the people of Belgravia do is show the *slightest* interest in anything. It's terribly non-U."

"You talked to Stallworth?"

She rolled her eyes. "No. I have *listened* to Stallworth. I didn't get the chance to talk."

"Who's getting this detail?"

"Stallworth says you are."

"What about Rowland? He's the station chief here."

"Our sector was always independent. Stallworth wants to keep it that way. Anyway, Rowland doesn't want it. I don't blame him."

"What resources do we have?"

"Removals. All the cleaning staff you need."

"Where do you fit in?"

"Whatever I can do."

"I guess Forensics has already been in?"

"Yes. Not that they found much. It was as if no one had ever lived here. The place had been thoroughly scrubbed. No prints. No fibers. No fluids. Forensics *did* say that a fire had been lit in one of the wastebaskets. It looked like—"

"A *fire*? Where?"

She inclined her head toward the bedroom door. "In there. Where *they* are."

"Didn't the fire alarm go off?"

"The internal system logged it. But then someone in the house pressed the cancel button—"

"They'd have to know the PIN number."

"They did. Otherwise the fire brigade would have come around to check it out. The security company saw the cancel order and called them off."

"What about the perimeter alarms?"

"They weren't activated."

"Porter had internal cameras everywhere. What do they show?"

"That's hard to describe."

"Try."

"Well, the hard disk can only store about a week's worth, and the program dumps the data every Sunday, so all we had was from Monday, the first of October. The film looks normal, Joanne moving around the house, the girls coming and going; the cleaning lady came in on Tuesday. The usual domestic activity, until . . ."

"Time marker?"

"Fourteen hundred thirty-nine hours on Thursday. October four."

"Okay. What happened then?"

"That's the thing, Micah. The images all went dark."

"You mean one of the cameras failed?"

"No. They *all* failed."

"They just . . . flicked off?"

"No. It started at the one covering the front door. You can see the street, see people going up and down Wilton, crossing the coverage area. Everything normal, and then the picture seems to fog up. No, more like *cloud over.*"

"Cloud over?"

"Smoke, it looked like. Or a dark fog. Anyway, first that camera goes. Then, in the downstairs hallway camera, you see Joanne going to the door, and she opens it—and everything goes dark on that camera as well. The rest go one by one. Same thing happens to all of them."

Dalton let that sink in for a time.

"Have they been checked?"

"Yes. All of them. They're . . . fried, I guess is the word. They're all digital, and the receptor has been . . . corrupted somehow. Almost like some sort of magnetic pulse."

"What about the remote disk?"

"Well, it would only show what it was receiving, wouldn't it?"

"Jesus, what could cause that? Do *we* have anything like that?"

"I wouldn't know. You'd be more likely to get that sort of gadget. The Langley boffins don't share well, especially with the foreign stations."

"I'll ask Jack about it. Pull the remote disk. I'll take it with me. You said there was a fire?"

"In the wastebasket. Someone burned something."

"Burned what?"

"It was odd. String. A section of string. That brown cord that they use to tie up packages. It had a bunch of little knots in it."

A section of raffia cord, with a burned end.

In Sweetwater's apartment in Venice.

"Knots? What do you mean?"

"Knots. Every few inches, a little knot had been tied in the string. Then it had been set on fire and dropped into the basket, along with some broken pottery. Like a flowerpot, sort of. We have it all here, if you want it."

He was looking through the closed wooden door but his mind was back in Cortona, in Naumann's rented room at the Strega hostel, and Brancati's description of what his men had found there.

"Mr. Naumann bought a bottle of Chianti and some cigarillos. He smoked the cigarillos and drank the Chianti and slept on top of the bed. At one point he smashed an old pot filled with morning glories, and then he made a small fire in the wastepaper basket—"

"He started a fire?"

"Yes. It set off the smoke alarm. The clerk went up. Mr. Naumann did not open the door. He said it was only a cigarette. He was very apologetic. The clerk went away."

"He broke a flowerpot?"

"Yes. It was full of *morning glories. Moonflowers. They were in one of those tall round things, like you would put white wine bottles into. To keep them cool.*"

"Did any of you *touch* the pottery?"

"Touch it?"

"Make skin contact with it. Breathe it. Any kind of close contact?"

"No. Our people always use masks. That's standard."

"Were there any flowers in the pot?"

"Flowers?"

"Yes. Flowers?"

"Yes. I think so. White ones. Large."

"Morning glories?"

"I suppose so, Micah. I don't do shrubbery."

"Where are they now?"

"The flowers?"

"Yes, Mandy," he said, sighing a bit. "The flowers."

"It's all in a sealed box by the door. Everything. Stallworth told Forensics to leave it all for you. They didn't like it much, but Stallworth made it clear to everyone that you were lead on this one. I had to sign off for it, but it's all there. The security tapes, digital shots of everything. The alarm company log. Photos of . . . of them."

"In my briefcase. The tan one by the hallway chair. I have a paper sack sealed inside an evidence bag. Inside the sack there are some pieces of broken pottery, a pack of Toscanos cigarillos, and a little leather bag with some kind of powder. Take everything you found here, and crate it up with the rest. Including the morning glories. All of it has to go to Stallworth at Langley in a diplomatic pouch. Mark the shipment with a Hazmat tag and send it triple-sealed in a vacuum canister."

"Why the flowers, Micah?"

"If you get a knock on the door and you see it's a man delivering flowers, do you open the door?"

"Depends on the flowers. Or the man. But probably yes."

"And if the flowers are morning glories?"

"I'm not following."

"Morning glories, at least the kind called moonflowers, are nocturnal. They only open their petals at night. In the daytime, the flowers are curled up tight. But at night, they open."

"And?"

"What if you put some sort of fine powder into the petals and let them close naturally. When they opened, in the middle of the night, the powder would be released into the air. If the house is air-conditioned, the currents would carry the powder everywhere. You follow?"

"God. Is that what happened here?"

"I think it's . . . possible."

"God. What was the drug? Pixie dust?"

"More like angel dust. Make sure nobody has any unprotected physical contact with it. Tell Stallworth it's all got to go straight to our Hazmat labs. If he asks, tell him I think it's what killed Porter."

"Was Porter *killed*? Stallworth says it was a heart attack."

"Maybe it was. But I want to know what *caused* the heart attack."

"Micah, do you think Porter might have committed suicide?"

He took a while to answer. Her eyes never left his face.

"No," he said, finally. "No. I don't."

"If it wasn't suicide, what was it? An accident?"

"No. It was no accident."

"Then it was murder? Do you have a target?"

Dalton didn't want to open up the issue of Mr. Sweetwater with Mandy—or with anyone else at London Station. And Stallworth had made it brutally plain: *whatever* he got, it all went straight to Jack, and no written reports. Verbal only, face to face in Langley.

"Maybe."

"But you're not going to tell me who it is?"

"No. I'm not."

"That's okay. I can live with . . . I can accept it. I'm just . . ."

Mandy's face showed relief and pain in equal parts. She had carried a torch (Dalton had always assumed an *unrequited* torch) for Naumann for years. Naumann's marriage had not been a happy one in its later years, and the girls had poisoned whatever peripheral joys might have been possible. Although Naumann had never admitted it, he held Joanne responsible for what the girls had become. Mandy had been afraid that Naumann had simply run wildly off the rails: perhaps he had killed his family in the middle of some kind of annihilating domestic rage, and then gone to Venice to commit suicide.

And it was true that Naumann had been completely off the grid for days. That was why Dalton had been sent out to find him.

But if he'd been *murdered*, then everything changed.

Murder, though terrible, absolved him.

"Okay," said Mandy, coming back. "The evidence bag overnight to Langley. Anything else?"

"Did they fix the time of death?"

"Tentatively. Stallworth wanted the bodies left in place for you to see, so Forensic couldn't do anything with stomach contents. But the degree of decomposition, lividity, internal temperature. They placed it on or about three or four days ago. Which fits with the time marker for the camera failure."

"Jesus. Four days. Are they still in one piece?"

"Yes. Feel how cold the house is? The air-conditioning has been left on Full for days. The master bedroom has condensation on the inside of the windows. The bathroom feels like a meat lock—like an icebox."

"So it was done on purpose? To preserve the bodies?"

"One would assume. It's summer. The scent of corruption would have gotten out pretty fast. This way, discovery is delayed."

"Any sign of forced entry?"

"No. The front door was dead-bolted from the inside. And we saw Joanne go to the door to open it. That's the last image. But the whole place had been wiped clean. Along with the door latch. There were no prints at all. Kitchen. Bathroom. Bedside tables. Nothing. Not even Joanne's. As I said, whoever wiped the place down was a professional. Flowers. You said she would have opened the door to accept flowers. Once the flowers were in the house, and the drug in the air, then the man could have come back later and gotten in, knowing that the people inside were . . . Would they be unconscious?"

"Possibly. All right. Good work. Thank you, Mandy."

"You're welcome." She sighed, turned to the door, her back stiffening and her face growing even more pale. "Okay, then. We might as well go in."

"You don't have to come."

"I owe it to *her*. Besides, I'm the one who found them."

"Please, Mandy. Stay here."

She wavered, her porcelain skin growing paler. She had a fan of delicate wrinkles at the outer edges of each eye, and her upper lip was incised with vertical creases that deepened as she tightened her mouth.

"Micah. I will *not* be sheltered."

Dalton let it go, stepping reluctantly aside as she opened the door to a large well-lit room with an elegant coffered ceiling done in tones of taupe and gray with wide crown moldings. A half-open door on the far side of the room led to a large master bath. The lights were on in that bathroom, and what looked like a large red towel was lying crumpled up in the half-open door. In the center of the great room, in front of a row of tall sash windows, was a large sleigh bed heaped with satin pillows. Dalton, who had braced himself for the room, stopped abruptly.

"Not here," said Mandy, close behind him. "They're in the bathroom."

They crossed the hand-knotted Persian rug on little cat feet, their shoes whispering, and stopped before the half-open door. The crumpled bath towel that lay just inside the door was holding back a red tide of blood. Pin lights from the halogen fixtures on the ceiling glittered like diamonds on the congealed surface of a lake of blood. He leaned over this clotted mess of fabric and fluid, pushed the door open, and stepped into the room . . .

. . . AND GRADUALLY BECAME AWARE of the fact that Mandy Pownall was holding on to his upper arm, her fingers digging in, her breathing ragged. He wanted her out of here, for her sake, and because she was a distraction.

"What can I do?"

"First of all, do not throw up. Go call Removals."

"Okay," she said, relief in her voice. "Don't forget the mirror."

She was gone, leaving Dalton alone with the bodies.

He stepped carefully around the matted bloody towels and moved in close to the knotted cords that had cut so deeply into Joanne's ankles that her feet had swelled into eggplant-colored balloons. He looked carefully at the knots themselves.

All three bodies had been strung up in the same way, an open-eye loop with the free end run in and pulled out to make a lariat, then around the ankles, then a running loop over the shower railing, and then . . . and then he did not care to complete the rest of this mental image. But it was range work.

Dalton had seen enough of this kind of casually efficient hand slaughter when he was a kid back in Tucumcari. It was cowboy work, done the way a man who was used to cleaning game would do it. Even the throat and abdominal cuts were practiced and efficient, a single vertical slice along the left carotid, and in the belly a low punching start with a deep circular rising sweep and a quick step back to avoid the avalanche.

Cowboy-style.

Dalton recalled Jack Stallworth's words:

"Sally says she's been pretty silent. Not a call for four days, and she's not answering her voice mail."

Four days.

Naumann had gone dark in Venice on the third of October, stopped filing reports, never picked up his e-mail, shut off his Treo. Typically, Langley hadn't sent Dalton out to try to track him down until the seventh. And sometime between Saturday night and Sunday, the seventh of October, Naumann died in Cortona. In the courtyard of San Nicolò. From unknown causes. Could Naumann have done this?

Yes.

It *could* have been Naumann.

An agency pro like Porter Naumann could get from Venice to London and back without leaving an obvious trail, and the European Union had made doing that sort of thing even easier in the last two years. But why would Naumann *do* something like . . . this?

This *atrocity.*

This wasn't even remotely like him. Naumann had done some very cruel things in the field, but that was combat, even if it was covert combat, and he'd done it to legitimate if undeclared enemies of the country. But what had been done here—this was . . . *savored.*

You could see the time that had been taken, the way in which the killing had been drawn out. Prolonged. There wasn't a chance in hell that Porter Naumann would do something like this; it just wasn't in him. This inner certainty wasn't anything he could have supported in a court of law, or even justified to his boss if he had been a homicide cop. But this wasn't a court, and he wasn't a homicide cop, and on-the-fly operational judgments were being made—had to be made—all the time.

There was no point tying up limited Agency resources doing due diligence and chasing down everyone in London and the continent with Opportunity and Means when your professional gut was taking you straight to the heart of the matter. Unlike the homicide cop and the DA in a civilian case, Dalton *knew* Porter Naumann, and Porter Naumann would not have been capable of this kind of killing, especially not with his wife and children.

Hell. Not *any* woman, anywhere.

He just wasn't *made* that way.

If not Naumann, then who?

Who do you really like for this, Micah?

He knew damn well. On Monday night, the eighth of October, Sweetwater was having dinner in Carovita, because Dalton saw him there. Carovita was Naumann's favorite restaurant—he ate there almost every night he was in Venice. It was reasonable to infer that Naumann and Sweetwater could have been in Carovita at the same time. It certainly put them in the same territory. Then Dalton sees Sweetwater at the same restaurant, and immediately afterward he slams into The Night of the Emerald Green Spider.

Next, on Tuesday afternoon, Dalton locates—no, he's led to—Cora Vasari's house on Calle dei Morti, and Cora says Sweetwater left her rental flat the day before, on the Monday, a timely and convenient departure, by the way.

Working it backward, it all could have started here, in London.

Dalton had spoken with Stallworth on the Monday, and Stallworth said it had been four days since anyone had heard from Joanne. Four days from Monday meant last Thursday, the fourth of October. Yes. Sweetwater could have been in London on the fourth.

If Naumann could have done it, then it could have been done by anyone, including Sweetwater. There was no reason to attribute this slaughter to Naumann just because he had gone dark around the time it was done. But other than Dalton's gut instincts, there was even *less* reason to hang this on Sweetwater, other than tenuous circumstantial connections, such as the presence of morning glories in Naumann's suite and later in Cora's flat, and the fact that Naumann and Sweetwater had both been in Venice around the same time. And in Cortona: the grocery bag they found in the trash can, that put Sweetwater in Cortona as well.

So what?

Lots of people were in Venice and Cortona all the time. It didn't prove a damn thing. All Dalton really had was what amounted to a strange gut-level obsession with a weird old man in lizard-skin cowboy boots. But it would not go away.

He sat down on the toilet seat lid and concentrated on the bodies, taking in the scene, trying to put himself in the mind of a man who was capable of doing something like this. What could a reasonable man—a sane man—infer from this kind of butchery?

First of all, the guy was a sadist all the way to his bone marrow, a true aficionado of human suffering. It was one thing to kill three people. Hit them and split. That was what a killer would do.

A *professional* killer.

So this guy, whatever else he was, was no professional.

He had spent far too long in the house, possibly all night. The cleanup. The wipe-down. Getting his prints and stray DNA, his skin cells and hairs and leavings off the surfaces, would have required at least a couple of hours.

No real professional would put himself into that kind of situation: you got in, wore protection, made the hit, got your ass out. You didn't hang around to . . . *enjoy* yourself; that kind of indulgence would get a pro caught and killed in a very short time.

So *definitely* not a professional hit.

But a hit that *could* have been carried out by a professional who, in this one instance, was not behaving like a pro.

And it was a good, highly skilled hit, in the sense that the entry and execution, although elaborate and prolonged, had been successful. The killer had gotten into the town house, disabled the security.

Spent his party time with the victims.

And gotten clean away without leaving a trace. A pro at entry, at stealth, at not being caught. Perhaps, in addition, someone with access to an electronic cloaking device, a magnetic field radiator capable of burning out the sensors of digital cameras.

Dalton had heard some vague rumors about gear like that; it was all high-level gear. Government gear.

Not necessarily *our* government.

The Brits could have gear like that. So might the Mossad, and some of the Pakistani counterintelligence outfits.

Also the Germans.

Another good question: Was this guy military. Or a spook?

If so, *whose* spook was he?

And we come back around to the chaos of the killing itself.

No reliable, well-trained spook would kill like that, at least not for any reason you could attribute to a recognizable intelligence goal. Neither Joanne Naumann nor the girls were very plausible targets.

If the idea was to destabilize London Station, to disrupt Burke and Single, then it made more sense to take out Naumann himself.

Or Mandy.

Or you, Micah.

If it wasn't a tactical hit, then it was . . . what?

Done for the sheer pleasure?

Certainly that element was here.

But why *these* targets? What made the killer pick these three women, out of a city of seven million people?

No, it wasn't random; they were *chosen*.

But chosen for what?

Only one reason was workable, in the sense that only one reason gave Dalton an operational handle on the killings.

Their connection to Porter Naumann.

So we have a possible spook killer who's in this for the joy of it, but he's not picking his targets at random.

There's an overarching strategy here: somebody's being *punished*. Was that somebody Porter Naumann?

Why him? And how did the killer know who Porter Naumann was in the first place?

No idea.

And what did this killer have against Naumann?

Again, no idea.

The longer Dalton looked at the three brutalized corpses, the more convinced he became that all of this had something to do with Sweetwater. For reasons known only to him, Sweetwater came to London, found the house in Belgravia, made an entry, killed the women.

Then he went to Venice.

He *must* have gone to Venice next, if he was acting alone—which Dalton had no reason to believe—because that was where Naumann was, and where he died.

But why go to Venice?

To *show* Naumann what he had done?

That would fit the pattern of a sadistic killer.

Fit the idea of the killings as punishment. Which means the killer *knew* that Naumann was in Venice. How did he know *that*?

He looked at Joanne's body. *She* would have known. And she would have told her tormentor. By the end, she would have told him everything she knew about Porter Naumann.

Mandy was at the door again, her eyes fixed on Dalton's face.

"The Removals van will be here in ten minutes."

"Mandy, did Forensics get any of Porter's DNA off the bodies?"

She shook her head, keeping her attention fixed on him.

"No. There was no mitochondrial DNA of any kind on them. Forensics figured they'd been hosed down with the showerhead."

"What about the drains?"

"Forensics pulled them; they'd been cleaned recently. There were traces of chlorine, a few hairs that were identified as Joanne's."

"Nothing else? No sign of Porter at all?"

"Not in the scene. His DNA and prints are all over the house, along with Joanne's and the girls'. But none at the scene."

"Mandy, do you know if Porter had a spike?"

"One of those GPS thingies, the little silver ones they stick under your skin?"

"Yes."

"No. He thought the idea of having a spike implanted was a security risk. Even if the locator output was encrypted, the very fact that you had one in your body was a tip-off to any foreign agency that you were definitely not just some kind of banker. Why?"

"I'm trying to eliminate Porter as a suspect—"

"I thought he wasn't!"

"He's not. But if I could *prove* he wasn't in London—"

"Prove it! To whom?"

"Mandy, he went dark on the third. We didn't find his body until the seventh."

"And you found it in *fucking* Cortona, Micah. If you're looking for suspects, how about me?"

"You?"

"Why not. I loved Porter. If his wife is dead . . ."

"Fine. And *did* you do this?"

"Would I admit it? If I had?"

"Yes. I think so. Have you ever killed anyone, Mandy?"

"Not yet, Micah. But if you keep on trying to lay this on Porter's grave, I could find some murder in my heart. It *wasn't* Porter, Micah!"

"I know, I know."

"You want to prove he wasn't here. What about his cell? His Treo? His laptop—if he used a Bluetooth it would show a location."

"Nothing. When Porter goes dark he doesn't screw around."

"Micah, you know Porter didn't do . . . this. Don't waste your time. Go find out who did. Find out who did, and then you kill him and anyone who helped, okay?"

"Yes."

"Promise?"

"Yes. I promise."

There was a strained silence. After a while Mandy looked at the bodies hanging from the shower railing.

"What do you want to do with . . ." She made a half-formed gesture in the direction of the bodies, the blood, the entire scene.

"This can't get out, Mandy."

"I've been giving it some thought. May I make a suggestion?"

"Please."

"We close up the house and put it about that Joanne and the girls are traveling."

"Won't their friends wonder? What about all this wireless stuff? Text messaging? Cell phones? E-mails? Chat rooms? If the girls just drop off the grid, won't their friends start to worry about them?"

Mandy gave him a look, raised her eyebrow. "Do ticks miss the dog? No. They move on and find another host. Mila and Brooke didn't have 'friends.' They had minions. Unindicted coconspirators. And Joanne's London crowd was always on the move. It would be *months* before any of them started to wonder where Joanne had gone off to. Then only in an idle, feckless way."

"What about her relatives?"

"Micah, all we can do is *delay* this. It'll have to come out eventually. How much time do you think you'll need?"

"God. How much can you give me?"

"Three weeks, maybe four. I still think this is the way to go."

She was right.

"Okay. It's a good idea. Try to make it four, if you possibly can. And Porter died 'in the line of,' so there wouldn't be a ceremony anyway. Another nameless star on the wall. We'll do it your way."

There was a soft call from the stairwell, Barney's voice.

"Sir, Removals is here."

"Are you up to this, Mandy?"

"Aren't you going to stay?"

"Yes. Of course. I wouldn't ask you to do this alone."

"Thank you."

Mandy was silent then, but Dalton knew what she was thinking. Dalton reached out to take her almost skeletal hand. Her face went through several emotions, her eyes welling up.

"I thought for a while that Porter might have gone mad."

"Did you have any reason to think so?"

Mandy went inward for a time, thinking about Dalton's question. "No. There was nothing . . . but . . . I mean, look at the mirror."

They both turned to look at the mirror, at the ugly scrawl there, done in some sort of thick black crayon, a vicious obscenity that had been scraped over the glass by a strong, angry hand.

"You actually thought *Porter* did this?"

"No. Perhaps. I don't know. I was . . . afraid," said Mandy. "For his mind."

They looked at the drawing for a time in silence. Something about the drawing resonated in Dalton's memory. He struggled for it, but it was too elusive, a trace only, now a fading wisp.

"Have you ever seen anything like this in Porter's papers?"

"No. Never."

"Have you looked?"

She hesitated. "Well . . . not thoroughly. I'd need clearance from Jack. I wasn't cleared for everything Porter was doing. Were you?"

"No. Jack says he was monitoring investment and trading patterns, looking for terror money on the move."

"Yes. That's what he was doing. I was his collector."

"I want you to go through his papers, Mandy—no, I want you

to *ransack* his papers. Turn his entire life upside down and dump it out on the desk. I want every e-mail, every coded file, personal papers, Agency stuff. I want to know who he saw and when he saw him, who he called and who called back, from where, when—the whole package. And I need it done by you, and you *alone*. Can you do that?"

"Do I need clearance?"

"You have clearance. I'm the cleaner here, and I'm giving you clearance, okay? Can you do it?"

"Should I talk to Jack?"

"I'll talk to Jack. You talk to nobody but me, here on in."

She nodded her head and said nothing. Dalton pulled in a ragged breath and immediately regretted it. He looked around the bathroom, half-hoping for Naumann's ghost to materialize in the room.

Where are you, Porter? Why aren't you here?

You were everywhere. Now you're the absentee.

Silence, then, as they stood there, looking uneasily at themselves in the mirror—both of them burning with the mortal shame of the survivor—and at the angry scrawl across the glass. The room smelled of toothpaste and lemons and perfume, as well as dried blood and spoiled meat.

"Do you want this . . . scrawl . . . left?" asked Mandy, after a time, and in a whisper, as if they were in the presence of something unholy.

"Forensics got a digital shot?"

"Yes. I was here when they took it. The camera's in the case by the door, along with everything else."

"Erase everything. Make it look as if this had never happened."

"But it did, Micah, didn't it?"

"Yes, sweetheart. It did."

His cell phone rang then, making them both jump.

"Dalton here."

"Micah, it's Sally Fordyce. I'm at Langley."

"Jesus, Sally. What time is it in D.C.?"

"Early, Micah. I came in to head off a tragedy."

"Tragedy? What kind of tragedy"

"The tragedy of Jack ripping your privates off with his bare hands, you utter dork. Were you using a Consular ID in Venice?"

"Venice?"

"Oh no! Don't you go all vague and loopy on me, Micah. Somebody's been trying to reach you through the Venice Consulate. The caller says you're attached to the CID branch there. The Venice station chief fielded the call and handed it right off to Langley. Duty desk at Langley tried to find Jack but he's off the grid right now—"

"Where is he?"

"Micah, Jack *runs* the Cleaners. He's always flying off somewhere lately, and he doesn't give me an itinerary, does he? And you're damn lucky he *was* out of touch, because I was next on the call list. So tell me. Did you use a Consular cover or not?"

Dalton stared at the wall, thinking fast. He *had* used a Venice jacket with Cora Vasari.

Christ, was *she* trying to reach him?

"Micah!"

"Yes, I did, Sally. Who was—"

"You're a complete and utter mutt, you know that?"

"Who was trying to reach me? Was it a woman?"

"Woman! My God, Micah. Have you been using Consular ID's to pick up *chicks*? What are you using for—"

"I know. We both know I'm pond scum. Who was calling, Sally? Was it a woman named Cora Vasari?"

"Vasari? Cora Vasari? No. It was . . . let's see . . . Zitti. Domenico. A guy. He was very upset. Probably her poor bloody husband, right? Said it was an emergency, something about an ambulance—"

"Ambulance? Where?"

"In some place called the Dorsoduro. There were people shouting in the background. Micah? Micah, hello? Hello? Micah Dalton, you *rat* bag *scum* sack *son* of a—"

But Micah Dalton was already gone.

wednesday, october 10
civic hospital in venice
10 a.m. local time

brancati, the Carabinieri cop, was waiting for him outside the hospital room, and of his former warmth and professional amiability there was no trace; his angular face was as stony as the walls of this ancient hospital overlooking the Arsenal, and his deep-brown eyes were flat and cold. He stood in the center of the long echoing hall and watched as Dalton raced down it, passing into and out of the pools of yellow light coming from the overhead lamps, Dalton's footsteps reverberating along the corridor, the sound of his rapid breathing audible from twenty yards away.

A uniformed sergeant, short, broad as a steamer trunk, stood a little to the left and slightly behind Brancati, showing Dalton another stone face, his right hand resting on his holstered sidearm, his hard black eyes fixed on Dalton.

"Major Brancati," said Dalton, coming up. "How is she?"

Brancati said nothing for a full minute, holding Dalton in a hot glare, his hand raised up, palm out. Dalton, wisely, said nothing. Seeming at last to master himself, Brancati let out a long ragged sigh.

"Cora Vasari has been assaulted, Mr. Dalton. Her injuries are not severe. She is in a nervous state, angry and afraid, yet still she calls for *you*. *Not* the police. Why is this so, Mr. Dalton?"

"I'd like to see her."

"And I would *like* her not to have been attacked by animals. I think what you would *like*, Mr. Dalton, is not very important to me. No, right now you will say *nothing*. You will speak no lying words to me. *Capisce?*"

Dalton locked it down and waited, his throat tightening. Brancati saw this unwilling submission in Dalton's face.

"Good. It was two men from Trieste. Does that interest you? I find it interesting. She was able to tell us this because she recognized their accents. Although it was difficult for her to speak. She is very brave. Anyway, she tells us they were Croats from Trieste. Young, well dressed. The one who called himself Radko was tall and slender, with a long face and skin that had been made leathery by too much sun, she tells us. His eyes were red from drugs or drinking and his voice was soft. They both had soft voices. The other one, who did not give a name, was short and extremely muscular and his head was shaved. He had broad, flat hands and a habit of biting his finger-nails. He had the air of a dockhand but was also very well dressed. They came to her villa in the Dorsoduro. Radko, who did the talk-ing, said they wished to see a room she had for rent. That she was known to rent rooms to good people. This room had lately become available, she tells us, and so she showed these two men, although they were Croatian and she does not in principle rent to Croatians or Serbs. Anyway, they seemed very polite. But once inside the room, it was of course quite different. During this time of threatening,

Radko asked her only one question. Do you wish to know what that question was?"

"Yes," said Dalton, in a toneless voice. "I do."

Brancati went some ways inward, closing his eyes as he did so in a distant, vaguely robotic way, an unnaturally slow movement, and Dalton could see that the man was trying very hard not to lose what little control he had left.

"Radko wished to know where a Mr. Micah Dalton was. These two soft-spoken Croatian men from Trieste. I find this Croatian motif most suggestive. Do you find this Croatian motif suggestive?"

"Of course I do. I'm not a fool. Why didn't she tell them?"

"At first she was merely angry at their tone. Then, after they had begun to threaten her, she wished only to defy them. She is a proud woman. I admire her. Of course, this could not last long. Few people, few women as lovely as this fine lady, few men, can withstand the threat of permanent disfigurement."

"Christ, Brancati—"

"You will say nothing right now. *Capisce?* Nothing."

Brancati waited to see if his warning had been heard. It had been heard all the way down the long hall and it was still reverberating thunderously down a distant stairwell. Nurses, doctors, other patients in the corridor had frozen in place. White faces were turned toward them, eyes staring. Dalton, whose own reptilian anger was now fully awake, choked his resentment down, but his expression was now as flat and cold as Brancati's. Brancati, if he noticed Dalton's anger at all, did not show it.

"She was *not* disfigured. She defended herself with a weapon she had concealed in her *borsa*—her purse. A little *pistoletta*, a very illegal *pistoletta*. With this weapon she shoots Radko in the face. A man who lives in her villa. A man named Domenico Zitti. He heard the angry voices. The sound of a shot, coming from the room, and he comes upstairs to see what it is about. The door is shut. He pounds on the door. He is a retired *pescatore* and very strong from hauling the nets for forty years. He pounds and shouts, the door is pulled open, and these two men from Trieste, one of them bleeding from a wound in his cheek, they try to push past him. He of course resents this. He is stabbed. His wound is grave. He falls. They step over him. He comes to his feet, sees Signorina Vasari. Her condition, the *pistoletta*. He runs to her and instead of asking for the Guardia Medica or the Carabinieri, she does not yet know that he has been stabbed, she asks instead for a Signor Micah Dalton of the American Consulate. Zitti is a gentleman of great courage. He makes the call at once. *Then* he calls the Guardia Medica. They call my friend Lucenzo, who is the captain of the Carabinieri for Venezia. He remembers the name Dalton from my report on the death of your Mr. Naumann. He calls me. I call your Consulate. They do not know you. Yet here you are. And I am here. Now you may speak."

"Did you catch these men?"

"No. Not yet. The report is that they came by a fast boat. A cigarette boat. Such as the smugglers use. They came from beyond the Lido. None of the doctors in Venice have been approached by a man with a face wound. We assume they have taken the boat to sea. We have in the air our *elicottero* searching for them. That was your question. Now for mine. It was you who assaulted those men by the Palazzo Ducale, yes?"

"Yes."

"Good. The simple truth, at last. I become less angry. You do not work for Burke and Single? This also is true?"

"I do work for Burke and Single."

Brancati sighed, and said nothing for a moment. Then: "I see. You are *equivoco*. You play a word game. You do *work* for them but you do not work *for* them. You are not *employed* by them."

This was not framed as a question. It was a statement. Brancati was a senior officer in the Carabinieri, and the Carabinieri ran the

Italian government's intelligence service. If Brancati tried hard enough he could find out who Dalton really worked for. Dalton assumed that he had. Time for clarity.

"No. I'm not."

"You are an agent of the United States government."

Again, not a question.

"I am employed by the United States government."

"Good. We progress. Was it United States government business, this matter of the two men in the square? Milan Slatkovic and Gavro Princip?"

"No. It was self-defense."

"A personal matter?"

"Yes. I was attacked. I defended myself."

Brancati smiled again, his eyes a little less sleepy.

"I wish you had not defended yourself with such *vigore*. Perhaps Miss Vasari would not be here in the hospital tonight. Perhaps she would not be facing an *atto d'accusa* from the police for having in her purse an illegal weapon. So you are perhaps involved in a vendetta with a pair of Croatian *sicari*, hit men, and *she* also is involved. Now you will please tell me *why* she is involved?"

"I was looking for a man. I was told he was staying at her villa near the All Saints' Cathedral. I went there to find this man."

"I see. While you were there you showed her identification papers that gave her the strong impression that you worked for the local American Consulate. May I see these papers now?"

"I don't have them with me."

Brancati's face did not register any form of surprise. Rather it seemed to confirm a private opinion already tagged and bagged.

"Of course. This accords with the fact that you are not registered with my government as a member of the American diplomatic service. And what was the name of this man for whom you were looking?"

"I was told his name was Pellerossa."

"Pellerossa is not a name. It is a kind of people. Your American redskins. Miss Vasari would no doubt have explained this."

"She did. She was under the impression that her tenant's name was Sweetwater."

"And did you locate this Sweetwater man?"

"No."

"You have no idea who he is?"

"Not yet."

"Why were you looking for him?"

"I thought this man might be able to tell me something about Naumann's death."

"And what gave you this impression?"

"Nothing. A hunch."

"*Come si dice? 'Nozione'?* This means a 'hunch'? You are equivocal again. Fine. I have consulted with our *dipartimento di spionaggio*. Also with my friends in your embassy. You are a spy. Spies must equivocate, as gulls must eat carrion, as dogs must lick themselves. I set this aside. In what way did Miss Vasari and this man come to be connected in your mind?"

"I first saw the man at Carovita. He stood out. His manner was strange, as was his clothing. He looked like an American Indian. I became interested in him. The next afternoon, I went back to Carovita and made some inquiries. I was told that this man was living in the Dorsoduro—"

"Who told you this?"

"An old woman who worked at Carovita. I didn't get her name."

"Carovita is closed. We looked for the owners. They have gone back to their winter home in Split, where we do not enjoy a formal relationship with the local authorities. Do you know where this is, this Split? It is in Croatia, on the Dalmatian coast. Does this Croatian motif now come to have some greater significance in your mind?"

Dalton absorbed this in stunned silence. This collision with Milan and Gavro? Was it more than it had seemed at the time?

For a thousand years, Venice had been the city of assassins. There was even a street in the San Marco region called Assassini. Was his encounter with Milan and Gavro far more than a vicious but random combat in the edgy Venetian night?

If it was more serious, what was the outcome supposed to be? Was it intended, by parties unknown, that he should die there, in what looked to be a random mugging?

"I don't know. I'd have to—"

"*You* have only to answer my questions. After that, you are to be escorted to Marco Polo Airport, where you will take your jet back to London or Langley or wherever you wish to go. You will not come back to Italy."

"What about Mr. Naumann's body? His . . . his effects?"

"Mr. Naumann's death is a matter for our security service now. In due course your government will be notified of our progress. His body will be more thoroughly examined by our best medical people. I no longer accept that his death was a simple *colpo apoplettico*. I wish to have a complete toxicological report done by our own people. When this is done, we will know what to do."

Drugs.

Brancati was suspecting a Croatian drug ring.

The Trieste connection had put this in Brancati's mind, and whether or not it was a valid lead, he'd play it out to the conclusion. Did he know about the trap that Sweetwater had set for him in Cora's apartment? What had Cora said while the adrenaline was still running through her veins? As if reading his thoughts, Brancati broke into them at the perfect moment with precisely the right observation.

"Miss Vasari has told us what happened to you, Mr. Dalton. I would like to hear your tale of this incident."

Vague.

And dangerously so.

Clearly a trap. But was it set with truth, with genuine knowledge, at its center? What had Cora told him?

"Tell him the truth, kid," said Naumann's ghost, stepping into the light from a dark corner of the hospital corridor.

"I think I was drugged, Major Brancati," he said, managing, with a violent effort, not to stare over Brancati's shoulder at the shimmering, vaguely luminous shape of Porter Naumann hovering behind him.

Stress could be the trigger, he decided. Perhaps he could control it by staying calm.

"Drugged?" said Brancati, without visible surprise. "How?"

If Dalton had any chance of staying in Italy longer than another two hours, he had to treat this Carabinieri officer with real respect. Anything less and he'd turn a man who was at the moment merely hostile into a settled enemy.

"That's right," said Naumann's ghost. "We need this guy."

We need this guy? thought Dalton.

Ignoring, with great difficulty, Naumann's presence, Dalton kept his eyes fixed on Brancati's face while he laid out in basic terms what had taken place in Cora's villa, withholding no detail but leaving out the exact nature of his own private journey back to Boston in those terrible seconds before Cora's Narcan injection had pulled him back to the living world. Brancati listened to his story without emotion and without interruption. When Dalton was finished, Brancati's heated aura seemed to be a degree cooler. "Yes," he said, for the first time with some sympathy in his tone, "this is what Cora Vasari also told us. You are recovered?"

Apparently not, Dalton said to himself, looking at Naumann's ghost. "I think so."

"Miss Vasari does not agree. She thinks you must go to the hospital. That the drug could have permanently damaged you. She tells me that in her apartment you admitted to her that you were seeing the ghost of your dead friend. This Mr. Naumann. Is this true?"

"Keep me out it," said Naumann.

"No, it's not. I was, but not anymore. I'm fine. No ill effects."

"I hope you are right. You do not look healthy. You look pale, you are staring at nothing as if you really had seen *un fantasma*. I suppose you have taken this *cilindro* back with you to London?"

"Yes. I sent it on to our people to be analyzed."

Brancati did not ask Dalton who his people were because he knew damn well who his people were.

"And the drug as well?"

"Yes."

"Have they determined what it was?"

"Not yet. Perhaps tomorrow."

"When you receive their report, I will insist on being told. I will insist on seeing it. This is a matter of concern to the Italian government. Anything less than full and frank cooperation will result in a formal protest to your Department of State. This would be out of my hands."

"When I know, you'll know."

"I have your word on this?" He smiled thinly. "As a spy?"

"No. Not as a spy. I give you my word as a soldier."

"Good. As a soldier. I hold you to it. We must talk further," said Brancati, "but not now. Do you wish to see Signorina Vasari?"

"I do. Very much."

"I see," he said, with a half smile. "You admire her. So do I."

He turned to the carabiniere by the closed door.

"Let this man through."

He looked back at Dalton.

"I give you ten minutes only. Are you hungry?"

"I am."

Brancati smiled, a full open smile, the first one Dalton had seen on the man since he first met him, no guarded quality to it.

"Good. I know a little place, not far from here. You will join me."

This was not a question either.

"I'd be happy to."

Brancati stepped aside and the guard knocked gently on the door before opening it onto a small, dimly lit and well-appointed private room in which a single pink lamp glowed softly on a bedside table.

"I'll stay out here," said Naumann. "You two probably need a moment alone."

IN THE ROSE-COLORED HALF-LIGHT Dalton could see that Cora was lying on top of a huge intricately carved wooden bed, her head on a single pillow, her hair a black tumble of silk around her white face, her eyes closed, still fully dressed—black slacks and a crisp white shirt-blouse, shoeless—her delicate hands folded across her gently rounded belly, her breasts rising and falling slowly as she breathed. Dalton crossed the soft carpet—reds and blues and golds—and sat down in a stiff-backed wooden chair, which creaked as it took his weight. She had been struck—struck hard—on the right cheek, just below the eye. A dark purple-and-green bruise had spread out across her cheek and into the shadow of her jawline just below her ear. One side of her mouth was swollen, the red lips puffy and distended at the corners. The sight of this pierced him straight through the heart, a cold iron bolt of self-hatred. Cora's eyes opened and she looked at him without delight. She closed her eyes again.

"So. Here is the International Man of Mystery."

Dalton reached out and placed his hand on top of her folded hands. She pulled them away, a flicker of distaste flashing across her fine handsome face before she composed it into a detached, expressionless mask.

"I hate a liar, Micah. Are you a liar?"

"Yes."

"If I ask you questions now, will you lie to me?"

"No."

"This is a lie."

"Brancati told me what happened to you. I won't lie to you."

Something crossed her pale white face then, a dark memory, a flash of pain, and when it was gone there was a sadness in the shape of her mouth and in the creases around her eyes.

For a long moment she looked old, tired, wounded. She opened her eyes and looked directly at him for a space of time that Dalton found hard to measure. He was aware of being considered. Judged. Not kindly. But there was no decision yet.

"I read, in the papers, about an attack upon two men by the Palazzo Ducale. Two nights ago. This man who did this, was it you?"

"Yes."

"I am told that both men are near death. One is in a coma."

"Yes. That's true."

"And did you know what you were doing? When you did this? Was it your intention? To hurt them? To kill them, if you could? Perhaps you were drunk? You drink a great deal, I think. Is this why you did it?"

"No. I wasn't drunk. I knew exactly what I was doing."

Dalton offered up no extenuations. He had done similar things to many other men in a state of stone-cold sobriety. He fully intended to destroy Milan and Gavro, and he had gone about it with every bit of skill he could summon. Of excuses, he had none to offer. She closed her eyes again and accepted this in silence, showing no desire to communicate with him. He had the impression of being interviewed by someone who was not physically present, a remote spiritual force.

As much as he wished he could say something reassuring, something to help her think better of him, he held his silence, aware that there was really nothing to be said.

"Micah, the men who came to my apartment, the men who stabbed my friend Domenico, do you know who they were?"

"No. But I'm going to find out."

"And when you find them . . . ?"

"I'll kill them."

"I see. And the man. The old Indian. Do you know who he is?"

"Not yet."

"His real name is not Sweetwater?"

"It may be. I don't think so."

"And whoever this Sweetwater is, you will look for *him* too?"

"Yes."

"And when you find him you will kill him also?"

"Yes."

"Is this what you do?"

"No."

"No? What do you do, then?"

"I'm called a cleaner."

"A 'cleaner'? What do you clean?"

"When something goes wrong in the company I work for, they send me out to fix it. No. Not to fix it. To clean up the mess."

"Was Mr. Naumann this kind of mess?"

"Yes. He was."

"Major Brancati says you work for the CIA. Is this true?"

"I work for the American government."

"This is the same thing. With you the lie is like a heartbeat. Are you still seeing the ghost of this Mr. Naumann?"

"Yes."

"When did you last see him?"

"A moment ago. Out in the hall."

"He is not in here? With us?"

"No."

"That is strange. What else do you see?"

"Nothing. Everything is normal. Except for the ghost."

"Can you do anything to make him go away?"

"I think that when I stay calm, when I concentrate on what is real, then he goes away. I was in London and he wasn't there."

"Why did you go to London?"

"It was business."

"What kind of business?"

Dalton told her the essentials of it, enough to make her understand the thing without illusions, no more. When he was through, her face was extremely pale and it took a time for her breathing to slow down again. Her hands, which had been tightly linked, her fingers white, became loose and she touched her forehead with her left hand, brushing away a lock of her hair.

"And the man who did this, this was the same man in my apartment? Mr. . . . Mr. Sweetwater."

"I have no proof yet. But I suspect it is, yes."

"Then I suppose someone should kill him."

"I intend to."

"This ghost who follows you. This means you are sick, Micah. It means that the drug this man has put in your brain has damaged you. There is treatment for this. I know the very best people. If you hope to find him, first you have to be cured. You can accomplish nothing until this is done. You are in great danger. You may have visions, hallucinations. Fugues. You cannot ignore this, no matter how much you want to. You must be treated. Cured."

"If I wait, Sweetwater is gone. So are the men who attacked you."

"I shot one, you know. In the cheek. The expression on his face was wonderful. Wonderful. Shock. Horror. Fear. I made him afraid that he would die. I do wish that I had killed him."

"Perhaps you did."

"No. I broke his cheekbone only. He took my father's *pistoletta* away from me. Father had it from the war. For a moment I thought the pig would shoot me, but then Domenico was shouting at the door and they ran away. Domenico was stabbed in the chest; he was bleeding. He is here in the hospital. They say he is in critical condition. I went to see him, but he is in surgery now. This is the world you live in, Micah? This is what you do?"

"Yes. It is."

"And no matter what happens, you will go on doing it?"

"I think so."

"Until you find this Sweetwater? And the two men from Trieste?"

"Yes."

"You are not quite sane, Micah. Do you know that?"

"My world is not quite sane either. I am sorry for bringing it to your door. I regret it very much. I would undo it if I could."

Cora made a weak but strongly dismissive gesture that Dalton found deeply wounding. "You regret very much, do you? I think you are a man who bears his regrets lightly, perhaps from having so many of them, and all of them hard-earned, so that you are used to them, the way other men grow used to a limp or the aftereffects of a wasting disease. Yet this does not stop you from collecting more of them. Without a strong desire to repair your way of living, your regrets are *una bagattella*. Flightless birds. You are attracted to me?"

"Yes. I am."

"And I am attracted to you."

Dalton's chest became tight and he began to speak. She raised a hand to stop him.

"But to what am I attracted? A spy? An agent of the American CIA? What right do you have to be drawn to me? You are not your own man. You are bought and paid for. You are not a free man. I think you also have a wife."

"Yes. I do."

"And yet you tell me that you are attracted to *me*? You betray your wife; then you invite me to share in your dishonor."

"My wife and I are . . . estranged."

"I see. Then of course you will tell me about the icicle?"

Dalton sat back in the chair. It groaned under his weight in a way that reflected the heavy stone he carried in his own heart. He was silent for a long time. Finally, he spoke. "No. I won't."

"Why not?"

"I . . . can't."

"You refuse, you mean?"

He leaned forward, moving closer to her. "Yes. No. I won't because I can't."

She sat up then, and swayed unsteadily for a moment, placing her head in her hands, wiping them across her eyes, brushing her hair back. She moved her legs and sat up on the side of the bed, taking one of his hands in both of hers, an act of gentle mercy that cut his heart in two.

She reached out and touched his right cheek, a delicate brushing touch using only her fingertips. He could smell her perfume and the scent of her body. Her eyes were dark and he found it hard to look into them. She leaned forward and pulled him closer and kissed him, softly, gently, her lips brushing his, her warm breath in his face, her body very close. Then she pulled back and let go of his hands and stood up, looking down at him.

"Good bye, Micah."

Dalton stood up and she did not move away from him. He could feel the warmth of her body. Her scent was a cloud of spice and lemons all around him and he could still feel the moisture of her lips on his, her sweet taste. He reached out for her and she let him pull her into his body. He held her for a time, gently but with strength, feeling her heart beating under his ribs, the rise and fall of her breasts against his chest.

"I'm sorry," he said, into the softness of her neck.

She pushed him away and looked up at him, shook her head.

"So long as you are false, Micah, you will always be sorry."

"SHE SAID THAT, DID SHE?" drawled Brancati, pushing a much-depleted plate of gnocchi arrabbiata away, his other hand hovering above his empty glass. He rapped twice on the little round table. Their waiter appeared, bowing, leaning in through the draperies of their little cubicle, his face beaming, red from the kitchen stoves, his hands folded in front of his spinnaker-size belly. Music from the outer rooms floated in over his shoulder. "Amarcord," by Nino Rota.

Brancati ordered a second decanter of wine and some *frizzante,* along with a bottle of sambuca, before turning back to Dalton's gloomy face in the candlelight as the waiter bustled off.

"Yes. I can't blame her for it."

"*Basta!* You are morose, Micah. You are tired. In the morning—"

"I won't be here in the morning."

Brancati waved that away with a glass. The wine came back, a crystal decanter, frosted, dripping on the pink linen tablecloth, and a bottle of sambuca, with two small thick glasses.

The waiter withdrew, bowing, mumbling, and Brancati refilled their glasses, so much wine that the surface of the liquid swelled a millimeter above the rims and trembled there, candlelight glimmering in a bright circle around the surface.

"Now you must drink," said Brancati, smiling at him. "If you can bring it to your lips without spilling, you will have your heart's desire."

Dalton tried, failed, the wine falling like little flame-shaped drops in the candlelight. Brancati laughed, reached for his own glass, brought it to his lips without a tremor, and sipped at it. Then he set it down and leaned back in his chair, wiping his mustache with a pink linen napkin.

"You are in love with this *signorina*? She is your heart's desire?"

"In love? No. I admire her. She is so—"

"Italian! Yes. If one leads a good life and dies well, God allows you to come back as an Italian, if only so that you can know the true meaning of remorse, and of virtue also. I too admire that woman, I too desire her, and I have three daughters and a wife and a mother *and* a mother-in-law, so I do not need to have another woman in my life, no more than a man needs more angry bees in his bathroom. Do you have three daughters and a wife and a mother-in-law, Micah?"

This cut right home, sliced right through his defenses.

"Yes. I mean, I did. One, that is. My daughter died. As a baby."

Brancati, horrified, saw that he had put a finger into an open wound.

Dalton held up a hand, offering an unsteady smile. "It was long ago."

"I am sorry. Forgive me."

"It was hard, yes. My wife never recovered from it."

"You are . . ."

"We do not talk."

Brancati shook his head, sadness welling up in his face. He was a sentimental man, thought Dalton. His feelings ran close to the surface.

"This often happens. I see this as a policeman. Many families do not survive a great tragedy, the loss of a child, a loved one. The survivors blame themselves. Blame each other. This is why I hate the bad ones so much. The ripples run out from a crime, run out through time and life together. There is no recovery, no complete forgetting.

The victims are always changed. Nothing is ever the same again, and in this strange new place the old ties, the old bonds of love and friendship, they wear thin, they fail. You do not blame . . . ?"

"I blame no one but myself."

"Yes. I see that." He lapsed into an uneasy silence, staring at Dalton over the rim of his wineglass. He sighed, set the glass down. "You will permit me to be . . . *scortese* . . . impolite?"

"Please."

"First, a question. Your rooms at the Savoia e Jolanda. The day you leave, yesterday, the maid tells us that you scrub the floors of the bathroom. The walls. The mirrors. The sink. Until they shine. This you never do before. Neither did Mr. Naumann, when he lived there. This is not something most men do at any time. Not in fine hotels, certainly. Then you take the linen towels away with you. Also you leave three hundred euros and a fifty-euro tip and a note apologizing for the bedcover, the missing towels, that they are stained from a very bad shaving cut, that you wish to repay for it. But there is no blood on the bedcover. Hearing this, our people used ultraviolet to look for blood in your rooms, but there was nothing, a few drops only."

He hesitated, shot Dalton a wary look, slightly ashamed.

"There is also some evidence that someone was in the room with you that night. Guests in the next suite heard voices—"

"Voices? More than one?"

"They could not say. Only that it seemed to them that a conversation was going on, the back and forth, pauses. More talking."

"Maybe I had a woman in the room."

Brancati smiled, tolerant, amused. Unbelieving.

"There was no . . . no sign of that. The maids always know. Also, in the wastebasket there were several ripped covers—for bandages— and the entire box of medical supplies was empty. When you paid for the room the desk clerk saw that your left wrist had a big bandage on it, and under the black glove there was a swelling, as if your hand was injured and you had wrapped it up. Yet I look at your hand here"—reaching out and touching his left hand with a fingertip—"and there is no injury at all. So here is the question—the impolite question. Your state of mind that night, it seems a little disordered. You imagine blood, but are not wounded. You converse, with no one in the room. You see a bloody bedcover where there is no blood. You clean where there is no stain. Is this because of the fight with Milan and Gavro?"

"Partly. The rest was fatigue. Too much to drink. Far too much."

"You drank before you met with Milan and Gavro?"

"Yes. And much more afterward."

"You were drunk, then, when you fought them?"

"I see where this is going. I wish I could go there with you. I can't. I had no excuse. I would have done the same on black coffee."

"Micah—I may call you Micah? Yes? Thank you. And you will call me Tessio, like my sons do. Micah, I do not know you very well. What I do know I begin to like. You do not seem to be *un uomo cattivo,* a man who enjoys hurting people. Do you not feel that what happened with Milan and Gavro—that maybe you should find something else to do for a while? I mean no offense. But I admit . . ."

"What I did offended you?"

"Not *offended,* no. How to say . . . it troubles me. Now that I know you a little better, I would say—with respect—it is not a natural thing for any man to sing Broadway songs and quote from *A Midsummer Night's Dream* while he kicks a man into a coma. If I told you this story about another man, what would you advise him to do?"

"Take a year off. Seek professional help."

"Yes. This would be the advice of a true friend. And will you?"

Brancati's tone was light; his question was dead serious. Dalton stared down at his glass, at the back of his left hand, resisting the urge to tell this man everything that had happened in the room, the emerald green spider, the bloody wound in his hand that was not there, above all the terrible *persistence* of these hallucinations.

Cora was right.

He needed medical help.

"Yes. I will. When this is over."

Brancati studied Dalton's face, looking for evasion, for equivocation, and decided after a time that Dalton was telling the truth, at least that he believed what he was saying to Brancati right now. Whether in the cold light of morning he maintained that resolve was an issue only Dalton himself could confront, and in the end what Dalton did about Dalton's demons was none of Brancati's business. He had his own, far too many, and would not care—in fact would savagely resent having them evoked, called up from the pit, by a stranger, even a benevolent one, even over fine white wine and a marvelous sambuca.

"Good. Enough. I intrude. Forgive me. Well, so you really were a soldier," he said, pouring some more sambuca into a glass, changing the subject without much tact but with charming determination. "I recognized this right away. I said so, did I not? And how, where, did you soldier?"

"Army. Special Forces, for a while. Then Intelligence."

"With your American Defense Intelligence Agency?"

"Yes. Before that I was a G2."

Brancati's polite expression showed no understanding of the phrase. Dalton realized that Brancati was too polite to ask.

"In our army, S2 mean an officer assigned to Intelligence. And G2 means that same thing, only at the Brigade level."

"Brigade-level Intelligence? And you saw action?"

"Yes. Some. Syria. The Philippines. And I was in the Horn."

Brancati took this in, his eyes widening slightly. "When?"

Dalton picked up his glass, sipped at it, looking at the candles, thinking about the Horn, about little fires in the black African night, stiffening corpses, knives in the moonlight, the feel of a man's face in your left hand, his beard rasping against your palm, the steel in your right hand vibrating as the blade cuts so deep into the throat that it grates against the man's spine. The gasping, the weakening convulsions, fresh blood on your forearm, warm as coffee.

"Ten years ago."

"During the Janjaweed Rising?"

"Unofficially, yes." A short answer, and as such a palpable hint, which Brancati deliberately ignored, his expression hardening.

"We were there too. My brigade. With the UN. An armored brigade of the Centauro Division. Under that Canadian general. We lost fourteen men. Taken as prisoners, abandoned by—by that Canadian—then butchered like veal calves."

"In Kismayo?"

Brancati had a blind look, his mind in the past.

"I was in that sector," said Dalton. "Your relief column got turned away."

"Sent back," said Brancati. "By that . . . clerk."

"You were supposed to have a safe passage. That unit, I mean."

"Ha! Guaranteed by that Canadian. His 'guarantee' was as empty as his huge square head. No matter. No consequences for him. He wrote a book and became a big man at the United Nations. He goes on television to weep about how difficult it all was for him, how much he suffers from the nightmares, from the guilt, although he insists that he himself did all that courage could do. No. His guilt is at one remove, he is only *remotely* guilty. For this the Canadian government calls him a great hero of their people. He sits in their government even now, smoking cigars, granting interviews."

"Bugger the Canadians," said Dalton.

"No. Tonight I will not bugger the Canadians, as so many of the best of them lie buried in little towns and villages all over Tuscany, killed fighting the Nazis in the last good war. But certainly tonight we must bugger the Horn of Africa. And we must not overlook the officers. Particularly we must bugger all the officers."

"You're a major yourself, aren't you?"

"Yes," he said, nodding, his expression grave. "Bugger me first of all. You too are an officer?"

"I was. I'm not in the Army anymore."

"No. You are a spy. Tonight we will bugger all the spies too."

"Well, technically, I'm not really a spy."

"You are evasive, Micah. I begin to think you do not wish to be buggered. No. I agree. In this you speak the simple truth. You are not a spy. You are too memorable. I have never met a memorable spy. Men who are memorable cannot become spies. Your true spy is always a half man. He is deformed in his aspect. He has bad skin. He is impotent. Stunted. Fat. Bald. *Abito che non calza.*"

"Suit but no socks?"

"Yes. They have no socks. It means they are . . . *come si dice?*"

"Out of place? Misfits?"

"Yes! Misfits. All spies are misfits. But not all misfits are spies. You are, although very handsome—such a *bella figura*—you are also a kind of misfit. I say this without offense, I hope. I too am a misfit. We do not fit our places. Our times. Our times are out of joint with us. Dante said that. Or perhaps it was Shakespeare, that black Irish thief. You are with the Central Intelligence Agency, but you are not a spy. What it is you do for them?"

Dalton, deciding not to debate the nationality and criminal propensities of Shakespeare, settled for "I think you know."

Brancati grinned, a flash of intense white in the rosy gloom of the cubicle, his mustache bristling above this like a thicket of thorns.

"*Tu fai pulizie.* You are a *ripulitore.* You clean up. You are a—"

"A cleaner. Yes. That's what I do."

"You will not take offense," said Brancati, leaning forward, coming in close, breathing sambuca on Dalton's cheek, "if I tell you that you are not so good at this cleaner job. With respect, you are something of a fornicator from upward."

Dalton could not work that out right away, so he said nothing.

"Perhaps your heart is not in it. You have taken Mr. Naumann's death very personally. It has deranged your judgment. Now you are exploded, a known spy, you are seen drinking with an officer of the Carabinieri, you have started a vendetta with the Croatians, and a magnificent Italian *fanciulla* rejects your suit of love. All this you have accomplished in only five days."

"Fornicator from upward? Do you mean I'm a fuck-up?"

"Yes! A fuck-upper! I said it wrong?"

Dalton raised a glass. "No. God, no," he said, laughing a good, deep laugh that felt like his first in a hundred days. "Here's to fornicators from upward everywhere."

"*Salute!* To you as well. And to me. We are all fornicator-ups in our own ways. *Allora,* I will help you, if I can, since I believe that you very much need my help. This Sweetwater man, you have a real name for him now?"

"No. I haven't had a chance to run him in the Agency databases."

"Why not? You were in London."

"London was pretty hectic."

"How will you 'run' this search?"

"I'll start with the name."

"Sweetwater?"

"Yes. See where it takes me."

"Good. A start. Cora—she has told me I may call her Cora—"

"So I see."

"Yes. What a woman! *Una ragazza magnifica.* If I were not married . . . but I am most powerfully married. Now, I have decided to help you. In whatever way I can. This depends on much. I expect you to . . . to share?"

Stallworth won't like that, Micah.

"As much as they'll let me, Tessio."

Brancati studied him for a time over the lip of his glass.

"Okay. *Allora.* Now I have something to show you, my friend."

He slipped an envelope out of his shirt pocket and laid it down on the table with a certain air, a flourish, as if to say, "Voilà!"

Dalton opened the envelope and tipped its contents out onto the table; six grainy color photos, each one showing a barred gate and a short section of hallway. In the first shot, the doorway, the gate barred, nothing showing. In the second, a shadow on the outside steps, as if from a streetlight. In the third, a black figure, shapeless, apparently surrounded by a black cloud. In the fourth, a black cloud filling the picture almost to the edges, and bars of white static, as if from an electrical interference on the power line. In the fifth, the cloud still, and the static fuzz, but both receding, shrinking, and the short section of the hallway reappearing around the edges. In the sixth, the black cloud is gone, the hallway is empty, but the barred gate stands wide open.

"Where was this taken?" asked Dalton, staring at the succession of images with a ripple of superstitious dread playing around the edges of his mind. The pictures seemed to show a shapeless form, almost a ghost, filling the frame, gliding through the frames, fading away.

"I listened to you, back in Cortona. I spoke with the desk clerk at the Strega, on Via Janelli, talked to him myself. He finally admitted that he had fallen asleep for a while. It came on very suddenly. He grew sleepy, put his head down. He may have been drugged somehow. This was at ten in the evening. At five minutes after ten, this dark figure appears at the door. The black cloud grows, and the static, the white noise as it were, and then it passes, and when it is gone, the gate is open. The gate is on a spring and very gradually it closes again. A while later the *blatta* girls in the next room hear two voices coming from Mr. Naumann's room. Not really voices. More like one voice and another sound, rather like bees droning. Then a crash and a fire alarm goes off and then . . . *niente*. Silence. An hour later, Mr. Naumann leaves the hostel—"

"Did the camera show that?"

"The clerk saw nothing. The camera stopped working. The rest of the night it showed only black. As if the eye had been burned out."

"What kind of camera was it? Digital or magnetic tape?"

"Magnetic. A VHS tape. You know something about this?"

"I've heard . . . rumors. At MIT they were working on a cloaking device. It puts out a jamming signal capable of doing this kind of thing to a video camera. It overloads the sensors with cross-spectrum broadband waves. It effects thermal imaging, infrared and ultraviolet sensors. The sensors react to this cloaking device almost as if it were a solar flare. It works on certain types of digital cameras as well. All you would see in the screen is a black formless cloud, and sometimes bars of electrical interference. People tend to think there's something wrong, some malfunction in the camera."

"Such a masking device, this would not be available to everyone? You could not buy it at your friendly Barracca della Radio in Boston?"

"No. This is very high level. State-of-the-art countersurveillance. Strictly covert operations at the federal level."

Brancati scooped up the photos and slipped them back into the envelope, his face closed, inward.

"Would this Sweetwater person have access to such a device?"

"I can't see how. But then I don't know who he really is."

"From whom would he get such a device?"

"I don't know. This is all just speculation."

"Perhaps from your own Agency?"

"This technology—if we have it, so could others."

"You think some other agency may be working this man?"

"I have no idea. Do you have access to the EU passport logs?"

"Yes. Of course. For all the good that does. Now that we have all this open-border European Union nonsense, an intruder can slip into some lawless piratical country like—"

"Like Croatia?"

"Yes. Like Croatia, and then simply walk across into Italy at Trieste. Or come ashore on a boat. A fast boat."

He stopped, considering, turning over the Croatian element in his mind. Dalton was ahead of him, but not at all of the same view. Naumann's death, the murder of his family, terrible though they were, had no obvious connection to Croatian drug cartels.

No *obvious* connection.

"What about the Croatian end of this. I don't want these guys . . . what were their names?"

"One was called Radko. The other one she did not hear."

"I don't want these guys going after Cora again. Is there anything you can do?"

"Have you ever tried to put a cat in a hatbox, Micah?"

"No. I haven't."

"I know the Vasari family. They are not the people who go into the hatboxes. Her grandfather was an airman. Very brave. He was murdered by a Fascist assassin during Il Duce's little adventure in Abyssinia. Cora will insist on being left alone. However, I will place some watchers on her."

"Thank you.

"What will you do? Now?"

"About the Croatians?"

"No. That is *my* business. I must insist on that. The Croatians you will leave to me. In Split there is a man named Branco Gospic— you remember him?"

"Yes. You told me about him. He runs a crime syndicate. Gavro's family, the Princips, they're connected to this Gospic character?"

"Yes. By blood. And by guilt. By debts. So Branco Gospic is the doorway to this. I will go after him. I give you my word that everything will be done to protect her. I ask about this Sweetwater fellow. You think he is connected to these Gospic people?"

"I have no reason to think it. But I can't rule it out."

"You have been back to London. Was it to look for him?"

"No. I think he had already been there."

Brancati sensed the meaning, raising an eyebrow. "No. More killing?"

Dalton told him everything, the complete report, not the edited version he had told Cora. Brancati asked one or two technical questions, but in the main he just sat there quietly and absorbed the data, entirely a cop at this moment. When Dalton had finished, Brancati was silent for a while.

"Such viciousness . . . it makes me wonder. Do you believe this butchery was done before the death—perhaps the murder—of your friend Mr. Naumann?"

"Yes. Forensics indicated that the time of death was around the fourth of October. Porter was in Venice at the time."

"So your friend died three days later?"

"Yes."

"And, as we saw, in a great state of emotion. Of horror."

"Yes."

"Such a state of horror that might be caused by images of the brutal torture and murder of your entire family."

"Porter wasn't a man to collapse under that kind of challenge."

"Not in his right mind, of course not. But suppose he was under the influence of some terrible drug—a drug that magnified all of his fears, his horror—would that not drive him to such an end?"

"Yes," said Dalton, thinking about icicles. "Yes. Quite easily."

"So we may be justified in thinking that whoever killed Mr. Naumann's family did so partly to have such terrible images to present to the husband, the father, at a time and place of this man's choosing."

"Such as a hostel in Cortona?"

"Yes. Exactly."

"This kind of planning, this sustained malevolence, this can only be for one of two things, Micah. For the joy of inflicting pain. Or for vengeance."

"I think it's both. So do you. It's a vendetta."

"Yes. Like the Croatians have against you. But you do not think this man has any connection to Gavro and Milan, to the Croatians?"

"I didn't. Now I'm not sure. I'm also worried about this connection with Carovita. I went there on Saturday night and I saw this Indian having a meal there, alone, at a table in the back. And I spoke to an old woman the next day, who told me where to find him. The fact that the people who ran the—"

"My information may not have been correct. I will check it further. I am not aware that Branco Gospic has any connection to this restaurant. Many Croatians run restaurants. They are not *all* criminals. Most. But not all. You have told me that Mr. Naumann had no connection to illegal drugs. I believe you are telling me what you yourself believe, although we see that at least one very powerful drug has been used against you. Nor have we been able to discover any in our own investigations. A man like that—with such connections; Burke and Single is known to us—if he had been involved in drugs, he would have appeared on our . . . on our radar screens, as it were. "Now, this does not mean that a clever man could not fool us, make us the dupes. You and I, we begin to think that Mr. Naumann and his family, they were killed for vendetta. The way they died, the cruelty—this speaks of vendetta. Here is what I offer you: I will follow the Croatians. The Serbians. This Branco Gospic and his friends. I do this for myself as well. They have assaulted two citizens of Italy. This is my duty. But I will also do it to see if there is any connection between Branco Gospic and Mr. Naumann and this Sweetwater man."

"Thank you."

"Don't thank me yet. There is a *contraccambio*—two ways. You reciprocate for me. In the end, I wish to know all about the drug that this Sweetwater man has used in Venice. Nothing held back by your 'people' in Washington. The whole story. From you, sitting in the front of me. I expect this."

He tapped his chest with his fingertips, and his face was hard.

"You'll get it."

"*La propria parola?* Your oath, as a soldier? *Di soldato?*"

"*Parola di soldato*. I wonder if you can look at something for me, while we're on this subject. Perhaps it would mean something to you?"

"*D'accordo*. Show me."

Dalton flicked through the images on the digital camera until he found the one he was looking for. He held up the screen.

Brancati stared at this through his reading glasses, pursed his lips, making his mustache bristle up. He shook his head.

"Sorry. It means nothing to me."

"You have never seen it before? A gang sign. A graffito?"

"Never. Where is it from?"

"It was scrawled across the mirror in the bathroom where Porter's family was killed."

Brancati looked more closely. "Print it out for me somewhere?"

"I will. The hotel has a printer. I'll—"

A shrill beeping cut through the smoky atmosphere. As if summoned by the sound, Naumann's ghost materialized behind Brancati's shoulder as Brancati fumbled for his cell phone.

Dalton stared at Naumann's ghost, wondering when, if ever, he was going to fade away. Wondering, as well, why Naumann's ghost never once asked him about London, now never even *mentioned* London, never seemed to be bothered by the brutal murders of his wife and daughters, or for that matter, by his own violent, horrific death, but seemed rather to be quite happily immersed in the same kind of jaunty insouciance that had been so much a part of Porter Naumann when he was in the living world.

No immediate insight occurred, and since any question posed to a hallucination must of necessity be purely rhetorical in nature, he simply watched with a kind of detached puzzlement as Naumann slowly made the sign of the cross, his face solemn, grave, composed, an effect of dignity and close military order only slightly undermined by the fact that he was now coming on to six days dead and wearing a pair of emerald green pajamas.

Brancati, quite oblivious to the presence of Naumann's ghost in their little cubicle, punched Risponda, said his name, and listened for a time to the tinny little crackle in his ear. His face altered, sagging. He aged in front of Dalton's eyes. Setting the phone down, his face grave, remote, he rapped on the table.

The fat waiter billowed grandly through the curtains; Brancati asked for *il conto, per favore,* and turned to Dalton.

"Domenico Zitti. He died on the table. An hour ago."

7

friday, october 12
cia hq, langley, virginia
5:30 p.m. local time

begonias! Brothel-creeping Jesus," said Stallworth to himself. "The pustulating sodomites are planting begonias."

Jack Stallworth was standing at the window of his inside corner office, muttering curses into the green-tinted glass. His was the only office in the entire CIA complex to more closely resemble a greenhouse than a branch of the Intelligence arms: a greenhouse stuffed to its moldy ceiling tiles with every kind of growing thing and generally maintained at a drenchingly humid eighty degrees, an office that smelled of black earth and frangipani and lilies. Immediately to Stallworth's left as he stood at his long window was a towering sago palm, and on his right a monumental glass-and-bronze terrarium in which floated pale clouds of mist drifting through a miniature jungle of orchids. Stallworth himself was a squat, blunt man shaped like an artillery round. His sinewy arms were folded across his broad muscular chest, his battered red face closed as a fist, daylight gleaming on his polished pink dome, his thick white brows pulled down in a ferocious frown as he glared out through the blinds at the workers digging up the flower beds by the atrium: *the fucking catamounts were planting begonias,* a plant he considered little better than a tuber, and a foul-smelling one at that. He was still contemplating this atrocity when Dalton, carrying a large ungainly package wrapped in flower-print paper, flanked by two guards and trailed by Stallworth's 2IC, a stunning and libidinous ex-sergeant of Marines named Sally Holyrood Fordyce, got himself frog-marched into the room.

Stallworth turned his head. The glare was unchanged, if anything intensified, the sunlight streaming in through the blinds and the window full of potted plants giving his forbidding face a distinctly tigerish look. He pursed his thin lips and emitted a half grunt, half snarl that could only be interpreted as a friendly greeting by a Barbary ape.

Dalton gave it a shot anyway.

"Jack," said Dalton, full of counterfeit cheer. "How the hell—"

"Save that honey-tongued crap for the disciplinary hearing, you gangrenous pustule. Right now explain just exactly *why* you kicked the living lights out of two unsuspecting Croatians in the Palazzo Ducale. Wait. Let me think. Did I? Or did I not? Oh yes. By golly. Now I remember. I *did* order you to stay in your goddam room, didn't I?"

Dalton opened his mouth to say something soothing, but once Stallworth had lifted off there was nothing much to do but sit back and admire the contrail.

"No, wait! Yes! It's *my* fault, isn't it? I guess I should have been more *specific*. I should have said 'and oh yes by the way please do *not* kick the living guts out of any goddam innocent Croatians, if you don't mind.' Next time I'll remember to mention that, not that there'll actually *be* a next time, because by the middle of next week you'll be stuck in D Block at Leavenworth wearing high heels and . . . and a . . . thong . . ."

He was beginning to lose altitude, distracted by whatever the hell was in Dalton's arms.

"Okay, you got me. What's in the fucking package?"

Dalton lifted up the parcel, grinned at Stallworth.

"A humble gift. For your collection."

Stallworth grunted, as if it was entirely usual for one of his agents to arrive at Langley HQ with an armload of potted present.

Which it was.

"Give it here."

Dalton handed the parcel to Stallworth, who swept aside a sheaf of papers on his desk and set it down carefully.

"What is it?"

"I think it's a kind of flower. They said it was very rare."

Stallworth's face altered from choleric rage to a pale avidity as he used an old Marine Ka-Bar sitting on his desk to slice the paper wrapping away, unveiling a towering moss-covered branch anchored in a large terra-cotta pot. The branch was studded with, in Dalton's considered opinion, alarmingly insectile bulbous-nosed corpse-colored flowers with bulging red penis-pistils in the center and soaring tiger-striped ears above, each one trailing a pair of twisted tendrils in spotted purple. In the sunlight streaming in through the window, the orchids glowed with a vivid unnatural light, a nacreous otherworld luminosity not unlike Saint Elmo's fire.

Stallworth sat heavily down in his chair, limp, an expression of lust and creeping suspicion spreading across his bulldog face.

"God. My God. Sanders' Paphiopedilum. Is it actually . . ."

"Is that what it is? I thought it was a gangrenous pustule."

"You have no . . . I'll tell you what it is."

His face went blank, his vision turned inward, and from his mouth in a kind of sacred drone there came a string of incantations:

"A medium-size hot to warm growing lithophytic species found on southeast-facing vertical limestone cliffs in Borneo at elevations of one hundred and fifty to six hundred meters that has four to five linear shiny green leaves and multiflowered blooms on a suberect terminal with purple two-inch-long pubescent inflorescence with elliptical-lanceolate leaves and red-brown floral bract carrying two to five simultaneously opening flowers. How did you time them to be open when they got here? How the hell did you do that?"

"Skill. Timing. Professional dedica—"

"Do you have *any* idea what this is? Never mind. This is simply the rarest and most expensive orchid in the world. You're not even allowed to pick— Christ, how did you get it into the U.S.?"

"I got this one in Florence, actually. The grower's name was Barbetta. He's supposed to—"

"Fiorello Barbetta? He *never* sells his Sanderiana. Never."

"These were a gift. He wanted you to try grafting one."

Stallworth's face took on a glow of uncomplicated pleasure.

"A *grafting* Sanderianum. From Barbetta *himself*? Really?"

"Really, Jack. Hope you like it."

Dalton smiled, enjoying Jack's rapt expression. As a matter of pure undiluted truth, the orchids were actually contraband, obtained by Dalton at painful personal expense—three thousand euros cash on the barrel—and then only after the sustained intercession of Brancati's wife, Luna, who happened to be a personal friend of Fiorello Barbetta's.

These flowers were from Barbetta's personal collection of Paphiopedila in the Boboli Gardens greenhouse, and then flown, in the seat next to Dalton, by company jet directly from Florence to La Guardia, where he used his Agency ID to bypass a truculent customs agent totally incapable of horticultural leeway.

And then personally conveyed directly to Langley in the back of Dalton's rented Town Car, which required a stop every fifty miles to spray the horrid little stinkweed with a misting bottle, not to mention maintaining the interior temperature of the Lincoln at a sweltering eighty degrees all the way down.

The price of peace in our time, thought Dalton—and from the dazed look on Stallworth's face, worth every penny of it.

"So you approve? Jack? Jack?"

Stallworth seemed not to hear. All of his attention was focused on the delicate tracery of green vine, the moss-covered branch, and the ghastly orchids on his desk, on fire in the slanting light. The look on his face was sacramental, an acolyte in the presence of the divine.

"I don't . . . know what to say. I'll write to him directly. Micah, I don't know how to—"

His expression abruptly altered, hardening.

"Say. If you think that—"

Dalton raised his hands, palms out, shoulders lifting.

"Nothing to do with Venice, Jack. I know that."

But Stallworth was gone again, already on his feet, looking pale now, patting at the tendrils, his lips pursed, his eyes widening.

"We've got to get these into the greenhouse. Here, you spray them," he said, handing Dalton a bottle of water, "while I get the top off. There, on the pistils. Not too much. Okay. Now the petals."

A flurry of brisk activity followed, Stallworth clucking away like a hen on the nest, Dalton lowering the orchids into a hastily cleared section of Stallworth's coffin-size terrarium; more misting, more fluffing of the tendrils, and finally the lid coming down—"easy, Micah, easy, you handless son of a bitch"—and then they both sat down in their respective chairs, breathing hard, Stallworth glancing hungrily from time to time at the new orchids in their dripping sarcophagus and Dalton sipping contentedly from a cup of hot coffee poured from Stallworth's espresso machine on his rosewood credenza.

Finally Stallworth tore his eyes away from Fiorello Barbetta's obscenely expensive orchids to stare thoughtfully at Dalton through the profusion of greenery on his desk (pots of dripping ferns, a spray of purple iris in a sterling silver bowl, pink tea roses in a flute).

"That was decent of you, Micah. That's a damn fine flower. And I thank you, I really do."

Dalton braced himself; sucking up in a manly way can only get you so far.

"But Micah, this shit's gotta stop, man. These guys in Venice. This Gospic mutt. You know he's got his thumbs up a lotta assholes."

"Jeez, Jack. I *don't* need that image."

"Well he *does*—and somma it's in our playpen. You follow?"

Dalton did not, but he was beginning to.

"Christ! He's not an asset?"

"No. But he calms the troubled waters for people we work with. In the Balkans. Cather's not happy Gospic is pissed at us."

"Gospic's pissed at *me*, Jack. Not the Agency."

Stallworth dismissed that with a flick of the hand, fell into a thoughtful silence while he considered Dalton over his glasses.

"This stuff with the dago. Cora Vasari. She's okay, is she?"

"She's not a dago, Jack, and yes. She's okay."

"Give it to me straight. You used your Consular jacket."

"Yes. I did."

"Why the hell did you need it?"

"I was looking for a guy I liked in the Naumann thing. I couldn't go around asking questions without some kind of legend. About Cora, Jack, you had to be there. She's a knockout. I lost twenty IQ points just staring at her. So would you."

Stallworth waved that off as well.

"These two Croats, the guys who showed up at her door later? This Radko mutt, NSA's got a voiceprint off a cell phone, could be him talking to Gospic."

"Why? How?"

"Call came from Venice right after the Vasari woman got smacked around. A cell tower down in the Dorsoduro. Call went straight to Gospic, so it got tagged and logged into sigint."

"NSA's tapping Branco Gospic?"

Stallworth rolled his eyes, lifted his hands heavenward.

"NSA's got a button mike in Hillary's dildo, Micah. There ain't *nobody* NSA isn't tapping. They got more taps out there than Restoration Hardware."

"A mike in . . . God, Jack, where does this stuff come from?"

"Nothing wrong with colorful speech, Micah. As long as you're precise. I'll have Sally send you the intercept voiceprint and whatever matches we can isolate; maybe you can use it to get a line on this Radko. If I ever let you back out in the field."

"What does that mean?"

"Micah. Think. We're in Iraq and Afghanistan and we're looking sideways at Iran. Now you got us at war with Croatia."

"I doubt Gospic's gonna send a crew all the way to America."

"You do, do you? Sometimes I wonder how the hell you got into the Agency in the first place. We should have left you with the DIA—they're all whack jobs in Army Intel. Gospic's already *got* people here, in Detroit, San Bernardino, Trenton. Most of the ports."

"You're not *really* thinking about taking me out of Operations?"

Stallworth said nothing for a time.

"Look. Right now, I need to know how operational you are."

"You mean with the drug exposure?"

"Yeah. We got the tox report from Hazmat. That's quite a cocktail you got in the snoot. Salvia, mostly, but also peyote, datura, and psilocybin derivatives. Easily vaporized. Very fine particulate mass, light as spores, totally sprayable. Dispersible as an airborne solvent if you work the matrix right. Outstanding tactical possibilities. One dose in the face and—this is the salvia part—you get this complete psychotic break. Like LSD, only immediate. Instantaneous. It gets right down into the cortex, unlocks the id, Pandora's box. Whatever you got in there, your personal demons—"

"I know that. But have they got an antidote?"

Stallworth studied Dalton's face for a while. "Not yet. You still seeing Naumann's ghost?"

"Not recently," Dalton said, lying like a Persian carpet.

"But you have? Right? The whole thing? An apparatus?"

"Apparition?"

"Whatever."

"Yes. Days ago. Maybe."

"That the truth?"

"May God strike me dead."

"Is he in here with us right now?" said Stallworth.

"Nope. Nowhere around."

Stallworth was looking decidedly undecided. "I don't know, Micah. You're starting to look like a medical risk out there. There are insurance concerns. Liability."

"I'm not gonna *sue* the Agency, Stallworth."

"No? Others have." He sat back, his expression neutral, looking at Dalton. "This salvia extract, Micah, the medics say it's in your limbic system right now, and it could kick out at any time. You admit that you've had several hallucinations, the last one only a few days ago."

Dalton wasn't going to give that puppy any air. "Stop right there, Jack. You took the SERE counterinterrogation course at Peary. The Biscuits dosed us up with LSD, other drugs, locked us up in cages for days, sleep deprivation. We all *saw* things. I got a dose and I had some visual things happen. They went away. I'm better. That's the end of it."

"We knew what to *expect* with acid. We don't know the long-term effects of this drug."

"I'm as stone-cold clear as a man can get. I give you my word. If I really thought I wasn't operational, I'd say so. You said it yourself. I'm a solid field guy. I get the job done. Yes, I had a bad time on this last detail. That's over. Don't take me out of the field. I mean it. I live there. Everything that *makes* my life is in this job."

Stallworth's face reflected some mixed emotions. The reference to the Survival, Evasion, Resistance, and Escape course at Peary—a nightmarish week filled with sleep deprivation, physical and emotional assaults, and disorienting nightmare mind games, often exacerbated by hallucinogenic drugs—left every course survivor profoundly shaken, almost broken. On the other hand, most of them went on to become superb field operators.

"I get your point. I really do. But your mental—"

"You Section Eight me, Stallworth, and I swear I'll walk."

"Ha! As if! You have no other life."

"That's my point! Send me to Walter Reed and I'll never get another field assignment. You know it. It happens all the time. You get looked at cross-eyed by your own guys. Nobody trusts you again. You can't get selected, because the rest of the team won't sign off on you, and even if they do they're always watching you while you sleep. You're operationally over. You end up down in Housekeeping with the rest of the walking dead, shuffling around in a worn-out bathrobe mumbling, looking under the bed for your pipe and slippers. I'm too young—"

"You're almost forty."

Dalton felt his anger rising, and under that his deep-seated fear of being left ashore, of being marooned on a clerical desert island, with nothing in his future but endless days of meaningless work, the loss of everything in his life that gave it its spark, its wild electric flow. "I understand that you're worried. I don't blame you. Hell, I'm worried too. But instead of booting me off to Walter Reed so I can go quietly bats, how about you give me some easy time?"

"What? Like a vacation? You just came back from a month off."

"No. Not a vacation. But something useful. How about it?"

"I don't know."

"Jack. Come on . . ."

"What kind of job are you thinking about?"

Dalton had his answer ready; he'd had it ready since he crossed the Chesapeake.

"Let me do a workup on this Sweetwater guy."

Stallworth's expression changed in some indefinable but detectable way. He held Dalton's gaze but in his eyes there was this . . . absence. An opaque quality.

"Sweetwater? *That's* the guy you like for Naumann?"

"And his family. How about it?"

"Why are you calling him Sweetwater?"

"It was the name he used himself. In Venice."

"Sweetwater?"

"Yeah."

Stallworth's face clouded up. "Man, this stuff is wack."

Wack?

"Micah. Micah, you coulda kept me better informed, you know."

"You *told* me: Nothing written. Person to person only."

"I did?"

"Yeah. You said it was policy. Straight from the Vicar."

Stallworth pushed his chair back, set his feet on the desk, templed his fingertips, stared at Dalton over the top of his reading glasses. Dalton thought the look needed a pipe but he kept his mouth shut. After a long while, Stallworth nodded slowly.

"Okay. I'll give you that. You stay in-country, right? No fucking off in the middle of the night to go to Serbia and start a firefight?"

"Scout's honor. Can I use the cubicle next to Sally?"

"Yeah. Mickey's in Gitmo. When do you want to do this?"

"Right now."

"Forget it. You look like a bucket of bat boogers."

"Jack, for the love of God . . ."

"Well, you *do* look like hell. You got a room?"

"I've got a suite reserved at the Regis."

"Jeez. A suite! At the Saint Regis? We're paying you too much."

"Nah. I put it on the Agency."

"When you wanna come in? Tomorrow?"

"I'll check in, get a shower, have dinner. How about later tonight?"

"It's *Friday* night, Micah."

"So go home to your greenhouse. I want to get this started."

"Okay. Your life to piss away. You'll have the entire section to yourself. What kind of access you think you'll need?"

"Need? I'll need *everything*."

"You're not cleared for *everything*."

"Okay. Give me everything except that."

"That? What *that*?"

"*That* being whatever part of everything I can't have. Got it?"

"I got it," said Stallworth, looking over at his orchid. His eyes grew soft and his face changed. He seemed to drift.

After a while, he looked back at Dalton. "You still here?"

8

friday, october 12
copper kings palliative care center
butte, montana
8 p.m. local time

Crucio Churriga's dying body was laid out in a hospital bed, the only occupied bed in an underused four-bed ward in the Bridger Wing of the Copper Kings center on Continental Drive on the eastern edge of Butte. Outside the window a blue shadow was crawling up the side of the Elk Park Pass, and the big white statue of Our Lady of the Rockies, her arms outspread as if she were about to take flight, was the only thing still illuminated by the setting sun.

Beside the bed a steel rack full of machinery pumped and whirred. A black plastic remote control lay in Crucio Churriga's upturned palm, his fingers lightly curled around it because, even in his deepest sleep, this remote was above all things precious and dear to him.

The remote controlled the IV drip of morphine that he needed to keep his skull from cracking open from the pain of the cancer that was eating his face off inch by inch under the wad of bandages that covered most of the right side of his head.

He had once been handsome, dark-skinned and sharp-featured with pale-brown eyes, rich black hair, and strong even teeth that made the ladies smile. But none of that had survived the thing that was eating him alive. His body was rack-thin, and under the pink sheet his ribs stuck out like a wrecked rowboat in a low tide. Crucio's body was in Butte, but Crucio's *mind* . . . his mind was far, far away.

In his dreaming mind he was standing on a white sand beach that curved around a mile-long bay and disappeared into a blue haze of low mountains on a distant curve of the ocean. Above him, rising up like the prow of a ship cutting into the shining blue haze of the Pacific, was Point Reyes Lighthouse, and down on the beach in front of him a young woman in a flower-print sundress was walking barefoot along the shoreline, the sun strong on her form, her full, ripe body visible as a shadow under the thin cotton of her dress. High above him gulls soared and dipped and the wind off the sea was clear, tangy, cooling his skin.

He came to this place as often as he could, borne to it on a river of morphine, and it was on this perfect crescent of sand and shimmering sea that Crucio Churriga hoped to spend his last days, waiting for death. He closed his eyes and felt the sun warm on his forehead, let the surging of the sea fill his senses.

He began to drift into sleep.

A sharp guttural cry from above; his eyes opened and he saw a large black crow strike at one of the gulls. It plummeted from the sky and landed at his feet, its throat ripped open.

Its head was nearly off.

Thick blue blood ran from the dying bird.

Crucio stepped back away from the dead gull and looked down the beach; the girl in the flower-print dress was gone, and in her place was a tall black figure walking toward him. The glimmer of the great booming ocean surrounded this figure, but he looked familiar.

In his dreaming mind Crucio raised his right hand to shade his eyes as he squinted into the glare off the water, trying to make out the features of the big man walking toward him.

He was wearing cowboy boots and a long black range coat and a Stetson with silver conches around the brim.

A name came to him.

"Moot?" Crucio heard himself saying. "Moot, is that you?"

The man came closer, and as he did so he held out his hand, palm out, showing Crucio what was in it.

"Where did you get that?" Crucio asked.

The man said nothing. He just looked down at it and then up at Crucio. He smiled. The smile was very strange, because although he knew he was looking at Moot, the smile on Moot's face did not belong to Moot; it belonged to a dead thing.

Now that Moot was here on the sand beside him, close enough to touch, Crucio could see that Moot's eyes were gone—there was nothing in the sockets but blackness.

Crucio decided that he didn't like this dream anymore.

Back in the ward in Butte, Montana, the body of Crucio Churriga began to move restlessly in the bed and his right hand closed over the remote.

The remote that was not in Crucio's right hand.

Back on Point Reyes Beach, back in Crucio's dream, he was standing before the tall man in black who was almost but not quite Moot. Crucio looked at the thing that was in the man's hand; it was the remote control that Crucio used to regulate the morphine drip, the remote that was his only reason for still being alive.

The remote that when he pressed the button would send a warm rushing river of ease and peace and joy and contentment flowing into his arm and from there out into all the rivers and streams and oceans of his body until he was floating, floating over the mountains, floating on a river that carried him all the way to the Point Reyes Lighthouse.

"That's *mine*," hissed Crucio, feeling the first stirrings of resentment. "Give it to me."

The man shook his head slowly, still smiling that cold smile.

The shadows of crows flitted around on the sand at the man's feet. He looked up to see a flock of crows wheeling in and around the gulls. A second gull fell from the sky and struck the sand to Crucio's right, hitting so hard its gray, speckled body split open and spilled pink intestines out into the sand. The blood ran into the sand and dried as it ran, leaving a dry lake of black beads that looked like shards of coal.

Crucio stepped back from the dead bird and looked up at the man who now stood in a cloud of flying crows. He reached behind his back and pulled out a long ivory-handled stiletto, turned the blade in the light. The glitter off the silvery tip lanced into Crucio's eyes. The light bit deep into his eyes and a red glow started up behind them.

The red glow turned into heat and the heat moved down the side of his face until it reached his jaw, reached where his jaw would have been if the surgeons had not sliced it off along with much of his upper palate and right cheekbone.

In the hospital room Crucio's right hand flexed and his fingers clutched at the remote that was never going to be there.

"Man, I *need* that remote. Please."

The man who wasn't Moot shook his head, and the leer spread across his face like an old wound opening up, showing stained brown teeth.

Crucio's rage had always been a few inches under his surface and now it boiled up like lava; he lunged at the man, who stepped easily to the right and plunged the tip of the stiletto deep—deep—into Crucio's cancerous jaw. The blade punched through the thick bandages and went in so deep that Crucio felt the tip scraping along the flat bone of his upper palate. The pain in his skull went from a red glow to a blue-white star that exploded behind his eyes.

He fell backward into the sand. The blue sky above him faded to white and the crows whirled around his head in a rattling, croaking swarm. He felt the ground as it slammed hard into his back.

He lay there for a time, gasping, staring up at a blazing match-head sun that bored into his eyes, the pain in his skull a white-hot blaze that seared through his mind.

A tall black shadow fell across him, cutting off the sun.

He saw a shape bending over him, reaching down toward him. The blade . . . Crucio's eyes snapped wide open.

He was back in his hospital room.

Sweat covered his wasted body.

The pain in his jaw was . . . immense. Like no pain he had ever felt in his long life. He could hear the beep of machinery off to his left. On the ceiling above him bars of dying yellow light glowed.

The remote.

Where was the remote?

His right hand probed the sheets beside him, fingers wide, his breath coming in short, sharp explosions.

Not there!

Not there!

He cried out in a slurred, mutilated voice. "Alice! Alice, where are you!"

Silence in the room. No whisper of rubber soles coming down the hall. The machinery beeping. The bars of sunlight inching across the ceiling. The pain *growing* . . .

He would have to get up and find the remote.

He set himself, sat up, his balance reeling, the IV stretching as he did so, the tall stand rattling. He swung his long hairless legs to the right and pushed himself to the edge of the bed, slipped forward on the edge; his bony bare feet touched something soft.

Warm.

He looked down.

Alice, the duty nurse for the six-to-twelve shift, was lying on the floor beside his bed, on her back, staring up at the same slow golden bars of yellow light that were inching across the ceiling of Crucio's hospital room in Butte, Montana.

She was not seeing them.

Her throat had been opened like the lid of a jewel box, showing a trove of rubies. Her eyes had been scooped out, and from underneath the fan of her white-blond hair a lake of bright-red blood was spreading outward. Crucio looked out at the open door into the hallway. Another nurse was lying there, her legs splayed open, thighs streaked with red, blood running from underneath her skirt.

Crucio recoiled, pulling himself back into the bedcovers. The phone. He moved to his left, reaching out for the phone.

There was a dark shape sitting in the chair in the corner of the room. In the half-light Crucio could see the phone in the man's lap. His leathery hands were folded over it. On his right wrist he wore a turquoise bracelet. His legs were crossed. He wore black jeans and cowboy boots tipped with silver. His face was in the shadows.

"Moot?"

The figure raised the phone and used a long-bladed, ivory-handled stiletto to slice the line. Then he stood up and stepped into what was left of the dying sunlight.

"Please. I need the morphine. I *need* it bad."

The black figure spoke to him, a whisper, hoarse and low. "Trinidad, Crucio. Do you remember Trinidad?"

"Trinidad? No. I don't remember Trinidad."

"You *will* remember it, Crucio. I will help you."

friday, october 12
cia hq, langley, virginia
butte, montana
10 p.m. local time

WARNING
ANYONE ACCESSING THIS SYSTEM
CONSENTS TO MONITORING

dalton sat back in Mickey Franco's chair in one corner of the huge cubicle-crowded Cleaners' Sector, sipping a black coffee and staring at the entry screen warning on his computer. He had decided to begin with facial-scan records of arrivals in London on or about the third of October, looking for anyone remotely resembling Porter Naumann. Although he knew in his gut that Porter had not killed his family, even the *remote* possibility had to be eliminated.

He brought up a full-face of Porter from his ID packet, and hit the scan button on the Entries portal. Fifteen minutes later he hit End Scan and logged out. Naumann had not arrived in any formal entry port anywhere in England, Ireland, Scotland, or Wales from the third of October until the seventh, and on the seventh he was dead in Cortona. That was at least some comfort.

If not Naumann, how about this old man in black going by the name of Sweetwater? With neither a face nor, in Dalton's view, a reliable name to start with, he had to narrow his search field.

Since Dalton's inquiry involved locating an individual who was possibly implicated in the death of a senior field officer, he felt reasonably justified in going into the IRS mainframe. He set up search parameters for a male, late fifties to early eighties, six feet or better, no obvious disabilities, typed in the name "Sweetwater" and hit Enter.

The mainframe response a few moments later surprised him. There were 1,638 living males in the age range selected going by the Sweetwater name, all of them scattered across the Great Plains states and down into the American Southwest. Rather than dig through the particulars of each case, he punched in a search for each subject's SSN card and waited for the mainframe to retrieve them. Each SSN card was linked to a digitized photo of the taxpayer in question. The sources for these were varied and often came from state driver's licenses or passport shots: it had been his experience that the shots were often out-of-date, but it was the best way he knew of to search for the face of a U.S. citizen, far better than the Department of State or each of the fifty-two state motor vehicle mainframes, because every taxpayer in America was in the IRS files. Not even God kept better records than the IRS. It occurred to Dalton that if the IRS had been tracking terrorists instead of taxpayers, the World Trade Center would still be standing.

While he waited for the shots to come up, he was painfully aware that he actually had no clear idea what his target looked like, having never gotten a good look at his face. Still, he had a gut feeling he'd know the man when he saw him. The screen flickered and he was looking at hundreds of digital shots, arranged by state and county.

He looked at every damn one; it took him forty-three minutes.

None of them looked even remotely similar to his target.

He had no idea why he was so certain he hadn't found the man's face somewhere in these shots, since he had never actually seen his target's face. But something was missing in all of these men.

Intensity.

Malice.

Some indefinable but unmistakable quality of latent aggression that the man in Carovita had radiated in his solitary silence, a quality that these men lacked.

Okay, thought Dalton, speaking half-aloud, let's take a look at the Bureau of Indian Affairs. See if they have any Sweetwaters on file. And they did. They had all 1,638 of them.

Useless.

Utterly useless.

Now what?

The guy was going by the name of "Sweetwater." But neither the IRS nor the BIA had any record of him. Yet Dalton was morally convinced the guy was a Native American. From the States, not Mexico or Central America.

And if this really was the guy who had shown up at Joanne Naumann's town house in Belgravia last week, he was also a pathological sadist.

It was true that most stone-cold killers are born that way. But the good ones, the ones who last, get training, they find some discipline and control, or it gets pounded into them by other equally hard men, either in the armed forces or the cops or in a federal prison. If they don't get discipline, they get caught and killed long before they reach seventy years. So perhaps our guy was either in prison or in the military.

He minimized the BIA and IRS search pages and logged on to the Military Service Records database. He typed in a search string for a Sweetwater, male, with an age-identifier range of sixty-five to seventy-five.

FILE NOT FOUND

Fine.

Not the military. The cops?

He logged over to the city, county, state, and federal law-enforcement personnel database and tried again.

FILE NOT FOUND

How about prison?

He logged onto the National Corrections database, which included state and federal prison records for the entire country.

FILE NOT FOUND

He *really* needed a picture, damn it! If he was going to run a facial scan through the Entries portal, he need a full-face shot of a series of suspects. Without a picture, he hadn't a hope.

It was possible the man did not *officially* exist. Not under that name, anyway. Yet he had used the name in Italy. Why was he using *that* name in the first place? Would the name carry some kind of special significance for the man? Or for his victim?

Naumann was a CIA employee.

Start there.

The CIA internal database carried a list of personal and operational names, often code names randomly generated by a mainframe in Langley, code names that were sometimes used for various operations around the world. Sometimes for foreign agents. Perhaps the name would ring a bell inside the Intelligence community. Unlikely, but worth a try. He went back to the Intel Link home page, logged on to the Umbra program, and typed in Sweetwater.

NAME RETIRED

Retired?

Retired!

That could only mean that at some point in the past, possibly the very distant past, the code name Sweetwater had once been an *active* Agency name, a name used in a previous operation of some sort.

Then why was an old Indian in Venice using the name out loud. Coincidence?

A message?

A message to whom?

To the CIA itself, of course.

Coincidences did happen in Intelligence, but nobody liked them very much. Let's review: Naumann is a CIA agent. He has possible contact with a man calling himself Sweetwater.

Now he's dead. Really quite sincerely dead.

Then Micah Dalton, another CIA agent, has probable contact, extremely memorable probable contact, with a man using the name Sweetwater, and he almost dies himself. This Sweetwater guy was becoming more interesting by the second. But he still needed to narrow this field. So how?

He reached down beside the desk and lifted up his suitcase.

Hazmat had left it in Sally's office for him, tagged with a CLEARED sticker and a list of the remaining contents.

Section of burned raffia cord—fourteen cm—clean
Dried moonflower petals—traces of SUBSTANCE UK present
(Neutralized—Inactive—see Hazmat report)
Organic material—seven pieces focaccia bread
(Neutralized)
Multiple sections of clay cylinder—terra-cotta
(Mineral scan—American Southwest—age indeterminate—less
    than one hundred years—hand-turned pottery—
    Comanche/ Apache/Kiowa style)
Burned paper items—Italian-made—grocery receipts, bus
    tickets, etc.
Fragment of carbonized paper milled in Omaha Nebraska.
Fragment of carbonized U.S. stamp present—franked.
Electron scan of carbonized paper fragment shows following
    image:

seco
Timp

A fragment of burned paper.

With traces of a U.S. stamp.

Was he looking at what was left of an address? If what he was looking at was part of the *recipient's* address, wouldn't it have some recognizable traces of letters that would be found in Cora's Dorsoduro flat in Venice? Calle dei Morti? Dorsoduro? Venice?

Actually, no, Micah. There was no special reason to think so, other than wishful thinking. The letter—if that's what it actually was—could have been in Sweetwater's possession for any amount of time.

There was no rational basis for believing that the image the techs had found would have any connection to Cora's apartment.

A dead end. But the image was all he had. Either his conjectures were on the point or they weren't. So give it a shot. Let's assume that "seco" and "Timp" form part of a *return* address. An address somewhere in the United States, since the techs seemed to believe that the stamp was American. This was all pretty slim, but it was something to run with, the only thing he had. He dug out a CD of Microsoft Streets and Trips and looked up every city, town, and county name in the continental United States that began with those letters.

He started with s, e, c, and o.

He expected to get fifty variations.

To his relief and delight, he got only one.

Seco, Kentucky

How about "Timp"?

His luck was holding. He got four.

Timp Ball Park, Utah
Timpie, Utah
Timpas, Colorado
Timpanagos River Park, Utah

All right.

What do we have? We have a Native American Indian. Let's agree that his *real* name is unknown right now. We can reasonably assume that he has a background of violence.

With a possible connection to the United States government.

Why do we think *that*?

Because he's running around using an operational name that was at some time in the past activated by an unknown branch of the American intelligence community. Weak, weak as cold tea, but so far his guesses were turning out to be more useful than his certainties.

Note to self, thought Dalton: Find out what agency had run an op known under the code name "Sweetwater."

We also have a fragment of pottery that the tech guys dated at around a hundred years old, possibly turned by Comanche, Apache, or Kiowa potmakers. That bit of data strengthened Dalton's hunch that the man he was looking for was a Native American.

Possibly Kiowa or Comanche or Apache.

Timpas, Colorado, come to think of it, is Comanche territory.

Utah is largely Ute, which makes sense, since that's why they named the place "Utah." They also had some Yakima and Nez Percé clans. But Colorado, certainly southeastern Colorado, is definitely Comanche country, as any number of slaughtered cowboys and butchered cavalrymen could tell you, if their mouths weren't stuffed up with two yards of prairie dirt.

Okay. A Native American male between sixty and seventy-five years of age—Dalton's subjective but professional estimate—with a connection to the world of intelligence and possibly from one of these five places in the United States.

How about we run a LexisNexis search? Dalton typed in a search string for INTELLIGENCE and NATIVE AMERICAN and TIMP BALL PARK UTAH or TIMPIE UTAH or TIMPAS COLORADO or TIMPANAGOS RIVER PARK UTAH and SECO KENTUCKY and hit Enter.

The screen blipped and he was looking at a string of useless hits, but one of them tagged a mention in a Pueblo paper called *The Colorado Miner.* He punched it up and got this:

NATIVE AMERICAN WINS SILVER STAR

December 21, 1952: A Timpas, Colorado, native was awarded the prestigious Silver Star for his service with the United

States Marine Corps in Korea. This native Apishapa Comanche has served with a secret intelligence unit of the USMC. The exact circumstances of his award cannot be released at this time. Even his Marine Corps name has been suppressed, since Indian intelligence operatives must operate in highly dangerous forward positions. The award was accepted in a private ceremony in Korea and word of it only reached this paper because his clan sister spoke of it to a reporter who later verified some of the basic details with the Public Affairs Office of the USMC. The man's family has refused to comment.

Somebody spoke out of school, thought Micah.

Probably another member of the same Marine combat unit, perhaps another Comanche serving in the same area of operations.

Okay. Progress.

Next, let's assume that this particular guy—we're still calling him Sweetwater—had been in a Marine Corps intelligence unit. Operating in a forward area. Put together "Native American" and "Military Intelligence" and it added up to—and this was only a guess, but it felt right to Dalton—it added up to Code Talkers.

Code Talkers, their very existence, had been one of the best-kept secrets of the Second World War. Dalton had no idea if they'd been used in the Korean War as well. But it stood to reason. What would work against the Japanese would certainly work against the North Koreans and the Chinese Communists. Whoever let that covert dog run loose had probably been promptly fired for the lapse. If not jailed.

But was this guy *his* guy?

Military intelligence was a great talent pool. It was entirely possible that a decorated Marine combat vet serving as a Code Talker would get a recruitment visit from an agent in the U.S. government. Probably the Defense Intelligence Agency, but not necessarily. Still, this definitely connected to Dalton's unknown target.

Okay. Back to LexisNexis:

COMANCHE and CLAN NAMES and APISHAPA.

Back came a string of about six separate clan names, all of them connected to the Apishapa tribal subgroup. Not one of them was Sweetwater. He had Knife, Escondido, Goliad, Red Bird, Sand Walker, and Horsecoat. But no clan with the Sweetwater name. That made sense. If his unknown target had actually been a Code Talker, then the Corps would have given him a cover name. He looked back at the list of clan names, and one jumped out at him.

Horsecoat.

The image on the fragment of scorched paper included the word "seco." Did that fragment form part of the word "Horsecoat"?

To be safe, he ran a LexisNexis search on all the clan names in the list. It took him another five minutes, his fingers flashing over the keyboard, each search cross-referenced to MILITARY SERVICE and COLORADO MINER ARTICLES. He got several hits.

One of the Knife clan members had joined the Army in 1967. Two kids from the Escondido clan had gotten scholarships from ROTC on the Denver State campus in 1971. One had died in some place called Anh Khe, which Dalton vaguely recalled was an Air Cav base in the highlands of central Vietnam. A Goliad clan member by the name of Consuelo had been killed in a multiple-car accident near the town of Trinidad, Colorado, back in 1997. Consuelo Goliad had been predeceased, in the charming obituary phrase, by her husband, Héctor Rubio González, a member of the Mexican Air Force Reserves.

A Red Bird clan woman had been found murdered in her double-wide outside Pueblo; the boyfriend, an AWOL Mexican soldier, had been indicted later. A Horsecoat clan member, first name Wilson, described in a back-page article under the heading "Crimes and Misdemeanors" as a "youth," was charged in 2004 with weapons dangerous and Possession for Purposes of Trafficking—disposition ROR, Released Own Recognizance.

And on April 9, 1948, a seventeen-year-old Timpas boy named Daniel Jeremiah Escondido, a clan member also known as "Pinto," had been charged with three counts of assault during a fight with three Air Force men from Schriever AFB in a bar outside Trinidad, Colorado.

This article carried a Colorado State Police Intake photo, a crisp black-and-white shot of a hard-looking slab-faced Native American boy with a bull neck and long silky black hair worn down to his shoulders. In the full-face shot, his small black eyes, deep-set in a blunt, angry pockmarked face, stared straight out at the camera as if he were trying to figure out the best way to skin, gut, and eat the cop behind it.

In the profile shot he had a prominent hatchet nose, a broad thrusting chin, an irregular blotch of pale pink skin showing just above his collarbone (source of the nickname Pinto?), and very small ears.

In the visible ear—he was facing to his left—he was wearing a small silver earring, a crescent over an iron cross. Exactly the earring that the old man calling himself Sweetwater had been wearing in Carovita, and, now that he was looking at it again, a design very similar to the crude drawing that the killer had left on the mirror in Joanne Naumann's bathroom, missing only the flowerlike scrawl above it. Dalton picked up the little digital camera and found the image again.

Whatever the *significance* of the scrawl, the *design* of the earring was too close and far too unusual to ignore it as a coincidence. And the boy's face *did* radiate, in a much cruder and more latent form, the same kind of malice, of brooding power that had surrounded Sweet-

water in Venice. The similarity of the silver earring to the crude scrawl in Joanne Naumann's bathroom, that was too much to disregard.

As he looked at the boy's face, Dalton's doubt, his investigative skepticism, his unwillingness to be led astray by a false lead, all of this slowly eroded in the presence of that flat reptilian glare, until his intuitive sense hardened into a moral certainty.

This was the man.

Daniel Jeremiah Escondido.

Known as Pinto.

To nail it down, he still needed a much more recent shot. Since this Pinto kid had already tangled with the law back in 1948, Dalton was prepared to bet it wasn't his last go-round. He logged onto the Bureau of Prisons database and typed in:

Escondido, Daniel Jeremiah, AKA Pinto
Born Timpas Colorado DOB Unknown

The BP mainframe seemed to take forever. Then the screen flickered and he was looking at a single closely typed page that seemed to be the record of a prisoner named Daniel Jeremiah Escondido, AKA Lucha, AKA Pinto Escondido, AKA El Cuchillo, file number 8929-030, a Comanche who had been convicted of drug trafficking and multiple homicides—three DEA agents had gone missing in southeastern Colorado and he had been implicated in the disappearances. Pinto had been convicted and sentenced to twenty years at hard labor in the Montana State Prison Facility at Deer Lodge.

When did he go in?

Date of incarceration: February 19, 1986
Released / time served: March 20, 2006

He'd been out in the world for over a year now, time served, no parole, no supervision. Gone. The man had simply sunk back into the great American desert like water from a busted canteen.

Daniel Jeremiah Escondido, commonly known as Pinto, had been born into the Escondido clan of the Apishapa Comanche nation near the town of Timpas, Colorado, on November 10, 1931, which put him well past the far end of Dalton's estimated age range.

According to his prison background file, he joined the United States Marine Corps in 1949. Service number 2543-773-010. He served with the Marines all through Korea. Awarded a Silver Star for conspicuous bravery at the Reservoir. Mobbed out in 1965 at the age of thirty-one with the rank of gunnery sergeant, and according to the IRS files, his last active service location with the Marines was in the brig at Parris Island, where he was apparently a guest of the Corps for three years before his—*get this*—his Dishonorable Discharge in sixty-five.

Dishonorable?

How does a Marine combat vet, a gunny with a Silver Star and *twelve years* of peacetime service, get himself an additional *three years* busting his hump at Parris Island before being tagged with a Dishonorable and tossed out onto civvie street in 1965?

Not surprisingly, there was no mention in the files of what his duties had been during those twelve years, where he had served them, in what capacity, connected to what unit. Or why he ended up in the brig. But the Code Talker Military Operational Specialty did bring him deep into the orbit of covert ops. It was time to look up his service records.

He logged on to Military Records, typed in Pinto's service number—2543-773-010—and the Naumann file immediately went totally weird.

FILE NOT FOUND

File not found?

Had to be a mistake.

He typed in it again, number by number, and hit Enter:

FILE NOT FOUND

And again:

FILE NOT FOUND

Oh yeah? "File Not Found" or "File Deleted by Yellow Rat Bastards Who Don't Want Anybody Finding Out About This Guy"?

Fine.

Our guy was in the Marines, but there was no official record of his service. In the brig at Parris Island for outrages unknown. Sent to Deer Lodge as an accessory to a possible triple homicide. And then released into an unsuspecting world over a year and a half ago.

In the back of his mind there was an uneasy feeling that he was poking around in somebody else's territory and if he did it long enough he'd attract some unhealthy attention.

On the other hand, the *hell* with them.

He was an agent of his government. He had every right to all the information he could locate, and if some pencil-dick bureaucrat in D.C. wanted to make a fight of it, he would be only too happy to oblige.

On the lower left of the Bureau of Prisons page there was an icon that read, Release Photo.

Dalton clicked on the Print icon under it.

The entire screen went blank, which sent a paranoid flash through his mind, but the page came back in a moment, the same prison record sheet, but this time there was a color photo in the center of the screen, the full-face and profile of a pockmarked, heavily tanned man with shoulder-length silver gray hair. In the head-on shot he was staring straight into the camera with what could only be called a killing stare, the dead-flat predatory regard of a bull shark, emotionless, yet full of malice, cold rage, and a terrible animal vitality.

It was the very same look that had been in his eyes in that Police Intake shot taken of a young Comanche boy charged with three counts of aggravated assault. Dalton felt a surge of triumph ripple through him. This was that same man, altered and brutalized by several decades of dangerous living. His face was full of angular planes and sudden cuts, as if it had been hacked out of a single slab of weathered mahogany by someone using an ax and a blowtorch.

Underneath his photo was his prison number: 8929-030. In the profile shot, his long silver hair had been pulled back to show the side of his face. *Nailed* you, thought Dalton, exultant.

There it was again.

The identical ear—small, flattened back onto his skull—and in it the same silver earring, or its exact likeness, the crescent over the cross. This was the man he had seen at Carovita, the man who was going by the name of Sweetwater.

Daniel Jeremiah Escondido, AKA Pinto.

Born in the town of Timpas, Colorado, on November 10, 1931.

Of the Escondido clan.

Of the Apishapa Comanches.

And the United States Marine Corps.

He looked at the picture of the man, a picture he had worked so hard to get, and decided to double his chances of keeping it long enough to run an Entries face scan for the London area.

He hit Print Screen, and while his printer chattered off a color shot of Pinto Escondido, he got up from his desk and stepped across to the box that Mandy had prepared for him last night.

He found the digital camera that Forensics had used to take pictures of the Naumann crime scene, pushed the ON button, and snapped a screen shot of Pinto's release photo.

All right.

Now he had a name and a head shot to hang it on and he was only a facial scan away from putting this same man in London on or about the time that Joanne Naumann and her daughters had been killed.

His only concern—and this was based on nothing more substantial than the kind of institutional paranoia that infected everyone in the intelligence game—was whether his fox-trot through the various Intel Link databases waving the Pinto flag had drawn any unhealthy attention from other agencies, perhaps from the people who had erased the links to this man's military records.

Well, it was too late to worry about that now.

If he did draw some bureaucratic fire, Stallworth would run interference for him. Stallworth bitterly resented any attempt to rein in one of his own men, especially an authorized cleaner running a high-priority search.

He used Edit to copy the digital shot of Pinto's release photo and pasted it into his Entries database scanner, cued it up, and keyed the Search for Matches button, using a time frame from October 3 to October 6.

And he got . . . nothing.

Some POSSIBLES that when examined in Zoom looked nothing like him, or who did not match the other physical parameters, or who could be disqualified on other grounds, such as solid-citizen IDs or—in one case—because he was a member of the British Labour Party.

Zip nada bupkes, as Sally Fordyce liked to say.

Okay. Not in London, or at least not *seen* to be in London in the time frame required. The next step was to try to find out if Pinto had traveled to Europe, especially Italy, in the last few weeks.

He logged back into the Portals database.

Since the man had been traveling under the name Sweetwater, Dalton entered that into the Scan parameters, along with the pasted-in prison shot of Pinto and the man's basic physical description.

He hit Scan and sat back, a wave of fatigue washing over him. He rubbed his face with his hands, stretched, never taking his eyes off the screen. All around him in the large darkened room other terminals blipped and beeped, and from somewhere down the outer hall he could hear the sound of a vacuum cleaner running. He glanced at the time marker in the lower right-hand corner of the computer screen.

3:12 AM

He had been up now for over twenty-nine hours straight.

The screen flickered, and then went blank, a flat screen of blue, with one row of red letters in the middle.

SESSION TERMINATED

Terminated! Session terminated!

Terminated by whom?

He leaned forward and typed in a string of letters.

Query termination order/root level/execute.

Nothing happened for a time. Then he got

GO HOME MICAH
IT'S LATE

Dalton stared at the screen for a while, and then typed in

Jack, is that you?
NO

Who are you?

DEACON CATHER
GOOD NIGHT, MICAH.

His machine whirred and clicked and the screen went black.
Dalton stared at it for a long time, and then he went home.

HE WAS BACK IN Stallworth's office at 0900 hours sharp on Saturday
morning.
  "Cather?"
  "Cather."
  "He was *monitoring* your search?"
  "I don't know, Jack. I know he ended it. Have you talked to him?"
  "Yeah. He never mentioned dogging your search string."
  "What'd he say?"
  Stallworth shrugged. "He says you did good work."
  "He said that?"
  "Yeah."

"Jack, can I ask you something?"

Stallworth's expression was closed and guarded. He spent some time sipping his coffee while Dalton twitched in his chair. "Sure."

"Have you ever heard of a CIA operation called Sweetwater?"

Stallworth's battered face softened as he took a few moments to adjust to the question, considering a variety of answers. "That's the name of your guy in Venice, isn't it?"

"Yes."

"Yeah, I ran it last night, myself. It was a cover name used by somebody attached to a part of the Echelon operation."

"You know the guy's real name?"

"No. That's an archive file now and they're very restricted."

"Can you get it?"

"Not likely. Data like that gets dumped from the After Action summary before it goes to Archives. You know about Echelon?"

"Everybody knows it. It's an NSA operation. Monitoring the trade in technical data, jet engines, metallurgy, communications gear, seeing to it that nothing of strategic importance gets sent to the wrong country. It's strictly passive. No metal-and-meat function. Right?"

"Yeah. That's right."

"So what about the Sweetwater link? Could just be a coincidence?"

Stallworth frowned. "Don't like coincidences."

"Neither do I. What part?"

Stallworth blinked at him. "What part of what?"

"You said Sweetwater was the name attached to a part of the Echelon operation. What part?"

Stallworth blinked some more. "I meant attached to it. It was *part* of the Echelon operation."

Dalton was picking up some evasion.

He marked it and filed it. "Okay. Sweetwater. What do you want me to do about it?"

Stallworth flipped a file across the table. "Cather handed me this, asked you to look into it."

Dalton picked up the file, scanned it. "Who's Willard Fremont?"

"Willard Fremont was attached to the Echelon program a few years back. Retired for substance abuse, but he was a good man. I knew him from Guam. Wild man, but a great contract freelancer. I got a call from the FBI last week. He's in a federal lockdown out in Coeur d'Alene. Seems he went all batshit a couple weeks ago, barricaded himself into a military-style stockade up in the Rockies, a few miles out of some backwater called Sandpoint, just south of the Canadian border. Shot at a postal worker trying to deliver a registered letter from the IRS. The Feebs took him down and now they got him in a lockup near Coeur d'Alene and he's using our name in vain."

"The Agency?"

"Yeah."

"What does this have to do with the guy who did Naumann?"

"You know *where* this Pinto guy is right now?"

"No. I was in the middle of that when Cather shut me down."

"Cather thinks this Fremont guy is where you should start looking."

"That makes no sense. No sense at all. I've got a photo ID on Pinto, and a sheet as long as my dick—"

"You're gonna need more than that."

"I'm trying to put him in London around the time Naumann's family got hit. I *know* I can put him in Venice and Cortona when Naumann got killed. I say we put him out all over the grid, get a location, and go nail his tongue to a door."

Stallworth shook his head. "Cather says no. He says you stay strictly continental."

"What? Why? No *overseas*? Why the fuck—"

"You want it straight? Medical. This salvia shit. You're not going global, Micah, and that's the name of that game. You follow? Cather's putting Serena Morgenstern on this Pinto guy. She's going to be—"

"Serena! Serena Morgenstern is a fucking infant, Jack!"

"She's twenty-nine. And she's a good street agent. Cather's giving her Mandy as field liaison. They're already out looking, Micah."

Dalton stared hard at Stallworth, who returned it just as flat.

"Jack. I *told* you I was okay."

"And we believe you. We just want you to stay inside the borders for now."

Dalton stared down at the file folder in his hands.

"This Fremont file, this is bullshit, Jack."

Stallworth shrugged that off as well. "Cather doesn't think so."

"Cather doesn't run your unit. And Serena's not a cleaner."

"He's 2IC to the director of operations, and Operations controls the cleaners. And Serena's a cleaner now."

"She is?"

"As of eight A.M. London time."

Dalton shut his mouth so hard it made his teeth hurt. He turned in the chair and stared out Stallworth's window at the atrium garden. Lots of activity for a Saturday. The begonias were being taken out.

"They're taking out the begonias, Jack."

"Fucking right they are. Come on, Micah. You're still operational. No section eight. You're just working a little closer to home. For now. Do this right and you're back in London Station."

Time passed. The begonias were plucked out one by one and thrown onto a cart. There really wasn't much that Dalton could do about any of this anyway. After a while, his breathing returned to normal.

"Mandy's working with Serena?"

"Yep."

"Not alone? Not out in the street?"

"No. Serena will have some muscle with her. Mandy's strictly liaison and computer backup. Searches, reporting. Once again, whatever she and Serena get, it comes straight to me. They've got your workup on this Pinto guy. They'll get him. You pull this end of it."

"I've never known you to keep such a tight hand on the wheel before. What's so special about this one?"

"It's not special. It's just policy. I told you—"

"Cather's policy."

"Yeah. *Cather's* policy. You don't like it, he's in his office right now. How about I give him a ring, you express your strong disapproval of all his works and days? Huh?" Stallworth lifted the phone up, held it in the air, raised his eyebrows at Dalton, waiting.

Dalton put his head back, stared at the ceiling.

Sighed.

"I *would* like to see some mountains again."

"Mountains? You just came back from mountains, didn't you?"

"Not like the Rockies. I was down in Tucumcari, at my uncle's ranch. But I was in Spokane last August—"

"Yeah. I remember. What was his name?"

"Bob Cole. Burned himself to death in his own garage."

"Yeah. Sad case. Ever find out why?"

"Money troubles, we figured. Couldn't find a note. Body was burned beyond recognition. Not even dental work. He used an accelerant. Burned white hot. We arranged for a pension for his girlfriend and their kid. I sent you the work sheet."

"My job is not to get bogged down in details. That's why they sent me over from the NSA back in ninety-five. CIA in those days was like that black guy on that ship, you know, admiring his own reflection in a bailing bucket while the whole damn boat sinks underneath him."

Dalton blinked at Stallworth, trying to work that statement out. He discarded several interpretations as simply too damn ridiculous before settling on one that was just plain loopy.

"You're not talking about *The Nigger of the Narcissus,* are you?"

"Yeah. That's right. The Conrad story."

There was just so much wrong with that literary reference that Dalton saw no easy way to untangle it. He sat for a time, in silent admiration of Stallworth's near-perfect ignorance on any subject other than rare orchids and complex international intelligence operations.

"Don't give me that *look,* Micah. Make a decision here. Willard Fremont. You want him? Go out there? See if he connects to Naumann. If he doesn't, you can always shut him up."

"Shut him up? You mean whack him?" said Dalton, trying for levity, still internally far off his balance.

"Man. First it's cowpoke stuff. Now you're Joe Pesci. No I don't want you to whack him. I mean, fly out there, see what his grievance is. If there's a link to Naumann, to this Pinto guy, find out what it is and tell no one but me. If the Echelon thing is just a coincidence, then do your cleaner gig. Cool him out. Smooth him down. Get him to stop flapping away like a broken fan belt, make him happy, even if it means springing him on a 62-14 and getting him down to the safe house in Anaconda. This is a very bad time for one of our old freelancers to go all Woodward and Bernstein on our collective ass. If you do have to yank him out of lockdown, babysit him for a few days in Anaconda and see if we can find a way to make him gurgle. Anyway, it's easy duty and you could use the rest yourself. Take him fly-fishing. Go for beers. Hire some hookers and catch a nice dose of chlamydia."

"God knows I've done *that* before."

"Tell you the truth, you're right about the psych thing. I can't afford to lose an operational guy without a damn good reason. I'm losing staff to Middle Eastern Operations every day."

"I know. I was glad to rotate out of there. I hated it."

"Me too. Remind me, next time we invade the Middle East, to just nuke the sons of bitches and call it a day. This whole War on Terror is sucking up resources, manpower, computer time—it's cramping our global reach, and all so a pack of camel-porking dune buggers can go to Blockbuster and rent Jim Carrey movies. And all the time the Chinese are sitting like vultures all along our Pacific Rim."

"September eleventh wasn't a distraction, Jack."

"I know it wasn't. But these Islamic terrorists, they'll always be with us. Like herpes simplex or Noam Chomsky. With them, it'll always be one damn thing after another. In the meantime, we got China rising up out there in the Far East like a tsunami while we diddle around in the dunes playing Lawrence of Arabia. You know China is shopping around in the Third World looking for high-tech rocket engines?"

Dalton did; he read the Intel Link dailies too. But there was no stopping Jack Stallworth once he got into high gear.

"All around the world, the Chinks are *hunting* missile tech. And what are we gonna do when they got three thousand nuke-tipped ICBMs dug in around Manchuria, two thousand miles from the coast, all their infrastructure buried way deep, immune to air strikes? And all of these ICBMs capable of taking out our entire Western seaboard? You don't think they're *watching* everything we're doing in the Middle East? What'll we do if the Chinese lob a nuke-tipped cruise missile into one of our Pacific carrier groups? How about the Chinese arrange a proxy missile hit on Guam? The North Koreans already have it sighted in with two of their Dong Two ICBMs. Make it look like some terrorist plot? I tell you, Guam is the new Pearl Harbor, Micah. Am I ranting here? Is this a rant?"

"Sort of. A bit. Actually it's more of a prolonged gripe, only your voice is real loud and your face is getting all red and sweaty and there's this big bulgy vein standing out right in the middle of your forehead."

Stallworth reached up and stroked his forehead absently.

"Yeah. I'm ranting. Sorry. I hate this war."

"How's Drew?"

"My son?"

"Only Drew I know."

"He transferred out of the Horn this September."

"He's a good kid. I always liked him."

"He's no kid anymore. Neither are you, I guess. Micah, I let you go look into this Willard Fremont guy, you gonna be . . . stable, like?"

"I just want to get back in the saddle."

"Cowboys again."

Dalton grinned, his first real smile in over an hour. Stallworth felt his own heart lighten; what the hell, it's a poor man who never rejoiceth. And maybe Micah would be okay. Maybe he'd even find a way to solve this Willard Fremont problem. Stallworth liked Dalton very much, and sincerely wished the best for him. As long as it didn't damage the Agency. Or in any way threaten his own pension.

"I was speaking metaphorically," said Dalton.

"You know I hate it when you start speaking metaphorically."

"Bullshit. You do it yourself. All the time."

"I do *not*," he said primly. "Metaphors are prolapse, and prolapsity is the enemy of precision."

"I think you mean prolix."

"Micah, no offense, I need you to go away now."

saturday, october 13
hayden lake federal holding center
coeur d'alene, idaho
6 p.m. local time

dalton read Willard Fremont's bulky jacket on the flight out, while thirty thousand feet below his porthole the landscape changed from a flat rolling sea of brown grasses to a wrinkled gray hide with here and there the silver thread of a river glinting in the sun, and then into a coat of dark-green lodgepole through which folded outcroppings and bare blunt teeth of granite thrust upward, and finally the cathedral spires and glittering snowcaps of the Rockies, rising up under the starboard wing. A hard landing in Spokane, and with the mandatory *bong bong* a galvanic, Pavlovian response rippled through the passengers; up before the plane had stopped rocking at the gate, butting into one another, shoving their elbows, their shoulders, their great corporate arses into Dalton's left ear as they unlimbered their cumbersome drag-ons, and then standing in a glum row like discontented steers waiting for the slaughterhouse gates to open.

Dalton, staying in his seat until the plane cleared, reached the conclusion that Stallworth hadn't been exactly correct when he called Willard Fremont "one of ours."

Willard Fremont was what they called in the darker arts a "bolt-on," a freelancer, attaching himself to one agency or another as the work offered, trading on personal references, a gypsy agent living the life of an underpaid and occasionally over-shot-at mercenary in the more disreputable outlying fringes of the intelligence community.

Now in his early sixties, Fremont had done a stint in the Navy. Mustered out as a loadmaster on the USS *Constellation* at the end of the Vietnam War. Spent some time in Guam, running his own machine shop and part-timing as an armorer for various intelligence agencies. Taken up full-time by the NSA in the late eighties as a kind of in-shop fabricator for various NSA units requiring special surveillance gear. Developed a kind of snap-on suppressor designed to work with subsonic rounds, got a patent on that, and then sold it to the Defense Intelligence Agency in 1992—for a song, it looked like. Declared personal bankruptcy in 1993, married, promptly divorced, banged into a drug rehab facility in Spokane for six weeks. Discharged allegedly cured, worked for a while as a long-distance trucker in the mid-nineties. And then apparently back in harness for the Sweetwater unit operating out of Denver. Retired in 2002, and his pension checks were signed by the paymaster general of the General Accounting Office, a meaningless detail, since everyone who had ever been in intelligence long enough to get a pension got paid by the PG of the GAO.

The photo accompanying his jacket showed a reed-thin but wiry whipcord of a man with sunken cheeks, an out-thrusting, pugnacious jaw, red-rimmed blue eyes, indifferent teeth, large ears that stuck out from his bony skull, a close-cropped military Mohawk gone yellowish-white, big knotted and capable-looking hands with enlarged knuckles, long ropy forearms: a man who had once been hard and useful but who had now sunk into a general air of decrepitude, disappointment, decay.

The ride in from Spokane was in the back of a tan Crown Victoria driven by an elderly and dyspeptic U.S. marshal in a wrinkled blue suit and a dirty white collarless shirt open to the third button. As the valleys and crests of the Rockies rolled by outside his window and the city of Coeur d'Alene showed itself in glimpses through gaps in the surrounding mountains, Dalton read and reread the final report from the HRT commander who had led the assault unit that managed to pry this grumpy old crab from his shell-like private compound up near the Canadian border two weeks ago.

It seemed that Willard Fremont, like Gollum, wearying at last of humankind, had retreated to a former Christian-Bible-school-turned-survivalist-camp and organized it into a no-go zone for all manner of living things.

Fremont had instituted a liberal policy of equal-opportunity sudden death, firing with intent on anything that flew, stumbled, crawled, or loped across a four-hundred-yard-wide circle of chemical deforestation and razor wire that ran right around his post-and-beam cabin tucked high up on a cliff face, complete with its own spring and a hydroelectric generator. None of which would have provoked any particular comment in this demented belfry of northern Idaho if one of those unfortunate skinless bipeds who happened to stumble into Willard Fremont's personal free-fire zone had not been an agent of the United States Postal Service trying to deliver a registered letter from Internal Revenue.

For his troubles he got himself duly fired upon—neither snow, nor rain, nor heat, nor gloom of night stays these couriers, et cetera, et cetera, but a couple of 30-30 rounds zipping by their earlobes will surely slow them down a tad. The postie hit the dirt face-first and belly-crawled the quarter mile back to his truck. Where, in a high-pitched shriek, he radioed out for the cavalry.

After that, as these things do, one thing led to another: bull-horns, Black Hawk choppers, the media frenzy pouring kerosene on Willard Fremont's burning resentments. The final federal ultimatum truncated by a burst of buckshot that took out the windshield of an FBI Hummer, the FBI's prompt reply, consisting mainly of tear gas and stun grenades, the collateral damage, including three dead dogs, a raccoon with an intermittent nosebleed, and any number of deafened bald eagles. In due course Willard Fremont was dragged from his smoldering lair, howling imprecations, wild-eyed, shirtless, all of which was very satisfying to the news crews, who filed their video by Wi-Fi and then broke for drinks at the Muzzleloader Lounge in nearby Sandpoint.

Once safely ensconced in the Hayden Lake Federal Holding Center—a squat limestone fortress surrounded by twenty-foot-tall steel fencing that was now filling up the forward windshield of Dalton's tan Crown Victoria—Willard Fremont had, like the turtle, found his voice at last, and was telling every turnkey and yard bull stupid enough to adjust his gun belt anywhere near Fremont's cage that he knew where every damn official secret since the Taft admin-istration was buried and he by Thundering Jesus was going to lead the international media right straight to the Elephant's Grave-yard of the Black Arts if somebody didn't call Langley and tell who-ever answered that Willard Buckhorn Fremont was calling for Jack Stallworth.

The Crown Vic rolled to a stop in front of the steel gates. No word of tearful parting from his chauffeur; as a matter of fact the old marshal hadn't uttered a single phoneme—other than the ones re-quired to burp up gas—during the entire trip.

The gates rolled back, the Crown Victoria rumbled into the compound, and the driver showed the uniformed guard his ID, then jerked his nicotine-stained thumb backward in Dalton's direction.

"This here's the spook from D.C." was all he said.

The guard, wearing those eternal bug-eye glasses that make them all look like steroidal locusts, grunted a reply and said not very much at all to Dalton. Nor did he find anything further to add as he led him through the sliding bulletproof glass and down an echoing confusion of cement-block walls painted in the official federal hues of Baby Shit Yellow and Cancerous Kidney Green, the two of them arriving finally outside a steel door painted forest green, where the guard ported his bull-pup Heckler and stuck a miniature walkie-talkie deep into his own ear: "Sector niner one zero. We're here."

"Roger that, niner one zero" came the munchkin-voiced response, and the steel door went up with a joyless noise, revealing a set of lime-green bars opening onto a steel-walled room—windowless— a stainless-steel table, two sheet-metal chairs on either side of the table, and the person of one Willard Fremont, clad in bright-pink paper overalls and wearing what looked like lime-green shower flip-flops.

Willard's head was down, his balding crown reflecting the light from a single overhead bulb in a wire guard, and he appeared to be reading a book from which the spine had been ripped.

"How long you want?"

"Give me an hour."

The guard closed the steel door behind Dalton and stalked away up the long dark hall. Willard never looked up from his book as Dalton came across the floor.

"Reading," he said. "Screw off."

Dalton tried to pull the chair out from the table, realized it was bolted down, and sat down opposite Fremont, folding his arms across his chest.

"You wanted a spook. Here I am. What are you reading?"

Fremont grunted an obscenity, then, leaning back in his chair, he shot the book sharply across the table at Dalton, who fielded it on the edge and lifted it up.

"*Heart of Darkness*? You're reading Conrad?"

No reply from Fremont, who was pretending an interest in the overhead bulb. Dalton saw the way his throat was working and realized the man was making a supreme effort not to lose control.

"Why Conrad?"

Fremont lowered his head and stared directly at Dalton, who was surprised to see a glimmer of intelligence in the man's expression.

"There's always something interesting in Conrad, asshole."

Then an invisible cloak came down and there was nothing but dumb insubordination, thick-witted bovine stupidity. "Who the hell're you, anyway?"

"My name is Micah Dalton. I'm with Stallworth's outfit."

"Jack's still on the loose, is he? Took you a while."

"We cut cards. It was you or gum surgery. I lost."

"What'd you draw?"

"Ten of spades. We understand you have something to say."

"Not to you. To Jack personally. Or I get me an agent."

"An agent?"

"Yeah. Doing a deal, gotta have an agent. Those New York publishers will skin you with a butter knife and then rape your cat."

"I'd pay to see that. What're you gonna call it?"

"Call what?"

"The book? Got a title?"

"Not yet."

"It's about the CIA, is it?"

"Yep. All about it. A real ex-po-zay."

Dalton shrugged, put the book down onto the table, pulled out a pack of Marlboros, drew one out, and offered the package to Fremont.

"Can't smoke here," he said, eyeing the pack with naked desire.

"You tried to skull-fuck a postie with a 30-30 Winchester," said Dalton, "so I don't think health issues are too high on your list. And the bulls around here can kiss my papal ring."

He lit up, and Fremont watched him inhale with an avid expression. The smoke rose up and curled around the light.

Dalton said nothing, but for a time he left the pack on the table. "I've read your file," he said, into the silence.

A flash of anger, immediately concealed. "Have you," said Fremont. "I hope you enjoyed it."

"I was riveted. You were a good field man. Now you're here. For reasons that elude me. You can't really *want* to go to Pelican Bay?"

Fremont's eyes flickered around the room, came back to Dalton. "No. Actually, I always wanted to sing in a choir."

A "choir boy" was Agency slang for a disgraced agent who submits willingly to a debriefing session at Camp Peary.

"Do you? You'd have to justify the tuition."

"Trust me. I can justify it."

Something in that tone, a note of resentment, of loss, caught Dalton's ear. He looked at Fremont for a while in silence and decided that the big ears and the red-eyed hillbilly dullness would make an ideal cover for a field agent; who would look for subtlety, for intelligence and operational skill, in such a weak, sour old man?

"Who's Verloc?" said Dalton, just to check his theory out. Verloc was the main bad guy in Conrad's *The Secret Agent*.

And Fremont knew it. He'd read it.

So this was no shoeless Okie fresh from the swamp. A look of instant recognition, a fleeting glimpse of his internal life, even of clear brilliance, a strong native intelligence, and then the dullness, the fixed flat eye, the veil came back down like a glaucoma. "Verloc? Don't know the guy."

Without moving his head, Fremont flicked his eyes around the room again; they came back to settle, steadily and without emotion, on Dalton's face. They were being monitored, the clear implication.

Dalton inclined his head once, conveying understanding; he'd assumed there would be mikes, and with that sign Fremont seemed to relax slightly, the stiffness, the braced quality, leaving his upper body.

He settled into his steel-backed chair, and a small smile played for a minute across his pinched, sunken features. Dalton, who was still holding Fremont's copy of *Heart of Darkness*, the only object that had been exchanged between them, opened the book where a folded corner had marked Fremont's place. The note written there was extremely faint, a feather-light shadowy script in very soft pencil:

synapse

Dalton read the word twice. "Synapse" was an old Agency code for a major, a critical, security breach, now out of common use but current when Fremont was on the job. He rubbed the faint markings away using the tip of his thumb. Nothing remained but a grubby smear when he put the book back down on the table. In Fremont's eyes there was a piratical gleam, almost triumphant, and his face was slightly flushed. Dalton stood up and walked over to the bars. He reached through and slammed a hand on the steel door behind it. At once a Judas gate opened, showing one pale-brown eye.

"What?"

"I need to talk to the key holder."

"Why?"

Fremont was still in his chair, leaning back now, arms folded, his dog-eared copy of *Heart of Darkness* shoved deep under his belt.

"I'm taking this man out of here."

"TAKING THIS MAN OUT OF HERE" required a great deal of urgent and occasionally heated cross talk in the office of the lockdown chief—a pale, scholarly looking man with a shock of white hair and a general air of resignation who was nevertheless capable of summoning up whole armies of argument against moving Willard Fremont so much as an inch, let alone entrusting him to the single custody of one purported CIA agent, no matter how impressive his credentials. It took a callback from Stallworth and a follow-up encrypted e-mail from the Intelligence branch of the FBI to convince the officials to let their prisoner change into civilian gear and shuffle out—still in leg irons and a waist restraint—through the sliding glass doors and into the back of the waiting Crown Victoria.

This time Dalton got in behind the wheel, after telling the old marshal that his vehicle was being commandeered in the name of Homeland Security, which was not well received.

"How the hell do I get home?"

"Frankly, my dear, I don't give a damn," said Dalton.

Willard Fremont was still chuckling over that when Dalton finally found his way out of the backwoods around Hayden, but he was sound asleep by the time Dalton got them onto Interstate 90 eastbound, Missoula, Montana, a hundred miles ahead of them and the CIA safe house near Anaconda another hundred miles beyond Missoula.

Dalton settled in at a steady 75, wheeling through the climbing passes with the Rockies rising up all around them, the police radio set to scan the state police frequencies. Near the little mining town of Wallace—marooned in a great dark valley between jagged granite peaks that fenced off the sky, their pinnacles dusted with the first of the coming winter snows, the little wooden town itself bisected by the sweeping ramps of the elevated Interstate—Fremont came struggling up from an uneasy sleep as they were climbing the final curve of a twenty-mile-long winding five-thousand-foot ascent that led to the crest of Lookout Pass. Not so much waking, that is, but jerking bolt upright with a gasping cry and sweat on his face despite the chill of the air-conditioning.

For a moment, lost in his nightmare, he stared around the car with real fear in his white face, his breath rasping in his throat.

Dalton, watching him in the rearview, thought at first that the man was having a heart attack, and asked if he was all right, but Fremont shook his head, bending down to rub his forehead with one tightly shackled hand.

"No. I'm okay. Just a bad dream. Comes and goes."

Dalton noticed that the farther away from Coeur d'Alene they got the less the man played the redneck hillbilly banjo-picker. His accent was flat, slightly nasal—Midwestern, possibly Kansas—but in no way raw or as uneducated as he wished strangers to believe. He left the man to his night terrors, having had enough of his own to know the devastating effect they had.

He kept the pedal down, turned the radio to a classical station, to the music of a piano sonata. The highway revealed itself to them in mile after mile of wide sweeping curves edged by shattered rock faces and pine thickets, the road soaring majestically upward as if on a course laid out by a condor, and the big Ford engine labored painfully as it hauled them up and up into the chill and thinning air.

In a while, soothed by Chopin, Fremont had repaired himself enough to straighten up, and now looked around him in a far more human way, curiosity slowly replacing the fading horror of his dream.

"Where are we?"

"Just coming up on Lookout Pass."

As he spoke they crested the craggy pass and drove under a large overhanging sign that read WELCOME TO MONTANA.

This seemed to comfort Fremont.

"Good bye, Idaho. I thought you guys would never show up."

"*Somebody* was coming. You made sure of that."

"I needed to get into a safe place," said Fremont, speaking more to himself than to Dalton. "That was the only way."

"You made a real production out of it. Why not just come to us?"

Fremont sat back and studied Dalton's face in the mirror.

"Yeah? To who, exactly? I needed a fixer, a guy who could roll with deeply weird shit. That's why I asked for Stallworth."

"How do you know Stallworth?"

"I used to be a mechanic for one of his NSA field teams in Guam. He'd come into the metal shop now and then, not too proud to talk to the hired help. I kept him in the back of my pocket. I was ever in a spot, I figured I could go to him. Everybody knows Stallworth ran his own field ops when he was with the NSA. He wasn't even in the CIA until a few years back. Tell you the truth, Stallworth's the only guy I trust."

Fremont's voice trailed away and he said nothing for a long time. He sat slumped in the rear seat, fiddling with his wrist shackles, staring out at the deep pine forest racing by his window.

Finally, "Look, you're *really* with Jack, right?"

"For my sins."

"Tell me something about him. Describe him."

"He's bald, round, and as mean as a warthog. He's uglier than an elephant's knee but he thinks the office chicks really dig him. Ignorant as a stump about anything but his work."

This description, which would not have delighted Stallworth, did seem to satisfy Fremont's lingering suspicions.

"Yeah. That's our Jack. Can I really trust you?"

"I don't know. You can't trust me to do anything that will compromise either me or my boss or my unit or my country. You can trust me to keep you safe and reasonably well fed until you make up your mind what you're gonna do with what's left of your time.

Stallworth sent me out here to smooth you out and to see if you had a problem that we could help you with. That's why I'm here."

Dalton left out the part about Sweetwater and whether or not Fremont's worries had anything at all to do with Porter Naumann's death. Fremont, shaken and off-balance, inclined to chatter, would get there on his own, if there was anywhere to go in the first place.

"That's what you do? Solve problems?"

"Stallworth runs the cleaners for inland work. And please don't tell the FBI. They think they're the only hard cases in America."

"Cleaners? I heard of you. Sometimes you just erase people."

"If I was supposed to erase you I'd have done it while you were twitching away in the backseat. You'd be floating facedown in a canyon creek right now, all your troubles at an end. You used the synapse code. That means—that used to mean—a security breach. A dangerous threat of some sort. How about you explain that part?"

Fremont worked that through, his thin lips moving as if counting off the odds in some obscure game of chance. Which in a way he was.

"All right. What else am I gonna do, anyway? Here's the thing. I'm being hunted. By somebody good. A contract guy. A pro. For over a month now, at least since the beginning of September. For a while I wondered why. I asked around, nobody could tell me anything. Finally, I figured out that the only thing that made me worth killing—I mean, by a solid professional shooter—was what I knew about Echelon. Echelon was the only really high-level outfit I ever got involved with. I figured somebody high up in Echelon, somebody right at the top, was sanitizing the record before he handed the operation over to a successor and took his retirement. Getting rid of the freelancers, the lowlifes like me, guys who never went to Choate. That way we never pop up in the news later to embarrass the guy in front of his golfing buddies."

Dalton, who had tried to get more up-to-date on Echelon before flying out, could not see the bureaucrats and forensic accountants and plodding computer dorks who currently ran it sending an assassin out to kill minor field hands like Willard Fremont, but he kept his mouth shut.

"Anyway, whoever the shooter is, the guy made two passes at me while I was taking a sorta vacation in a friend's cabin up in Bonners Ferry. Sniper shit, both near misses, big magnum. First time, September third or maybe the fourth, I'm fishing on Upper Priest Lake, I bend over to gaff a pike—zoot!—round goes right by my ear, I roll out, and I'm in the water, swimming for my life. Second time, three days later, the seventh, I'm in the outhouse, communing with Mother Nature, this great big round punches straight through, hums by my ear like a bumblebee. Please don't ask me where I was hiding when the shooter came down to check out the privy."

"Did you see his face?"

"Where I was, a patch of white with two wide blue eyes looking up would sort of stand out. No sir. I kept my head down and dug in as deep as I could go. Heard him walking around up there for another forty minutes. Then nothing. Then gas and flames. He set the privy on fire."

"How'd you get out of that?"

"Contrary to what you may have been told, sewage doesn't burn. It kind of bakes, though, which I do not want to get into either. He made another, the last—most recent, I mean—when I was over the border into British Columbia. Got a smoke?"

Dalton fished out the Marlboros, lit one, leaned back over the seat, and placed it in Fremont's mouth. He sucked on it until the tip glowed like a firefly and a cylinder of ash fell onto his shirt.

"Thanks. Anyway, I mean, I'm in *Canada* for Christ's sake, land of the eco-weenie-pansy-pacifist Birkenstock-wearing furry-legged hippity-dippity crap they believe in up there. I figured I was safe. I was wrong. It was in later September. Make it Monday the seventeenth, which means if it was the same guy who took that last run on me in Bonners Ferry on the seventh, it only took him *ten days* to find me in Canada. And I'm a guy really knows how to flee. Fleeing is kinda my military operational specialty. So I'm now laying way low, on my guard, dog-sitting for a friend who was doing a hitch for armed robbery down in Winnemucca, real nice out-of-the-way cabin up in the Canadian Rockies. Dog goes nuts one night—a big bitch mastiff named Trudy. I go out for a walkabout with my sidearm. When I come back in, Trudy's dead on the carpet—ear-to-ear, almost decapitated. The cutter took her *eyes* out, man. That part really freaked me. I mean, who would *do* that?"

The same kind of guy who would string up three women and gut them, thought Dalton, wondering how the hunt for Pinto was going. But he just nodded. The world was full of sicko killers. Too full.

"I just turned on my heel and bolted," said Fremont, coming back from a dark memory. "Got into the woods and spent three days with him right on my case. Never saw him, but I knew he was out there. Made it to the Interstate and hooked a ride with the first truck I saw. Slid back into Idaho, got myself bunkered up in that old fort around the eighteenth of September. Figured at least I'd see him coming."

"Wearing a post office uniform?"

Fremont grinned at that, a rueful twist.

"Yeah. Sorry about him. I'd been up there for two weeks, talking to nobody but my dogs, and even they were starting to avoid me. I saw the movement along the perimeter and fired away at it. Don't know how I missed him either. Two rounds and no kill. Not like me at all. When I heard the postie on the scanner, squealing for a chopper and sobbing like a girl, I knew I'd gotten my ass into it. I figured, let the Feebs come and get me. Either they'd kill me, in which case my troubles are over, or they'd take me alive and put me in a lockdown where I'd be safe for long enough to contact Stallworth and ask him for help."

"Any idea who this guy is?"

"Don't know. But like I said, he's good."

"You don't have *any* idea what he looks like?"

"No idea. I didn't know everybody in Echelon. It's a big outfit. Hell, to be honest, I don't even know if this has anything at all to do with Echelon. I made some enemies on my own. But like I said, nobody with this kind of skill set. Guy may not be a perfect shooter—missed me twice—but my how he likes to work in close. You should have seen what he did to Al Runciman, down in Mountain Home."

"Who's Al Runciman?"

"You don't *know* him? You don't know what happened to Al? What's your name again?"

"Micah. Micah Dalton."

"Micah? Not Michael?"

"Micah. As in Formica. I was conceived on a bar top."

"Listen," said Fremont, breaking off, "is Stallworth gonna be there? I really need to see him. Did he say he was coming?"

"He said to get you to the safe house. That's all I know. How do you know the guy who was after you is the guy who killed Runciman?"

Fremont gave him a sideways look. "We were both with Echelon. It was the only thing that linked us, the only operational thing we had in common."

Operational? thought Dalton. Echelon isn't operational. It's strictly forensic accounting attached to data-mining surveillance software.

"Man, everybody in our district knew Al Runciman. He was famous, one of the very first Echelon contractors, before they ever set up shop in Lordsburg. I met him the week I got taken on, we worked together a whole five years out of the Lordsburg office—"

Lordsburg? Echelon is in Lordsburg?

"—covered the whole of New Mexico down to the border, most of eastern Colorado, even got into the Four Corners a few times, if the business required—"

What the hell was Fremont talking about?

"Anyway, Al was one of the best carjackers I'd ever seen. Also good with any lock, even better with alarm systems. Great cook too, which counts if you're wintering in a safe house up in the Absarokas. He was as good a saucier as ever popped a cork. A friend too. I hadn't heard from him in over two weeks—"

"How'd he communicate?" asked Dalton, plucking the burning cigarette butt from Fremont's lips just before it scorched his nose.

"MSN chat. Through a cloaked server. His persona was a thirteen-year-old schoolgirl. New name every week. Tell you the truth, Al was kind of a free spirit. His off-duty hobby was trolling the Web for Short Eyes. Half his in-box was chat messages from pedophiles. He'd string them on for weeks, months, then arrange a meeting in some out-of-the-way place somewhere."

"He beat them up?"

"Al wasn't a mean guy, 'less you pushed. No, he'd mark them."

"Mark them? How?"

"In Lordsburg me and Al came up with this spray, only showed up in certain kinds of light—laser, some ultraviolet, certain fluorescents. We used it to tag containers, freight cars, trucks. We had laser sensors installed at rail yards and truck stops and we'd kind of keep an eye on individual shipments. It was great stuff. Permanent. Bonds on a molecular level. You get it on your skin, it's worse than a tattoo. You have to peel the skin off right down to the fat to get rid of it. I mean, radical cosmetic surgery. Nothing else works."

He raised his hands against the restraints, wiggled his fingers.

"I got it on my fingertips. You need a black light to see it. Anyway, Al's sister had a daughter, eleven, she was stalked and raped by one of these Internet cockroaches. Guy got two years, gets out, six weeks later he's at it again. Lures this thirteen-year-old boy into a meeting and just goes all medieval on his . . . well, it was real bad. Boy lived, in a way, but he eventually hung himself in his bedroom. So Al thinks there's gotta be a way to tag these creeps for life. We had access to NCIC in those days, so Al would search out all the guys who were registered offenders—all this in his spare time—find his MSN chat name, set him up, take him down in a park, the woods, an alley, coldcock him, strip him naked, truss him up, and use this adhesive latex stencil he had worked up to mark the guy's forehead with I AM A CONVICTED CHILD MOLESTER. U.S. Army–style letters. Guys came to, all they'd know is that they'd been mugged. Wouldn't know what was on their foreheads until they went into a bar or someplace that had the right kind of lighting. Peeler bars. Laser tag places. Airport security. Dentists' offices. Any bathroom with old fluorescent lighting. But when that tag lit up, you should have seen their faces. Al tagged nineteen repeat sex offenders before he had to stop."

"And why did he have to stop?"

"Al was a great guy, but he could show you a mean streak if you pissed him off. He turned up one guy who he'd tagged once already. The guy was right back at it, surfing the Web. So Al gelded him."

"Castrated him?"

"Yeah. The whole apparatus too. Steve *and* the Twins, all at once, Bob's your uncle. Guy didn't feel a thing. At least, not until he woke up, anyway. I guess it woulda smarted a bit then. Al wore surgical gloves, had everything sterilized like it was an operation. He used a real honest-to-God sheep-gelding tool on him. He said the wound bled way less than if you used a razor or a knife. Said it was more humane. Anyway, off they come, snippety-snip. Fed the guy's dick to a dog and threw the guy's orchids into a bark-chipper. Didn't want to leave a mess."

"I think body parts are biodegradable, Willard."

"So I'm told. Anyway, Al didn't want to kill him. He just wanted to relieve him. Of his sex drive. Which this procedure usually does. Al's mistake was letting his sense of fun get loose. He left a business card pinned to this guy's shirt."

"*His* business card?"

"No. No, from a veterinarian's office in Twin Falls. Dr. Franz Kaltvasser. He's a real guy too. Al stole a pile of his cards from his front office a long while back, when he had to take his dog in for surgery. Kaltvasser was a horse doctor, specialized in gelding stallions. His slogan was 'The Kindest Cut.' Al thought the cards were a hoot, he used to hand them out at bars, pretend he was the guy, just to see the looks on people's faces. He'd tell 'em to just call him Fritzie, go into detail about all these horses he'd gelded, play it real straight, string the folks along. Got himself too famous, and since what Al did to this molester—guy actually kind of died, not from the gelding but from a clot a week later, which Al figured any ER doc could have prevented with some heparin—well, it was too much for the Idaho Staties. *Tagging* the perps was okay, but gelding them was kind of bad PR for the law-enforcement side of things. The Agency got him off the manslaughter charge, but Al had to promise to retire his hobby. Like I said, Al was kind of a free spirit."

"What happened to him?"

"Over two weeks go by and no MSN message. It wasn't like Al. I was in that cabin up near Bonners Ferry—this was before I knew I was in the shit, before the shooter made his first run on me. I was worried about Al a little. He'd been drinking, kinda running to seed. I figured I owed him a drop-around, at least."

Fremont's voice trailed away.

"And?"

"And I found him in his double-wide on the outskirts of Mountain Home, laid out on the fold-down table. Dead maybe a week. Skinned alive. You can tell. Gutted. Al died hard, from the look on his face, which I'll take to my grave. Walls all covered with graffiti. Damnedest thing I'd ever seen. Nothing I could do for him but to torch the place, give him a Viking funeral you know, and run like the hounds of Hell was on my heels."

His voice trailed off and Dalton heard him moving around in the backseat with an audible clinking sound.

"Look, I don't mean to complain, but these shackles are chafing me fierce. Okay if we slip 'em off? I'm not going anywhere."

Dalton, caught up in the Al Runciman saga, had completely forgotten that Fremont was still bound up in irons and a waist belt. He looked up the road. They were passing through a deep granite defile blasted through the living rock and just passing a slow-moving RV in the curb lane. There was a big green road sign just ahead, which Dalton strained to read.

"Christ. Yes. I think there's a rest stop a mile up. We'll pull over and get them off. Sorry. I forgot all about them. What'd you do about Runciman?"

"I told you. I torched his trailer and ran like hell."

"You didn't wonder who killed him? Tortured him?"

"Sure I did. But what was I gonna do, on my own?"

"You coulda gone to the cops."

Fremont was silent for a time. "Yeah. You're right. I coulda. Maybe I shoulda."

"But you didn't."

"No. Look, this is no excuse. But it's an answer."

"I'm listening."

"Covert. We were all covert. Our unit. Going to the cops, that's not your first instinct when you're off the grid. You get a man down, doctrine says you put some distance between you and your guy. Way Al died, it looked like . . . like vengeance. Retribution."

"You have a guilty conscience, Willard?"

"Don't you?"

Dalton had no answer for that, other than silence. The silence ran on. Fremont was right, about the doctrine. Covert operators didn't work for justice; they worked for government, a very different thing. And Fremont had been right to run, as it turned out, since a short time later someone had spent most of September trying to kill him.

Fremont, his early adrenalized chatter having burned him into a daze, as Dalton had expected, lapsed into a reverie, and neither man said anything else for the next few minutes, staring out the window at the canyons and valleys rushing by as they plummeted down the eastern slopes of the Bitter Root range, hypnotized by the stream of SUVs and RVs they were passing. At the next stop they got Fremont out of his shackles and squared away—they both did what was necessary in the rank, dank echoing urinals—and in a few minutes they were back out on the Interstate, both men having fallen into a thoughtful silence, immersed in entirely separate worlds, worlds that were related only by the enigmas that bound them together.

The big car wound its effortless way through Lolo National Forest with the sun slipping down into a turquoise evening sky behind the black peaks of the western Rockies, long purple shadows crossing the road, the slender needles of lodgepole pines pricking the narrow gap of twilit sky above them, an eagle circling lazily far above, the liquid gold of the setting sun bright on its motionless wings, the tires drumming on the blacktop, the radio hissing and popping with cross talk from the state patrol cars as they moved into and out of range. The easy rhythm of driving, the sense of being in a timeless middle passage with the road uncoiling ahead took them both deep into their separate minds.

As they swept in a wide arc of Interstate around the tableland that held Missoula, Fremont's head, nodding these last ten miles, sagged forward onto his meager chest. His breathing grew deep and regular, tidal. Dalton glanced at him from time to time, feeling a certain kinship: the man was under a terrible strain, living with the fear of death for weeks, but for the moment, this brief moment, here in this drumming silence, Fremont was at peace.

Dalton envied him.

THE "SAFE HOUSE" WAS a rambling post-and-beam construction set far up an unmarked and well-camouflaged dirt lane that led, through a thick screen of blue fir and cottonwood, into a broad upland valley in which a meandering tributary of the Clark wound a snakelike path. Its stony riverbanks were choked with bending reeds, nameless wild birds wheeling above, bats flitting in the violet half-light under a few cold stars. In the far north a pale-yellowish aura marked the lights of the hardscrabble old mining town of Anaconda.

Their heels crunched in pea gravel as they stepped out of the car, their breath frosting in the chill mountain air. The house itself was low-roofed and dark, with a long veranda running the entire width of the front, the windows shuttered with heavy planks, the thick oaken door fortified with iron bands.

Fremont got his bag out of the trunk and shuffled up the steps, his head turning this way and that, as nervous and wary as prey, not taking a breath until Dalton got the door opened, led him inside, barred and bolted it shut again. Even then, Fremont stood with his back against the door and waited while Dalton, a big Colt Python in his hand, did a walk-about through the entire Mission-style ranch house.

He came back and flicked on the lights, revealing a large main room lined in pine, a massive fieldstone fireplace, the fire set and waiting for a match, three big plaid couches and matching plaid armchairs, a braided rug on the stone floor by the fireplace—a warm, comforting room done in the Santa Fe style favored by Hollywood stars who move to Montana and try to pass for normal in towns like Livingston and Bozeman.

"Nice place," said Fremont, sitting down in one of the chairs while Dalton lit the fire. There was a high-mountain frost in the night air and it had seeped down into the bones of the house, which had been shut up unused for over six months.

Dalton, watching the tender shoots of flame beginning to spread out in the dried thatch, felt himself drawn into the fire. The smell of pine smoke filled the room, and white smoke began to billow outward from the fire.

"Jiggle the flue," said Fremont.

Dalton twisted the wrought-iron handle set into the stones just under the mantel. There was a puff of in-drawing wind and the fire flared up, pulling the smoke back in and sending it up the chimney. Dalton got up, dusting his palms, picked up his luggage, and walked over to the huge pine sideboard along the interior wall.

He pulled out his laptop, opened it, and plugged a DSL cable into a wall jack. The screen cycled up, and after a few clicks he was looking at a computer-generated video schematic of the safe house and the surrounding woodlands. In the bright field of green-and-blue detail, the rectangle of the house itself glowed a warm yellow, and inside the rectangle there were three vivid red objects, a few feet apart, one rounded and indistinct, the other two man-shaped; the thermal images of Dalton, Willard Fremont, and the open fire.

Dalton looked at the rest of screen, the green-and-blue area. A few small pale red objects drifted through it, and one larger shape, glowing a deeper red. A small foraging bear, from the shape, and two smaller red blobs, probably her cubs, about a hundred and fifty yards northeast of the house, heading down a long treed slope toward the deep silvery-blue thread of the Clark Fork.

Dalton clipped a remote alarm beeper to his belt and opened the pine cabinet, looking at the interior, bottles of scotch, bourbon, a built-in fridge stocked with mixes, cold beer.

Fremont had gotten up while Dalton was setting up the laptop, and now he was standing beside him, staring down at the screen with envy but also with the professional appreciation of a skilled technician. "What kind of perimeter controls do you have?"

"This laptop is connected to a mixed-receptor array on the cliff face of that peak we saw when we came in. The array gives us a very wide field of coverage, including the entire house and about three hundred yards of perimeter. Sensors all over the terrain, cabled to the array and hardwired to this laptop through this DSL connection. Hackproof program. Gear shielded from EMP and jamming. Motion, infrared, thermal. Carbon dioxide. And night video. Right now we're looking at a bear and two cubs. They're moving down the hill toward the stream, maybe a hundred yards to our north. This beeper lets me know when the system sees something more manlike."

"A bear is a manlike object. How does it tell the difference?"

"Bears stink. Men don't."

"You never bunked up with Al Runciman."

"Remind me not to. The house itself is fully awake, in the sense that a central computer monitors every window, all the doors, even the roof. Servo-assist cameras. Relax, Willard. Have a scotch."

"Just a beer, if you got it."

Dalton popped a Lone Star for Fremont, poured himself three fingers of twenty-year-old Laphroaig, dropped two cubes into the heavy crystal glass, and handed Fremont his beer. They crossed the fieldstone floor and dropped with heavy sighs into opposite couches on either side of a big slice of lacquered redwood that served as the coffee table.

Dalton lifted his glass in a weary toast, Fremont replied in kind with a nod of his grizzled head, and as they drank the ghost of Porter Naumann flicked into being, sprawled, boneless, at his languorous ease, still in his green pajamas, on the third couch of the square.

Dalton dropped his glass, spilling the contents all over himself.

"What's the matter?" barked Fremont, sitting upright.

Dalton sent Naumann a vicious look—which Naumann returned with a jaunty salute—while he mopped at his wet crotch, cursing.

"Just a twitch. Sorry."

"Man," said Fremont, "you jumped a yard there."

"It was nothing," said Dalton, getting up and going back to the cabinet to pour himself another scotch. Naumann had been gone for so long that he had begun to believe that he was fully recovered. Now he was back, and Dalton began to believe instead that he was going to have this problem for the rest of his life, a recurring visible delusion that he'd have to work around each and every day, like a man with Parkinson's or the effects of a crippling stroke.

"Pour me one too," said Naumann. "I'm dying over here."

"Go away," snapped Dalton, without thinking, near panic.

"Say what?" said Fremont, in an injured tone.

"Not you."

"Who, then?" said Fremont, staring around the room.

"Him," he said, nodding in the direction of Naumann's ghost. Fremont squinted at the empty couch and then looked back at Dalton with new eyes.

"Who's . . . him?"

Dalton finished building his scotch in silence, poured a second one precisely the same, walked over to Naumann, and set it down in front of him with a hard glare. Fremont watched this entire exercise in silence, and sat back in his chair only when Dalton was sitting down across from him.

No one spoke for a while as the fire grew in strength, filling the low masculine room with dancing shadows and a warm flickering light. Fremont drained his Lone Star and set it down on the redwood slab.

"Micah, are you . . . seeing things?"

Dalton nodded once, staring at the untasted scotch in his hands.

"What kind of things?" asked Fremont, his voice unnaturally low and calming, as if soothing a flat-eared horse.

"Just drink your beer, Willard."

"Good advice, Willard," said Naumann.

"You're not here," said Micah, to Naumann. "I know that."

Fremont sighed theatrically, got up and walked over to the cabinet, picked out another Lone Star, popped the cap, and came back to stand in front of Dalton.

"You know, I don't mean to be a weak sister, but you're sort of freaking me out here, man. I'm kind of depending on you to keep me alive, and right now you're not looking all that reliable."

"I'm fine, Willard. Really. I've been on another detail for over a week. I haven't gotten much sleep. We'll have something to eat, watch a DVD. In the morning, we'll talk to Stallworth—"

"How'd he like the orchid?" said Naumann, cutting in.

"He loved it," said Dalton, after a long taut silence.

"Told you he would."

"Yes, Porter, you did."

"Who's Porter?" asked Fremont.

Dalton just shook his head and sipped at his scotch.

"Man. You do sound like you really *are* talking to another guy," said Fremont. Dalton looked up at him, and then back at Naumann, who lifted his hands, shrugged, leaned back into the couch, and put his bare feet on the table.

"I guess that's what it sounds like, Willard."

Fremont sat down. He took a pull at his beer, considering Dalton. "Is this guy, like, dead?"

"Very dead."

"He was a friend?"

"Yes. A good friend."

"That's rough," said Fremont. "How'd he die?"

"He killed himself—"

"Like hell," put in Naumann. "Don't believe him, Willard."

"Killed himself? How?"

"Stabbed himself with an Art Deco hat pin, actually."

"Very funny," said Naumann.

"How can a guy kill himself with a *hat pin*?"

"Wasn't easy," said Dalton, smiling at Naumann. "Took him several hours. Had to keep jabbing away. Squealed like a girl all the way through it too."

"You really are an asshole," said Naumann.

"Where did he do this?"

"In Cortona, Italy, about a week ago."

"Yeah? Why'd he do that?"

"I'm still trying to figure that out."

"Suicide, huh? And this guy, this suicider, he's here now?"

"Yes. Over there. On the couch."

Fremont studied the couch for a time, narrowing his eyes.

"Can't say I see him all that clear. What's he look like?"

"Six two, one-ninety, big build. Pale-blue skin. Used to be tanned. Now kinda moldy. Good-looking in an advanced-state-of-decomposition-crawling-with-maggots sort of way."

This wasn't completely accurate. Naumann was looking reasonably good, for a corpse. As a matter of fact he seemed to have improved quite a bit—he looked almost "fresh"—but the chance to heat Naumann up was just too good to pass up.

"I am *not* crawling with maggots, you lying snake."

"Got on a pair of emerald green pajamas."

"Green pajamas. That what he was wearing when he died?"

"No. Matter of fact, I don't know where he got them."

"In Hell. Shop called Dante's," said Naumann. "Near Nel Mezzo del Cammin di Nostra Vita. Tell 'em Virgil sent you."

"I knew a guy was haunted, once," said Fremont, in a detached conversational tone. "His name was Milo Tillman, one of our guys, worked out of the Lordsburg division, over there by the Arizona border? Tillman was in the Marines, went to Vietnam, did what was required, Silver Star, Purple Heart twice. On the way home in the Braniff jet, he's sitting beside this guy, Regular Army, name of Huey Longbourne, got a MAC SOG patch, fruit salad all over his chest, looks like he earned every stitch of it. Huey and Milo took a liking to each other, got themselves a little pissed, talked out some of the uglier bits of the war. They're getting ready to land, Huey says he's gotta go to the head. Huey never comes back. They land, go through customs—no sign of Huey. Milo gets the pilot to read him the manifest. The seat next to him was listed empty. No Huey Longbourne on the passenger manifest. But his name was there on another list. The cargo manifest. He'd been killed on a Lurp near Anh Khe the week before. His body was in the hold, along with ten other ex-grunts. After that, Milo saw Huey Longbourne off and on for years, mainly in the evening, or when he was tired. Got reconciled to him, I guess."

"Does he still see him?" asked Dalton, deeply interested.

"Hard to say. Milo got himself disappeared years back, lost somewhere in the foothills of the Rockies, down in southeastern Colorado. Winter of ninety-seven, I think. A very bad winter. Lost in a storm, we think. Never come back from a field op."

"You never found him?"

"We looked. Scoured the whole sector around Trinidad, all the way up the Purgatoire to Timpas, up along the Comanche grasslands. Got as far as the Kansas border, but that kind of looking sorta draws the cops and we were trying to keep a lower profile those days. It might even be that Milo's not dead at all. I like to think he just decided it was time to walk away. He might be sitting in a cantina right now, down in Tularosa, talking about the Nam with the ghost of Huey Longbourne. I hope he is. Anyway, my point, Milo was haunted and it never got in the way of his job. So I figure, you got a ghost, you still look like a competent guy. I'm okay with it."

"Sporting of you, Willard," said Naumann. "I like this guy."

"He likes you," said Dalton. Fremont smiled, waved in the general direction of the empty couch, lifted his beer.

"Here's to you too." Turning to Dalton, "Porter?"

"Naumann. Porter Naumann. Porter, meet Willard Fremont.

"Nice to know you, Willard," said Naumann.

"He says it's nice to know you."

Dalton topped up his glass and decided there was no room for ice, a situation he felt he could find it in himself to accept.

"Can I ask it a question?" asked Fremont, looking cagey.

"I'm not an 'it,' you wizened old zygote."

"Porter says, By all means. Feel free. He'd be delighted."

Fremont stared in Naumann's general direction, looking myopic and unfocused as he searched for something to fix his eye on.

"Mr. Naumann—"

"Porter," said Naumann. "Call me Porter."

"He says you can call him Porter."

"Okay. Thanks. Porter. My question is, do you ever tell Micah here anything that he doesn't already know?"

"I'm prepared to bet good money," said Naumann, grinning wolfishly at Fremont, "that almost *any* topic you could possibly raise with this fine young lad here is a topic about which he knows not one rudimentary iota. And if he *does* know something about it, you can rest assured that what he *thinks* he knows is dead bang wrong."

"Basically," put in Dalton, "he's saying no."

"Yeah? Well, that's kinda significant," said Fremont, musing.

"Why?"

"Because if he never tells you anything you don't already know, then he's probably not a real ghost."

Naumann seemed to be ignoring the slander. He looked as if he had gone inward and was now wrapped in deep thought. Fremont was looking quite satisfied with himself. The discussion interested him on a professional level; he had never debriefed a dead man before.

"Have you ever met any real ghosts?" Dalton asked Fremont.

"Not while I was sober. But Milo Tillman's ghost—"

"Huey Longbourne."

"Yeah. Longbourne used to tell Milo all kinds of things. Told him all about secret MAC SOG operations. Milo checked them out later; they were all true. Things Milo could not have known but Huey could. That's how you tell you got a real ghost. What you got here—"

Naumann, who had evidently figured out what was bothering him, broke in here, talking right over Fremont's dire warnings about demons . . . warlocks . . . Rosicrucians . . . something about white chickens . . . rock salt and a moonless night . . .

"I did so tell you something you didn't know!" said Naumann, a note of definite triumph in his voice. "I told you that Milan and Gavro were severely injured. Crippled. In a coma. You didn't know that."

"Jeez, Porter. I was *there*. I'm the one who did the thing. When I was through I had a pretty good idea they weren't gonna get up, dust themselves off, and go for lime rickeys."

"Where's Lime Ricky's?" asked Fremont.

"Willard, how about you stay out of this for a second? Porter, you can't tell me anything I don't know and you can't remember what happened to you in Cortona because *I* don't know. If I really knew, then you'd remember it. Don't you get it, Porter? You're not real. You're not here. If I can get you to see the truth of it, then you'll go away, like those people in *A Beautiful Mind*. Once the guy figured out they couldn't be real—the little girl never got any older—his delusions went away."

Fremont was shaking his head. "Actually, they didn't—"

"Willard," said Dalton, rounding on him, "stay out of this."

"We've been over this ground before, Micah."

"Then how come you never tell me anything I don't know?"

"My point exactly," said Fremont.

"Tell you the truth, I think it's against the rules."

"Rules? What rules?"

"Rules of Engagement. I break them, I can't stay."

"Why not?"

"I start to affect outcomes. Tamper with destiny. I'm not qualified to do destiny."

"Isn't it tampering with my destiny to tell me to go see Laura? Isn't it 'affecting outcomes' to say I only have three weeks to live?"

"You've only got three weeks to live?" asked Fremont, in an anguished bleat.

"No," said Naumann, primly. "That's more your dire warning from beyond the grave. Apparently we do that all the time. They tell me nobody ever listens."

Fremont was now quite emotionally involved, since if Micah Dalton was going to be dead in three weeks, his being dead was going to dramatically reduce his effectiveness as a bodyguard for one Willard Fremont, the Dearly Beloved. He uttered another plaintive bleat. "Is he really saying you're gonna *die* in three weeks?"

"Actually," said Naumann, looking at his empty wrist and then swearing softly, "that was a week ago. He's only got two weeks left."

"There you go again," said Dalton. "And you say you're not allowed to tamper with destiny. That's a neat excuse you got there."

Naumann shrugged that off, and then brightened. "Wait a minute, I did tell you something else you didn't know. Back in Venice, after Cora got knocked around, you were having dinner at that café on Campo San Stefano. I told you that Domenico Zitti had died. Next thing Brancati's cell phone rings."

"Oh for Christ's sake. You crossed yourself, that was all."

"I made the sign of the cross. Like you do when people die."

"Thin. Thin as watered whiskey."

"There's no persuading an unwilling mind."

"Mind if I cut in here?" said Fremont. "With respect, you two boys aren't getting anywhere."

"Not at all," said Dalton. "Feel free. I've made my point."

"Jump right in," said Naumann, crossing to the bar and filling his glass with a huge wallop of single malt, an activity that was not visible to Fremont, who was still staring at the place where Naumann wasn't.

"Okay," said Fremont, warming to his argument, "we need to get down to basic ghost psychology. Whether or not this Mr. Naumann is a real ghost or just a mental problem *you're* having, nine times out of ten, when a guy's haunted, or *thinks* he is, there's something behind it."

"Behind what?"

"There's a reason for you being haunted with this guy. Or *thinking* you are. He ever tell you why he's hanging around like this?"

Dalton did not like the direction this conversation had taken. He drank off half the scotch. It burned down inside him like molten gold.

"Go to it, Willard," said Naumann. "Now you're on the scent."

"You don't want to answer that question?"

"Not really, Willard."

"None of my goddam business?"

"In that territory, anyway."

"Too painful?"

"Yeah," said Dalton, staring at his glass.

"Fine. I don't need to know what it is. The point is, *you* already know. That's what counts here. This thing you don't want to talk about, Porter—Mr. Naumann here—this is the thing that he wants you to do something about? Right?"

"Way to go," said Naumann. "Buckle down, Winsocki."

"Yes," said Dalton, after a long pause.

"This something that he wants you to do, is it something that can actually be done? It's not something like crazy hot sex with identical lesbian triplets in a bathtub full of ranch dressing or simplifying the tax code. It's a thing you could actually pull off if you wanted to?"

"Yes. Well, perhaps. I mean . . ."

Fremont put his beer down, held his palms out. "So?"

"So, what?"

"So, whatever it is, go do it."

"Thank you!" said Naumann, smacking the redwood table hard enough to make Dalton jump, which may have been what made Fremont jump at the same time, spilling his beer again. At this stage of the debate and in his mildly inebriated state, Dalton found it hard to tell.

"What'd he do?" asked Fremont.

"He smacked the table and said thanks."

"So he agrees with *me?*"

"Looks like it. And I'm so glad you two are really hitting it off."

"So? Are you? Gonna?"

"I don't know."

Fremont threw up his hands, got himself another beer, killed it in three gulps while standing at the cabinet, dropped the frosted corpse into a box, got himself another, and came back to his couch, visibly frustrated. He took another long pull in a sustained silence while Dalton and Naumann watched him, and then turned to Naumann—turned in Naumann's direction anyway.

"How about you throw something in the kitty here, Mr. Naumann?"

"Me?" said Naumann, touching his chest.

"He's listening," said Dalton.

"Like what?" said Naumann.

"He says, 'Like what?'"

"Like . . . like you promise to go away if Micah here promises to do whatever it is he's supposed to do as soon as you're gone."

Naumann looked confused. So did Dalton, but it sounded like a fair deal to him. Fremont sat there, staring at a curved and vaguely green-tinted space in the air that was becoming more visible the drunker he got.

"Is this a deal?" said Dalton, looking at Naumann.

"You'll go see Laura? If I disappear?"

"Damn straight."

"You'll make things right with her?"

"I'll do what I can."

"Your word?"

"My word."

"How long do I have to disappear for?"

Dalton turned to Fremont. "He wants to know how long he has to disappear for."

Fremont, who by some sort of cosmic triangulation of ectoplasmic vectors had become the sitting magistrate in this case, considered for a while, blinking slowly.

"Seven days," he pronounced, after due deliberation.

Naumann looked dubious. "You'll really do it, Micah. Go see her? Make it right?"

"I'll go see her. Making it right is more your department."

"When?"

"On the morning of the eighth day."

Fremont savored the poetry in that.

It was . . . epic. Biblical.

Naumann looked wary, studying Dalton's face as if he were looking for some intent to deceive, to play the coyote.

"He's given you his solemn word, Mr. Naumann," said Fremont, staring at this curved space in the air that was centered more or less around the third couch. There was no doubt in his mind now. It was definitely taking on a man-shaped outline. Apparently there was more to Lone Star beer than met the eye. Could it be that beer was actually a cosmic portal, a door into the spirit world? It occurred to him that this was why the wise old ancients in their wise old ancient wisdom had called alcohol a spirit since the very dawning of time.

He maintained his fixed regard on this curved green-tinted space even while managing to crack open another beer and take a very long pull. Dalton kept his eyes on Naumann as well.

Naumann, after a long and presumably introspective silence, took a pull of his scotch, set the glass down hard, wiped his dead lips, and stood up, brushing off his green pajamas. "Okay. Fair deal. See you on the eighth day."

"The eighth day."

"Carmel Highlands?"

"Carmel Highlands."

"Dr. Cassel?"

"Dr. Cassel."

"Word of honor?"

"Word of honor."

"Because if you—"

"I know. I know. Bed knobs and broomsticks."

"Damn straight. The fire and the fury. All right, then. I could use the break. Manifesting yourself all over the damned globe is harder than it looks. Willard, I tell you frankly, you're a clever guy."

"He's talking to *you* now. Frankly. He says you're a clever guy."

"Yeah," said Willard, rising to his feet, his rough-hewn face composed into a bleary solemnity. "Thank you, sir."

"Willard, you're a gem. Not many guys can broker a deal between a vapid cretin and the walking dead. You should have been a literary agent. Micah, as they say in the song, I'll be seeing you."

"You take care, Porter. And get those PJs dry-cleaned."

Naumann smiled, snapped to attention, sliced off a military salute, and abruptly flicked out of existence.

Dalton blinked at the empty space for a while.

The fire had burned down low and red sparks were snapping and hissing in the ruins. The ice in his glass popped and turned slowly over, like an iceberg rolling in the deep southern oceans. The long silence ran out, a hymn with neither words nor music nor rhyme nor melody, a symphony of nothingness, of the void, of serene emptiness.

"I take it he's gone," said Fremont, after an indefinite period.

"Yes," said Dalton, with deep relief. "He's gone."

"There you go," said Fremont. "What's for supper?"

THE ALARM BEEPER on his bedside table woke Dalton up out of a deep dream of peace: Cora had been sitting at a table in that large light-filled room in the Dorsoduro, nude, writing in a book of gold.

The remote, set on Vibrate, was buzzing around on the night table like a rattlesnake's tail. By the clock on the dresser across the room it was a little past four in the morning. In one smooth motion he rolled out of the bed, plucking his big Colt off the table, and silencing the remote. He glanced at the bulletproof window.

Total darkness beyond it. The night pressed up against the window like the hide of a black bear. In jeans, shirtless and shoeless, he padded down the hall past the closed and locked door behind which Willard Fremont was having another one of the nightmares that had lately made his life a grinding misery that he heard nothing as Dalton passed swiftly down the hall and out into the living room.

His laptop was still open, sitting on the pine cabinet. The room smelled of stale beer, cigarette smoke, and the steaks Fremont had grilled, expertly and efficiently, in spite of his advanced state of drunkenness, at the end of the long, long evening.

The image in the laptop screen showed the house; there were two red man-shapes, one of them Fremont, moving restlessly in his bed, and the other of Dalton, here in the living room.

But there was another large formless shape, crossing the river, approaching the house. Dalton switched the screen over to the night-shot lens.

The image showed starlight flickering on the surface of the Clark, starlight shimmering on the leaves of the cottonwoods along the banks, a lightless void under them, and the same indistinct shape moving slowly up the nearer bank of the river, an oval shape, the surface of which seemed to shimmer with moving light, with a darker and much more solid shape contained inside it.

Not obviously a man.

But manlike enough to trigger the alarm.

Dalton stared at the image, at the way it was moving, puzzled. The object was alive, that much was clear, and something in the way it covered the ground suggested stealth, deliberate predatory stealth, but it had no discernible details at all, as if it were a wisp of fog or a marsh light. Dalton dialed up the resolution to maximum.

The stones of the riverbank leaped into vivid detail, each boulder sharp-cut, the surface of running river scintillating with pinpricks of starlight, the branches of the cottonwoods spidery and black under their moving cloak of silvery leaves.

While Dalton watched, the object moved away from the river-bank, crossed the broad sand shoals, floated over the boulders, and as it touched the deeper blackness under the cottonwoods, merged seamlessly with the shadows, as a separate drop of water will melt into a pool. *Cloaked*, thought Dalton, recalling the black fog that had drifted into the hallway of the Strega hostel in Cortona.

This was actually someone who was using an infrared cloaking device, a device capable of masking the outlines of an infrared or thermal image. Whoever this guy was, he had to be working for the U.S. government. No one else would have access to this kind of technology.

And no one else would know that this was a safe house belonging to the CIA. This guy was here to take out Willard Fremont.

Which meant that someone back in Langley had betrayed them both. But the only guy who knew where they were was Jack Stallworth, and Stallworth was no traitor. There was a sound, movement in the hall. Fremont, awake, dressed, rounded the corner and froze in place, staring into the muzzle of Dalton's Colt.

He blinked at Dalton, his mouth working. "What is it? What's up?"

"There was something on the screen," said Dalton, his face lit from beneath, glowing with blue light from the laptop screen.

"A man?" said Fremont, staring into the picture, seeing only the ripple of light on the bending river, the tops of the cottonwoods waving with silver light over the impenetrable shadows below.

"Yes. I think so. He's gone now. Into the dark under the trees."

"How far away is he?"

"Two, three hundred yards out. Near the cottonwoods."

"Have you got any remote mikes in that area?"

"Yes," said Dalton, touching an icon on the screen.

The speakers flared up with the sound of rushing water, leaves rustling in the wind. He turned the volume up to full. The room filled with the hissing and rattling of the woodland, the sighing of the wind, the bubbling of water racing over stones.

And another sound, far deeper, a sound that Dalton knew, a sound that chilled his heart and tightened his belly. A sound at the lowest edge of hearing, more a sensation than a sound, a deep rising and falling sound, a low, ponderous vibrato, but with a living, breathing rhythm.

"What's that?" asked Fremont, staring at the screen.

"No idea," said Dalton, but his mind was back in the Dorsoduro. He was standing in that light-filled room watching the cylinder spin, the cylinder that growled and hummed and buzzed all at once, with exactly this same rising and falling note, like a big cat purring.

"Stay here," he said. He padded back down the hall. When he came back he was wearing a black jacket, jeans, and soft-soled shoes.

Fremont saw the big Colt in his hand and his face hardened. "What is it, anyway? What did you see?"

"I think it's a man using a cloaking device."

"What? Like an EMP?"

"No. It's new. But I think I've seen it used before. In Italy."

"He's here for me?"

"I'd say so."

"How would anyone know we're here?"

"Great question. I have another one."

"Sure."

"This guy out there, he's a pro."

"Obviously."

"Why is so much time and effort going into killing *you*?"

"I been asking myself that for weeks. I wish I knew."

"This goes beyond Echelon. Echelon is a major NSA operation, known to a lot of the general public. No matter how sensitive some of your Echelon work was, this kind of sustained high-tech stalking, using a killer of this caliber, on American soil, this is simply not something that the NSA does. There's got to be something else going on here. Can't you think of any other reason?"

"You think this guy's one of ours? An American?"

"I'm not certain. But who else has this technology?"

"A lot of people," said Fremont, staring at the screen. The formless glowing shape drifted out into an open area under the trees and then slipped back into the dark, now less than a hundred yards away and closing in on the safe house.

"Why is *anybody* trying to kill you, Willard?"

Fremont shook his head as he watched the screen, fear, uncertainty, dawning suspicion in his face.

Dalton stepped back from the screen. "Okay, whoever he is, let's take this guy down."

"I'm going with you."

"No. I need you here, on the monitor. Take this."

He handed Fremont a small Special Forces com set, a throat mike on a neckband and an earpiece. Fremont slipped it around his neck, set it in place without a word. Dalton put on another set, then looked at Fremont, who did a click test to see if the two units were communicating.

"Watch the screen. Whatever you see, let me know."

"I'd rather be out there," said Fremont, his face grim. "Last time I was in this situation, it was the one who stayed behind got her throat cut, not the guy who went to look."

"You're not a dog, Willard. I'm going to try to take this guy alive, but if you lose radio contact with me for longer than ten minutes, don't come looking for me. Call the duty desk at Langley and tell them you need an extraction. They'll recognize the phone line. No one can get in here, not without an Abrams. Sit tight. Wait it out."

"What if you're the guy taken alive? Got a gun to your head?"

"You know the answer to that."

"Yeah. I do. But a piece of my own would comfort me greatly."

"There's a bolt-action 308 in a glass case in the master bedroom. Box of rounds in the slide drawer underneath."

Fremont assented in silence, his face stony.

Dalton liked him for his steel. No whining, no complaint. None of that phony hillbilly twang either. Whatever he was or had become, he was still a solid field man, and Dalton was glad to have him around. Fremont put his hand out. They shook hands, said nothing.

Dalton went back down the hallway to the side door, slipped on a set of night-vision goggles, eased the locking bars out of their slots, opened the well-oiled steel door, and slipped out into the shimmering green night.

The woods, glowing green in his night vision, had been cleared out to a distance of fifty yards all around the house, for obvious reasons, and he crossed the stony ground in a quick soundless rush, the Colt out, slipping into the green shadows under the trunks.

Above him, through the tangle of black branches and leaves, he could see bright-green patches of open sky. A few pale stars glittered in the moonless night. The cottonwood leaves hissed and rattled in the cold wind and he could see his own breath, a pale-green misty glow in the starlight.

"I see him," Fremont's whisper in his right ear. "He's come out into the light about forty yards south-southwest of your position. What the hell is this guy using? I've never seen anything like it."

Dalton checked his wrist compass and moved out slowly, feeling his way through the trees, stepping carefully through the dried thicket and dead branches under his feet. He'd covered about twenty yards in the direction of the target when Fremont came back on the radio.

"Micah, he's closing. He's back under the trees now. I can't see him anymore, but he was definitely heading your way."

Dalton stopped in place, in a low crouch, his back up against the bowl of a sagging cottonwood. Something slid across the toe of his deck shoe, something heavy. By the weight and the speed of movement, a damn big snake. In Montana some of the snakes are harmless. These snakes are usually eaten by all the snakes that aren't.

Dalton tried to ignore whatever venomous reptile it was that was flowing heavily over his toe in a muscular coiling glide, because now he could hear that deep rising and falling vibration, coming closer.

Out in the cold air the sound was more dense, more alive. It reminded him of a cathedral organ, that deep booming vibrato that shakes the pews. The sound was so strong, so resonant, that Dalton could feel it drumming on his skin, beating against his ears.

Perhaps because of the drug he connected with this kind of sound, or even some lingering effect of the salvia, his heart was hammering inside his chest, his mouth was dry, and when he tried to swallow he bitterly regretted it. This was fear, chaotic and compelling fear, with an undertone of superstitious awe, but it was not yet panic.

He pulled in a deep, silent breath and let it out through his nose, clearing his mind and readying himself. The bass organ sound was very close now, and he could see a great formless shape moving between the glowing trees. He raised the Colt, lined up the three red glowing dots in a level row, and laid them over the pale-green luminous blob that was now moving out from the shelter of a fallen cottonwood.

The shape hesitated at the edge of the clearing, pulsed in place for a while as the vibration changed into a slower, deeper note. Then it moved out again, entering the clearing, now less than thirty feet away and still coming directly toward his position.

"I see him," whispered Fremont. "He's close, man. Real close."

In Dalton's outstretched hands the Colt was steady, his grip firm, but he could see the effect of his breathing, his rapid heartbeat, in the way the three red dots were pulsing, the two dots on his rear sight moving into and out of line with the single dot on his foresight blade.

What he really wanted to do was to turn and run, keep running until he could run no more, roll over and lie there in the dark— disgraced, ashamed, alive. In a hidden place in his heart he hated his sense of duty, hated his suicidal sense of honor, and he hated Willard Fremont for needing his protection and devoutly wished him dead.

The figure was fifteen feet away and the humming vibrato was in the air all around him. He tightened his finger on the trigger, feeling the sear deep in the frame as it ticked across the oiled and polished surface of the hammer, the straining of the hammer spring, the incremental motion of oiled steel on steel. He stared into the cloud and saw a distinct shape, a solid central form, tall, perhaps six feet tall, broad as a barrel, wrapped inside the shifting, flowing cloak that surrounded it.

Although the humming was in him now, a deep vibration in his chest, in the electric air he breathed, he willed his world into silence, forcing his rising panic down, easing his adrenaline rush until his mind was still and he could see nothing but that hard dark-green shape deep in the heart of the swirling light-green cloud, hear only his heartbeat, feel only the gridwork of engraved lines on the broad blade of the trigger. The three red lithium dots were rock steady, lined up and centered over the heart of this solid shape.

Ten feet away, and as if he had sensed Dalton's presence, the figure had stopped moving. Dalton slipped off his goggles: the muzzle flare would blind him for thirty seconds if he kept them on.

He blinked as his vision adjusted to the sudden dark, centering his sights on the target, now only barely visible as a moving black shadow in the pale starlight. The bass organ sound increased, driving into Dalton's mind like a dentist's drill. The sear inside the frame of the Colt ticked another micron across the surface of the hammer cog.

And another, a steely heartbeat deep inside the revolver.

The figure hesitated, and then came rapidly forward, a sudden gliding advance straight at Dalton.

The idea of taking this man alive, if man it actually was, seemed quite suicidal at this taut moment, so he fired, three quick rounds in succession, each one a distinct earsplitting thunderclap, the big gun jerking as the round exploded out the muzzle, the red bloom of the muzzle flare lighting up a churning seething mass of tiny glistening forms, the world snapping into darkness again, the image still burning on his retina, the trigger pull harder now that he was back in double-action. A tiny metallic click as the sear released and the spring drove the hammer down. Another booming flash. In his eyes the same cloud of glistening red-tinted particles, shards of shiny black mica in a breaking beach wave. He pulled the trigger one last time. The Colt jumped in his hands. The solid cloudlike shape broke into a million particles, reformed itself like liquid mercury, and rose straight up into the night, a writhing tornado of spinning, buzzing particles, spreading itself out across the tops of the trees.

Then fading, dissolving, disappearing against the stars.

For a time, Dalton could hear a distant vibration, receding, dying gradually away into nothingness. Then silence, complete, deep, stunned, nothing but the sound of his own rasping breath, his carotid pulsing in his throat, and a high-pitched incessant ringing in his deafened ears.

"HONEYBEES?" SAID FREMONT. "A swarm of honeybees? Nuts. Couldn't be. They don't travel at night. Anyway, it's too damn cold."

"I've seen it before," said Dalton, wrapping his fingers around his cup of coffee, inhaling the rich, deep scent. "Sometimes if a grizzly breaks a nest open, the main queen gets alarmed, she'll swarm them up like an army and they'll move just this way. Even at night."

"Bees," said Fremont, shaking his head. "Scared the—"

"Me too."

"You're lucky they didn't swarm you. They can kill a man."

"I saw a swarm kill a young Kodiak once, when I was a kid in Tucumcari. They got into his muzzle, blinded him, smothered him."

"Yeah. Ugly way to die."

"Very."

Behind Fremont's shoulder the light was changing in the eastern windows of the house, going from milky gray to pale pink. Fremont followed Dalton's look, then turned back to his fried eggs and bacon. "Morning soon."

"Yeah. Long night."

"I kind of wish it hadn't been bees."

"Why?"

"If it had been the guy who was trying to kill me, maybe we mighta found out something. We're still in the dark."

"Any more thoughts? On Echelon?"

"Yeah. Quite a few. I think this *has* to be about Echelon. Echelon was the only intelligence op I was ever on that had any real importance. Micah, I'm a small-time field man. Married. Divorced. A bankrupt. If it isn't Echelon, who is it? My ex-wife's lawyers? My bookie? My creditors?"

Dalton sensed a building panic in the man and decided that now was a good time to see if he could be led around to the delicate subject of Sweetwater. He poured himself another cup, offered the pot to Fremont. "I thought Echelon was just a technology-monitoring operation. What the hell *were* you guys doing for the NSA, anyway?"

"Okay, we were what the NSA called 'the remedial arm' of Echelon. You're right. Echelon's brief was—still is—to monitor all kinds of communications worldwide, looking for a lot of things, but in our case it was mainly the illegal movement of prohibited international technology. Weapons-grade electronics. Advanced jet-propulsion systems capable of being reverse-engineered into engines that could drive a nuclear missile. Anything contrary to our national security, our military superiority. Although we were technically CIA, we were kind of seconded to the NSA. Anytime they detected a company, a person, a charity, a political organization, any entity that was trying to move prohibited technology to an enemy, they sent us in. We were the ones who got our hands dirty."

"Like what? Assassination?"

"No. Hell no. At least not intentionally. This was years before September eleventh. We lost some people accidentally—foul-ups, civilians wandering into a running op—but nothing on purpose. Mainly we set up complicated stings, false networks, suckered the target into showing his play, and then we took him down hard. Al Runciman and I also did detailed surveillance, basic financial workups, got the domestic life of the target figured out, searched out the background of the company. We managed the gear, the electronics; whatever needed to be specially built, we'd fabricate it ourselves. It was a great outfit, like the special-effects unit on a film crew. We had a string of major successes. One way or another, the leak would get plugged, the technical exchange derailed. Sometimes the people trying to get the prohibited technology out would never even know where it was really going—the end user—or why the deal never got done."

"And if that failed?"

Fremont shrugged. "Like I said. We were the remedial arm. We'd set them up for the FBI, or for the local cops, and put them out of business entirely, find some way to frame them on other charges. Used the IRS sometimes, the way they got Capone. Most times the targets would never know why they were set up—the real reason, I mean. But we did what was necessary. Get them in prison if we could, but anyway stop them from selling critical technology to our enemies. Whoever was involved. Directly, culpably involved, I mean. Root and branch, like cancer surgery. However far down it went, we sliced it out."

"By any means necessary? Short of outright murder?"

"Damn right," said Fremont, his face hardening. "And I'd do it again tomorrow. This is a great nation. It deserves to be defended. I have nothing to apologize for. I'd still be doing it if . . . if I could."

"I didn't think you needed to apologize. And I agree with you. How many guys were in your unit?"

"Globally, I have no idea. Might have been a hundred separate units around the world, doing the same kind of work for the NSA. Our guys, our unit, we were six guys, and we were mainly responsible for the Southwest. We handled anything that came up from Southern California, Arizona, Nevada, New Mexico, Colorado. We were based in Lordsburg mainly, but we went anywhere we had to go. We were a tight crew too, all real good guys. Al Runciman you heard about. And Milo Tillman, who we lost in the high desert in ninety-seven—"

"The guy you think might still be alive. Drunk in Tularosa."

"Yeah," said Fremont, looking a little uncertain.

"Who else?"

"Crucio Churriga. But you can write him off."

"Why?"

"Crucio's dying of cancer. Got it from sticking that Skoal tobacco snuff under his lip. He's in a . . . what do they call it? Where you go to die and they give you painkillers and aromatherapy massages and shit but you better not adopt a kitten or buy any green bananas?"

This took awhile to decode. "You mean palliative care?"

"Yeah. That's it. Palliative care, last I heard, in a clinic in Butte— just down the Interstate from us. There's not much point in going to see him, though. He can't even talk. They took most of his lower jaw off. And he's in a kind of self-induced coma most of the time.

They got him on one of those computerized drip things so he can control the amount of morphine he's getting. So he takes all he can handle. Which is funny, since Crucio was a *major* doper when we were in the unit. Me and Crucio, we used to . . ."

Fremont's voice trailed off and he looked down at his coffee cup, his eyes hooded. Dalton didn't push it.

"Anyway, then there's Pershing Gibson, named after the general. He was our shooter, our main guy with weapons. Big guy, over six feet, very strong, an ex-Marine. Sorta scary. We used to call him Moot, on account of him always saying that something was a moot point."

"A shooter? A long-range sniper?"

Fremont, anticipating the drift, shook his head. "No way. Moot's no back-shooter. If he wanted me dead, it'd be easier to invite me to his ranch in the Bighorn Valley, bust my skull with a rock. He's got a spread out there, right next to the Jim Bridger Trail, high desert so flat you can watch your dog run away for three days, Rockies a hundred miles off in the west, the Bighorns fifty miles in the northeast. Got a pack of feral dogs who howl down the blood moon if they smell a live man walking. Moot's safe enough, I guess."

"Moot Gibson? Like Hoot Gibson, back in the twenties?"

"Yeah. Cute, huh?"

"And he's still alive?"

"So far. He retired from active duty with our unit seven years ago. He's real hard to reach, hates technology, went deep into this kind of Indian spirit stuff years back, stays far away from people. Very tough, very vengeful guy. Scary if you got him real pissed off. Good with guns, good with a knife. I figure, of all of us, Moot'd be the hardest guy to kill."

"Al Runciman, dead in Mountain Home. You. Crucio Churriga— dying of cancer in Butte. Milo Tillman, who's been missing since . . . ?"

"Ninety-seven. Drove into a snowstorm and never came out."

"Milo Tillman, and this Moot Gibson guy. That's five."

"Last unit guy is Pete Kearney. Also retired. Got a place not all that far from Moot's ranch, only on the eastern edge of the Big-horns. A little cabin on an outcrop overlooking Ranchester, right where the Tongue runs down into the Powder River country south of Sheridan. Got a cliff at his back and a view out his front window that goes all the way to South Dakota. Not even your friend Porter could sneak up on him. Pete's family goes way back down there. His great-grandfather was Phil Kearney, the cavalry general. From the porch of his cabin Pete can see the site of his great-grandfather's fort, Fort Phil Kearney, right down there by the Bozeman Trail. Pete was our wrangler. Anything to do with horses, he's your man. He's my age now, but in great shape. What they call a real range cowboy. A hardhanded man. Know what I mean?"

Dalton did. He thought of the scene in Joanne Naumann's bath-room. That was range work, something done by a range cowboy. On the other hand, fifty thousand cowboys lived within five hun-dred miles of this safe house in Missoula.

"And these guys—Moot Gibson, Crucio Churriga, Pete Kearney—they're all still alive?"

"I haven't talked to Pete or Crucio in weeks, but if something had happened to either of them, I'm pretty sure I would have heard. Crucio's got all the nurses charmed in his ward and one of them woulda called me. And Pete, he's no hermit, not like Moot. He's got lots of friends in Ranchester and Dayton. Somebody would check on him. Far as Moot's concerned, I *know* he's still alive be-cause he's still using his ATM card."

"His ATM card? How do you know that?"

"Moot used to have a much bigger ranch, out there near Hardin, a ways past Billings, a real sweet spread. Took his retirement in one go and poured every dollar he had into this horse-breeding opera-tion. Down in Custer country, near where the massacre happened, but Moot went bankrupt two years ago, after that big drought. Could have stayed on his feet, the creditors were all willing, but the IRS forced him into selling everything. Moot took it pretty hard—he truly loved his horses, and most of them went to slaughter. He took it especially hard after all that 'service to his country' stuff at his retirement party. We'd used the IRS to break a target so many times that he saw the IRS as just another branch of the CIA. He even asked the Agency to help him out with the IRS, and they did try, but there was no calling those dogs off. They went for his blood and by God didn't they get it, too. Ruined him."

It struck Dalton that Moot's grudge against the IRS could, in a bloody-minded man, easily expand into a generalized rage. "But he still has a place in the Bighorn Valley, doesn't he?"

"Yeah. I helped him out there. I been bankrupt myself, so I knew how to work it out that you got to hide some of your assets, whatever you could keep from the feds. I put Moot onto a guy named Dick Poundmaker, he was my bankruptcy trustee, half-Yakima Indian and crookeder than a sink trap. Dick had worked out this cheat system for probably a hundred of his clients. Dick gets hired as the guy's trustee, and the guy—in this case Moot—promises Dick a cut of everything he's got left, medical disability checks, welfare, investment property, whatever the guy has managed to hide. Since Dick's acting in the name of the guy's creditors—in Moot's case the IRS—he sends the creditors a couple bucks to keep them happy, puts the principal into one of a whole bunch of different bank accounts he's got set up under his own name in Coeur d'Alene, Spokane, Seattle, all over the Northwestern seaboard. Dick's client gets an ATM card linked to one of these accounts, and he takes out his cash whenever he needs it. If it weren't for Dick Poundmaker, Moot wouldn't even have his little old ranch in the Bighorn Valley. I talked to Dick when I was in the holding pen in Hayden Lake and he said Moot was still drawing cash money out his special account as of last Friday."

They fell into a thoughtful silence, considering the implications while Fremont brewed another pot of coffee. He set a full cup down in front of Micah, took his chair, and sat for a while, looking at the lines and creases in Micah's face. The guy was older than he looked, or he was carrying some damn ugly memories. Either way, Fremont liked him.

"How you feeling? Seen your friend Porter, at all?"

"No. Not a glimmer."

Fremont picked his coffee up, leaned into the creaking old ladder-back, tilted it up on its rear legs. It groaned under his weight but Fremont ignored it, grinning at Dalton over the rim of his cup. "Guess I oughta go into the exorcism business."

"Maybe you should."

"Mind if I ask you a question?"

"Ask me and I'll tell you."

"You unnaturally prone to being haunted, at all?"

"No. First time."

"You *do* understand the guy wasn't real, don't you?"

"Yes, Willard. I do."

"Why do you think he went away?"

"No idea. They say you can talk sense to a schizophrenic, if he has a willing mind. And I was. God knows I need that problem gone."

"Don't get mad if I ask if you do, ah, recreational drugs?" he asked, his manner tentative.

"Not unless we're including champagne."

"Because in my troubled youth, I dabbled in that sort of thing."

"Seeking the path to enlightenment?"

"That too, of course. But mainly to score with chicks."

"Sex can lead a man to enlightenment, or so I'm told."

"Well I can't say the drugs improved my sex life much, but they sure enlightened the hell out of my wallet. Reason I went bankrupt, in the end. But what I took, especially the hallucinators, acid, mushrooms, crystal—hell, even now, years and years later, I still get these flashbacks. Your ghost, maybe it's a flashback, a vision, like?"

"No idea, but I think the same drug may have killed Porter."

"You said he committed suicide?"

"It looked that way at the time."

"And he did it with a *hat pin*?"

"I was just heating him up. Actually, it was real ugly."

"How ugly?"

"You don't want to know."

"Sure I do. I can take ugly."

Dalton told him.

"Damn. That *is* ugly."

"Yes. It is."

"But now you're not so sure? That it was a suicide?"

"No. I have reason to believe that he was exposed to this drug. The same drug I was exposed to, during my last job."

"What kind of drug was it?"

"We didn't know at the time. We sent it in to the Hazmat unit to have it analyzed. It came back as a salvia derivative."

"Salvia? Never heard of it. And I know my mood-altering substances, my friend. No one knows 'em better."

"Well, we think there was more to the mix than just salvia. But one of the effects of salvia is to effectively short out the cortex, and many times the effect is to induce a major psychotic break. The effects are instantaneous. I had a small packet of it explode in my face—"

"What? Like a booby trap?"

"Yeah. It was inside a terra-cotta cylinder. Spinning. The noise it was making was a lot like the sound we heard last night."

"Like a swarm of bees?"

"Yes. Exactly. Only much louder, and with a strong underlying rhythm to it."

"And the sound was coming from this spinning thing?"

"Yes. The cylinder turned on a big twisted sinew, wound up like a coiled spring, as thick as my wrist. The cylinder got shattered but the Hazmat boys rebuilt it, figured out how it would work. If it was set up in a strong wind, the holes and slits cut into the cylinder would act like a primitive flute. Out would come this sound—"

"Funny. What you're describing, the materials involved, they sound prehistoric, but the mechanism, the idea of *creating* sound that way, that's real advanced."

"The Egyptians had primitive electric batteries. The Greeks knew what atoms were. The Vikings found the New World five hundred years before Columbus, and they did it without a compass. I think this cylinder started out as some kind of musical instrument. When you think of it, the sound it makes is a lot like throat singing."

"You mean like the Indians? The Plains Indians?"

"Yeah. Exactly like that," said Dalton, thinking of Pinto.

"Jesus. Fascinating stuff. I'd love to hear one of these things."

"I hope I never hear it again."

"Who made this thing?"

"I don't know who cast it. I'm pretty sure that the guy who used it on me was a Comanche Indian from Timpas, Colorado."

"Timpas, yeah. That's Comanche country, all right. I knew a lot of Apaches when Al and Moot and the rest of us were working out of Lordsburg. Never met any Comanches, though. A touchy folk, the Apaches around Lordsburg. Come to think of it, drugs were a big part of their religious life down there. Drugs and chanting. . . ." Fremont trailed off into silence.

"Man. Goyathlay's Throat. That's what this sounds like. Goyathlay's Throat. You ever hear of the Native American Church?"

"Of course," said Dalton. "It's a big deal in the Southwest. Supposed to be over a quarter million members, all of them either Apache or Kiowa or Comanche. Started down in Central America about three thousand years ago."

"That's right. Grew out of a thing called the Peyote Cult. For them, Peyote was a god, and the visions you had were supposed to clean your spirit, purge you of your sins. Show you the way to truth. Like I said, I had . . . an interest . . . in the drug culture and some of the guys I knew were into all this Carlos Castaneda stuff. Remember him?"

"Yeah. Wrote a couple of books about Don Juan, he was supposed to be this Yaqui brujo, a sorcerer, who got Castaneda turned on to the Peyote Cult way back in the fifties. Pretty loopy stuff."

"That's the guy. Moot Gibson was really into Castaneda's books, and he used to talk about this secret peyote ritual—a purification ritual. It involved a lot of prayers. Chanting. They used this kind of long clay tube, and he called this tube Goyathlay's Throat. When Moot retired he got real involved in this spirit cult, adopted some Indian name, went completely native. He used to talk about Goyathlay all the time."

"Goyathlay? Was he a god, something like that?"

"No. Goyathlay was the Bedonkohe Apache name for Geronimo. In Apache the name means 'one who yawns.' Geronimo was a big deal in the Native American Church. His spirit was supposed to speak out of this thing called Goyathlay's Throat. I always figured it was just an expression—Moot and his Apache buddies sitting around chewing peyote and seeing visions of the infinite, like in that old movie, *Altered States*—but this spinning cylinder you're talking about, maybe Goyathlay's Throat was a real thing."

"It sure as hell was real to me. I grew up in Tucumcari. They were mostly Kiowa around there, and they had these secret religious meetings too. When I was a kid I tried to sneak into one, almost got my throat cut for it. They used the mescal button, I think, because peyote wasn't found in those parts. It grows naturally down in northern Mexico, and the ritual required that the singers had to go out and find it themselves. But the Kiowa used to get it by mail order."

"Mail order? Like from Sears?"

"No. From mescal growers. But it was legal to mail it—"

Dalton broke off suddenly, remembering the fragment of burned paper that the Langley techs had examined, the return address of Timpas. Was somebody named Horsecoat *mailing* the ingredients of Sweetwater's drug to Venice?

"Anyway, from what I remember about their beliefs, the Native American Church was all about finding peace, with harmony and the purification of the spirit. I do admit I'd like to pay a call to the Horsecoat clan in Timpas and ask them how they happen to be mailing letters to a guy in Venice, Italy, calling himself Sweetwater."

Fremont's face changed, his features going slack. He looked up at Dalton with a narrow, pinched expression, a wary, hostile look. "Sweetwater? Where'd you get the name *Sweetwater*?"

Dalton leaned back and studied Fremont's face.

"I may be a dried-out drunk," said Fremont, standing up and bracing himself, "but I damn well won't be *handled*."

There was no sign that Fremont's anger was in any way forced, and no indication that he was trying to hide anything. His reaction was straight and simple and it had the unmistakable ring of truth.

"Actually, I've been waiting for you to bring it up."

"Me? Why?"

"Because I think there might a connection between this guy calling himself Sweetwater and what's been happening to your unit."

Fremont, his anger subsiding a little, sat back down in the chair and stared at the cup in his hand. After a time, he set the cup down.

"Okay, yeah. The name did freak me a bit. It was a cover name and we kept our cover names pretty close. Sweetwater. Yeah, one of the guys in our unit, he used the Sweetwater jacket. We all had legends. I was a guy named Fetterman—"

"Who used the Sweetwater jacket?"

"Before I tell you who, you saw this guy? Describe him."

"He looked like a lot like an American Indian. He was tall, tanned, over six feet, heavy-built, with long silver hair all the way down to his shoulders. He wore lizard-skin cowboy boots and had a lot of heavy silver jewelry on him. He also wore an earring, a cross under a crescent moon. This sound like anyone you know?"

"A silver earring? Real small, in his left ear?"

"Yes."

"The guy you're describing is Moot Gibson."

"And Gibson's legend was Sweetwater?"

"Yeah. It was."

monday, october 15
interstate 90 eastbound
ten miles east of butte, montana
7 a.m. local time

they had gotten out of the safe house before first light, a cold pink day with a hoarfrost on the cottonwood trunks and the windows of the Crown Victoria as delicately ice-etched as saloon glass. They were doing a steady 85 eastbound on I-90 as the first sliver of the rising sun cleared the eastern ridge of the Bridgers. The trunk was full of gear; Dalton's briefcase and his laptop, a blue canvas Nike bag with what little clothes Fremont still had, the com sets, two Steadicam binoculars, rough-weather gear, the big Remington bolt-action, six big boxes of hollow-point rounds and the Leupold ten-power scope, Dalton's Colt, and a 1911 collector's-grade .45 semiauto with a gold frame and mint-fresh bluing that Fremont had claimed as his own as soon as he saw it in its hardwood case. They picked up fresh rounds for the .45 and a change of clothes for Fremont at a Conoco truck stop in Butte and pulled out of the realm of the Copper Kings with egg-salad sandwiches in their hands and steaming-hot coffee in the armrest cup holders between them.

The Interstate was empty for a Monday, now and then an eighteen-wheeler rolling out of the Rockies on the long continental down-grade that runs from the eastern foothills of the Rockies all the way to the Minnesota border. A mile this side of Whitehall they passed a long lumbering train of slow-moving RVs with Alberta plates, their drivers goggling stupidly at the purple Rockies in the south, the ragged granite peaks tinted pink by the rising sun.

Wearied by a night of bee swarms and tense inconclusive talk, neither man had much to say and a lot to think about as they squinted into the sun and listened to the police cross-talk on the radio.

Dalton had been checking his cell phone for a connection. The screen had read NO SERVICE ever since they left the safe house, but a few miles west of Bozeman he found he was getting a strong signal. He punched in Jack Stallworth's number (it would be 9:45 on a Monday morning in Langley) and finally got through to Sally Fordyce after a long wait.

"Sally, this is Micah. Jack there?"

"Jack's out of the office, sweetie."

"Where's he gone?"

"Didn't say. Just told me he'd be unavailable for a couple of days. He left some information for you, and if you really need to speak to him he's going to call in every evening for messages."

"This is a damned strange time for him to go dark."

"You know our Jack. He took your butt-kissing orchid with him, by the way. What a beastly thing, like a pug dog with the mange."

"Thanks. It only cost me four grand U.S."

"Want the info?"

"Yes. Go ahead."

"You're not gonna like this, but the guy you think got to Porter and his family, this Pinto guy? Well, it looks like he's more than slightly dead."

"Pinto's *dead*?"

"Extremely dead. Dead enough to qualify for burial, which usually resolves any of those lingering ambiguities. Died near a place called Comanche Station, near Timpas, in southeastern Colorado."

"How long ago?"

"About a month?"

"About?"

"Yes. As in 'on or about.' Serena and Mandy were doing a prelim search on the guy yesterday and they turned up his death notice. Called me from London. I called Colorado. According to the state troopers, he was found in a pickup parked way out in an area called the Comanche National Grassland. He'd been there for at least a month, but maybe even as long as six weeks, according to the local smokies. Pretty chewed up by the wildlife, and dried out like an old corn husk, according to this Captain Bondine guy. He's the CO of the local Crowley County Sheriff's Office. They took the call from the state guys and went out there to police him up."

"What killed him?"

"Bullet."

"Don't go all laconic on me, Sally. You know what I mean."

"Bullet from gun."

"Sally."

"Sorry. I talked to this Captain Bondine for an hour yesterday afternoon. He talks like that, like he has to pay for every consonant he uses out of his own salary. Reminded me of Gary Cooper in *High Noon*. I kind of liked him. Captain Bondine says the autopsy showed a single entry wound in the left temple, a big round, from a brand-new forty-four-caliber Smith and Wesson revolver."

"How'd they know that?"

"Your good old-fashioned police work, plus the gun was still in the man's lap, his left hand around the grip. Round blew his left eye completely out of the socket and ruptured his right. Most of his brains and a big section of the right side of his skull ended up on the passenger window, which also had a major hole in it."

"Suicide?"

"You're so good at all this manly spook stuff, aren't you."

"How'd they know it was Pinto?"

"They brought in people who knew him, a kid named Wilson Horsecoat, kind of a clan cousin of the local Escondido Comanches. And an aunt named Ida Escondido. They both made positive IDs. And the truck was registered to Daniel Escondido, which is Pinto's real name. Had a wallet in his jeans pocket stuffed with ID, Bureau of Indian Affairs card. Colorado driver's license with his picture. Patient card from a walk-in clinic in La Junta. Pictures all matched the shot you gave Jack before you left. But the main thing was a personal ID from two of his clan members."

"What did the guy look like?"

"Before or after the crows got at him?"

"Before."

"I'm looking at a coroner's photo Bondine e-mailed to me right now. Hard Indian-looking face, what's left of it, anyway, which is not much. Long gray hair down to his shoulders. Big man, over six feet tall, and real heavyset. Strong hands like a cowboy. Looks mean as a DI on a fifty-mile hump. Last meal was chiles rellenos and beer. Cowboy boots, silver jewelry. This your guy?"

"It's him exactly. Dammit. Did he have an earring?"

"Let me see . . . yes. Small silver earring, through the left earlobe. Some sort of cross-shaped thing with a moon over it. A crescent moon."

"But that's the same earring I saw on the guy in Venice."

"I'm sorry I have to be the one to tell you this, Micah, but sometimes you'll find they make more than one copy of an earring. They've even been known to make them in pairs, the cunning bastards."

"Why the clinic card?"

"Captain Bondine called the clinic in La Junta. It seems Pinto was being treated for lung cancer. Had it bad, so I understand. Prognosis was real poor. Looks like he just decided not to wait for the cancer to kill him. This sounds like bad news."

"It is. Tell me, did Jack find out whether or not Pinto had traveled to Italy or England in the last few weeks?"

"Man did not have a passport. You can't travel very far in today's world without a passport, even if you *are* a Marine."

"So no connection to Italy?"

"He may have ordered a pizza once."

"How about any linkage to intelligence ops?"

"Now, that part was weird. I tried running a search on his military service and got a 'file not found' message. Yet he was carrying a Reserve card and Marine Corps ID."

"I ran into the same thing."

"Did you? So I pushed it a little further and called a guy I knew in Marine Corps Intelligence. He grumbled about it but after some digging he called me back to say that Pinto had been a Code Talker in Korea, so his records were suppressed. Routine."

"That was all?"

"Yeah. They did it for all the Code Talkers. And the U.S. Army often firewalls the IDs of personnel who've worked in intelligence."

That was true; Dalton had requested that his own military records be sealed against all public inquiries, and then had them tagged with a silent Report All Hits alarm that would trigger an e-mail notice back to him if anybody asked about his records.

He should have figured that out for himself.

"Thanks, Sally. So he was never into any intel work? I mean, after the war?"

"Nope. I've got his printout here. Into the Marines at nineteen, Korea, Code Talker, Silver Star, in the brig, a three-year beef for unlawfully disassembling an MP in a bar fight. Pulls his time. Mobs out with a dishonorable in sixty-five, gets into drugs, using and dealing. Made a pile of cash and became a big deal around Comanche Station. Ran the local church, even. What you would call a religious leader. Very highly respected at Comanche Station, according to Bondine. The DEA launched an op against him in eighty-four. Something went very wrong and three of their agents disappeared. They made a circumstantial case against him for that, he was their last known contact, so in eighty-six he goes to Deer Lodge for twenty years. Got out in oh six, time served, no restrictions, moved back to Timpas last year. Lived a humble quiet life. In reward for changing his evil ways and becoming a pillar of the church, God gave him lung cancer and he shot himself in the head six weeks ago. Warms the cockles, a story like that, right?"

"No connection to *any* American intelligence agency?"

"Zip. Nada. Bupkes. Why is it so much fun to say 'bupkes'?"

"Not even as an informer? A freelancer?"

"Sounds like you made the wrong man, Micah."

"You have a phone number for this Captain Bondine?"

"Sure. Office line is 719-384-2525. If he's out on the road they'll patch you through. I told them they might be hearing from you. You going to go there, check it out?"

Dalton wrote the numbers out on a section of napkin, holding the phone in the hollow of his neck.

"Okay. Got it. I'm on the way to Colorado now. I'm eastbound on I-90. We're going to a place called Cloud Peak, in the Bighorns."

"If you're headed to Colorado, that's a little out of the way."

"There's a reason. I also need you to go our personnel files and pull out anything you can get on a part-timer name of Pershing Gibson. He was in this Sweetwater unit with Willard Fremont. Also known as Moot. His DOB was . . ."

"November thirteenth, 1939," said Fremont, after a pause. "El Paso, Texas."

Dalton repeated the numbers, waited while Sally read them back, and said, "Gibson was in the Marines. So was Pinto. See if they ever served in the same unit, or even in the same AO. I need to know if they ever crossed paths. Basically I need everything you can get on Pershing Gibson. And another thing—"

"I live to serve, sweetie."

"Cross-reference both these guys with everything we have on Porter Naumann. See if they intersect at any point."

"You really think any of this connects with Porter?"

"I have no solid link yet. It's just what I'm running into out here. If it's a unicorn hunt for you, I'll make it up any way I can."

"Promises. Promises."

"Have I missed anything?"

"Do you have a current location for this Gibson person?"

"Yes. He lives on a small ranch near Greybull, Wyoming. We're going to head there after we talk to our man in Cloud Peak."

"Do you want me to ask the local SAIC to send a car out to Greybull and sit on this guy until you get there?"

"The FBI? Jesus, no."

"How about the local state guys?"

"Much as I admire the county constabulary, I think I'd like to leave this guy under the impression that all is right with his world. A couple of nineteen-year-old ex-linebackers cooping in a plain brown wrapper a half mile down the road from his ranch would mitigate against this blissful state of mind. Have I missed anything else?"

"Well, what I wore to bed last night was pretty spectacular."

Dalton snapped the phone shut.

Fremont was shaking his head. "I keep telling you. Moot is not your guy."

"How do we know this?"

"How do we know *any* guy? I worked with him, risked my life with him. And why would Moot want to kill the guy who put him in touch with Dick Poundmaker and saved his ass from the IRS?"

"Do you have a number for this Poundmaker guy?"

"Yeah. What time is it?"

"Going on eight-thirty. Seven-thirty in Coeur d'Alene."

"Dick'll be up. He plays the NYSE and he hates it that they have a three-hour lead on him. What do I want him for?"

"Ask him if he can get a printout of Moot Gibson's ATM use for the last thirty days. I need locations, specific bank addresses."

"Dick's not gonna want to hand out that kind of info."

Dalton sent him a look. Fremont received it.

"I'll see what I can do."

"You do that."

IN THE END, Dalton had to get on the line and rain down holy federal thunder to convince Dick Poundmaker, Trustee in Bankruptcy, Attorney at Law, Holistic Surgeon, and Certified Doctor of Homeopathic Medicine, that his long-term financial interests, not to mention his choice of permanent residency, depended entirely upon a prompt and full disclosure of any and all banking records pertaining to the ATM usage of Pershing "Moot" Gibson that he could download and fax to a Sally Fordyce at CIA HQ in Langley—

"The CIA in Langley?" bleated Mr. Poundmaker.

"That's where we keep it. Got doors and a roof and everything."

"Yes sir. I'll get on it as soon as we hang up."

"Excellent."

"May I speak with Willard?"

"No."

"Will you kindly relay a message, then?"

"Sure."

"Tell him I regret to inform him that we are no longer friends."

"I'll do it, but it'll break his heart."

"One more question—"

"Shoot."

"Am I going to jail?"

"Not if you do what you're told."

"Will you report this to the FBI, Mr. . . ."

"Dalton. Micah Dalton. If those banking records are in Langley before I get to Billings, this will stay between us, Mr. Poundmaker."

"Where are you now?"

"Bozeman."

"Dear God—"

Dalton shut the phone off.

"Jeez," said Fremont. "Remind me not to piss you off."

"Just don't kill a friend of mine."

"You really think Moot had anything to do with the suicide—"

"The death."

"With Porter Naumann's death?"

"I can hardly wait to ask him. By the way, Dick asked me to tell you that he regrets to inform you that you are no longer his friend."

"He said that?"

"His words precisely."

"Dick's a dick."

"That was my impression."

THEY WERE FORTY MILES farther east when Dalton's phone rang.

"Dalton."

"Micah, it's Sally again."

"That was fast."

"This isn't about the faxes. I'm still waiting for those. I was doing a run on the rest of the guys in Fremont's unit and I turned up something."

Dalton gave Fremont a brief sidelong look. "Yeah?"

"Your guy Fremont? He mention a Crucio Churriga?"

"Yes."

"Where are you right now?"

"Just coming up to Butte."

"That's what I thought. You might want to stop in there."

"Okay. Why?"

She told him.

He thanked her, shut the phone down, and then he told Fremont.

Thirty minutes later, they were pulling off 90 and turning north onto Harrison. The old town of Butte was a tangled grid of dusty red Victorians that climbed up the ocher slopes of a ragged mountain, behind the crest of which lay an abandoned slag pit that was now the home of the world's largest toxic-waste pond.

Below the steep grade of the old town, spreading out into the valley to the south and west, ringed in by snowcapped peaks to the north and east, was the suburban sprawl of the new town, a maze of shopping malls and trailer parks and cardboard housing gnawed all winter by storms off the Rockies and baked all summer by a blistering dry heat. Back in the 1880s Butte had been the home of the Copper Kings. Now it was the home of the Burger Kings and any number of hardscrabble peeler bars with names like Double Deuce and Trigger Time. A gen-

eral air of resignation and gloom lay over the town, relieved from time
to time by little explosions of domestic violence or clashes between
what was left of the Indians and what was left of the miners. The pa-
tron saint of the town, and still its most famous son, was Evel Knievel,
who honored his birthplace by getting out of town as fast as humanly
possible—in his case on a Harley—and never going back.

The Copper Kings Palliative Care Center on Continental Drive—
so named because the Continental Divide was a few miles up the
mountain ring, on the far side of Elk Pass—was a fairly new complex
of low limestone blocks scattered about the stony hillside under the
spreading arms of Our Lady of the Rockies.

Dalton pulled the Crown Vic up under the portico and shut the
engine down. A Montana state trooper pushed his way through
the green-tinted double-glass doors and walked over to meet them.
He was a big slope-shouldered man in his late fifties with a barrel
chest, ruddy cheeks, careful blue eyes, and a snow-white handlebar
mustache. His handshake was as hard as his face and his uniform
would have made a Fort Bragg DI glow with admiration.

"You're Mr. Dalton?"

"I am. This is my associate, Mr. Fremont."

Fremont shook the trooper's hand, looking a little worried. The
trooper gave Fremont a once-over, looking skeptical. A cutting wind
carrying yellow dust was swirling around the entranceway, stinging
their eyes.

"I'm Bo Cutler," said the trooper—a captain, by his silver bars.
The biting dust seemed to have no effect on him. "Nice to meet
you. I got your call from D.C. You boys are with the Federales?"

Dalton shook his head.

"No sir. Not the FBI. We're with another agency."

Cutler's eyes narrowed and he showed them broad yellow teeth
under his massive mustache. "That's what I thought. Mr. Churriga's

medical insurance and his pension checks were sort of a clue. Okay. Let's get this done."

They both nodded. Cutler led them through the doors and into a broad lobby with a floor of limestone blocks. A cluster of nurses stood together in one end of the lobby, under a huge oil painting of a buffalo herd flowing over the plains under a lowering veil of thunderclouds. Cutler nodded to the nurses, whose faces all wore the same shattered, shell-shocked look, and led the way down a long hallway that smelled of iodine and stale piss toward a set of stainless-steel doors at the far end. Two young troopers stood on either side of the doors. When Cutler got to within some sort of critical distance known only to the troopers, they braced up and snapped out a pair of salutes, palms flat, faces set and blank. The doors were marked CCU.

Cutler bulled through the doors and turned left into a darkened room. Another trooper was sitting in a chair beside a hospital bed. He got to his feet and saluted as Cutler came into the room.

The bed was inside a large clear plastic tent. In the bed, under a crisp pink sheet, lay a skeletal figure, bony chest rising and falling. A rack of monitors beeped and whirred behind the trooper, and a tall IV drip stood beside the tent. Tubes ran into the man's arm and another snaked out from under the sheet, dripping into a receptacle under the bed. The room smelled of ozone and blood and antiseptic.

Fremont came forward and looked at the man in the bed. The man's face looked like a heap of raw meat. The lower part was a horror, a gaping red maw with a few pink molars showing. Fremont stood looking down at the man for a long time while Dalton and Cutler waited in silence. Finally Fremont turned away and looked at Cutler. "What happened to him?"

Cutler sighed deeply, making his gun belt creak. "Like we told you on the phone. Looks like the attacker peeled his face off. Skinned it, from the hairline to what was left of his jaw. The docs had already taken off a large section of Churriga's lower jaw and some of the cheekbone, as you can see there. But the rest was pretty intact. Cancer was . . . aggressive. Rapid spread, so the docs say. But the cutter was— I guess he'd done it before. Worked fast but good."

"No one . . . heard?" asked Fremont.

"Nobody to hear," said Cutler. "Only two nurses on the ward at the time. Both of them were dead. Throats cut. Mutilated."

"Before or after?" asked Dalton.

"The guy spent some time with them before he cut their throats."

"Enjoying himself," said Dalton, not as a question.

Cutler nodded, his face grim.

"This is about as bad a business as we've had in Butte for years, Mr. Dalton. Whole town is in a state. Anything you can tell us?"

Dalton looked at Fremont, whose face was rock-hard and set. "I don't know. What do you have right now?"

"Lone man. Came down from up there near Elk Pass, from the boot trail. Big man, cowboy boots, left one with a worn-down heel. Figure the guy has a limp, pronates the heel a bit. He came in through the window of Mr. Churriga's room. Patient was alone in the ward, heavily sedated. On a self-monitored morphine drip. His mind was . . . somewhere else. The cutter buzzed for a nurse, took her as soon as she walked into the room. Went to work on her. Finished up. Buzzed in the other one. Did her out in the hallway. Party time, you follow?"

They followed.

"Then he did something to Mr. Churriga's IV drip and that brought Churriga up out of it. We figure he spent maybe an hour with Churriga. Cutter had no fear of being caught."

"Any cameras?" asked Dalton.

Cutler shook his head. "No. It's a hospice, not a bank."

"What about the drugs?"

"Yeah, there's drugs. But no one's ever made a run at them before. Our Lady of the Rockies has a big facility and of course they have all kinds of security. This is a private clinic, not real well known."

"He's breathing," said Fremont. "Is he awake?"

Cutler shifted in his stance, his face closing. "No. How you can tell? He's not screaming. The nurses can't handle that, not anymore, considering. I know you want to bring him up, see what he can say, but we've already *done* that, and to be honest I don't think any of us has the heart to do it again. All the muscles of his face are sliced off, eyes gouged out, flesh and skin all gone. That's living bone you're looking at there. But if you want to, we'll do it."

He stopped for a moment, breathing deeply. Then he looked hard at them, from one to the other and back, his pale-blue eyes glittering. "But . . . it's not right," he said finally.

"Was he able to speak?" asked Fremont.

Cutler shook his head. "How could he? No lips. No tongue. Jaw all hacked off."

"But he gave you *something*?" said Dalton.

"Yeah. We brought him up far as he could stand it. He's a brave man. Tougher than I am. One of the nurses held his hand. We asked him questions and he squeezed her hand. Once for yes. Twice for no. Took about an hour and then the nurse had to leave the room because the pain was getting pretty bad and the noises he was making . . ."

"What did you get?"

"Cutter was male. Big. Not a stranger."

"Crucio knew him?" said Fremont.

"We think so. We asked him, was it someone from his past, somebody from his work. He indicated yes. We tried to spell it out, you know, start with 'a' and work through, but he kept going in and out. We got a few letters, we think. Definitely a 'g' and an 's.' That mean anything to you boys?"

Fremont glanced at Dalton and then away.

"No," said Dalton. "Were you able to establish a perimeter?"

"For what?" asked Cutler. "By the time the nurses came in for midnight, the guy was long gone. In and out. Gone. The cutter was here sometime around dusk Friday. We didn't even try asking Mr. Churriga for a description until late Saturday afternoon. You heard what we got."

"Did the cutter leave . . . anything?"

Cutler gave Dalton a sharp searching look. "Semen on the nurse in the hallway. Prints too."

"A lot of tissue was taken from Churriga's face, it looks like."

Cutler's expression twisted into a grimace. "Yeah. Several ounces, according to the ME."

"Where did it go?"

Cutler looked down at his boots and then back up. "You know what 'anthropophagi' means?"

Dalton and Fremont looked at the cop for a time.

"Jesus Christ," said Fremont. "The guy *ate* it? What the fuck makes you think *that*?"

"Not all of the tissue taken from Churriga's face was sliced off. Some of it was torn off. There are teeth marks. On Alice's body, there's also some bite marks. Same radius. Same dental pattern. Tissue taken there too. In chunks. Some of it we found elsewhere on the body. Showed signs of being— The docs called it 'mastication.'"

"Mother of God," said Fremont, his face bone-white.

"Yeah," said Cutler. "Me too."

The image stunned Dalton and Fremont into silence. Cutler let them work it out for a time, and then said, "He left something else."

"I thought he might have," said Dalton.

Cutler gave him a sharp searching look. "You want to see it?"

"Yes."

"Then come with me."

He turned to leave the room.

Fremont reached out and stopped him, holding his arm.

"What about Crucio? What happens to him?"

"You kin to him, by any chance?"

Fremont shook his head, his eyes red and moist.

"Then he stays where he is until he either dies or a relative shows up and gives us permission to ease him on through. Sorry."

"Can I stay with him a while?" asked Fremont.

Cutler looked at him steadily, his face softening.

"Sure. Alone?"

"Would that be all right?"

Cutler nodded to the trooper, who picked up his Stetson and left the room. When he was gone, Cutler looked at Fremont for a time. "He was a good friend? Mr. Churriga?"

"Yes," said Fremont, straightening his spine.

"You ever in the service, Mr. Fremont?"

"He was," said Dalton.

"Guess I won't ask which branch," said Cutler, smiling briefly at Dalton before he looked back at Fremont.

"I can give you fifteen minutes," he said. "No more. You follow?"

"I follow," said Fremont.

Cutler turned away and led Dalton out of the room and down the corridor into a dead-end section sealed off with crime scene tape. He lifted the tape and held it while Dalton slipped under it.

"It's the room at the end there," said Cutler, leading the way. The door to the ward was closed and sealed with a sticker carrying the crest of the Montana Highway Patrol. Cutler pushed the door open and walked into the ward room. Four stripped beds stood in the center of the room. The room smelled of Lysol and Dustbane.

"It's in the corner, where his bed was."

Dalton walked around the beds and over to an open space beside a wide window, through which he could see a broad slope of stone mountain rising up six thousand feet. Halfway up the slope was a tall white statue of the Virgin Mary. He turned away and looked at the thing on the wall above the place where Churriga's bed had been.

Cutler was standing close behind him now. The man smelled of gun leather, raw anger, and stale cigarette smoke.

"This mean anything to you?" he asked, after a silence.

"Yes," said Dalton. "You?"

"It looks like *sign*," said Cutler. "Indian sign."

"Indian? What kind of Indian?"

"What *kind* of Indian?" said Cutler, in a snarl, his barely suppressed rage, his deep resentment of Dalton's evasive answers, his soul sickness at the horror that had visited his town and left it forever scarred: all of this boiled up in a rush.

"What kind? The twisted motherfucker psycho cannibal kind, I guess. You *knew* this thing was gonna be here. You've seen it before. You got anything useful to say to me, Mr. Dalton? You fucking well better. You better be ready to put me within arm's reach of this cocksucker so I can rip his own fucking face off and feed it to my dogs. I got two dead girls and a lot of very upset people here. This town will never be the same. Hell, I'll never be the same."

Dalton turned away from the scrawl and faced the cop. "You're right. I think I know who the cutter is."

Cutler nodded, as if Dalton's words had only confirmed his instinct. "I figured you did. And now you're gonna tell me."

"No. I can't."

Cutler's face seemed to freeze over.

"*You* do not leave this room. I *will* take you apart, mister."

"Anything I tried to do for you would get shut down by Langley."

"*You're* not in Langley, Bucky. You're right here in front of me."

"I *can* give you something," said Dalton.

"What?"

"My word."

"Your word?"

"Yes. My word that your cutter will be dead in a week."

Cutler's rocky face did not change. Threat, violence rose up around the two men like smoke from a fire. Dalton held his look.

Finally, the trooper sighed. "This guy? He's on a tear?"

"Yes. So far we think he's killed a man in Mountain Home, three more victims in London, another man in Italy. Now Mr. Churriga. And he's getting . . . crazier. This *eating* thing . . . he's losing himself. Coming apart."

"And you're on him? I mean, solid leads? You're . . . *close*?"

"Yes. Real close."

"I don't know you, Dalton. I don't know how good you are."

"I'm good enough to take this man out."

Cutler's look was searching, as if he was trying to see into Dalton's soul. After a while his features altered.

"I'll want *proof.* Courthouse *proof.* DNA. The knife he used. Something I can show the families. There will be no . . . *ambiguities.*"

"You'll get it."

"DNA, Dalton! Tissue. Blood. Take-it-to-the-hangman proof!"

"One week."

"Seven days."

"At the longest."

Cutler turned and walked to the window, stared out over the mountain slopes for a while. He spoke after a time, still looking out the window, but seeing only what was burned into his memory forever. "Something you should know about me, Mr. Dalton. One of those young nurses this cutter mangled up was a girl named Alice Foley. My daughter Ellen grew up with Alice Foley. Alice was in our house every day. Like a second daughter. Her mother and I were close once. Long ago, when we were both young. Close. You understand me?"

Dalton nodded, said nothing, and waited.

"I don't forget much, Mr. Dalton. You fade on me, you break this word to me, I *will* find you. And that will be a bad day for both of us, but not as bad for me as for you. You follow?"

"I follow," said Dalton.

DALTON AND FREMONT WERE fifty miles west of Billings, running down a steep, winding grade with the twelve-thousand-foot peaks of the Absaroke-Beartooth Range rising up in the southwest, the rolling grasslands of eastern Montana opening up before them, and the yellow cloud of refinery smog that always hovers over Billings barely discernible on the eastern horizon.

A long, haunted silence had gathered the two men up in separate solitudes since they left Butte, and now they were listening to a piercingly sad Rachmaninoff concerto. It came to an end.

Fremont sighed and looked over at Dalton.

"What did you do?" asked Dalton.

"I took his hand. I put the morphine controller into it. He tightened his fingers down on it. I pressed the feed button and I held his hand tight around it. After a few minutes his breathing got real slow. The monitor alarm started to beep so I turned the volume down. This nurse came to see what was going on. I shoved her out and closed the door on her. Locked it. Crucio flatlined a couple minutes later. I pulled the sheet up over him and walked out. The nurse and the trooper were standing there. She started to say something but the trooper put his hand on her shoulder and nodded to me. I walked out to car, waited for you."

Dalton looked at Fremont briefly. Since there was nothing to say, they agreed to say nothing, and they both went back to pretending to concentrate on the road ahead.

Ten miles farther down the line and the clamor of the cell phone made him jump.

It was Sally.

She had the faxes.

"This Gibson guy gets around. He used his ATM all over the Northwest in the last two months. He's averaging two hundred a day. Must be paying cash for everything, because there are no debit-card payments. Just these cash withdrawals. In the months of August and September he went from Cody, Wyoming, to Mountain Home, Idaho, then to Missoula, and then to Coeur d'Alene."

"When was he in Mountain Home?"

"Ahh . . . let's see. He took out five hundred dollars from a First Idaho Credit Union ATM on Two Moons Way on Thursday, August thirty. At four in the morning."

"Can we get video of the withdrawal?"

"From the ATM? Probably not, not after all this time. They usually loop the tape. And even if they still had it, we'd have to ask the FBI to do it, which Jack will never go for."

"Okay. What's this tell us?"

"It tells *me* the highest amount of cash activity was in the final days of September and the first two days of October. He drew out four thousand dollars, at five hundred bucks a pop, going from Helena to Butte to Livingstone, back up to Bozeman, then Billings, Hardin, Sheridan, the last at some place called Shell, Wyoming."

"Four thousand? How much money did he have in the account?"

"Close to fifteen thousand."

"I thought he went bankrupt."

"Yeah. He was. I got the record of it, then I called this Poundmaker guy back. He pranced around the issue for a while but I got the impression that Gibson had used the ATM card to *deposit* over twenty thousand dollars cash in the middle of August."

"Did he say where Gibson got this twenty thousand?"

"I didn't have the time to push him. You want me to?"

"Yes, if you can, after we hang up."

"May I get biblical on him?"

"Please."

"Now I do have something here that connects to him to Porter. There's every reason to believe that Gibson was, at the very least, in England around the time that Porter's family got killed."

"I knew it. Thank you, Sally. Thank you."

"Well, let me lay it out for you. I checked his passport records and he flew United coach from Denver to Gatwick and was entry-stamped there by the Brits on October second. From there he passes out of mortal ken until he resurfaces back in Greybull, Wyoming, on October eleventh. Four days ago," she added, helpfully.

"Anything since then?"

"He withdrew a thousand over two days in Greybull. That's the end of the records. I pulled his file from Personnel."

"Any contact with Porter?"

"None on the records. Most of the stuff in it is all about his beef with the IRS. He wrote fifty-six letters over a two-year period, starting in oh three. They went out to various honchos at the NSA,

State, even wrote a few congressmen and the junior senator from Wyoming. The last one was written about three months ago, and it's mostly scrawled gibberish. Across the top he's written 'culebra' and 'purgatoire,' on the bottom he's written 'atone,' references to something hidden, to a struggle—'die born'—what looks like a U.S. flag with a skull—'snake eater'—all of this in block capitals—the word 'messenger,' and it's all clustered around this weird drawing . . ."

"Describe it for me."

"Well, just a mad scrawl, but there's a daisy, or some kind of flower, over a crescent moon and what looks like a cross. Now that I look at it, I guess they're a lot like that earring you were talking about earlier, the silver earring?"

"Do you actually have these letters?"

"I do. I have the whole stack right here. The tone of these letters is very odd. They start out calm, polite, reasonable, and then they gradually go totally mad. Spelling deteriorates. He starts writing in big block capitals. Then these drawings start to appear. By the last one, that's all there is. Scrawls. Doodles. I'd say the guy was slowly going mad. If I had been getting letters like this, I'd have called in the FBI."

"Did anybody?"

"I guess it got referred back to our own security people here, because somebody in HR sent Gibson's file over to the Vicar."

"Cather? Cather got a bullet?"

"Yes. Why?"

Stallworth's office, last Saturday morning.

Jack and Dalton.

"You know where this Pinto guy is right now?"

"No. I was in the middle of that when Cather shut me down."

"Micah, you still there?"

"Yes, Sally. Sorry. Anything come back from Cather?"

"Not on paper. But then if the Vicar's unit took care of it, it wouldn't exactly make the *Times,* would it?"

"Christ, I don't want to go poking around in Cather's crypt."

But you are, aren't you, Micah?

"Me neither, sweetie."

"So what you're saying is—"

"I think we can agree that Gibson's an unstable freakazoid who was in England and Italy around the time you and Porter were there. I mean, we can't prove Italy, but England's right across the channel."

"Any sign that he crossed?"

"If he did, he didn't do it as Pershing Gibson."

"How else would he clear the borders?"

"There are no borders. There's the EU. And he's a CIA-trained field man. That's what you guys do. Frankly, I'm a little surprised he used his own passport to get into England in the first place. Micah, can I ask you a question?"

"I'm holding my breath."

"Are you going to go over to Greybull and take this guy on?"

"Yes."

"Alone?"

"No. I've got Willard the Bold, my trusty sidekick."

"Great. Where's Pal the Wonder Dog?"

"He called in sick. Did we hear from Stallworth?"

"No. But the day's not over yet. Where are you now?"

"Coming in to Billings."

"How did it go in Butte?"

"It was ugly."

"How's Willard doing?"

"Better than expected."

He glanced over at Fremont, who was staring straight ahead, unseeing, his mind back in that hospital room in Butte.

"Micah, if you're going to Greybull, will you let me call in some reinforcements? Nicky Baum and Delroy Suarez are in Lawrence, Kansas. They can get on a jet and meet you in Greybull. I checked, there's an airport there. Long enough to land one of our Gulfstreams."

"You talked to them?"

"Not yet."

"What are they doing in Kansas?"

"Taking a course. At the university there."

"What's it called?"

"Motifs of Moral Decay in the American Espionage Novel."

"You're making that up."

"I wish I were."

"I sure don't want to drag them away from that. But it's nice to know they're close. Have them stand by in case I change my mind."

"I'll do more than that. I'm sending one of the Gulfstreams to Topeka. It'll be there for Del and Nicky if you want them in a hurry."

"Stallworth will freak. That's very big money."

"Jack's not here. I am."

"You watering his plants?"

"With my very own tears."

AROUND NOON, THE SUN high overhead in a cloudless sky, they were rolling southward as the Interstate curved down-country beyond Hardin, and at a little past twelve-thirty they reached the town of Crow Agency. The land around them was open grassland with here and there a few stands of cottonwoods and poplars.

On their left as they passed Crow Agency the grassy hills rose up into a rounded crest, where a tall stone cairn stood above a long rectangle of golden sweetgrass marked off by a low wrought-iron fence. Scattered down along a falling slope that led into a wandering river valley thick with cottonwoods stood a collection of white marble gravestones, some of them single, most in groups of two or three, while inside the iron fence there were sixty or seventy gravestones gathered into a tight formation.

A warm wind stirred the tall sweetgrass, moving in wavelike ripples across the low hills and shallow valleys. Both men fell silent as the car raced past this little cemetery where George Armstrong Custer and the men of the Seventh Cavalry had died in less than thirty minutes of savage hand-to-hand fighting against over six thousand Sioux and Cheyenne warriors.

Fremont craned his neck to take in the battlefield as the car sped southward down the highway, the mounded blue domes and the purple valleys of the Bighorn Mountains becoming more visible along the southwestern horizon. In the end, as the low bank of golden hills dropped out of sight behind them, he turned back with a long sigh.

"Bad business, that" was all he said.

"Worse if you were taken alive," said Dalton, thinking about the charming old Sioux custom known as *kakeshya*. "You remember what Kipling said?"

"I do," said Fremont. "When you're down and wounded on Afghanistan's plains, and the women come out to cut up your remains . . ."

"Just roll to your rifle and blow out your brains . . ."

"And go to your God like a soldier."

"Amen," said Dalton.

Neither man spoke for another fifty miles, each man thinking of what might be waiting for them at Pete Kearney's cabin high up in the eastern ledges of the Bighorn Mountains. The feeling of moving deeper into history, deeper into the still-surviving remnants of an ancient and unending war between the whites and the Plains Indians, oppressed both men, and they had little to say to each other until they crossed the border into Wyoming. The mood in the car rose once they were well into the lush rolling terrain of the Powder River country, and in a while they turned west off the Interstate, heading west toward the supply town of Dayton, sitting on a big slow bend of the Tongue River, in the shadow of the Bighorn Mountains.

Fremont directed them to a squat square building, made of cinder blocks, sitting on the western edge of the town. A hand-painted sign over the sagging wooden doors read, incongruously, HANOI JANE'S. They parked the car in the meager shade of a dried-out two-hundred-year-old cottonwood and walked up the rickety wooden stairs. Inside the deserted bar, in the dank gloom and the smell of spilled beer and old cigars, they paused to let their eyes adjust to the darkness, and then they crossed the creaking floor of rough hand-sawn planks and sat down at a battered mahogany bar, into the surface of which had been set at least five thousand silver dollars.

Behind the bar was a tall antique sideboard groaning with dusty liquor bottles. A large stainless-steel cooler clattered and wheezed in a corner, next to a bank of new-looking video poker terminals. Other than the moronic electronic tweedling coming from these machines, and a distant radio scratching out a country-and-western tune, the place was silent. Above the bar fifty different versions of the Vietnam-era Huey chopper, each one made out of a different brand of beer can and strung up on fishing line, turned and bumped lazily in the dusty wind off the street. In an ornate Victorian frame next to the antique sideboard there was a copy of a black-and-white photo of Jane Fonda, wearing a North Vietnamese helmet—badly—and giggling away like a complete horse's ass in the gunner's chair of a North Vietnamese antiaircraft piece, a profoundly vapid and arguably treasonous stunt that if pulled by a North Vietnamese woman visiting America during the same war would have resulted in the immediate slaughter of her entire village.

After a wait, during which the faint sound of the radio was suddenly cut off, Fremont rapped on the bar top and called out.

"Katie, you home?"

"Hold your water" came a raspy female voice. In a moment a door at the rear of the bar slammed open, propelled by a kick, and a tall, thin woman in a cowboy shirt and black jeans came in carrying a case of Miller High Life. She banged the door shut behind her with a practiced boot heel and crossed over to the bar to set the box down, where, in the better light, they were able to make her out as a strikingly attractive, or rather a strikingly *handsome* woman. In her deeply seamed, fine-boned, and weathered brown face a pair of clear calm light-blue eyes looked out from a fan of wrinkles, considering Fremont through narrowed eyes.

"Willard Fremont, in the flesh. You owe me forty-seven dollars and eleven cents."

"Katie, I want you to meet a friend of mine. This is Micah Dalton. Micah, allow me to introduce Katie Horn."

"Nice to meet you," said Katie, taking his hand in a steely grip and giving it a firm shake before spreading her hands out on the bar top and leaning on her braced forearms in the classic bartender pose.

"What can I get you gentlemen, assuming that one of you boys can pay off Willard's tab here first?"

Dalton went for his wallet, grinning at Fremont, who laid a bony hand on Dalton's arm and pulled out his own billfold. He extracted a large wad of cash, peeled off a faded fifty, and set it down on the bar top with a degree of smug satisfaction. Katie eyed it with some suspicion, picked it up, and held it under a black light just below the edge of the bar, and then showed them a set of brilliant white teeth as her face creased into a net of deep lines around her eyes.

"Where'd you get all that cash?" she asked, with some affection.

"Stole it from my young friend here," said Fremont, giving voice to Dalton's unspoken suspicion: Fremont had been dead flat broke when he pulled him out of the Hayden Lake holding center.

"Found it in the hall safe," explained Fremont, "while you was out terrifying those poor unfortunate bees."

"The hall safe was locked and armed," said Dalton.

"So it was. Katie, my sweet desert rose, I believe I will have a long cold Stella. And my friend's money is no good here."

"That *is* my money," said Dalton, smiling at Katie.

"It pleases my young friend to be jocular, Katie. Ignore him."

"He's too good-looking to ignore," she said, flirting openly.

"I'll have a Stella too," said Dalton. She collected three from the wheezing old cooler, popped them in a graceful succession of practiced wrist flips, and poured them out with some ceremony in a neat row on the bar top. She set them down on flat cork disks with the phrase "God Created Men and Women but Sam Colt Made Them Equal" printed around the edge. They raised their glasses in mutual salute and set them down again, Dalton eyeing the framed shot of Jane Fonda. Katie followed his glance and grinned.

"Named the place after her," she said, a bit redundantly. "She and her husband at the time—that network guy, got close-set beady eyes—"

"Ted Turner?"

"They were looking to buy a spread over there near the Wagon Box fight."

"You figured naming the place after her would bring in the celebrity trade?" asked Dalton.

"Hell no. But I figured it would sure keep *her* away."

"Katie's husband was a chopper pilot in Vietnam," said Fremont. The "was" needed no elaboration, and no one offered it.

After a silence, Dalton made a point of admiring the Huey models over the bar, and Katie plucked one down and handed it to him, a large version of the Huey made out of what had at one time been a can of black powder.

"You can keep that one," said Katie, finding much to approve of in Micah Dalton, her appreciation for him blatantly physical. "Maybe it'll bring you back sooner. What brings you boys to Dayton, if you don't mind my asking?"

"We were hoping to use your phone," said Fremont. "We want to go up to see Pete, but we don't want to just drop in unannounced. He won't answer his phone unless he knows the caller ID, so we figure if—"

Katie's expression became uneasy, even guarded.

"Pete's lit out for the Territories, we figure. Nobody's heard from him in two weeks. I got worried after calling him a few times, drove up to his cabin last Friday, place was deserted, doors locked down, windows shuttered. His truck is gone, and both his dogs too."

"When's the last time you spoke to him directly?"

But her suspicions had been aroused by the question. "You two don't look so good. What's up?"

"We're a little concerned—" began Dalton, but she raised a hand to stop him.

"No offense, Micah, but I don't know you real well yet. Willard, before you ask me any more about Pete, maybe you can tell me why you two look so damn worried about him?"

Fremont looked at Dalton, who shrugged and said nothing.

"We think Pete might be in some kind of trouble. It could be that somebody is looking for him, and we—"

"The Indian?"

Their reaction was impossible to miss, and she frowned at them. "Last time I saw Pete he was in here—maybe the second of October—had a couple of drinks, all cooped up in the booth at the back there, sitting with his eye on the door, and he was carrying that big old Ruger of his. He looked like he had a lot on his mind. I left him alone for a time, till the place emptied out, and then I sat down to have a beer with him. We talked about this and that and then he asks me if I had seen anybody new in Dayton, was anybody asking for him? Nobody was and I told him so, but this didn't seem to settle him. I asked him what kind of trouble he was in and he said it was no big thing but if I happened to see a big man, looked like an Indian, with long gray hair down to his shoulders and lots of Navajo silver on him, well he'd appreciate it if I were to give him a call up there in his cabin. Last time I talked to him, and that was"—she glanced at a calendar behind the bar—"that was thirteen days ago now. I called him a few times since but never got an answer. Left messages but he never picked up."

Fremont's face had been closing down during this report, and Dalton's passive expression did not hide his growing concern from her.

"Okay, I said my piece. How about you two fill me in?"

Fremont opened his mouth to speak but Dalton cut in.

"You know anything about Pete's past, Katie?"

"I know he did government work. He never went into details. We don't push people on their past around here. It's not polite."

"It's possible that someone from Pete's working years has gone off the rails and it may be that he's out looking for him. This man would be tall, well built, in his late seventies, a man who's seen a lot of outdoor work, but he wouldn't necessarily look like an Indian. He might look like retired military. Have you seen anyone like that?"

"Without you narrow it down a bit, you just described half the old men in the Powder River country. But we know most of them. Wyoming's only got one person for every five hundred square miles, so strangers get noticed. I talked to some of Pete's friends around here, and he asked them the same favor, to let them know if they saw anybody like the man he described to me. Same man you described. But nobody has seen him. Just what is it you do for a living, Micah?"

"I'm with the government."

"So's my mailman. You look military, even though you got all that long lovely blond hair just like Jennifer Aniston. There's something hard about you, and I know Willard here's got a lot more sand than he wants you to think he has. Also you're both wearing sidearms and you look damned worried. So if it's all right with you I think I'd like a better answer."

"I think you've got all the information you need."

Katie shook her head, as if Dalton's answer had tipped a scale. She pushed herself off the bar, reached down under it, and came up with a gleaming Winchester carbine.

"Yeah. I expect I do. Come on, help me lock up."

"Where are you going?" asked Fremont.

"With you two. Up to Pete's place."

"Sorry. There's no way you're coming with us," said Dalton.

"I'm not?" she said, smiling thinly at him. "Tell you what. You two go on out to your government car out there and get a head start while I call up a couple of Pete's friends, and then we'll see just how far up the highway you get without me. How's that sound?"

AT HER STRONG INSISTENCE, they took Katie's sixty-two Lincoln Continental convertible, which had once been gleaming black and which had probably come out of Dearborn with a front windshield that did not have an unexplained large-caliber bullet hole through the passenger side. Katie was at the wheel, Dalton next to her, with Fremont rather grudgingly installed in the backseat, Katie wheeling the huge machine expertly through the long sweeping curves of the two-lane blacktop that led upward into the Bighorns.

The road climbed, in a series of switchbacks and narrowing hairpins, past the tumbling waterfall that was the source of the Tongue River, past a valley strewn with limestone obelisks called the Fallen City, but climbing, always climbing, a rise of over six thousand feet above the sunlit valleys that fell precipitously away below them.

Dalton, trying to appear calm while Katie raced around a curve with a drop on his side of a thousand feet, stared back over the shrinking landscape of the Powder River country and realized that a thin greenish tint of uneven land at the farthest reaches of the eastern horizon could very well be South Dakota.

The engine was laboring and the heat gauge was bumping against the red line when she made a hard right turn at a sharply inclined gravel road and headed up an impossible grade, a grade intended for horses, and sure-footed horses at that.

The rear wheels were spinning out a spray of gravel and the men in the car had become strangely silent as Katie fought the wheel and swore softly to herself in a low growl. After an endless climb over rocky ground, the trail shrank down to a narrow path between encroaching brush and pines, stiff thorny branches scraping along the paintwork and clutching at Dalton's sleeve. The temperature dropped almost ten degrees, and now there was a distinct chill in the clear air.

"You boys doing okay?" asked Katie, taking her eyes off the road at a point in a goat-track hairpin curve that was already forcing Dalton to recall Naumann's prediction that he had less than three weeks to live, and wonder if this car trip was exactly what Naumann had in mind.

"Just fine," he said, through gritted teeth, as the huge car lurched across a steel-slotted grate laid over a six-foot-deep storm ditch, pushed its blunt snout through a stand of twisted mesquite and stunted firs, and came to a grinding, bouncing halt in a clearing.

On the far side of the clearing a narrow graded road, reasonably well finished in coarse sand, led in a blind curve around a cliff of yellow stone that soared upward, easily two hundred feet, its sawtooth peak lost in a gathering mist.

"We better walk from here," said Katie. "Can't turn this beast around at Pete's front yard and I don't like backing up on the goat walk he calls a driveway. He usually leaves his truck here."

This sentiment found much favor with Dalton and even more with Fremont, who had spent the last ten miles holding on to the handle of the back door, ready to open it and leap for his life before Katie drove the Lincoln off a cliff, which he was morally certain she was going to do at any moment. He peeled his bone-white trembling fingers off the latch and shoved the door open, cursing quietly to himself.

Katie pulled her Winchester out of a scabbard sewn to the interior of the driver's door and pushed the door shut, staring across the clearing at the narrow track that ran around the curve of the cliff face, a sandy track without a mark on it, not even the tracks of her own boots from her last trip up here only five days ago. She crossed the clearing, levering a round into the Winchester, and crouched down at the beginning of the road.

"Nobody's been here," she said, touching the dry sandy soil with a fingertip and putting the tip to her mouth, tasting it. "Wind up here's been blowing hard all weekend. Tracks are all gone."

She stood up and looked at the two men, Dalton with his Colt Python in his hand and his canvas cattle coat pulled in tight against the chill, and Fremont looking taut and white-faced, his pale skin contrasting oddly with his bright-red nylon vest. Fremont's .45 was in his right hand, the hammer cocked.

"There's only one way in," she said.

"I know it," said Fremont, "I been here before."

"Okay. How you want to do this?"

"I'll lead," said Dalton, stepping forward. "If anything goes wrong, Willard knows who to call."

"That I do," said Willard, happy to have a man back in charge, even if Dalton had no idea what was waiting for them around the curve. Katie followed the men at a distance of thirty feet as the three of them came slowly around the long slightly inclined grade cut into the wall of the cliff. Through a thin screen of brush on their right they could catch brief glimpses of a far blue country spread out below them and thin wisps of pale cloud a hundred miles away.

The sand was gritty and their boots crunched faintly, the sound blowing away on the strong cold wind that was flowing straight into the cliff face. Halfway around the curve Dalton caught—they all caught—a strong whiff of corruption, something very large and not too long dead, coming from close by.

Dalton pulled the hammer back and stepped to the outer edge of the trail. The smell was very powerful now, carried to them on the wind flowing up from the valley. Katie was at his side, her Winchester in her hands. She leaned over and peered down through a long drop, a cliff face dotted with short spiky shrubs, a few needle-tipped pines jutting out like quills.

"There," she said, pointing the muzzle of the carbine at an outcrop of rock sixty feet down the face. Something red and broken lay on the ledge, partially impaled on a pine branch, white bones showing through torn pink flesh and purple entrails, a fan of shattered ribs bared to the sky like teeth from an ivory comb.

"It's a buck deer," said Fremont, standing a little ways off and holding on to the branch of a pine as he leaned over the cliff's edge.

"Been there quite a while," said Katie. "Should have smelled it last Friday, I guess, but the wind was coming the other way."

Dalton was studying the carcass carefully. "It's been skinned," he said, in a low voice.

Katie squinted at it.

"Yes," she said, shaking her head. "What kind of a wasteful fool would skin a buck carcass and then just throw all that venison away?"

Fremont and Dalton exchanged a look, which Katie caught, but they said nothing as they trotted around the last of the curve, where the ledge opened up to a plateau of flat yellow limestone about thirty feet wide. The whole of the Powder River country stretched out before them, hundreds and hundreds of miles of open grassland fading into a deep, hazy blue. In the valley the long shadows of the Bighorns behind them were creeping out toward Ranchester as the sun ran down into the west. They turned and looked at Pete Kearney's cabin, a stout, solid fortress of a home built out of square-cut timbers and roofed in slate, set hard up against the cliff face, a sheer rise that went soaring up a hundred feet before disappearing behind a thatch of scrub pine.

The front of the cabin, sheltered by a low beamed porch, was shuttered with thick pine slabs, and the door, a flat panel of solid pine, was crisscrossed with steel bands. The cabin looked dusty, and dry leaves had blown up all along the windward face, as if the last man who had lived there had boarded it up and gone west in the dying days of the last age. A shrill cry from overhead made them all look up as a golden eagle circled far above them, three long sweeping passes traced against the pale blue sky, before he decided that they were not prey—at least not easy prey—and he wheeled away to the south, peeping absurdly.

Katie walked up to the cabin door and kicked it hard, hard enough to make the dust bounce off the planks. Grit drifted down off the underside of the porch, glimmering in the late-afternoon light.

"Pete! You in there? It's Katie."

Nothing. The wind rolling in across the plateau. From an unseen spring bubbling up in the cliff face came the hissing murmur of racing water. In a stand of trees at the far end of the ledge a crow cursed them and then laughed raucously, joined in a moment by others of his kind—from the sound they made, a multitude, all of them well hidden in the trees, their cries echoing off the face of the cliff.

"I don't like all them crows around," said Katie. "Isn't natural. Now what, trooper?" said Katie, looking at Dalton quizzically.

Dalton lifted the Colt Python and blew a fist-size hole in the upper-right hinge plate, the wood chips flying, the boom of the gun sending a huge flock of crows soaring into the blue sky, braying and screeching madly. Another shot into the middle hinge, and a third into the lowest one, followed by a fourth round into the door latch. In the deafened silence that followed the only sound was the oiled metallic ratcheting as Dalton reloaded his Colt.

Katie kept her Winchester leveled on the door. Fremont, his back to the two of them, was watching the curve of the road, the trees at the far end of the shelf, the open plateau, his .45 in both hands, the muzzle slightly lowered.

Dalton stepped up to the door, put a gloved hand into the gaping splintered hole where the door latch had been, set himself, put a boot against the frame, and gave the door a massive pull. It groaned against the timbers, shifted a half inch, and then flew right out of the frame, the huge door slamming to the ground with a thunderous clap and narrowly missing Dalton's boots as he stumbled backward off the porch. Katie caught him in a wiry grip to keep him from falling. The doorway loomed open, the interior as black as a mine.

Katie stepped forward, but Dalton caught her by the arm.

"No. Wait. Listen."

Katie stopped, her head cocked. A low murmuring buzzing, rising and falling, deep, almost at the lower limit of hearing. The sound—terrible and frighteningly familiar—flowed over Dalton like a wave, stopping his breath. Fremont stood a little way behind them, listening to the same sound, his face going pale and his eyes widening.

"What the hell is that?" asked Katie, shaking Dalton's hand off and walking up the stairs. "It sounds like—"

A single green fly flew straight out of the middle of the open frame, buzzing aggressively around them, followed by two more.

"Katie," said Fremont, "you better—"

And then a torrent, a storm cloud of flies, a living horde of buzzing fat flies, their distended bellies glistening blue and green, their wings a shimmering blur, poured, literally *poured* like black oil out of the open doorway of the cabin. The three of them bowed down under the stream of flies like people in a strong wind as the swarm flowed over them, and flies crawled down their necks, and into their eyes, and rustled up their open sleeves, slipping into their mouths as they gasped for air, buzzing and rattling deep in their ears, crawling busily over their eyes, in their hair—

They all three broke and ran, stumbling away from the river that was pouring out of the interior of Pete Kearney's cabin and spreading out across the open ground of the plateau, crawling, flying, buzzing, an unspeakable sickening flood. They beat the air around themselves as they staggered away from the cabin, Katie screaming as she ran, Dalton grimly silent, his lips set tight against the greasy flies he could feel crawling over his mouth, crawling up his nostrils, Fremont close behind, bellowing like a bull.

They covered a hundred feet before the swarm diminished, before they could breathe without inhaling flies, and there they stopped, panting, stunned, horrified.

In five long minutes the torrent of flies had slowed to a stream, and then to a trickle, and then to only a few bloated flies buzzing around the doorway, and a few more crawling up the outside walls, on the underside of the overhanging roof.

The deep organlike note of their buzzing diminished into a constant burring sound, the chatter of their wings or the rustling sound they made as they rubbed up against one another in clusters, their bodies glimmering with gasoline colors in the dying light.

The wind from the valley floor had been gaining in strength as the evening came on, and now it was racing across the plateau and into the open door, driving away the clusters of flies around the cabin, blowing them into the air by the thousands.

The three of them stood there, in shocked stillness, staring in bleak horror at the cabin until the wind had cleared most of the flies away, a time out of mind that turned out to be, by Katie's watch, no more than ten minutes.

A kind of suspended calm came back to the little plateau and the space around the darkened building, and in that false calm they walked slowly, warily back across the open ground, stopping at the foot of the stairs. Now an overpowering stench, the stink of dead meat and rotting flesh, drifted out through the door, forcing them back again. From inside the cabin they could hear a low, busy, murmuring hum.

"Oh good Christ," said Katie. "What're we waiting for?"

She raised the Winchester and strode firmly into the darkness. Dalton and Fremont looked at each other, and then both men followed her inside. Into the suffocating stench, the cloying reek of putrefaction. The interior of the cabin was as dim as a crypt, the only light coming from the open door, but they could see a large shape in the middle of the room, wrapped in a seething cloud, and the buzzing noise was very loud. The walls were moving, and the boards under their feet were thick with black cockroaches, their wings chittering and whirring. Fat cold slugs dropped onto their heads from the rafters, and tiny biting flies flew at their faces. Katie, her face set and hard, bone-white but steady, turned to Fremont. "Get those shutters open."

"Katie, I'm not sure I—"

"Open the goddamned shutters, Willard!"

Fremont went to the nearest window, his boots skidding on the crunching, slippery floor. He hammered at the steel lever and the shutters flew outward and away, and hard flat sunlight streamed into the cramped little room. The air was alive with buzzing flies. They crawled on every surface and hung from every fixture. They swarmed and buzzed and scuttled across the huge scrawled drawing spray-painted right across the rear wall of the cabin, the drawing that Dalton, in the recesses of his heart, had been afraid that he would find here ever since they left Butte.

And they swarmed in their millions around a huge shapeless mass in the middle of the room. Barely visible under the crawling layers of busy biting flies was the bloody hide of a big buck deer, and the hide of the buck had been wrapped tightly around what looked to be the figure of a man, although his shape was only vaguely human.

"Oh . . . Pete . . . ," said Katie, softly, her voice breaking.

"Katie," said Dalton, gently, "we have to get out of here."

12

tuesday, october 16
greybull air force museum
greybull, wyoming
7 a.m. local time

the CIA Gulfstream came in low out of the rising sun, skimming down the western slopes of the Bighorns and racing across the stony plains of the eastern Bighorn Valley less than a thousand feet off the ground, the banshee howl of its jets shaking the windows and rattling the nerves of everyone in the high desert village of Greybull.

Watching this approach, the tower controller picked up his third coffee of the morning and said, "Fucking carrier pilot jet-jockey cowboy assholes" in a hoarse rasping voice.

Across the room, Fremont and Dalton, sitting in ladder-backs and watching the same jet, said nothing, but they nodded in silent agreement. Far, far away in the ultimate west, the Yellowstone Rockies had caught the rising sun a full hour before it reached the broad valley, and the two men had sat there, stunned, silent, weary beyond belief, staring in a dull, hypnotized daze as the first rays of the sun touched upon the snowy peaks of the Beartooth Range and they flashed out suddenly, a blazing diamond-sharp light, the pine fields on their eastern slopes glittering like a forest of silvery spears, while the broad sweeping valley below them lay covered in a pale violet shadow.

The air down on the plains was cold and sharp; the first bitter tendrils of winter hoarfrost had crept across the car windows during the night, and in the tower the overheated control room smelled of boiled coffee, cheap cigars, and the controller's stale sweat, none of which bothered Fremont and Dalton in the slightest; they had spent most of the drive across the Bighorns trying to get the ruined face of Crucio Churriga, the smell, the sights, the sounds of Pete Kearney's cabin, out of their clothes, their minds, their skins, with no success at all.

They had talked, briefly and without enthusiasm, about the drawings on the wall of Pete Kearney's cabin and the one on the wall at the hospice in Butte.

Fremont confirmed Dalton's intuition that the same drawing had been written across the kitchen wall right above Al Runciman's flayed body in Mountain Home, and that the ATM records of Moot Gibson's travels seemed to coincide with Runciman's death, with the abomination at Pete Kearney's cabin, with the mutilation of Crucio Churriga in Butte, and with the series of attempts on Fremont's life.

A trail of tears.

And then there was Katie Horn.

She had seen them off, *run* them off, to be more precise, in the face of all their objections, their solicitude, all of which was firmly and at last vehemently rejected, and their final memory of her was as she walked across the empty street and climbed the stairs of Hanoi Jane's in Dayton, moving like an old woman, her shoulders bowed, her crazed-porcelain skin waxy and pale, her face dull and tearstained.

She had turned just as she reached the screen door and stared back up at the long-shadowed slopes of the Bighorns, where a column of dense smoke was still rising up into the very last of the sunlight, up into the high wind off the plains, where it was caught and whipped away in a long delicate thread, stretching out into the west and finally disappearing over the dome of Granite Pass.

She stood there for a time, watching the blue smoke rising, and then, with a final listless wave to Fremont and Dalton, she went inside and closed the door. Dalton and Fremont had climbed into the Crown Victoria without a single word passing between them. In that same brooding inward silence they headed back up the mountain, staring at the smoke coming from high up in the hills as they went by the entrance to the gravel track, then looking blankly straight ahead as two state patrol cars and a volunteer fire truck came racing toward them in the oncoming lane a mile later, then, much faster, speeding away westward over the Bighorns on the Cloud Peak Highway, with the Flower Duet from Lakmé on the radio.

They cleared Granite Pass around midnight, stopping for dishwater coffee and circular wads of cold clay that the pimpled, chinless, pig-eyed clerk stubbornly insisted were country-fresh doughnuts, and then they descended the treacherous ridges and jagged red cliffs of Shell Canyon in the early-morning hours, rolling down out of the Bighorns and out onto the desert plateau that ran all the way west to the Yellowstones, finally reaching Greybull a full hour before sunup.

It was now past seven, and the company Gulfstream, carrying Delroy Suarez and Nicky Baum all the way from Topeka, was right on time. The plane flared up and touched down like a leaf on a pond, flaps lowered and jets howling loud enough to rattle the windows, and they got up, thanked the sullen controller for his hospitality—getting a prolonged parting belch for their trouble—and were standing on the windblown tarmac at the end of the runway when the jet rocked to a stop fifty feet away and the side door popped open. Two men came down the folding gangway, both of them short, muscular, one darkly Hispanic, with a shaved head, the other a pale, pink-looking man with bright-red cheeks and a bit of a beer belly, both men wearing leather jackets, cowboy jeans, and dusty combat boots, both men carrying long military-issue rifle cases.

They saw Dalton waiting by the tower, his hair flying in the crosswind, his cowboy range jacket pulled in tight, and Fremont next to him, looking pinched and wary, his red down vest buttoned up tight and his arms crossed against his chest. They came across to meet them, the Hispanic man grinning broadly.

"Micah Dalton, as I live and breathe," he said, his lively black eyes bright with good humor, his lean face creasing up as he smiled.

"Delroy," said Dalton, genuinely pleased to see him, and grinned as he shook the man's hands. "Always a pleasure," and, with a little less warmth, as he turned to Nicky Baum, whose closed unwelcoming face had changed into a hard, suspicious, cold-eyed glare as he got closer to Willard Fremont, "And you, Nicky. How's the wife and kids?"

"Last time I saw them they were fine, Micah. Who's this?"

Dalton did the honors. Fremont was ready to be judged and excluded by these new arrivals, who, by the hard flat look of them, were not that long out of Army Special Forces. He was also somewhat reluctant to give up Dalton's exclusive attention. He tried his best to be civil, but it wasn't until they were all safely stuffed into the Crown Vic and rolling west along a bumpy two-lane goat track passing itself off as Wyoming State Highway 14 that he relaxed enough to comply with Dalton's request to fill the men in on what had happened back at Pete Kearney's place on the far side of the Bighorns.

Fremont told it straight, sparing no details.

When he was finished, both men sat in the back and stared

blankly at Fremont for a full thirty seconds. Finally, Nicky Baum, a beefy pink-skinned man with pale-brown eyes and, of the two men, the one with the most pronounced air of latent aggression, sighed theatrically, and said, "Micah, this old fart actually reliable?"

Fremont, who had been preparing himself for precisely this, turned around and faced the road, his thin, sharp face hardening into a remote, cold glare. Dalton shook his head and sighed.

"Nicky, Willard here has seen more operational time than both of you put together. He's been working this part of the country for twenty years, and before that he was NSA in Guam, working under Jack Stallworth. While you were still hoping to make third-string safety for the Nittany Lions, Willard was out here in the wild keeping your pimply teenage butt safe from America's enemies. You can either find your manners, Nicky, and speak to my friend with respect, or you can go right back to Kansas."

Baum's pink face had brightened into a full-blown apple red during Dalton's short, sharp rebuke, delivered in a flat and businesslike tone that lacked for nothing in force and conviction. When it was over, the atmosphere in the car was taut and electric.

"Nicky . . . ?" said Dalton, clearly waiting.

"I'm sorry, Mr. Fremont," said Baum, in a strangled tone. "I didn't know your background. I sincerely apologize."

"So do I," said Delroy Suarez.

"You didn't insult him," said Baum. "I did."

"I was apologizing for my choice of partners," said Suarez, smiling at Baum. "Excuse Nicky, Mr. Fremont. He's a tad insecure meeting new people on account of his mother was a lowly ungulate and he's afraid people will hold it against him. I keep telling him that these sorts of bestial couplings happen all the time in Pennsylvania—"

"Shut up, Del," said Baum. "Micah, this guy Mr. Fremont has been telling us about, this the *same* guy we're going to see right now?"

"Yes."

"And he was one of . . . he was company too?"

"Yes. He was a member of Willard's Echelon unit."

"And this is true, about him wrapping this Kearney guy up in a fresh deer hide and leaving him to get eaten alive by maggots?"

"That isn't the kind of thing a healthy mind makes up."

"Where would a guy even *get* an idea like that?"

"Plains Indian trick. The Comanches did it all the time."

"This Gibson guy's a Comanche?"

"No. But he's studying real hard to become one."

"The guy's fucking insane," said Suarez. "What's his story?"

Dalton laid out what they knew—or hoped they knew—about Pershing Gibson's struggle with the IRS, about his slow descent into madness, about Al Runciman's death, last Friday evening's attack on Crucio Churriga in Butte, and the earlier attempts on Fremont's life up in northern Idaho. The two men listened intently, exchanging only a few sidelong glances, until Dalton got around to the death of Porter Naumann and his family.

"I knew Porter Naumann by reputation," said Baum. "It's hard to believe that anyone, even an ex-Marine Recon, could get to him."

"Well it happened," said Dalton.

"So why is this guy killing guys from his own unit?"

"We haven't a freaking clue," said Dalton.

"Mr. Fremont—" Suarez began.

"Call me Willard."

"Did your unit have any contact with Porter Naumann?"

"Not as far as I know."

"Then why'd this guy go all the way to Italy to kill him?"

"That's why you're here," said Dalton. "We're going to take him alive and then we'll ask him. How's that sound?"

"Can't we just call in an air strike?" said Nicky Baum, only half-joking; their assessment of the target's threat level and operational skills had been cranking up with every new detail.

"No. But we'll keep it in mind. Show them the map, Willard."

Fremont pulled a well-thumbed terrain map from the glove compartment and spread it out on the backrest. Both men leaned forward to look at it.

"This here's the road were on, Highway 14. And here, about thirteen miles west, there's this little town called Emblem. We turn off there and go south until we cross the Greybull River."

He traced the route with a tobacco-stained index finger, drawing a line that led out into a huge flat high-desert plain bisected by the meandering course of the Greybull, bounded in the north by a chain of peaks known as Elk Butte and in the south by Sheets Mountain, a solitary volcanic peak that rose five thousand feet off the valley floor. He tapped a point in the middle of a wide flat nowhere about halfway between these two mountains.

"This here's where Moot's got his spread. Nearest town is Meeteetse, six miles to the west, and then there's Worland way off to the southeast. Land around there is hardscrabble, small rocks and sagebrush, and the wind is always blowing in from somewhere, so it gets in your eyes, your gear. Nasty fighting ground. There's every kind of crawling biting stinging thing you can imagine—"

"I can imagine a whole lot," said Suarez, who had a deep fear of scorpions. "Any scorpions at all?"

"A few. The little brown ones, mainly. But they only come out after dark. Just don't kick over a rock without a stick. Also rattlers, sidewinders mainly, and a few copperheads. Now, this—"

He pulled out a drawing he had made, from memory, of the layout of Moot's ranch, the outbuildings, the type of fence, and everything he could recall of the main house.

"This here's the basic layout. The main house here, its all on the one floor, but Moot dug a storm cellar under the summer kitchen at the back, which could be a hidey-hole for him, so when we go in, bear that in mind. Two front rooms, dining room and living room, and a third, which is his bedroom. Whole building's about thirty-foot square—"

"What's it made of?" asked Baum.

"Cinder block mainly, but he poured gravel in a latex compound into the chambers, so they will stop most long-distance rounds short of a fifty or a big magnum, and the roof's flat adobe on plate iron, so's he can catch the rainwater and run it off into a cistern by the rear of the house. Two small windows in each room and he fixed up some two-inch-thick solid-steel shutters—complete with fire slits in a cross shape so he can elevate as well as traverse—to bolt down over all the windows. Place is a right little fort, gentlemen."

"How about the perimeter alarms?"

"Moot keeps dogs, four of them. Better than any electronic system you can devise. They live in this outbuilding here, far side from the privy, two mongrels, a half-blind mastiff he keeps chained up, but his main dog is a wolf-shepherd cross name of Irene, and she is a serious piece of work. Weighs a hundred pounds, scary-smart, can't be tricked, won't take strange meat, can hear a flea fart in a sandstorm, smell a man a mile off, and she can run like the very wind itself. I saw her run down a hare in a fifteen-minute chase. She never gave up until she had her teeth in his guts. She *likes* to kill, once she's coursing, and if she gets you on your back she will have your throat out before you can say how do you do."

Dalton, listening, privately noted that Willard Fremont's response to the new arrivals was to slide back into his cowboy hillbilly persona, if only out of defensive habit.

"Other than these dogs, Moot had some trip wires laid out at a hundred yards off, all around the area, but these plains get a lot of antelope and the occasional rogue elk, so the trip wires got ignored, as they tended to go off a lot. Mainly this is a low, flat, heavily forti-fied bunker surrounded by three hundred yards of high-plains desert with very little brush and no man-size trees, and the fellow who lives there is a serious killing hand."

There was a silence while Baum and Suarez studied the terrain map and Fremont's detailed sketch. Then Baum, with a tentative look at Suarez and something of the air of a conjurer, reached into his kit bag and pulled out a sheaf of photographs, which he handed across to Fremont with a slightly sheepish air.

"I know this is operationally risky. I tried to make the request look routine. But I got a friend at NRO to e-mail me the most re-cent overfly shots of this area from the Condor Nine bird—"

"Condor Nine," said Dalton. "How'd you do that?"

"She's kind of a personal friend," he said, blushing.

Since everybody in the car except Fremont knew that Baum was married, the detail was lightly passed over in a diplomatic silence.

"Anyway, these were taken yesterday at 1633 hours 19 seconds. Here's the infrared readout from a quadrant that includes this place here."

He tapped a glossy blue-tinted photo taken from fifty miles up and then magnified a thousand times. It showed a flat, pebbly ter-rain dotted with a few scrub bushes and a cleared area around a low flat bunkerlike building and two smaller outbuildings. A tiny mean-dering driveway led up to the main building. Long shadows were trailing eastward from the shrubs and buildings. Beside the main building was a pickup truck with a dim red oval on the hood. Another brighter red oval showed inside the main house, and a series of smaller red blobs in the larger of the two outbuildings.

"These are infrared readings from the sector. As you can see, it looks like the truck had been used a little while before, because the engine is still cooling off. Inside the house I figure that's one man, or at least one man-shaped heat source. And I guess these other red returns are his dogs, penned up in the outbuilding. These other shots . . ."

He fanned out three more, in varying degrees of magnification, showing the house in straight black-and-white high-resolution shots.

"These give us a look at the immediate area, maybe a range field of five hundred yards. You can see a fork of the river here—"

"The Greybull," said Fremont.

"Yes, the Greybull, running here in a diagonal across the top right sector. You can see by the shadows that the river has carved out a series of arroyos and one of them runs to within a hundred yards of the house. Since it's in shadow, where the house is still lit up from the west there, I figure it's deep enough to let us come in pretty close before we make our run."

"Nice work," said Dalton, grateful for any tactical data that would help him frame an assault plan that wouldn't get them killed. Or, even worse, unthinkably worse, taken alive.

"Thanks," said Baum. "What've we got in the way of arms?"

"Remington 308 bolt action with a Leupold and match-grade rounds with armor-piercing jackets. Colt Python with all the rounds. A 1911 Colt .45, ported and stabilized, and fifty rounds. And you?"

"I've got a scoped Barrett 50 and a big box of match-grade rounds. Del has an M249. We've both got Beretta nine-mils. And we brought along some shape charges and a couple of stun grenades."

"You brought a Barrett?" asked Dalton.

Baum shrugged, gave him a sideways smile.

"I took a look at a map when we were back in Kansas. This is a flat and empty land, just like Mr. Fremont says. I figured we'd need a guy to stand off and punch a lot of heavy-caliber bullet holes in stuff."

"I couldn't agree more," said Fremont, looking out at the broad flat plain and thinking about the way the changing light was lying.

THEY GOT WITHIN A quarter mile of Moot's place by a little after two, bumping along a shallow depression that ran by the course of the Greybull River, and left the car at the last bend, covering it with fresh-cut brush and coarse river sand to hide the gleam of metal.

They held a brief counsel of war: Wait until twilight, until the shadows come out strong and a hard western light would lie right in Moot's eyes. Nicky Baum, with the Barrett, would provide long-range covering fire, taking an OP on a little crest of rising land about two hundred yards to the west of Moot's place, with a clear sight line to Moot's front door, in the west so the setting sun wouldn't blind him if he had to make a long, difficult shot in a tearing hurry.

Usually the long-range sniper would have a spotter, partly to tell him where his rounds were going, but also to cover his back, since the attention of a sniper was of necessity often a thousand yards away. But there was only one target, not multiples, so they decided against it. Which left Del Suarez, with the Remington bolt-action, free to work his way around to the rear of the house to take up a blocking post about fifty yards out, in a small stand of pine they had seen through the binoculars.

Fremont, with the SAW, would check out the smaller outbuilding and the privy, making sure no ambush was waiting for them, and then hold down the southern sector for Dalton's final approach, taking a stand near a lone creosote shrub a hundred feet from Moot's side wall.

A hundred feet, because that was the outside limit of the SAW's effective combat range, and not too close to the solitary creosote bush, of course, because bitter experience has taught the infantry soldier that any bush or rock that looks like good cover to you will also look like good cover to your enemy, and will either be booby-trapped or so well sighted-in with aiming sticks that the defender could drill out the location with full-auto rounds even in the pitch-blind dark.

Dalton would be the entry man, with the Python and the .45. He would clear the other outbuilding and then, carrying the shaped charges, make the final dash across the front yard. Suarez and Baum, as the snipers, would use whatever suppressing fire was necessary to cover Dalton's final approach to the house, then Fremont would come up on the run—again, covered by the snipers—when Dalton was ready to go through the door.

They all had com sets, wound packs with morphine in case things went bad, and canteens filled to the brim so they wouldn't make noise. They calculated three hours for Suarez and Baum to get into position—easily that long, since the idea was to get into place without being seen. Once there, they'd check in on the com sets.

They all shook hands, wished one another luck; Baum and Suarez moved out with hardly a rustle of gravel, disappearing into the low brush in a few seconds, leaving Fremont and Dalton to wait the long wait in the stony arroyo near the Greybull River.

While they waited, watching the light change slowly on the land, Fremont and Dalton talked quietly of various things, places they had seen, men and women they had known, talked of Guam and the Horn and Stallworth's obsessive love of orchids, about this never-ending war, a few wry reflections on how things were better when it was just the Russians they had to worry about. The quiet talk flowed easily on, both men thinking of the coming action and wondering whether their theoretical tactics would withstand a bench test out in the mortal world.

As it usually happens to men facing a fight, the talk ran to other memories of combat, either declared or covert, that they had experienced, which, naturally enough, brought them around eventually to the here and the now, and Fremont asked Dalton if he thought that Baum's Barrett 50 was the right weapon for suppressing fire.

"Great question. My platoon sergeant when we were in the Horn had a list he called 'The Rules of Combat.' The first rule was that the single most dangerous thing in a combat zone was an officer with a map. Today, that would be me. Number two was 'No battle plan ever survives contact with the enemy,' which is about to be proved again. And number three, to answer your specific question, was that suppressing fire only works when it's used on abandoned positions."

"That has been my experience," said Fremont, laughing. He was a man whose natural state was reasonably sunny, and he looked around the valley with real appreciation of the present beauty it was offering.

He looked up as a flight of birds passed over, a thousand feet up, black chevrons against the fading light—they might be swifts or swallows—and in the west an orange fireball sun was sinking through a gray storm squall high over the Beartooth, while a delicate pink afterglow was slipping away into the east, chased by a violet dusk.

The cold had been building since late afternoon, a damp, biting chill with the smell of dry pine and wood smoke inside it. In the far distance a coyote sang a solitary song for no reason other than to let the rest of the world know he was still in business. Fremont breathed it all in and said, "Lovely country, isn't it? A man with a good heart could be real happy in this valley."

"There is an hour," said Micah, pausing to call the memory up complete. "There is an hour wherein a man might be happy all his life, could he but find it."

"That's right. That's very damn right. That yours?"

"No. George Herbert."

"Walker Bush?" he asked, with some disbelief.

"No. Not that one . . ."

His voice trailed off then, and in his mind Dalton went far away to a long-ago summer afternoon in Cortona: Fremont let the silence run. The day was dying fast now and long blue shadows were creeping out from the cottonwoods. A few pale stars glittered in a cloudless arc of deep blue. The comfortable silence spooled out until the com set crackled once, and Dalton touched his throat mike.

"Nicky?"

"I'm in, Micah. I've got the house in my scope. Nothing moving. No lights. Truck's right where it was in the satellite shots. No heat signature on the truck. One heat signature in the house but from this angle I can't say where. I can hear a dog barking but I can't see him."

"Del?"

"Just digging in. Okay. I'm set. I've got my shot. Let's go."

"We're moving."

"Come ahead," said Baum. "I got you in the palm of my hand."

Dalton signaled to Fremont, who got up into a crouch, his lean face lit by the setting sun, making his right eye gleam like a shard of bottle glass, the left side of his face in darkness. He hadn't shaved in two days and his hollow cheek was covered with short white stubble. He looked tired and old and Dalton felt a rush of affection for him.

"Willard . . ."

"Yessir?"

"Why don't you just stay—"

Fremont's thin face hardened up and his one sunlit eye glittered.

"Moot Gibson killed my best friend. The man needs to die."

His hard look softened, and he smiled at Dalton. "Know what a friend of mine named Pascal once said? He said that the sole cause of a man's unhappiness is that he does not know how to stay quietly in his room. If Moot had managed just that one little thing, sit quiet in his room, then Al would still be alive and Pete would still be running packhorses up to Medicine Wheel and Moot Gibson wouldn't be going to die today. But he didn't. So let's go."

THEY HAD A LOT of ground to cross and they crossed it at a flat-out dash, Fremont veering south, heading for the outcrop by the creosote bush, moving well for a man his age, the SAW at the ready, his boots heavy on the stony ground, Dalton running lightly, his eyes searching the terrain as he moved up toward the little collection of buildings. As he closed in on the house, he instinctively tightened up in the expectation of a round singing past his ear followed by the harsh crack of the weapon, but no shot came.

He reached the side of the larger outbuilding and rested for a moment there, sheltered from the fire line of the main house. Through the thin wooden walls of the shed he could hear the sound of a large dog growling and barking. He watched as Fremont, bent low, slipped into cover behind the rocky outcrop, vanishing from sight.

He moved around to the side of the outbuilding and found a small quarter-glass window. He braced himself and smashed the pane with the butt of his Colt. From the interior of the cabin came the hysterical howl of a badly frightened dog, but no rounds whacked through the walls and into his cringing belly.

He risked a quick look and saw a large pen, in the middle of which was chained a large shepherd cross, her muzzle covered with bloody foam, her eyes wide and the whites showing as she howled her fear and her rage at the timbers of the roof.

Around her were the bodies of three other big dogs, all of them horribly torn and bloody. There was nothing else in the shed but a few tools and some sacks of animal feed. He slipped back to the edge of the building and pulled in a long breath, letting it out through his nose, willing himself into stillness. The moment hung there, suspended, and on the chill air he could smell the sharp tang of wood smoke.

A thin blue wisp was rising up from the chimney stack, slipping away on the wind. The setting sun lay full on the front door and the two shuttered windows, a flat shadowless look, giving it an ominous air.

He had a hundred feet of ground to cross and every foot of it was wide open. If Moot Gibson was waiting for Dalton to cross that ground, the chances were very good that Dalton had just begun to count off the last sixty seconds of his life on this earth.

He knew that as soon as Moot fired, Nicky Baum's Barrett 50 would blow a football-size hole in whatever place the round had come from, but until Dalton moved and until Moot fired, Baum would have nothing to shoot at, and since the whole idea was to try to take Moot Gibson alive, and that first shot could very easily be the one that blew Dalton's brains out the back of his head, the tactical problems were huge. Dalton understood only too well that he really did not want to try to cross that last fifty feet.

Not at all.

There had to be a better way. Maybe they could try talking him out? Yes. That's the ticket. It sure as hell worked with Saddam Hussein. Reason with him. Think like the United Nations.

Just ask him real nice if would please pretty please—

Dalton cleared the corner in a convulsive leap and raced across the ground, his eyes fixed on the gun ports, braced to take a round in the head, thinking *not in the face not in the face,* as combat soldiers often do, cutting cards with death.

He slammed up against the wall beside the heavily barred door, dropped into a crouch with the Colt at the ready, and clicked twice on his com set mike. In a moment Fremont came lurching around the corner with his SAW, grinning at Dalton.

He crossed to the far side of the door and held his hand up, shaped a fist, his face running with sweat.

Dalton nodded, reached up, slapped a shape charge against the upper hinge and another against the lower hinge.

They both turned away as Dalton clicked the trigger: two massive deafening cracks and the door blew into pieces.

Before the smoke had cleared, before the sound had stopped echoing from the distant mountains, they were through the door, Dalton going left with his Colt up, Fremont going right, covering the room with the SAW. They were in.

There was no one there.

"NICKY."

"I'm here, Micah."

"We're in. We've cleared the whole house. He's not here."

"I see you. Willard says there's a storm cellar—"

"Already cleared it. The place is empty."

"Is it mined?"

"If it was, we wouldn't be having this conversation."

"You want me to come in?"

"No. Hold your position. If you see anyone coming, let us know. Del, you there?"

"I am. Nothing moving in my sector. I might have a scorpion up my pant leg. Other than that, I'm fine. Want me to come in?"

"Yes. Come up. We still have to safe the outbuildings."

Suarez was with them in forty-five seconds, panting heavily, his lean Latin face gritty with dust.

"You and Willard check out the other buildings for IEDs. And there's at least one dog alive in that wooden shed there. She's out of her head and if you have to you put her down."

"Is it the wolf dog?" asked Fremont.

"Looks like it."

"That's Irene," he said, looking at Delroy Suarez. "I'll see to her. You check the other building. You going back in there, Micah?"

"Yes."

"Moot had a thing about his personal effects. If you're going to turn over his drawers and things, watch out for blades and fishhooks."

"You've got to be kidding."

"Nope."

The men moved off to secure the shed and the equipment shack. Dalton stopped in the doorway to raise a hand and wave to Nicky Baum, who very likely had his crosshairs centered on Dalton's forehead right now. Thinking about trigger pull, resistance factors, and every harsh thing he had ever said to Nicky Baum, he turned away and stepped back through the open door into Moot Gibson's home.

He had been expecting one of those serial-killer nest scenes, a squalid ruin with the look of a crack house, the walls covered with newspaper clippings, scrawled obscenities, filth-strewn floors, all the outward signs of Moot Gibson's slow descent into savagery and madness. Instead, after he had moved through the place again and opened up all the steel shutters, he found himself in a crisp, clean, sparsely furnished four-room home that looked as if it had been decorated by Shakers; simple wooden walls, a spotless hardwood floor with a few colorful Navajo rugs here and there, a few pieces of simple pine furniture; in the dining room, a long trestle table gleaming in the half-light from the setting sun.

In the kitchen, a galley fit for a wooden sailboat, with a row of copper pots—graduated and gleaming—hanging over a center island, a small icebox in the corner, and by the sink a stack of neatly folded dishcloths and a fresh square of Sunlight soap.

In the bedroom, a single hard cot dressed barracks-style with a taut white sheet folded down over two soft Navajo blankets, and under the bed three pairs of black combat boots, each one polished to a dazzling shine and the laces squared away. On the far side of the room, a tall dresser made of rosewood, as polished as every other wooden surface in the home, and on top of the dresser a standing mirror shaped like a gothic window, two bottles of Old Spice cologne, and next to the mirror what looked like a framed piece of ancient antelope or deer hide, butternut brown, into which had been burned—branded—the same familiar drawing that he suspected he would find in this place:

He reached out and took the picture down—it was surprisingly heavy, the hide being quite thick—holding it in his hand and feeling himself at the edge of a revelation. He turned the picture over and was in no way surprised to find a message taped to the back, a phrase he had first heard seventeen days ago in Venice, coming from the lips of a dead man's ghost standing in the curtains that led out onto a balcony with a view of Saint Mark's Basin:

To get the answer,
you must survive the question.

HE DID A THOROUGH SEARCH, which delivered up no insight other than that Moot Gibson ate only organic grain and home-tilled vegetables, that he had standing subscriptions to *Harper's, The Atlantic Monthly, National Review, The Economist, Soldier of Fortune, Jane's Defense Review,* and *Utne Reader,* that his taste in fiction ran to K. C. Constantine's Mario Balzac books, and that he had $21,533.71 in the bank after a withdrawal of $500 at an ATM in a store called Picketwire Guns and Archery Supplies, according to scraps of ATM receipts he found in the half-burned trash outside the back door.

The trash also contained a tangle of knotted wooden twine and a bowl-shaped half of a hollowed-out gourd, on the surface of which had been painted a string of indecipherable pictographs: a sun, what looked like a daisy, little crosses. The figures had been executed with far more care than the drawings he had found in his global pursuit of Moot Gibson, but they shared the basic iconography of a crescent, a flower, and a cross. The underside of the gourd was coated with a thick black substance. He put the gourd to his nose and recoiled—the sudden flashing picture of the sunlit room in Venice and the spinning terra-cotta cylinder filled his mind and sent a bolt of terror through him.

He stuffed the gourd and the ATM receipts into a leather sack hanging on a chair in Moot's bedroom, picked up the framed drawing, and left the house at far more than just a walk, with the muscles across his back tightening painfully and what felt like a hundred yards of gleaming hardwood floor to cross before he reached the shattered smoldering rectangle of the blown-open door.

He stepped out into the soft light of evening and found Delroy

Suarez and Willard Fremont in the front yard, crouching solicitously over the trembling form of a large black-and-tan dog with a low blade-shaped head and teeth like a *T. rex.*

The dog was panting heavily in between tentative sips of water taken from Fremont's cupped palm and she watched Dalton coming with one white-rimmed eye.

"Micah, I'd like you to meet Irene. Irene, this is Micah."

Dalton knelt down and after a guarded look at Suarez and Fremont, held out the finger he was least unwilling to lose to this slit-eyed, wolfish bitch.

She rolled her eyes, whimpered at him, and then sniffed at his knuckles. Her muzzle was hot and her breath was foul. She smelled of what she had been eating, possibly her kennelmates, but in her manner there was only an intense sense of gratitude and a readiness to please.

Suarez, standing up and walking Dalton a few yards away, nodded toward the dusty black Dodge pickup sitting in the front yard, and said, "I checked that truck out. There was a can of Sterno sitting under the engine hood. Flamed out a while ago, but it would have been burning around the time Nicky checked the satellite shots."

"I found another Sterno can in the fireplace. It was still hot. How long does a can of Sterno burn?"

Suarez shook his head. "Never used it. But a big one like the one under the hood, set on low, might burn for a couple of days."

They both watched Fremont stroking the dog, who had now stopped quivering and was smiling up at him, both of them happy to see each other. They looked like old retired pirates at a reunion.

"What do you think?" Dalton asked, after a silence.

"Think? I think we've been outthunk," said Suarez.

"Looks like. Willard," he said, "say good bye to the dog. We gotta go."

Fremont was standing up, his mouth open and formulating the first appeal on behalf of the dog (Dalton could see it coming) but Dalton was already on the com set.

"Nicky, you there?"

Fremont was walking toward them now, his face set and his manner determined. "Look, Micah, we can't just leave—"

"Nicky, come in."

"—her here to starve. She's a good old—"

"Nicky . . ."

"—dog and she'll be no—"

There was a hum, a definite humming burr, and a solid silvery flash. A heavy rifle round struck Fremont in midstride with a sound like a sledgehammer hitting a side of frozen beef.

The round blew him literally in half: his lower torso, legs still obscenely working, traveled another pace toward them while his midsection blew out to the left, an eruption of flesh and bone, guts, his belt buckle, three inches of spinal cord striking the wall of the house. The expression on his face as he died was shocked, indignant.

Then the sound of the shot, the deep reverberating boom of a .50-caliber rifle, came rolling across the desert from Baum's position two hundred yards to the west.

Suarez and Dalton went for the house, Dalton a few feet in the lead, Suarez right behind him. Dalton heard Delroy Suarez clearly say "shit" just before something wet and hot and solid struck the back of Dalton's neck.

Another crack of distant thunder.

The Remington clattered through the door as he crossed the threshold, tripping him up. He fell forward and rolled as another silvery humming blur cracked the air a foot over his head and the kitchen table in the back room exploded in a spray of splinters before the round punched out through the kitchen wall.

A flash of motion darkened the door and Irene came racing in, her paws scrabbling on the hardwood floor just as a fourth round exploded through the wall just beneath the right-hand window.

Dalton could see a piece of evening sky through the gap. Then came a fifth round that carved a furrow across the floor before punching through it and smacking into the rocks beneath the house. Then . . . silence . . . and Irene huddled up next to Dalton's leg, her body shaking convulsively, uttering tiny yelping whimpers.

Of course.

Five rounds in the magazine of a Barrett.

He'd be reloading now.

How many rounds did Nicky Baum say he had for his Barrett?

A box of match-grade rounds was what he said.

How many rounds in a box?

No idea. Probably fifty.

But there was nothing, not a single thing, not even the engine block of that Dodge pickup out there (even supposing Dalton could reach it), that would stop a round from a Barrett 50 at two hundred yards. Not the cinder-block walls, even if they were filled with gravel in an energy-absorbing matrix. Not the fieldstones of the small fireplace. And Irene's touching faith in the round-stopping ability of Dalton's body (she was now shoving her damp bloody muzzle deep under his thigh) was sadly misplaced.

If this shooter— Face it, Micah: Nicky Baum was lying out there somewhere with his throat cut; the shooter was Moot Gibson. And if Moot Gibson wanted to empty the whole box of rounds into this place he could *literally* tear it apart.

The Remington lay on the threshold, just a few tantalizing feet away. In a last ray of the dying sun he could see spatters of Delroy Suarez's blood on the wooden stock.

He gathered himself, leaned into the opening, and snatched it back. Great. Now he could die with something to hang on to other than his dick.

He thought of the storm cellar, a stone-lined pit six feet deep under the floorboards in the kitchen. He decided against burying himself before he was actually dead. It seemed only fair that Moot would have to do the spadework, if that was how it turned out. One thing was certain, Moot Gibson was *not* taking him alive.

He looked at Irene, who had pulled her head out from under Dalton's leg when the shooting stopped. He'd shoot her first, he thought, because God only knew what a thing like Moot Gibson would do to a dog that had gone over to the enemy.

He leaned back, breathing hard, and considered the flat ceiling above him. Fremont said the roof was steel plate, and flat to catch the rainwater. As dangerous as that 50 was, there was still only one of them out there, which meant that if he could get out by the defilade side and climb onto the roof, he could at least see where the rounds were coming from, and with the Remington he had a fighting chance of taking out the shooter.

It took him three minutes to get Irene into the root cellar and himself up onto the roof. He belly-crawled over to the western side and raised his head to look over the shallow concrete lip.

He got a brief glimpse of the flat plain in front of him, glowing in the starlight, the black mountains a sawtooth line against the stars, a soft wind playing in the brush.

He saw a flicker of bright white light at the top of a shallow defile about three hundred yards out. He cradled the Remington and rolled to his right as a heavy round smacked into the ledge, blasting out a hole the size of a rain bucket.

He set himself up, moving fast, laid the Remington on the lip, got the crosshairs centered on that distant point, and fired off three quick rounds, working the bolt, feeling the rifle kick, sighting in again.

The rounds kicked up bits of stone and gravel in a tight circle around the spot where he had seen the muzzle flash.

Ten yards to the left of this spot he saw another white flare.

Moot had rolled away as soon as he had fired but it had taken him a few extra seconds to steady that oversized gun. The incoming round blew up a section of concrete about a foot from Dalton's head. The distant rumble of the rifle shot rolled across the plain.

Then silence again.

The wind sighing in the brush, and Irene howling below.

No more rounds from Moot's position, and therefore no returning fire from Dalton.

Given the tactical situation, the terrain, the absence of suppressing fire, Moot could not close in for a kill without exposing himself, could not fire without revealing his location, and could not stay where he was for long, since he had every reason to believe that Dalton would call for reinforcements.

In combat, a defender has the advantage, so long as he has food and water, morale, and ammunition. To attack requires three men for every single defender. Similar but not identical tactical problems now confronted Dalton.

Stalemate.

TIME PASSED.

The last glow of sundown faded away behind the Rockies. No more rounds came streaking in. No more cracks of distant thunder rumbled across the Bighorn Valley. Dalton stayed in place until it was completely dark, and then he climbed down off the roof and went in to comfort Irene, who had not ceased to howl since the firing had begun.

He showed a target, deliberately, to draw fire, if fire was to come, but in his heart he knew that Moot had pulled out a long time ago, probably a half hour after their final exchange of fire.

They came out of the house like the last two survivors of a plague, glad to be alive, afraid of what they would see, ashamed to be living among so many undeserving dead.

Irene, who seemed to be more of an optimist than Dalton, trotted over to Fremont's crumpled body and began to lick his upturned face.

If Fremont had been alive when he hit the ground, Dalton thought, then the last thing he would have seen was that fading sunlight high up in that deep violet sky. The idea gave him some comfort, although it in no way masked his pervading sense of complete and utter failure, his bitter realization that he had been outthought, outfought, outmaneuvered, and that he had not only failed in his original mission, which was to keep Willard Fremont alive, but that he had managed to contrive the senseless and pointless death of two more good men at the same time.

Delroy Suarez was lying on his left side, a heap of distorted limbs in a lake of thickening blood, just to the right of the door. The wall had been spattered with what had been inside his chest and neck when the enormous round plowed through faster than the speed of sound. He reached out and touched Suarez on the shoulder.

Suarez was still blood-warm, which meant that he had probably died about an hour after he was hit, which was quite an achievement for a man who had just taken a .50-caliber round.

Behind him Irene lifted her head to the sky and began to howl at the gliding crescent moon. She was still howling when Dalton threw the first shovelful of gravel onto Willard Fremont's upturned, staring face a long time later.

He buried Fremont and Suarez together, under the shade of the creosote shrub, and while he was doing it he took some grim satisfaction in the three solid hours of brute suffering it required to open the stony ground deep enough and wide enough to keep the two men from being dug up and defiled by coyotes and crows, or worse.

He did not put up a marker, and he disguised the graves as well as he could. If he lived through the rest of the week, he'd know the place when he came back.

If he didn't, he wanted to keep them safe from Moot Gibson.

After a rest, and a brief search, he found Nicky Baum's body under a stunted sage about twenty feet away from his sniper position.

His throat had not been cut.

He had been shot in the back of the head from some distance away, a single tiny entrance wound just where the spine meets the brainstem. No exit wound.

Probably a silenced subsonic single-shot long-barreled .22 pistol (the Agency favored the Ruger Mark 2) firing a hollow-point round, a classic covert-ops weapon. Although Dalton scoured the area in a fifty-yard radius, he never found a piece of brass.

It took a long time to bury Nicky Baum where he lay.

The Barrett was gone. There were some slight scuff marks in the soil, but Dalton was no tracker. All he could say for sure was the shooter had been alone, he was a very big man, he moved lightly, he wore cowboy boots, and the heel on the left boot was worn down on the outward side, which meant the man had an ankle problem and his gait was slightly pronated.

The same pronated left heel mark that Captain Bo Cutler of the Montana Highway Patrol had seen in the hillside outside Crucio Churriga's window in Butte last Saturday.

He followed the tracks backward to a hide about two hundred yards from Baum's body, a hollowed-out trough roughly the size of a big man. Cut sage branches had been set aside, and there were signs—including human scat, a urine-scented shrub, ashes from a cigarillo, and the traces of a small grain meal eaten cold—that told him the man had been lying in this position for two, perhaps three days.

In precisely the right position to counter the tactical plan that Dalton had laid out. Moot had seen it all coming: the placement of a long-range sniper in a spot where he would be firing out of the sun, the slow infiltration required to put two more men in blocking positions, and of course the need for an entry team to make the final assault.

It showed a professional grasp of small-unit tactics, and it also showed cold calculation; the Sterno cans in the truck and the fireplace, to fool overhead sensors, either satellite or light plane or a rifle-mounted infrared scope: drawing them in, setting them up.

Dalton stood looking down at this shallow gravelike depression and thought about what kind of man would lie in such terrible ground, tormented by every crawling thing, baking in the sun and freezing in the long starry night, cradling his covert .22 and feeding himself on crazy hate. What would drive such a man, what he would not expect, how he might be killed. The man's tracks faded into hardpan a few yards to the west, in the general direction of Mee-teetse. There was no point in trailing him in the dark. Dalton would just wander into a trap and die like a hapless fool. And although he felt that this would only be what he deserved, he now wanted to kill Moot Gibson far more than he wanted to assuage his guilt at still being alive.

Dalton policed up the spent Barrett casings, collected Baum's Beretta and his ID and what few personal effects he had brought to Wyoming, added them to his expanding collection of similar relics of the recent dead in the sack, picked up the framed drawing, shouldered the Remington, and walked away in the direction of the Greybull River.

Irene watched him go for about fifteen minutes, until he was little better than a darker shadow on a dark land. Then she looked around at the place, shook herself violently, and trotted off in the same direction. Irene was walking slowly behind him, her head down and her tail lowered, when Dalton reached the Greybull River. The car was still there. So were the keys. He had no idea why this should be so. He decided it was obvious that he was intended to live, and to go where he was led, for reasons that seemed right and fitting to Pershing "Moot" Gibson. This is called "hubris," after the Greek, and it is often fatal.

13 | wednesday, october 17
greybull motel
greybull, wyoming
8 a.m. local time

the phone woke him from a dreamless sleep, a black coma, jerking him upward from the blessed dark into a sun-filled motel
room with a bilious shag rug and an ancient Admiral television put
high up out of harm's way on a rusted metal shelf bolted to a dun-
colored concrete wall. He rolled over a large shapeless breathing
mound as he picked up the handset and sat on the side of the bed,
staring dully out through the blinds at a pale, winter-colored sun.

"Dalton here," he croaked.

"Micah. It's Sally."

"Hey . . . Sally."

Irene pushed her blood-matted shark-shaped head out from under the lime-green comforter, licked her lips, and whimpered at him.

"Is someone there with you?"

"Yes. Her name's Irene."

"Oh, Micah . . ."

"She's a wolf-shepherd cross. She didn't want to stay out at Moot's place. I guess she's sided with me. Have you talked to Jack?"

"No, and I haven't heard from him since the day you left for Idaho. I'm beginning to worry about him. I've tried his beeper, his cell, I even called his ex-wife. Did you know her name is Peach? She is not at all a peach, by the way. I'm thinking I should bring in Security—"

"Don't do that. Not yet."

"Why?"

"Because either Jack or Deacon Cather is playing some kind of game here. I know it. Jack set me up with Willard Fremont and now he's holed up somewhere hoping I'll take care of the problem."

"You're not saying that Jack has gone off the reservation?"

"No. But he's running me somehow. Who's in our loop on this?"

"Nobody. Other than Losses. For now . . ."

There was a long taut silence while she gathered her attention and forced her tears down. There would be grieving and recriminations and consequences—but not yet. Not quite yet.

"Well . . . sorry I'm snuffling . . . this is so hard. We haven't told the families yet. Nicky Baum was separated from his wife. Del's parents are in Tuscany right now, but we're not going to tell them what happened until we can figure out what did happen. Officially, I mean. This will all go to Losses and there'll be a hearing on it. Fremont was a bolt-on but Nicky and Del were fresh out of the Snake Eaters, and what happened to them will end up going all the way to the director of operations. But not yet, not as long as it's still an ongoing action. I told the duty desk that Jack Stallworth was running this from the road. I have no idea why. I guess I wanted you to have a free hand."

Dalton was grateful that Sally had not added the obvious "for all the good you've done with it."

"So this is still between you and me?"

"And Jack, when I reach him. Yes. Just the three of us."

"Do you still have those letters that Gibson wrote?"

"Yes. I do. They're right here."

"Can you dig them out for me?"

"Sure . . . just a minute . . . okay. Got it."

"In the final letter, you said Gibson was basically sending these incoherent scrawls, but you also said there were phrases. Names. Can you read them off for me?"

"I can fax the whole thing, if you want."

Dalton looked down at the desk phone, saw a sign for in-house fax service. "Yes, fax it to me here. You have the number. In the meantime, can you look up something for me?"

"Sure."

"It's a phrase. Write it down. 'To get the answer, you must survive the question.' Got that?"

"I do. What is it? Sounds like the Spanish Inquisition. You know, getting put to the question?"

"Yes. It does. Can you run it by someone in the geopolitical section? One of their cultural analysts? Someone with a good background in Native American religious beliefs?"

"Sure. I think Zoë Pontefract is in today. Vassar class of ninety-seven. She did her postdoctorate in Meso-American Studies."

"Perfect. Send her the drawing too."

"I will. And I'll fax the letter right now. Where will you be?"

"Here for another half hour. I have to shave, get some breakfast, figure out what to do with this dog here."

Irene, hearing the tone if not the reference to her, blinked at him expectantly, as if she understood. Or maybe she just knew what was usually meant by the word "breakfast."

"Then what? Because I hope you're not going—"

"Not directly at him, no. I need to find out what's in his head. What he's doing makes perfect sense to him, the way it does to most people who are insane. Killing Fremont, Runciman, what he did to

Pete Kearney and Crucio Churriga, probably the murder of Milo Tillman, all these acts have been highly organized, not the work of a disorganized schizophrenic. There's a map in his head. I want to be able to read it. If I can, then the next time we run into each other, I'll be there first, waiting for him."

"Why alone?"

"Because Gibson wants me alive. He'll kill everyone else."

"Why does he want you alive?"

Dalton had a brief flash of Pete Kearney's ruined face, the sockets of his eyes seething with squirming life, the walls of his cabin crawling with bloated flies in all the colors of spilled gasoline.

"I'll make it a point to ask him. Send the fax, Sally."

IT ARRIVED AT THE front desk of the Greybull Motel ten minutes later. The young Eastern Shoshone girl running the machine stared at it as she handed it across to Dalton, obviously curious and quite unashamed to show it. She actually craned her neck to look at it as Dalton held it in his hands. Dalton, his attention fixed on the letter, missed her intense interest. Although the letter was exactly as Sally had described it, what had been missing from the description was the violence of the line, the coarse brutality of the letters, the way the words had been carved, gouged into the paper itself.

"That's a weird drawing," she said, smiling at him, her broad, dark-skinned face and high cheekbones framing lively gray-green eyes.

Dalton looked up at her and realized that he had been lost in the letter. "Yes. Damn weird."

"Are you a sociologist?"

"A sociologist? Why do you ask?"

"I'm working for my degree in Bozeman. We had eight units in cultural anthropology and the professor was a sociologist. He looked just like you. He was interested in the Native American Church too."

"Was he? And how did you make that connection?"

She touched the center of the fax page.

"That's the symbol for Peyote, the Messenger. I mean, not the whole drawing, and it isn't very well done. Normally the roadman— he's like the priest? He does a very careful drawing of the god Peyote, sometimes in the sand. See there, it's just a kind of flower-looking thing and it's supposed to be a button. That's the button of Peyote. It's placed on a cross—I guess that's what this thing here is supposed to mean—but the cross is leaves of sage. The button and the cross of sage are placed on this—the crescent shape here. That's the altar. The altar is always shaped like a crescent. Then Peyote is covered with a scraping gourd, because Peyote likes the sound. Don't you already know this stuff?"

"No. I had no idea. What about the rest of this? Does it mean anything to you?"

She considered the scrawled words, the lines and arrows, chewing the inside of her plump cheek. She smelled of mint toothpaste and green-apple shampoo and he had a vision of Cora Vasari pushing her hair back from her fine-boned face as she counted his shaky drug-addled pulse in her villa in the Dorsoduro.

"Nope. Although I guess the stuff about answer, and question, and atonement, that would be part of the ritual. That's at the heart of the Native American Church, the ceremony of atonement."

"You mean, like a confession?"

"Sort of, but not like in the Catholic Church. In the Peyote ritual the priest hears your sins, each one, and for each one he ties a little knot in a piece of string. One sin, one knot. As many as it takes. The idea is you have to speak your sins out loud, in front of the others at the ceremony. That means you are releasing the evil spirit that lived in that sinful act. The sin goes into the string, and then they burn the string in a bowl. They call it asking the question, and if you answer falsely, then Peyote will punish you. If you want to hear Peyote's answer, you have to be pure, to have made your confession and to promise atonement, or you will not survive the question. Not like you'll explode or anything. But you could have a very bad experience under the influence of the drug itself, if Peyote is not pleased with you, or if you are false in your confession. But people usually pass this test—unless they've done something very, very evil—because Peyote, the Messenger, is a loving god. Then you're ready to hear Peyote's words, his message, as a new soul, someone without sin. But first you must confess and atone."

"Atonement is different from confession?"

"Oh yes. Confession is simply to declare your sins, whatever they are, no matter how terrible. Atonement means to try to make things

right, sometimes through your own suffering, or sometimes by going to the people you have hurt in your life and trying to undo that
hurt. I guess whoever made this drawing wants to make things right."

Dalton stared at the young girl as a passing eighteen-wheeler
drowned out all possibility of conversation. There is a hidden rose
by every dusty mile of road, he thought, deciding not to actually
kiss her.

"Well," he said, folding up the letter, "I learned a lot here. I can't
tell you how much I appreciate it."

"You're not a sociologist at all, are you?"

"No. Just a tourist."

She shook her head, smiling at him.

"No. Not a tourist. You have a shadow around you. You have been
with darkness. Perhaps you are a policeman. Can I say something to
you? It's none of my business, but I think you should know."

"Sure. Anything."

"This drawing at the top here, the word 'culebra' with those arrows pointed at it? That's called 'sign.' The arrows mean that there
is danger, and what the arrows point at is the source of that danger.
'Culebra' means 'snake' in Spanish, so the danger comes from a snake,
which could be a man or an animal—but the sign definitely means
danger. Like, mortal danger, you understand?"

Dalton, who knew what "culebra" meant, had not known the
meaning of the arrows, although the entire page literally shrieked of
lunatic killing rage. She drew back and regarded him with a gentle
but searching expression on her round, intelligent face.

"Well, I've said enough. I don't get a good feeling from that
drawing. There's stuff in there that goes way beyond the Native
American Church. I'm not a member. Shoshone are plains people.
We were in Montana long before the Sioux, the Cheyenne, and those
ugly Arapaho ever got there. We do the Sun Dance. Peyote belongs

to the Kiowa, the Apache, the Comanche. Many of these folk have maggots in their heads. You need to be careful around them."

HE WAS IN THE ROOM, packing, remembering the last time someone had used the term "maggots in the head," while Irene rapidly devoured a plate full of *huevos revueltos* and a side of refried beans.

He was trying to get the plate away from her before she ate that too, getting an accusatory look from her as he did it, when the phone rang again. It was Sally.

"I talked to Zoë Pontefract. She tells me the central drawing is the symbol for the god Peyote. He's the—"

Dalton stopped her, with some effort: she had done a lot of work and was not happy to be robbed of the chance to lay it out for him. He managed to fill her in on what the Shoshone girl had told him.

"Was she pretty?"

"Stunning. Did Zoë come up with anything beyond that?"

"Essentially, no. Although the ceremony your Shoshone girlfriend describes varies quite a bit from the chronicles of Fray Bernardino de Sahagún, who studied the Chichimec and Toltec versions—"

"But she would agree with what this girl is saying, basically?"

"I got the impression that Zoë thought the person who did the drawing was crazier than a bog rat. And I wanted to remind you, in case you have also forgotten, that this reference to 'snake eater' on the upper left? That's the Army term for Special Forces. You were one yourself, weren't you? So think hard about what that means. And Zoë says that the Native American Church does not encourage 'atonement' but only the forgiveness of sins and peaceful coexistence with your neighbors. Peaceful coexistence does not strike me as Moot Gibson's personal creed. Now what? Do you have to go join a Peyote cult?"

"What did she make of the stuff about Purgatoire and Culebra? Why is Purgatoire in French, for one thing?"

"She noticed that. She thinks the word refers to a river called the Purgatoire, which is in southeastern Colorado. The funny thing about the name is—"

"Where in southeastern Colorado?"

"Where? It starts in the Rockies, down by the New Mexico border, ends in the town of Lamar, up by the Kansas border; it flows mainly northeast through the Comanche National Grassland—"

"But this is where *Pinto* lived."

"Yes. That's right. As a matter of fact, the Purgatoire runs sort of parallel to the Timpas River, which runs parallel to a little creek called the Apishapa—"

"This is right in the *middle* of Pinto's territory."

"Yes, I think we've already established that. You may recall that we've also established that the Coroner of Munchkin Land, who thoroughly examined him, says he's not only really dead, he's really quite sincerely dead. Pinto, I mean. Not the coroner. Anyway, as I was saying, the Purgatoire runs northwest through the town of Trinidad—"

"Trinidad. One of Fremont's unit guys got lost in a storm in the hills around Trinidad. Milo Tillman. This is all *connected*. I know it."

"Connected to what?"

"These names. Trinidad. Goliad. The Purgatoire. *Horsecoat*. Wilson Horsecoat. He did the ID on Pinto's body, didn't he?"

"Wait a minute . . . yep. Wilson Horsecoat and Ida Escondido."

"These names. They fit together. Somebody with the Horsecoat name was writing letters to Sweetwater when he was in Italy. Trinidad. Goliad. I've seen them somewhere else. They're . . . damn, I can't *remember*."

"Micah, if you think this is vital, I can run a search string."

"Can you? Can you do it now?"

"Sure. I'll run the name Goliad, cross it with Trinidad."

"I need this right now, Sally."

"And you'll have it. Goliad . . . how do you spell it?"

Dalton spelled it out for her, and waited, staring absently, unseeing, down at Irene, who was staring right back up at him while using all of her considerable powers of telepathy to convey three simple words to Dalton:

Must.

Go.

Out.

The phone beeped and crackled for a time, and he could hear Sally's fingers on the keyboard, rapid-fire, staccato, and the rustle as she picked up the handset again.

"Okay. Maybe this is it. Dateline Monday, November seventeen, 1997: at five forty-five local time in eastern Colorado, a Consuelo Luz Goliad, age forty-nine, was killed in a multiple-car crash while traveling northbound on Interstate 25, near the town of Trinidad. Does this mean something?"

"Yes. I just don't know what."

"Well, there's a cross-reference to an article in . . . in the *Simi Valley Clarion* . . . by somebody named Barbra Goldhawk. Dated June fifteenth, 1998. I can only get the extract—wait—okay, this Goldhawk person was calling for the FBI to investigate what she was calling the suspicious deaths of Consuelo Luz Goliad and her husband, Héctor Rubio Goliad, who was a pilot in the Mexican Air Force. Any more? No, that's it. Nothing else. No FBI follow-up. And this Goldhawk woman is never heard from again, according to this."

"Simi Valley? That's near Los Angeles, isn't it?"

"Yes. Why?"

"Can I borrow something?"

"Sure. Name it?"

"The Gulfstream?"

friday, october 19
friendly village mobile home park
689 ridge view drive
simi valley, california
5 p.m. local time

t he brown-and-cream double-wide trailer was studded with large wooden butterflies the size of pterodactyls and was surrounded by a white picket fence made entirely out of recycled plastic. The creaking gate opened onto a large concrete rectangle painted lime green, along the edges of which sprouted dusty, faded bunches of plastic daisies and tulips and begonias and a flight of steps made of stacked blocks painted orange that led up to a rusted screen door with pink flamingoes for a frame. From inside the darkened interior he could hear a tinny radio playing "In the Mood" by Glenn Miller.

As he stood there listening, a large calico cat oiled up to his leg and began rubbing herself against him. Dalton was not fond of cats and he wished that he had brought Irene with him instead of leaving her back at Van Nuys Airport with the ex-Marine pilot who had made the flight from Greybull so gosh-darn memorable that, at several points en route, Dalton had considered shooting him in the back of his skull.

He gave the cat a not-so-discreet shove that lofted her into a patch of plastic petunias. Turning to face the door again, he found himself staring up into the disapproving glare of an age-spotted woman wearing a very loud Hawaiian shirt in coral and powder blue, pale pink terry-cloth short shorts, a hunchbacked crone with a corona of bright pink frizz around a thin liverish face deeply marked by sun damage, a face out of which shone two small black eyes bright with intelligence and ill-will.

She had a clear plastic oxygen tube that was looped around both ears, the tube running under her nose and down into a portable oxygen canister on rollers, and she had a raw-looking trachea implant that was partially covered by a filthy white neckerchief.

She glared down at him through the screen, raised a clawlike hand in which burned a Marlboro, stuffed the cigarette into her trachea implant, sealed her lips, pinched her nose shut with the other hand, and pulled a long lungful into her through the trachea port, doing so with obvious relish and clearly enjoying the effect this performance was having on her visitor. Then she exhaled it through her trachea tube again, a plume of pale-blue tobacco smoke that poured out through the screen and wandered off on the hot dry wind out of the nut-brown slopes of the Santa Susana Range far away in the northeast.

"Miss Goldhawk? I'm Micah Dalton."

She pressed a spiky knob-knuckled index finger against some sort of device attached to her tracheal implant and emitted a droning buzz that Dalton realized was electronically synthesized speech.

"You the spook? Let me see some ID."

Dalton showed her the impressive-looking ID the Agency gives you to show to people to whom the Agency does not want you to show your not-quite-so-impressive actual ID.

She had a pair of glasses—huge pink plastic ones with green parrots sitting on palm trees forming the frames—hanging from an amber-beaded necklace. She finally got them fixed in place and blinked down at his folio ID with rheumy eyes. She grunted and shoved the screen door open.

Dalton followed her into the cool, dank dark of her double-wide—a long barren room furnished in garage-sale odds and ends, smelling badly of the hanging stink of her Marlboros.

There was a kind of galley kitchen—surprisingly, quite spotless and clean—and beyond it, dimly seen through the haze, a narrow bedroom with a well-made bed and clothes hanging in orderly rows in an open closet. The entire front section of the trailer, and the only part of it in any kind of disarray, was taken up with a long table covered with stacks and heaps of paper: reports, drafts, letters, computer printouts, in the midst of which sat a brand-new pearl-gray Dell Inspiron laptop.

In front of the Dell was an old wooden office chair excessively padded with ripped and yellowing foam rubber. An ashtray beside the laptop was overflowing with stubbed-out butts and tubes of gray ash. A greasy tumbler half-filled with some amber liquid sat next to a large black cat with a chewed left ear, sitting on top of a stack of books and licking itself—a strong, lushing sound—with the kind of contemptuous disregard that only cats can convey.

The tomcat paused for a moment to consider—and disapprove of—Dalton, with one green eye and one yellow eye over a vertical hind leg, and then went back to his business, pink tongue rolling. Barbra Goldhawk put a finger to her voice box and buzzed at him.

"Fuck off, Woodstein. Company's come."

The cat straightened up, flared out, bared his oversized yellow fangs, hissed at her, and then flowed down off the desk, scattering her papers across the threadbare carpet. She dragged her little blue-

and-silver oxygen tank behind her—Dalton had a fleeting image of what R2D2 would be doing after he retired—and set it upright next to her chair, where, through a series of practiced gyrations, she got herself safely sat down without strangling herself on the oxygen tube. She leaned back in the chair, lips smacking, looking like a grizzled old Munchkin Madame about to broker a deal for a kinky night with Dorothy—Toto ten francs extra—staring at him through her glasses, her huge brown eyes blinking . . . blinking . . . blinking . . .

Dalton looked around for a chair, saw a milk box full of newspapers, dragged it over, and sat down.

"Writing a book," she buzzed at him. "Sorry for the mess. Beer's in the icebox, if you want one."

"No, thanks," said Dalton. "I appreciate your taking the time to see me. What's the book about?"

"You boys. Spooks. What complete fuckups you are."

"Can I help? I know a lot about fucking up. It's my life's work."

She blinked at him awhile, trying to figure out if he was being saucy, and decided that he was. She showed him her unnaturally even Chiclet-size teeth and clacked them at him again.

"Funny. I guess you were doing your stand-up routine in Vegas while those raghead muff-uckers were taking their flying lessons."

It took Dalton a few seconds to successfully decode "muff-uckers" and one more second for him to conclude that whatever else Barbra Goldhawk was, she was no *Paphiopedilum sanderianum*.

"No. I was in the Poconos. Got a publisher yet?"

"Yes. Me. I'm doing it myself."

She pushed some papers aside and showed Dalton a shiny computer CD.

"Seven hundred and sixty-three pages of pure muff-ucking Pulitzer. Unless you're here to try to stop me, son. Don't even try."

She leaned down and reached into the wastebasket, coming up with a small stainless-steel Llama .32 pistol with ivory grips and a gold-plated foresight. Dalton felt his vitals retracting as he stared down into the unwavering black dot of the muzzle.

"Not at all," he said, in an unsteady voice, thinking that if he died this way they'd bury him with his ass in the air and a plastic daisy stuck where the sun, in any decent, God-fearing world, ought never to shine.

"Good," she buzzed, lowering the muzzle and resting the little pistol in her lap. She crossed her legs and took a pull at her cigarette. "Well, what do you want? This about Connie Goliad?"

"Yes. Consuelo Luz Goliad. Died—"

This triggered a long dissertation in that electric buzz.

"Consuelo Goliad. Died in a multiple-car crash while traveling northbound on Interstate 25 near the town of Trinidad, Colorado, on Monday, November seventeen, 1997, at approximately five forty-five Mountain Time. I know her. I know a lot more than you think I do. And I got it filed away where you can't get it too."

"Look, Miss Goldhawk—"

"Call me Barbra, like the singer."

"Barbra—"

"You like Streisand, son?"

"Well . . ."

"Me neither. You ever hear of a place called Red Shift Laser Acoustic?"

"No. What is it?"

"It's a tech business, laser research, big outfit over there on Tierra Rejada Road, on the way to Ventura. They do government work, laser analysis. Pour me some of that Jamaica there, will you?"

Dalton looked around for the bottle.

"In the icebox," she buzzed at him, shaking her head sadly.

He opened the refrigerator and saw a half-full bottle of 150-proof black Jamaica rum lying on its side in a nearly empty fridge that gleamed as if brand new. He pulled it out and poured her a tumblerful. She found another tumbler on the floor beside her and offered it to Dalton, who filled it to the very brim.

She took a long, loving sip, smacked her lips, clacked her teeth together again—Dalton was going to pay for her implants out of his own retirement if he ever had to talk to her again—and then leaned back into the creaking old chair, gathering herself. Dalton lifted his own tumbler to his lips and took a tentative sip.

"Okay," she croaked, crackling a bit, "Red Shift Laser. Short story, they do real high-tech stuff, contracted out to Lawrence Livermore, CalTech. If you're really CIA you know exactly what I'm talking about. I was working for the *Clarion* at the time and this Consuelo Goliad calls me up one day—I was the feature reporter and I'd just done a big series on how screwed-up the security was at Livermore—which by the by the networks stole from me . . ."

She stopped to pull in some air and recharge.

". . . which they . . . stole from me . . . so Consuelo figured I'd be interested in what she had. Wanted me to meet her at some motel way out on the coast. I drove out there, she was this heavyset matron-looking woman with all this Navajo silver on her—a real Comanche she was, honest-to-God Indian—well, she was real upset . . ."

A gasping sigh . . . another . . . *please God don't let her die yet.*

". . . and I figured, well here's another one, you know, one of these cranks with a bug up her ear, all this la-di-da about government conspiracy, but I stayed to hear her out. You ever hear of Goyathlay's Throat?"

She might have been far older and even less redeemable than the glory of old France, as well as four-fifths into the crypt, but she was a reporter and she knew a poorly suppressed reaction when she saw it.

"I see you do. I find that interesting. I find that illuminating as all hell. Well, long story short, Connie Goliad was a member of this church, called the Native American Church—"

"I know it."

"Yes, I expect you do, if you know about Goyathlay's Throat. Anyway, not the regular branch of this church, but what you might call a breakaway sect. She didn't tell me all this at once, mind—I sorta got it outta her—but talking makes me tired. I had more stamina before the Internal Revenue folks cleaned me out."

"They did?"

She shot him a hard, cold look. "You know damn well they did," she buzzed at him. "And it was no muff-ucking coincidence neither. Happened right after I got onto the Goliad story—all of a sudden I'm being audited, three years in a row. They force me to go back nine years, nine muff-ucking years, young man. They bankrupted me, they ruined my . . . Anyway, that's all over with now, another sorry-ass old-broad story.

"This break-away sect, they had these things they called Goyath-lay's Throat, long clay tubes, about two feet long, real old. Ancient. Connie said they were turned on a wheel in the same tent where old Goyathlay would have his sing during the Peyote ceremony. She really believed that, you know, she revered this thing just like a Bible Belter would revere the personal pickled pecker of Jesus muff-ucking Christ himself. Anyway this clay tube she had, it was a gift from a roadman—a priest of her kin clan—"

"Did she tell you his name?"

"No, I don't think so. I was surprised that Connie was telling me all this, but it had to do with something she had seen going on at her company. She worked as an acoustic laser technician at Red Shift. Far as I could tell from what she told me—she was given to prattle, the dizzy old bint—anyway, Red Shift techies was trying to figure out what sort of coating would work to stop laser surveillance from reading what was being said inside a room. You know, it reads these tiny variations in the movement of the window, from a thousand yards, and it can hear what's being said. So Red Shift had come up with this film, looked like ordinary window tint, but it prevented all kinds of gear from peeping in on secret meetings. It's on the Pentagon glass right now, why it looks green."

Dalton waited her out, sipping at the rum, savoring the rich, dark tang of it. She had excellent taste in liquor, he decided.

"What this had to do with Goyathlay's Throat, she got it into her head that since this cylinder had been cast right in the same tepee as old Goyathlay was living in, then it stood to reason that the sound waves from Goyathlay's actual voice would sink into the wet clay as it was being turned on the wheel. You know about Hatshepsut's Tomb, over there on the banks of the Blue Nile?"

A hard left turn, but since he'd flown in from Greybull with a pilot who flew the way Barbra Goldhawk talked, he stayed in his seat. "Not really. What about it?"

"There's a big picture on the wall there, painted two thousand years before Christ, and it shows the Ka, the soul, of Amun himself, being turned on a potter's wheel by the ram-headed god Chin-um. Right there next to a portrait of old Queen Ahmose. Interesting, isn't it? So this is sorta like what Connie and her clan believed. That the soul, the voice, of Goyathlay himself had seeped right into the walls of this cylinder."

She stopped short, and went a long way inside herself, her skin going blue-white and her cheeks flushing.

"Get me my puffer, will you, son?" she said, after a long silence.

"Where is it?"

"In the bedroom . . . table . . . by . . . the . . ."

He stumbled to the back of the trailer, scattering kittens and cats, and found the blue plastic ventilator on a TV tray by her cot. She had her hands out as he came down the hall and stuffed the mouthpiece into her tracheal tube, pressing down on the plunger. After a few gasping heaves her skin grew less deathly and the flush faded from her cheeks.

"Sorry. Not smoking enough, I guess. Say it'll kill me, but it hasn't yet. Pass me a cigarette, will you?"

"Maybe you should hold—"

"Maybe you should hold your tongue, kiddo. Pass me a smoke."

Dalton reached for the Marlboros, pulled one out. He even held the lighter like a gentleman as she sucked the cigarette alight through her tracheal implant. She laid her hand on top of his and flashed him a ghastly coquettish leer as she did so.

"Okay . . . now . . . what all this has to do with Red Shift is that Connie Goliad figured—this was back in early ninety-seven—that if she could find some reason to stay late a couple nights (she sorta ran her own bench with nobody over her shoulder so long as she got her reports in), then she would have access to this top-secret laser scanner thingy that could read the most minute variations in the surface of things. She figured if she set this Goyathlay's Throat thing into the machine, she could find out if there really were sound waves embedded in the clay."

"And were there?"

"Hard to say. She got a lot of random variations that the machine translated as white noise. Tried the same thing with the cylinder spinning at the same rate as it would have spun while it was being made, and she *did* get some weird rhythmic sounds out of it, kind of a droning singsongy sound, sorta like somebody tuning a church organ. She played me a tape of it and it did sound sorta like chanting. But that's not what her real beef was. While she was there in the lab running this stuff, her husband, Héctor, he was a pilot trainer in the Mexican Civil Air Patrol, he was wandering around the lab, waiting to drive her home, and he happens to be sitting at this computer trying to make it access the Net, when he looks up and he sees through the window that the manager's computer has turned itself on. All by itself. You follow?"

Dalton said nothing, although the idea that a computer would turn itself on in the middle of the night did not, in this Microsoft world, strike him as more sinister than his McAfee program doing exactly the same thing at four in the morning to a billion other computers.

"So he calls across to Connie, who goes into the office. Security there was lousy. And she sees that this remote computer is talking to the manager's machine. She pings the remote and sees all these interval linkages come up. Well, here she told me a lot of technical bull crap that she might as well have told to old Woodstein over there—for Chrissake leave off lickin' your dick, Woodstein, 'fore you wear it to a nubbin! But it seems like she was able to determine that some machine in Paris, France, belonging to an Anglo-French consortium called FrancoVentus Mondiale—she Googled them and found out they designed turbojet engines—she realizes that this machine was exchanging what looked to her like encrypted technical data with the Red Shift mainframe."

"Did she think this was routine?"

"No. And it damn well wasn't either. She knew the entire Red Shift client list backward, and besides, Red Shift had what she called an Umbra-level security wall that directly forbade them from having any direct Internet linkage with any foreign firms. It was designed to prevent the illegal transfer of technology that might end up in the wrong place, North Korea or China for instance."

"I know something about it."

"I'll bet you do. So do I. It's called Echelon, isn't it? Run by the NSA. Don't bother shining me on with those movie-star looks. I know a con artist when I see one. Anyhow, Connie decides that the security of Red Shift has been broken. They been hatched into by a hatcher—"

"A hacker?"

"Hatcher, hacker, tallywacker. Some freaky-geeky spy boys of some sort. Her husband agrees with her, and they, being poor ignorant beaners and redskins and not knowing Penobscot from the Pentecost, well don't they get all patriotic and call up the Red Shift chief of security, this Latino ex-FBI dorkwad named Zigismond D'Escarpa—known in the Red Shift cafeteria as Sigmoid O'Scopa, because he was always looking up somebody's ass for security breaches. There's a good one in there somewhere. Security breaches. Security britches. Well, when it comes to me, I'll call you. Anyway, Sigmoid, he comes down on them like a ton of bricks."

"Not grateful?"

"Grateful? It was all Connie could do to hold on to her job. Tampering with the mainframe. Use of company facilities without permission. Breach of confidence. Espionage—"

"They didn't believe her?"

"No. Sigmoid and the techies ran a complete hard-drive scan and rechecked all the traffic logs going back six years. Turned Red Shift upside down for three and a half months, during which she was suspended without pay and her husband had to go back to training pilots in Guaymas to pay the mortgage. In the end it all came to nothing: they declared that there had been no breach and they told Connie to just forget all about it. Even let her come back to work."

"And that was the end of it?"

Goldhawk sent him a look. "She's dead, isn't she?" she beeped at him in that robot voice. "'Long with Héctor, who has himself a— But I'm getting ahead of myself. More rum."

Dalton filled her up again and took a sip of his own while she gathered her narrative line again, her wrinkled old face bright with cheerfully malicious intelligence.

"Thanks. Smackety-smack, eh? Nice stuff. One-fifty proof too, goes down smoother'n an altar boy on the Bishop of Nîmes. Where was I?"

"They let Consuelo Goliad go back to work?"

"So they did, and for a time it looked like that was all there was to it, except that she started to have problems at the bank. All of a sudden her line of credit is being 'reconsidered' by the bank and a couple of her cards are called. Short story is she realizes that the Red Shift management is trying to destroy her. Héctor gets demoted down there in Guaymas from flight instructor to maintenance pilot, all these little things going wrong, and she figures, okay, this is a covert thing here. The brass at Red Shift, the manager anyway, is a spy. She figures he's selling critical defense data to these folks at Franco-Ventus in Paris—"

"Why them?"

"They're frogs, aren't they? Cheese-eating surrender monkeys. So bent they can piss around corners. All that European Union crap, standing up to the good old United States of America? Like I said, she was a true patriot, the sap. So she figures she's gonna take this to another level. Screw the Feebs, she's gonna do a Bunny Berrigan—"

"Bunny Berrigan?"

"The rogue priest who stole a bunch of government secrets and took them to the press. The Pentagon Papers? Like that."

"Bunny Berrigan was a band leader. I think you mean Daniel Ellsberg?"

"There you go. So she's gonna do an Ellsberg, take this to the press, like, so she comes to me with the whole sorry sack of grief."

"What did you do with it?"

"That's my point. I was working up the pitch to my editor, getting my sources nailed down, and checking Connie's story. Much as I could: Red Shift wouldn't even return a phone call. Then I get this message from Connie: her husband Héctor, he's flying a check-out night mission on some kinda single-prop job they use for skimming the grow ops they got down there along the border outside of San Ysidro. What you call an instrument flight? Whammo! He flies right into a transmission tower outside of Ojos Negros and gets fried like a jumbo shrimp. You ever wonder why they call 'em jumbo shrimp? I mean, a shrimp is supposed to mean tiny, right. Like a shrimp, but then they—"

"When was this?"

"When was what?"

"When was Héctor killed?"

"Wednesday, October twenty-nine, 1997. Well of course Connie's hysterical. She's convinced that the Red Shift boys have somehow rigged this thing. And she's sure she's next. Now I'm trying to calm her down. I need her to hold her act together, because my editor is saying he won't print word one until he meets with Connie up close and personal. Says this story could sink the *Clarion*. But Connie can't be gentled up on this. She says she's got all the papers, got the proof right there, and she's gonna hightail it up to Comanche Station and go to ground there."

"Consuelo was part of the Goliad clan in Timpas, wasn't she?"

"That's right. And that part of Colorado is wide-open grassland with nothing but other Comanche clans around. She figured she'd be safe there, stay low and let me work out the tactics here in Simi Valley. . . ."

Her buzzing narrative trailed off and her skin color changed from a hectic flush to a shiny yellow like old parchment.

"Are you okay? Can I get you something?"

She looked at him for a while through her thumb-stained glasses and Dalton could see that her eyes were welling up.

"I'll tell you something, son, I was a good reporter. I may not look it now, but I took my job for real. I know I was just a small-timer for a sellout rag, but this story meant something to me. Story like this comes along maybe once in your whole career, and this one was mine, and I liked Connie. Not just as a source, but for what she was. She cared about her work. She loved her country, and she come to me looking for justice. And all I did was get her killed. Course they made it look like an accident, a big pileup in the snow over there on I-25. Her Jeep rolls over and she breaks her neck. But it was a killing, plain and simple."

"Who was behind it?"

She rallied a bit, wiping her eye with a tissue and then balling it up and throwing it into a corner.

"Who you think? Those sons a bitches at Red Shift. They killed her, sure as gnats got nits. Set her up neat as napkins. In the doing of it the careless pricks also killed five innocent people and left three others crippled for life. Got their names by heart too. Wanna hear 'em?"

"Yes. I do."

Let's see . . . Aside from Connie Goliad, dead at the scene, there was Alice Conroy, twenty-nine, research doctor on her way to Denver for a new job in advanced pediatric oncology. God knows how many lives she mighta saved if she lived. And in the red Fiat with her a guy named Declan Hearne, a thirty-five-year-old ski instructor she was engaged to marry. And Jewel Escondido, thirty-six, along with her one-year-old daughter Amber, they were in a pickup got pushed right off the bridge and fell a hundred feet into the Purgatoire—"

"Jewel Escondido?"

"Yeah. Escondido. She was a bank teller from Pueblo, on her way down to Raton to visit her mother, who was in a cancer hospital down there."

"You happen to recall what her mother's name was?"

"Jeez . . . it's in my files. She was at the funerals. I'd have to—"

"It wasn't Ida, was it?"

"Ida? Ida . . . Ida . . . yeah, it could have been Ida. Why?"

"No reason. Just trying to make it real."

Barbra gave him a hard look then, her eyes narrowing, and opened her mouth as if to push the question, but she let it pass.

"Oh it was real enough. Little baby Amber fell all the way to the river's edge still tied up in her car seat. Hit facedown. I saw the shot from when the state boys turned the carrier over. Little girl's face was so much raspberry jam. One of the cops threw up, so they told me. And another woman—odd name, Silken Kir—she went into a coma on her way to the hospital and died six weeks later. She left three kids under ten and an unemployed husband who had both legs amputated after his combat patrol took a mortar round in Basra. Crippled for life were Tadeo Hiruki and his father Takeo, along with an old priest from Mission San Labré out in Montana. All that grief, you know? All of it going out in ripples, like. Kills me to think of it, even now. They got clean away with it too, those shits at Red Shift. Still have, all these years later. You go on over to Tierra Rejada Road and see for yourself. Can't miss it. This big mission-style bunch of buildings all done in adobe like they was the Alamo. Sixteen miles of razor wire all around it and you can't even drive up the road to the gate without a big old Hummer stuffed with pumped-up yard bulls cuts you off sharp and asks you to state your fucking business. No, they killed her, sure as death and taxes."

"Didn't you follow up?"

"Didn't I follow up? I called the FBI, I called the CIA, I even called *The New York Times*. Never even got a call back. Not one. You know how I know they killed her? She had all her papers sent along to FedEx? Everything she had printed out from Red Shift, records of this remote computer in Paris, the whole shebang, with the instructions to hold on to the packet until she gave instructions on where it was supposed to go. The Colorado cops jerked it away from FedEx and put it in storage, all righty-tighty. In January of ninety-eight Red Shift filed a claim to recover the documents, but I raised a lotta hell, called the court clerks so often the judge told the deputies to keep her stuff in storage until the ownership could be decided. And in February of ninety-eight the place was robbed. All her documents, everything that was in her Jeep? It was stolen. Nobody was ever caught. Stuff was never seen again. If that doesn't sound like an inside job, I don't know cat piss from soda pop. No, you run it all together, look at the timeline, you see it plain for what it was."

"An assassination?"

"Yep. To cover up a spy operation right spang in the middle of one of America's most important high-tech sectors. Right here in Simi Valley. And I couldn't do a damn thing about it."

"You could have written the story anyway?"

"Tried, didn't I? Tried my damnedest. Editor said without the witness, without the papers, it was too risky. He was right too. Anyway, after that, I sorta lost heart. I was being audited by the feds by then, like I told you, and the editor was hired away to work for the *L.A. Times*. The *Clarion* got new owners. Things started to slide for me personally. I got fired for drinking, or so they said, although I never missed a deadline. Well, I suppose the biggest news story of my life just fizzled out. Which is the story of my actual real life too, I guess."

Here she came to a natural pause and sat back, exhausted by her story and by the excitement of his visit, by the chance that after all these years vindication had come calling. She drained off her glass, set it down on the desk, placed the little pistol beside it, and buzzed at him.

"So what you gonna do with all I told you, son? You really gonna get the CIA off its ass? It's not too late, you know. I could let you have my files. They're all on this CD here. Everything there is to know about that accident, personnel records from Red Shift. You could take it all to Langley. Nail those treasonous bastards."

She held up the CD, breathing hard, and Dalton knew the book she was going to write was never going to happen. He took the CD from her skeletal fingers and she closed them over his hand, pressing hard.

"You're more than just a pretty boy, else I would never have blabbed on like I did this afternoon. This thing here, it's all I have left to give to anybody. Kids don't call. Friends all dead. I'm in the end of days here. I was gonna win . . . a Pulitzer. . . ."

She released his hand and fell back into her chair, her eyes closed, wheezing through her trachea implant. Woodstein jumped up on her desk and stared at her for a while before turning his impassive gaze onto Dalton.

"Barbra . . . ?"

She opened her eyes, waved him away, and went deep inside herself again. A hot wind stirred the drapes and the cooler ticked away like an old clock in the corner. Her lips were blue and her eyes, when closed, looked purple and sunken. The image of death itself was almost visible there, just beneath her skin, like a face rising in a pool.

Dalton pulled her laptop around, placed the CD inside the slot, put a blank disk in the burner, copied it, and placed the original on the pile of papers in front of her. He reached out and stroked Woodstein a couple of times. The cat arched, pressing against him, and then pulled away. The cat crept slowly into her lap, she placed one bony hand on his back, and in a moment they were both asleep. Dalton turned the fan on them, touched her cheek with the tips of his fingers, and left.

AIRBORNE AGAIN, rising up over the Rockies with the sunset a thin turquoise band far behind them, Irene staring out the porthole as the earth turned beneath them like a whale sounding in a limitless ocean of the purest blue, Dalton put Barbra's CD into his laptop and opened it up.

It was all there: her notes, scanned in and perfectly organized, cross-references, websites noted, copies of transcripts, letters, all of the material laid out and charted through a general menu.

Clearly she had been—still was—a great investigator, and given any chance at all she would have made this story a national sensation. But of course she never had any real chance at all, because the entire intelligence community was lined up against her.

She was lucky to be alive.

Halfway down the menu he came across a file marked "Accident Photos." He clicked on it and found a file folder filled with JPEG images of the multicar accident scene on Interstate 25, some of them images from the Accident Reconstruction Team of the Colorado State Police, and others apparently done by a stringer for one of the local papers.

Taken from various angles, they showed a tangle of cars and trucks, dimly seen through a screen of flying snow, a close-up of a Mercedes, its rear end crushed by the blunt nose of a flatbed trailer, another shot of a cube van sitting literally on top of a small red Fiat, another that showed a wide gap in the barrier, apparently torn open by a vehicle, another shot, taken from the bridge, showing a pickup truck lying on its roof on a shoal of boulders at the edge of the Purgatoire River a hundred feet below, a smaller red plastic object close by it.

More random shots of people standing around, looking stunned or avid or simply curious, depending on their natures, here a shot of the first patrol cars arriving. Cops deploying. Now the ambulances. A fire truck: a hundred different images showing the long line of cars and trucks lined up on both sides of the Interstate.

And a medium shot of a man standing beside the open door of his eighteen-wheeler, part of the door visible, a sign saying FREIGHTWAYS. The man's expression was unreadable, opaque, even guarded, as he stared into the lens, his mouth half-open as if to voice some objection and his other hand halfway to his face as if he had intended to shield it from the camera.

Under this shot was a notation that read:

DALE FRANCIS FETTERMAN??
FREIGHTWAYS DRIVER / MATERIAL WITNESS??
CURRENT LOCATION UNKNOWN??

Dalton stared at the image of a much younger Willard Fremont for a long while. Fremont had told him that "Fetterman" was one of his operational covers.

Somebody in the Agency had decided that Consuelo Goliad had to go away (the reasons for that weren't yet clear—something to do with Red Shift Laser Acoustics and FrancoVentus Mondiale)—but it was damned clear to Dalton that they had put Fremont's unit on the job.

Fremont had told him that they had never actually executed anyone, but they sure as hell killed Consuelo Goliad. Along with a whack of other people. Bystanders. Innocent bystanders, including two members of the Escondido clan, one of whom was related to Ida Escondido.

And Ida Escondido was one of the two people who ID'd the corpse of Pinto Escondido out there at Comanche Station.

The other one was a kid named Wilson Horsecoat.

Comanche Station.

Dalton reached up, touched the intercom buzzer.

Irene turned to stare at him, her jaws wide, her eyes white around the rims. She had been scrubbed and cleaned and fed and walked and given a mild tranquilizer but she still look terrified and lost. He rubbed her behind the ear and she licked his wrist.

"Yes sir?"

"We're not going back to Langley yet, Mike."

"No problem, sir. Where to?"

"Southeastern Colorado."

"How about Colorado Springs? We can land at Schriever Air Force Base?"

"No. I need a civilian airport."

"Nearby?"

"Near as you can make it."

"Okay. Let me punch it up. Will Pueblo do? They got an airport there that can handle a Gulfstream."

"Pueblo's fine."

saturday, october 20
comanche station
two miles west of timpas, colorado
comanche national grassland
7 p.m. local time

there was a bank of snow cloud resting on the distant peaks of the Rockies far off in the west, but out here on the edge of the Great Plains the air was hot and dry as Dalton wheeled his rented pickup into the haphazard little collection of shacks and trailers and bungalows at the end of a long arrow-straight gravel road. The wind stirred up a sea of long yellow grass, a great golden plain that reached out for miles in every direction, an ocean of rippling light as the day was closing. He parked the truck in front of a low wooden structure that had once been whitewashed but was now the color of bleached bone.

In the shade under the porch roof three ancient leathery-looking men, all in faded jeans and dusty boots and cowboy hats or rumpled ball caps, leaned back in their chairs, their hard, pinched faces closed and wary, watching grimly as Dalton climbed out of the truck, fol-

lowed by Irene, who trotted off across the dusty hardpan to investigate a stand of stunted cottonwood trees.

A flag bearing the profile of a Plains Indian surrounded by rays of
light and embroidered with the words "Comanche Station" flapped
in the wind, and from inside the building came the sound of country music, a Dobro endlessly moaning as a woman with a drawling
sensual voice lamented her taste in lovers as she lay fearfully awake in
her double-wide listening to an angry drunk pounding on her door.
Dalton climbed the withered old stair boards and stopped in front
of the three old men, who looked up at him without any sign of life
or interest.

"I'm looking for a boy named Wilson Horsecoat," said Dalton.
"I'm told he can be found here most evenings."

"Who's looking?" said the man on the far left. His skin was as dry
and cracked as a Gila monster's and he had small, sharp teeth stained
golden brown. He seemed to have the power around here, and the
other two looked blankly out at the sea of yellow grass as if Dalton
had simply snapped out of existence.

"The name is Micah Dalton."

"That she-wolf yours?"

Dalton looked back into the street. Irene was sitting a few yards
away, on her haunches, staring up at the porch.

"She's with me. But she's not mine."

"What's her name?"

"Irene."

"She looks snake-mean. I like a snake-mean dog. No use else
they snake-mean. Buy her from you, if you want. I'm Bill Knife. This
is my place. No whites allowed in here. No offense."

"None taken, Mr. Knife. Is Wilson Horsecoat inside?"

"Might be. Might not. Can't say. What you want with him?"

"Just some personal business."

"You federal?"

"Yes."

"What kind of federal?"

Dalton reached into his leather jacket and pulled out his Agency ID. He leaned down and held it out. Bill Knife leaned forward to squint at it, and then looked back up at Dalton.

"You ain't a Goddam Feeber then?"

"No sir."

"Hate the Feebers. Terrible folk. Deaf. No ears on 'em at all."

"That's been my experience."

"Has it?"

"It has."

"Well. What's a spook from D.C. want with that young fool?"

"A talk. Nothing more."

Bill Knife studied Dalton for a time, recognizing incoming trouble and mildly curious to discover its precise nature.

"Wilson is in there, if you want to go bring him out."

"I can go inside?"

"My place, isn't it? Watch his hands there, son."

Dalton sketched a salute to Bill Knife, looked briefly at the other men, who continued to stare impassively out at the moving sea of grass, and then he called to Irene, who snapped her panting jaws shut and came racing up the steps to stop beside him, looking tense and eager.

He pushed open the screen door and held it for Irene, who padded into the cool dark of the interior. The broad wooden-walled room was filled with a scattering of couches and wooden chairs, facing every which way, with a few card tables here and there, an ancient fridge wheezing away in the corner.

The four lean, rangy young men inside—there were no women visible—had all fallen silent as Dalton and Irene came into the room. The radio had been turned off a while back so they could hear the conversation out on the porch. They were now leaning back in their chairs, staring at him, using the same slack-jawed hard-eyed war face that young men all over the world have copied from the movies.

They all looked range-hard and capable and frankly Dalton didn't give a bucket of horse spit how they looked. In the center of their circle there was a low, rough-hewn table filled with empty beer bottles. The shabby room was thick with hanging smoke. It smelled of sweat, chili, and beans. Warm beer. Teenage testosterone.

"Afternoon," said Dalton. "I'm looking for Wilson Horsecoat."

"That your wolf bitch?" said one of them, a lean Comanche boy, rather horse-faced, with red-rimmed staring eyes, his long greasy black hair held back from his high pockmarked forehead by a silver conch.

"You Wilson Horsecoat?"

"Who the fuck is he?"

"You are."

"Who says."

"Mr. Knife."

"Bill Knife can suck my cock."

The other three hooted at this and the boy with the long black hair showed Dalton his teeth, fine and strong and vivid against his muddy brown skin. His eyes were twitchy and his pupils too small for a dark room but he seemed to be reasonably straight. Dalton looked at the boy's hands, veined and knotted, and at the butt of the Ruger pistol they were resting on. Irene, who had been sitting near Dalton's leg, got to her feet and started to emit a low purring growl. The laughter stopped.

"You leash that bitch," said the boy, "or I'll shoot her."

"Get up."

"What?"

"You're Wilson Horsecoat. Get up."

"So I'm Wilson Horsecoat. So fuck you."

No one saw him move; it was as if Dalton's Colt had just materialized in his right hand. He leveled it at Horsecoat's nose.

"You," he said, looking at one of the other boys. "Reach over and lift that Ruger out of his belt. Put it on the floor and kick it over."

The boy leaned over, tugged the pistol loose, holding it with the tips of his fingers, set it down on the scarred floorboards, and shoved it across to Dalton, who had never taken his eyes off Horsecoat. Dalton picked the Ruger up and studied it for a moment.

"Where did you get this?"

"It's mine, fuck-nuts. I had it for years."

"This is a silenced Ruger Mark Two. It fires subsonic 22-caliber hollow-points. It's a covert assassination weapon and simply being in possession of one will get you a federal twenty years. It can't be bought anywhere in America."

He hefted it, glancing at the slide.

"This particular weapon was modified for the CIA by a custom armorer in Alexandria, Virginia. This broad arrowhead is his personal trademark. This weapon was taken from an agent of the CIA and the fact that you have it opens you up to a charge of murdering an intelligence operative in a time of war. The penalty for that is death. And I have reason to believe that this weapon was used a couple of days ago to shoot a Special Forces soldier in the back of the head. Stand up."

Horsecoat stood, knocking his chair over, trying for cold icy threat but barely reaching surly. The other three men stayed put, looking down at the table, hands in their laps. Dalton got the impression that Wilson Horsecoat had no friends in this room.

"Let's go."

"Go? Go where?"

"For a drive."

"A drive the fuck where?"

"You're going to show me a grave."

"Whose grave?"

"Pinto Escondido's grave."

THEY DROVE WEST into the rising night, across miles of rolling flat-land, following two narrow ruts worn into the hide of the earth it-self. In the far west the Rockies were a towering wall of peaks, black against the evening sky. The pickup pitched and bounced across the plains. In the space behind the front seat Irene sat quietly, staring hungrily at the back of Wilson Horsecoat's head. Horsecoat sat slumped against the passenger door, unsuccessfully affecting disdain and contempt, his left knee jumping rapidly.

Dalton pulled out his cell phone, dialed Sally Fordyce.

"Micah? Where are you?"

"Colorado. I need you to run a serial number for me."

"Sure. Hold on . . . okay. Let me have it."

Dalton lifted the Ruger up and read the maker's markings off the slide, and the serial numbers under it. Horsecoat was staring at him, his face bony and frightened.

"Okay. Got it. It's out of our armory at Alexandria. Suppressed Ruger Mark 2. Issued to . . . Agent Milo Tillman. Requisition franked by Bob Cole. Tillman's unit commander. Both men marked deceased. Weapon lost in 'ninety-seven. Never recovered."

"When was it issued?"

"Let's see . . . September seventeenth, 1994."

"Thank you, Sally."

"You're welcome. What are you doing in Colorado?"

"Hunting," he said, and he closed the phone.

"Was that about me?" asked Horsecoat. "What did they say?"

Dalton stared out at the oncoming grassland and said nothing. Hard dry grasses whisked and rustled along the underbody of the truck, and out here away from the town the air was cool and clean and smelled of sweetgrass. Wilson Horsecoat smelled strongly of fear. After a few miles, as Dalton expected, Horsecoat had to speak, if only to find some comfort in the sound of his own quavering voice.

"Come on, man. What's this all about, anyway?"

Dalton said nothing.

"You can't do this, you know. I got rights."

Nothing.

"Man, you know, you're so *totally* fucked, man."

Nothing.

"You don't know who's coming for you, do you? I got heavy people on my side, man. Hard guys. You think you're a hard guy? You're a fuckin' pussy."

"How far?"

"How far to what?"

"Pinto's grave."

"It's just up there, by the Little Apishapa. See it?"

Dalton stared out at the plains, into the cones of his headlights. There was a low rocky mound a thousand yards out. Some sort of pole had been stuck into it, and a scrap of cloth flickered in the wind. Irene began to whimper. Dalton turned to stroke her flat blade-shaped head. She was shaking now and her nose was working, her nostrils wide, breathing in, her broad chest heaving, her eyes wide.

"What's with the bitch?" asked Horsecoat.

"She smells something."

"Fuck yeah," he said, with a honking snigger. "Fucking corpse, man. Guts bubbling. Worms crawling. Eyeballs rotting. That's what that cunt-dog is smelling."

They reached the mound in a few minutes. By now Irene was trembling violently and her mouth was wide open, her pink tongue working. Dalton brought the truck to a halt a few yards from a mound of river rocks about five feet high and eight feet long. A pole had been driven into the top of the mound and a small flag, red, carrying the crest of the United States Marine Corps, shredded by the endless prairie winds, fluttered and snapped at the top. As he opened the driver's door Irene scrambled out of the cargo space and vaulted out of the truck. She raced across the sweetgrass and clambered up onto the rock pile, her head low, snuffling and growling. Out in the darkness a coyote yipped. Bats flicked and whipped in the sky, small fleeting patches of utter black against a glowing field of countless stars.

Horsecoat got out of the pickup and came around to within a few feet of Dalton, staring at the mound, watching Irene as she padded up and down the mound, whimpering, scratching.

"What's with your dog?"

"She's not my dog."

"Whose dog is she?" he finally asked.

"She belongs to the man in that grave. Moot Gibson."

Horsecoat's body tensed and he said nothing for a time. "Yeah?" he said, defiantly. "And who's Moot Gibson when he's at home?"

Dalton looked at the skinny young man, his hands shoved into his back pockets, his face shiny with sweat. Irene stopped moving, sat back on her haunches, lifted her muzzle to the stars, and began to howl. The skirling, soaring wail rose up and echoed across the plains. The far-off coyote stopped yipping and the bats fluttered away.

Irene, settling deep into her grief, howled and howled.

"Shut her up, will you. Cunt-dog's giving me the creeps."

"You talk like that again and I'll knock you down."

They stood there, listening to Irene, for a long while, and then Horsecoat shook his head.

"Can I say something?"

"If it's polite."

"You're CIA, right?"

"That's right."

"Are you here for Pinto?"

"You told the Colorado state cops that Pinto was dead."

More silence, while Horsecoat tried to work out a way of dealing with his present situation; although barely twenty-seven, he'd had years of practice in the deceitful arts, honing his manipulative powers on a succession of band counselors and social workers and youth justice advocates and probation officers, and although he wasn't brave he had a lot of low cunning, which is sometimes a lot more useful, at least in the short run.

"That true, what you said about the Ruger?"

"Yes."

"I can go to death row just for having it?"

"Absolutely. And I will personally guarantee it."

"Did a guy really get shot in the head a couple a days ago?"

"Yes. With this gun."

"But I didn't *have* it a couple days ago. I loaned it to a friend."

"What friend?"

"What's in it for me if I talk to you?"

"I won't kill you."

Some sort of sly internal voice persuaded Wilson Horsecoat that now was the right time to show Dalton a little 'tude, a touch of moxie.

Horsecoat was poorly advised.

"Hey! Lick my dick, you fag. You can't do nothing to me."

Dalton looked at him, at the young man's bony underfed body, his thin pretense of street fighter's toughness. He backhanded the boy across the cheekbone, knocking him backward into the sweet-grass.

He scrambled to his feet and backed away from Dalton.

"I told you not to swear," said Dalton, his tone gentle.

"Are you *nuts*? Do you *wanna* die?" he said, his voice breaking, his round eyes showing white. "I'm not the problem. It's not me. It's Pinto. He's the *problem*. I talk to you, Pinto will come for me."

"Pinto's not here. I am. Why did you kill Moot Gibson?"

"I didn't. Pinto did it."

"Why?"

Dalton watched while the young man worked out the angles, the desperation clear in his pale wet face. There had to be a way to handle this, he was thinking, some way to get around it. He looked at Dalton's stony face, his cold hard stare, and saw nothing there but sudden death. It was either die now or *maybe* die later, and *maybe* dead later was way better than certainly dead here and now. Hell, it really didn't matter *what* he told this mean-tempered son of a bitch, because Pinto was going to gut and flay the guy before first light no matter what happened here. The idea here is stay alive, keep the guy talking, and shuffle the deck. He shrugged, wiped his face with both hands.

"Okay. Why not? Pinto needed the guy's *life*. He needed to *be* Moot Gibson. So he could move around and do what he had to do. Pinto's an ex-con, got no passport. Gibson had all of that. They were about the same size, and Gibson had real tanned skin, wore his hair long, dressed like a Wannabe Indian, so Pinto killed him. Made it look like a suicide. Out there in that pickup. Windows open so the crows would fuck him up. Me and Ida told the cops it was Pinto's body. We had to, or he'd have killed us."

"Pinto had a passport with Gibson's name on it. How?"

"Pinto knows guys from when he was in Deer Lodge. Guys in that business. They also give him a Wyoming driver's license. He and Gibson looked a lot alike anyway, same build, same size."

"And the money? Where does all his money come from?"

"The church. Our church. Pinto . . . Pinto is a priest. A roadman, for our church."

"What church?"

"Goyathlay's Throat."

"Goyathlay was Bedonkohe Apache. You're Comanche."

"Yeah, but now we're all part of the same church, all of us, Kiowa, Apache, Comanche. We all serve Goyathlay, who speaks through Peyote himself. Pinto is the new voice of Goyathlay. Pinto made a new way of calling Peyote. Instead of mescal buttons he had something new—datura root, also crystal meth, and this plant called salvia. Pinto used to run a meth lab over in Colorado before the DEA got on to him, and he studied on ways to make Peyote stronger. He found a whole new Peyote to preach with. So the word got around and our church grew. People began to come from everywhere, and Pinto charged a lot for the ceremony. I helped. We made good money."

"How?"

"People will pay a lot to talk with Peyote. Also from their confessions, when they see the god Peyote. Some people talk too much when Peyote is in their hearts. Pinto listens. Later, he tells them that the way to atone for the really bad sins is to give their money to our church. If they don't give the money, Pinto says that Peyote will come to the sinner's family, Peyote will tell the family what he did. If their sins are bad enough, the sinners will always pay."

"What does this have to do with Moot Gibson?"

"Like I said, Gibson was a white man who wanted to be a Comanche. He came down here six months ago, from up in Wyoming, he was angry with the U.S. government, they took away his horse farm, whatever, and he wanted to find out how to have magic power against them. He had heard about Goyathlay's Throat from some Apaches out in New Mexico, and he came here to see about being a part of a sing. Pinto let Gibson into a sing. They shared the new god Peyote. I don't know exactly what happened, but Gibson said something during the telling of sins, and Pinto went totally nuts."

"What did he do?"

"He took Gibson out to a hut near here, doped him up, real nice and respectful, got him to talk all about what his sins were—Gibson was like you, he was CIA. That's why you're here, isn't it? Pinto told me later that Gibson had killed his little sister Jewel and his niece Amber. Down on Interstate 25, maybe ten years ago, back in ninety-seven, they were trying to kill someone else—another Comanche, a woman named Consuelo Goliad. Anyway, Pinto got it all out of Gibson: who the other guys were, where they lived, all except the guy who went into the Jeep and broke her neck. Gibson called him 'the man in the long blue coat.' Swore he didn't know the man's real name. Said he was called 'Cicero.' Like a code name. Cicero. Gibson told Pinto that only Goliad was supposed to die, but things went haywire."

"Did Gibson name the man who was running the operation?"

"Somebody named Cole. Bob Cole. Something like that."

"And who was the actual killer? The man in the long blue coat?"

"*Cicero* was all he could get out of Gibson. Gibson never knew his real name. He wasn't a full-time member of their unit. Gibson called him 'the parachute pro.' Said he wasn't needed. Pinto talked him into trying to find out Cicero's real name, said that he couldn't be pure and find his spirit power unless he atoned for all of his sins."

"When was this?"

"Maybe three months ago. Man, by that time, Gibson was a real head case. Pinto dosed him up almost every day while he was getting the story out of him. Pinto can be real nice, talk low and soft, he can make you think he's a sweet guy, but he is *not* a nice guy."

"Did Gibson find out who the inside guy was? The man in the long blue coat?"

Horsecoat shook his head, lifted his palms. "No. And Pinto pushed him hard. Even when he was talking to Peyote himself, the guy had no idea. Pinto told him that there would be no forgiveness without atonement, and that could only happen when *all* the people who helped to kill Amber and Jewel were dead. But Gibson couldn't find out. He tried. Gone for days. But there was no way."

"That's not true. The man in the long blue coat is dead."

"I know. Pinto told me. Pinto went to England to find him."

"But you don't know how Pinto got Cicero's real name?"

"No. Maybe it was something in the wreck?"

"What wreck?"

"There's a big old Suburban down by the Apishapa. Been there for fucking years. Black. Has a corpse in it. That's where I found the Ruger, man. Honest. I didn't know it was illegal. I found it in the wreck."

"You found the wreck? Not Pinto?"

"No. I found it. I showed it to him later."

Dalton gave the man a long hard look and decided he was telling the truth. It made no sense, but it had the ring of truth.

"Okay. Where do I find Pinto?"

Horsecoat laughed, a strangled, mirthless rattle in a tight throat.

"Find Pinto? Pinto'll find *you*, man. He'll find us both."

"Where's this wrecked Suburban?"

"Like I said. Down there by the Apishapa. About a mile."

"Show me."

IRENE WOULDN'T LEAVE Moot Gibson's grave. When Dalton tried to take her by the collar, she bared her teeth at him, so Dalton left her there. It was deep-blue dark under a sky full of stars by the time they reached the dry wash of the Little Apishapa, a broad gully worn out of the grassland by the meandering course of the creek.

He stopped the pickup truck at the edge of a drop-off and they got out, Horsecoat walking a little ahead. A low line of sorrel and sage marked the edge of the arroyo. Horsecoat stopped there and looked back at Dalton, his eyes glittering in the glare of Dalton's flashlight. He extended his arm and pointed down.

"It's down there. Been there for ten years."

Dalton shone the beam downward into the darkness. The undercarriage of a large SUV, rusted and scaled, four tires coated in mud, part of a side panel that had once been black.

"You first."

Horsecoat led them as they slipped and slid down the bank, holding on to shrubs and skidding on their boot heels. Dalton came up hard against the rusted side of the Suburban. The ground was littered with broken glass, scraps of faded blue cloth, pieces of bone.

Dalton shone the flashlight beam into the interior of the truck. The skeleton of a large man was hanging upside down in the overturned truck, still strapped in. The skull had dropped off the vertebrae long ago, to be carried away by some large animal, and the torso had been attacked by crows and other foragers. Dalton looked at the rags and bones still suspended from the ceiling and knew that he was looking at the remains of Milo Tillman. He pulled his head out of the truck and stood there, looking at the wreck, while Horsecoat slouched against the bank. Did Milo Tillman get lost while going cross-country to avoid the cops? Did he just blunder into this arroyo and die here?

Or had he been killed by Porter Naumann, just to seal the case shut. Dalton figured he would never know.

One truth remained: Porter Naumann was the man in the long blue coat. The killer brought in to make sure Consuelo Goliad died in the accident. That's what Naumann did for years, before being reassigned to Burke and Single. Fremont's unit were not trained killers. But in this case they needed one and Langley had provided.

Dalton had read and reread Barbra Goldhawk's notes on the ac-

cident. It had been witnessed by hundreds of people. A man named
Lewis Dolarhyde, one of the witnesses, told the Colorado state police
that he had seen a man, a large middle-aged white male, tanned and
muscular, with blue eyes and a prominent, sharply beaked nose, very
well dressed, wearing a long blue overcoat, coming out of Consuelo
Goliad's wrecked Jeep. The description matched Naumann perfectly.

Consuelo Goliad's neck had been snapped, and the EMS crew
had noted that there were glove marks on her cheeks, marks still visible in the coating of explosive residue from her deployed air bag.
One hand on the cheekbone, the other under the victim's ear. Set
yourself, two or three hard jerks, down and up and down again—a
broken neck. Any strong man, any man trained to do it, could accomplish it in seconds.

He pulled out the fax sheet and held it up to the beam.

While he was staring down at the fax, Horsecoat pushed himself off the bank and came over to look.

"Where'd you get that?"

Dalton ignored the question. "What else did you find in this truck?"

"A big bag, full of papers. And some broken bits of pottery."

"Where is this stuff now?"

"The papers were all rotted. I tried to thaw them out, but they just turned into mush. What I could read was all numbers—groups of numbers—so I just took them out to the trash and dumped them."

"Where?"

"Big dump site back of Comanche Station. Covered over years ago. Gone. Long gone. Sorry."

"There's a big peak, in the Front Range. You can just see it from here. Way off in the southwest, but it stands out. What's it called?"

"That's Culebra. Fourteen thousand feet above sea level. Maybe more. Biggest peak in southeastern Colorado. We Comanches call this Culebra country. Snake country. Who did this drawing?"

"Moot Gibson."

"He drew that?"

"Yes."

"When?"

"About three months ago."

"That's Peyote, you know, in the center. But Pinto would never have let him draw something like that."

"Why not?"

"You never name the roadman."

"The roadman? The priest?"

"Yes. His real name is a secret. A sacred secret."

"Is Pinto's name here?"

Horsecoat tapped the sheet. "Yeah. Here . . . and here." He touched the word "hidden" and the word "struggle."

"That's his name," he said, speaking in a whisper.

"Pinto? His given name is Daniel Escondido."

" 'Lucha' was the name he took when he was sixteen. Like you say, his original name was Daniel. He named himself Lucha. *Lucha* is Spanish for the struggle. For the fight. And Escondido means—"

"Hidden."

"Yes. That's his clan name. They got it from the Mexicans, for killing so many of them and then just slipping away into the grass."

"What does this word mean? 'Deadead'?"

"I guess that's for Pinto."

"Deadead means Pinto?"

"No. It means DEA Dead. It's for those three federal agents who disappeared. Why they sent Pinto to jail. The DEA agents. Pinto liked to say that when they came down here they were DEA and when he left them they were DOA. He strung them up to a big old cottonwood over there by the Huerfano. Naked. Even the woman. Sliced off their eyelids and let the sun roast them. The woman lasted the longest, only because Pinto gave her water. Pinto used her a lot, so Bill Knife says, while she was hanging there, because it made him feel happy to hear her crying like that, her begging not to die, offering him whatever she could think of, praying for mercy. She did stuff to him, took him every which way, at the end Pinto says she told him she really loved him and would never ever tell the cops on him, but she died anyway. Pinto loves to hear people do that, asking for mercy, crying, saying they'll fuck him, suck him, do whatever he wants, whiny, pitiful, sorry shit like that. Pinto says he likes to breathe in the souls coming out of people while they're dying, says he can taste them on his tongue, breathe them in like sage smoke. It makes him smile. We used to go look at their bones when we were kids, but Bill Knife scared us off, told us never to go back there again, that it was a dead place, full of angry unhappy spirits."

The look on Dalton's face must have been more revealing than he intended, because Horsecoat shrugged his thin shoulders, raised his hands: "I know. I know. That's what Pinto does."

Dalton folded the paper up. "Let's go."

"Where we going?"

"Back to Moot's grave. To wait for Pinto."

"Man, we can't do that. I can't be there."

"Why not? You said he'd come for you?"

"Yeah. He'll come for both of us."

"You're part of his church. He won't hurt you."

Horsecoat shook his head. "You don't know him. Pinto's crazy. If he thinks I talked to you like I did, he'll kill me too. Bill Knife says Pinto has maggots in his head. I can't be here, man. Really. I can't be here."

"Then go."

Horsecoat looked around the arroyo, and then back at Dalton.

"I can leave?"

"Yes."

"Can I have the Ruger? Just in case Pinto doesn't believe me?"

Dalton racked the slide, clearing the magazine, and handed the weapon over. Horsecoat clutched it to his chest, as if it were a talisman that could really save him from something like Pinto. He knew that handing the kid a gun was an insane thing to do. Dalton didn't really care. He was half-mad already. He was the walking dead, and in the land of the half-mad, the walking dead is king. Besides, if the pistol gave Horsecoat the courage to go find Pinto, then it was worth the risk.

"How do you know I won't just go tell Pinto where you are?"

"I think that's what you should do. Maybe he'll let you live. You go out there and find him and tell him I'm here waiting."

"And you're just gonna sit there? Let him come for you?"

"Yes."

"Then you're a dead man."

"Yes. I'm a dead man. You tell Pinto that a dead man wants to see him. Tell him I'm waiting for him. Now go."

Horsecoat stared at him for a time, and then turned and ran, vanishing into the sweetgrass. Dalton heard the hissing of his passage through the dry grass, the thud of his running boots. After a while this faded to nothing and then there was only the faint ticking of the truck's engine cooling and the deep slow beating of his own heart.

FULL NIGHT; Dalton alone by the rock mound.

Irene lying asleep a few yards away, her side heaving, twitching in a dog's dream, her paws jerking as if she were chasing prey. The pickup truck engine had cooled enough to stop ticking long ago. The cold wind had increased, slicing down out of the Rockies, out of Culebra Peak, the jagged knifelike crest of the mountain cutting a black slice out of a sky filled with stars, filled with the wide, slowly undulating pink curtain of the Milky Way. The sweetgrass was hissing and tossing in the wind and a silvery light lay on the land. The air was sharper, colder, carrying the promise of snow.

Dalton was leaning back on the mound, the rough river stones still giving off some of the day's heat, his range jacket zipped tight, his collar up, holding the Colt in his left hand and feeling the slender shaft of a disposable hypodermic needle in his right. The needle was filled with Narcan. Maybe it would help. Maybe not. He was hungry and afraid and thinking about Florian's in Venice, about the light on Saint Mark's Basin, the taste of cold champagne on a hot afternoon. He did not expect to live through the night, but he found he could not leave. The world needed Pinto dead, and the work had come to him. Irene sat up and sniffed at the wind, whimpering. Dalton stood up and looked to the west, the breeze ruffling his collar as he faced into the wind. He saw a dark eddy in the waving grass.

He cocked the Colt.

He smelled eucalyptus and a nameless spice on the wind.

The world changed.

The sky grew very bright and he could feel the electric hum of the Milky Way on the back of his hands as it shimmered in the night sky. All the tall grasses around him turned into golden snakes, writhing and coiling. There were strange voices in their hissing, a song he could not quite understand, although the meaning seemed to float just beneath the surface of his mind, and he felt that if he concentrated on the song, the meaning would suddenly be revealed, and that revelation would be shattering, would open his soul to God and make him perfect.

Under the singing of the snakes he heard the clicking of the beetles busy in Moot Gibson's grave. Irene was beside him now, quivering, as a tall broad shape, surrounded by a corona of emerald green light, rose up out of the long grass on the far side of Moot Gibson's tomb. All the golden snakes faded away into silence, into a perfect stillness, so complete that Dalton could hear his own heart beating, a ragged fitful drumming.

"You're the man from Venice," said the figure across the grave, the deep voice low but carrying, a whisper full of menace and power.

"I am. You killed Porter Naumann."

Pinto shook his head and green flies buzzed up in a great cloud around him. He spoke out of the swarm, in the buzzing voice of a hive. "Peyote killed him. He could not survive the question."

"And the rest?"

"Rabbits are for eating. Who cares about them? Why should we talk? You have nothing to tell me. You have been given the breath of Peyote. I scattered it on the wind, while you sat there and dreamed about Italy. I could tell you to shoot yourself now, with that Colt in your hand, and you would do it. I could tell you to strangle that she-dog and you would do it. I told your friend to tear his face off and he ran away to do it. In a while I will tell you go to sleep and when you wake up I will have found something interesting to do with you."

Now Pinto's voice was no longer the voice of a swarm. It had changed into a deep drone, like a huge organ. He felt Pinto's spirit walking around in the bridges and streets of his skull, his boots echoing off the bone the way they had echoed off the cobblestones in the streets of Venice. His mouth was stuffed with cold wet clay, as if he were lying beside Moot Gibson already, and there were shining green beetles feeding in his brain.

Dalton slid a careful hand into his jacket pocket, closed it around the disposable hypodermic needle.

"Where's your spirit friend?" Pinto asked. "The green man."

Dalton searched for his voice, found it at last, a dry croak. "He's gone away."

"Too bad. He was with you in Venice."

"He saved me from your spider."

"You liked the spider? Here, a gift—"

He threw something across the rock mound, something green and on fire, spinning legs of green fire. It landed with a thump on the ground at Dalton's feet—a huge green spider.

Dalton squeezed his fist tight around the needle in his pocket, drove the tip deep into the palm, pressing the plunger. The Narcan rushed into his system, flooding it, driving everything before it.

Dalton stepped forward and crushed the green spider into the earth with the sole of his boot, feeling it pop under his sole.

Irene ran up the rock mound and launched herself at Pinto. Pinto slashed at her with a knife—Dalton saw the blood drops spray sideways across the sky, a constellation of rubies.

He lifted the Colt up. The gun kicked back. The muzzle flared, an expanding corona of fire that blazed like Andromeda.

Two.

Three.

Four.

Five.

Six rounds off, the big Colt leaping in his hands, his shoulders jerking back. Then the hammer, clacking and clacking and clacking on the empty chambers. Dalton stood there for a timeless period, blinking, his retinas still imprinted with the flaring galaxy of the muzzle blast, and then he stepped up onto the top of Moot Gibson's grave and looked down at the sweetgrass on the far side.

There was nothing there.

In the starlight Dalton could see a swath of crushed grasses, leading away into the open plains. He stepped off the mound and knelt down beside Irene. Her mouth was open and she was panting rapidly. He touched her ribs. Her heartbeat was faint but steady. The wound along her side gaped, and pink ribs showed. Dalton used his belt to wrap her chest, pinching the wound shut.

He patted her, stood up, took a ragged breath, and passed into the long grass with a hiss and a rustle, following Pinto's path. In the distance he could hear the sound of someone racing through the grass, and when he looked into the middle distance he could see a black shape, stumbling now.

He reloaded the Colt.

Kept walking.

Far overhead a crow soared, a black flutter against the star field. Down on the starlit grass plain beneath the crow's wings, the crow saw two dark figures moved through the waving grass, one man stumbling and staggering, the other man following, moving easily, coming on.

The crow wheeled higher and flew off toward Culebra.

AFTER A LONG TIME Pinto reached a stand of cottonwoods by an arroyo where the Little Apishapa used to run. By now Pinto's boots were full of blood and they squelched as he staggered forward toward the stand of trees, their bare branches pale in the starlight.

Pinto reached the clearing and fell forward against the trunk, wrapping himself around it, his bloody hands leaving black smears on the rough bark. He let his body slide to the ground, twisted; the pain in his belly was ferocious, like a wolf ripping at his guts.

He got his back against the tree and pulled out the long ivory-handled stiletto he wore in a sheath at his belt. Far out in the grassland he could see the tall figure of the man pursuing him.

Pinto lifted the Ruger, aimed the muzzle at the figure, pulled the trigger, a dry click. He threw the pistol down, laid the stiletto across his blood-soaked thighs, pulled in a long breath, and waited.

A few minutes later, Dalton walked out into the little clearing around the cottonwood tree, the Colt out, the muzzle steady.

Pinto looked up at him, his eyes dark, but two pale glints inside them. When he opened his mouth to speak, a black bubble formed, broke, and a ribbon of blood ran down his chin.

He began to laugh, a dry rattle.

"You know where you are?" asked Dalton.

"Yes. I am at my altar. This is where I tasted the government people. This is where I took the woman again and again. Her bones are here. And the two others."

"Why did you come here?"

"I like it here. It smells . . . good."

He pulled in a snuffling breath, like a dog taking a scent.

It ended in a wet cough.

"Three in my belly. You are a good chaser. I thought I had you, back in Wyoming, but you got onto the roof. I had to let you go."

"Here I am."

Pinto lifted the stiletto, turned it in the starlight.

Dalton could see the blue flicker along its edge, and beyond it Pinto's bloody smile in the darkness.

"I breathed your friend in. While he died. In that little church-yard. I leaned over him and sucked out his soul. He lasted a long time while I used this on him. I breathed him and I tasted him. He died hard. His pain was great. My face was the last thing he saw in this life."

"Why the women?"

"Rabbits are for eating. And I needed the pictures. While he was still with Peyote, I showed him what I had done to his wife. He took that with him when he died. I could see it in his face. It was . . . *fine*."

Pinto leaned forward, put a hand on the ground, got a knee un-der him, and pushed himself to his feet, bracing his back on the cot-tonwood trunk. His chest was heaving and his long silver hair hung down limply over his brutal face. He was drenched in blood from his chest to his knees; Dalton could smell his blood across the clearing. The stiletto glinted in his right hand and he lifted it into the starlight.

"I make no excuses. They killed my sister and her baby. Not that I cared much for them. But they were mine and not to be killed by anybody else. And killing all those people, that was pleasant. Did you find the one in Butte, the one I left alive? I enjoyed him very much."

Pinto jerked his arm.

Dalton moved to the left.

The stiletto hummed through the air.

Dalton brought the Colt up, but before he could squeeze the trigger, Pinto jerked suddenly forward. His chest blew wide open. Dalton saw thousands and thousands of glowing green maggots fly-ing out of his body. Bits of lung and bone spattered wetly on Dalton's boots.

From a long way away came the thunderclap sound of a heavy ri-fle, and then wind again, sighing in the sweetgrass.

Dalton walked over and looked down at Pinto.

His eyes were open and his mouth was working.

Dalton bent down over him. "Bill Knife says there are very bad spirits here."

Pinto was staring up at him.

"The spirits of the people you hung in the trees here."

Pinto's eyes grew wide.

A bubble of blood burst from his lips.

"I'm going to send you to *them*, Pinto. They are waiting."

Pinto opened his mouth to speak, but all that came out of it was a river of black blood. Pinto moved his head weakly, one hand raised, palm out, his eyes glimmering wetly in the starlight. Dalton placed the muzzle of the Colt against Pinto's forehead, pressed down hard, and squeezed the trigger. His face was the last thing Pinto saw in this life.

HE WAS STILL THERE, standing beside Pinto's corpse, when the old men came silently out of the sweetgrass, three of them, two carrying long Winchester rifles, their faces barely visible in the starlight.

One of them stepped forward, looked down at Pinto's body, and then up at Dalton.

"You okay, son? Not shot?"

"Not shot. I'm not quite right in the head."

"Pinto laid his powder on the wind. You'll be okay in a while."

"Why did *you* shoot him? I had the Colt."

Bill Knife looked down at Pinto's body. "He knew how to make Goyathlay speak again. But we saw that he had maggots in his head. He killed young Wilson Horsecoat, just over there, a blood-simple boy, but he was kin to us, and he was a Comanche. Pinto never killed a Comanche before. So we figured it was time for him to go. Where's the dog?"

"She's back at the grave. Pinto cut her up pretty bad."

"He did? Well, we'll go take a look at her. I got a question?"

"Sure."

"If the dog lives, can I have her? I do like a snake-mean dog."

Dalton gave the matter some thought.

"Tell you what. I'll trade you."

"For what?"

"An ax."

"Don't have an ax. Will a hatchet do?"

"That'll do."

The morning of the eighth day . . .

16

monday, october 22
carmel highlands home
pacific coast highway
carmel, california
4 p.m. local time

d alton drove slowly up the long curving driveway, through the wrought-iron gates, and into the cobblestoned courtyard, coming to a stop at the foot of a wide curving staircase. Dr. Cassel— a tall, white-haired woman with a high, clear forehead, sharp brown eyes, and a hawklike nose—stood at the top of the stairs, her pale-pink linen dress ruffling in the ocean wind. Behind her the carved Spanish doors stood open under a broad portico, the old mission-style hospital rising up behind, pink adobe walls and carved wooden window frames, balconies, vines climbing up, heavy with bright red and blue flowers.

As he climbed out of the car, she smiled and came down the steps to meet him, her slender hand out, heavy gold on her wrist. She folded him into her frail birdlike body and kissed him in the French manner, a touch of the lips on the left cheek, and then the right, while holding his shoulders with her surprisingly strong grip. She smelled the way the sea did, salt and cypress, flowers and the tangy scent of cedar smoke.

"Micah, so wonderful to see you."

Her expression altered as she looked up at him.

"You look terrible. Where have you been? No, no—I know you can't tell me. Come upstairs, I have a table set on the veranda. Have you eaten? You really need to . . ."

She talked away at him, a stream of comforting trivial chatter while she walked him up the stairs and into the cool dark of the lobby, the floor of polished terra-cotta tiles gleaming in a shaft of sunlight coming in from the seaward sunroom, curved dark beams rising up into the darkness above, the smell of fresh flowers, coffee, a few patients staring down at them from the upper landings in that detached appraising way that the very sick or the very old have, the feeling of having stepped aside, of being raised above the bittersweet onrushing tide of everyday life. Dalton waved at the bent figure of an old man in a navy blue blazer and pressed gray slacks, a crisp white shirt. The old man may even have recognized Dalton—he lifted an empty pipe with a thick gold band and waved back to Dalton, smiling broadly.

Dr. Cassel walked him out through the greenhouse solarium and onto a wide flower-filled stone veranda encircled by thick pillars of pale pink marble.

Down the cliff and through the cypress trees, the broad Pacific boomed and roared, green waves curling up and crashing down against the cliffs, white spray flying, while beyond this the thunder and boom of the endless sea, rolling away to the uttermost ends of the world.

She sat him down at a green-painted wrought-iron table with a pink linen tablecloth and poured him a glass of wine from a dripping silver decanter, another for herself, and sat back to smile at him over the rim of her goblet.

"I was so sorry to hear about Porter. He was a lovely man."

"He was."

"Will there be a funeral? I don't mean to pry. I know how delicate these things are in . . . in the company."

"There isn't, usually. But we've arranged a little ceremony in Cortona. That's where the body is. The Carabinieri have been holding it for us. A Major Brancati, he has arranged for a mass at the church of San Nicolò—"

"I know it. That scruffy little hut, without a steeple, high up in the town. Why there, for all love?"

"It's where Porter died," said Dalton, pressing down the image that the words brought flowing into the top of his mind. Dr. Cassel saw the pain in his eyes and regretted the question.

"Well, that's very lovely of the police there. Was Major Brancati a friend?"

"He became one. He was a great help in the investigation."

"When do you leave?"

"The mass will take place on the Wednesday. The thirty-first. Then I'll fly back with Porter's body on the first of November. There'll be a ceremony inside Langley and he'll go to his family's vault in Alexandria."

"So many deaths. His entire family?"

"Yes. And too many others."

"But you . . . you found the man? The killer?"

"We did."

There was a silence, and it drew out. They sat there together and watched the Pacific churning, the soft light far out on the sea.

Finally, Dr. Cassel spoke.

"Micah, are you sure? About Laura?"

He continued to look out at the ocean for a time, his face unreadable, thinking about Porter Naumann's ghost, half-expecting to see him materialize in the shining ocean light that filled the broad sunlit patio—perhaps a little disappointed—and then he reached for his glass.

"I am. I've thought about nothing else for days."

"It was a terrible, terrible thing. And so very much sadness . . ."

Her voice trailed away and Dalton let his mind follow hers. Racing through the front hall of his house in Quincy and out into the snowstorm, Laura's white stricken face, her hands clutching at him as he brushed by her, the emerald green carriage, the bundle of bright green blanket, and the two-foot-long icicle, tapered and glittering, falling like a lance from the overhanging eaves.

The baby pierced right through, the bright red blood bubbling up. Then the police, the hospital. The heavy silence of the empty halls in the half-light of dawn. Then came the recriminations, the accusations and counteraccusations, the searing guilt.

And months after their separation, the long silence, the unanswered calls in the middle of the night, her last message to him—asking him to come home.

The sealed garage and the dusty Cadillac running . . . running . . .

"Would you like to go and see her, Micah?"

He closed his eyes for a moment and then they got up and walked through the glass doors and back into the cool, dark interior. Up the curving stone stairs and down the long hall, their steps echoing, and into a bright sun-filled room, painted white, the gauzy curtains flaring inward on the warm wind off the sea, and Laura on her bed.

Pale, shrunken, turned on one side, in a pink-floral nightgown, her thin red hair brushed, her powdery white cheeks shining in the sunlight—the hiss and pump and chuff of the breathing tube, the machine in the stainless-steel shelving beside her, clicking and beeping and wheezing.

Dalton knelt down beside her and touched her cheek. Her lips were dry and cracked and the ventilator tube looked huge, obscene, where it punched through her throat. On the far side of the bed an

IV rack dripped fluids into her, and another tube ran out from under the sheets, draining into a tall plastic bottle.

Her eyes were closed—they looked sewn shut, like a mummy's, and the lids were pale blue.

"Shall I leave you for a while?" asked Dr. Cassel.

"Yes. For a while."

"You know what to do, don't you?"

"Yes."

"And you're sure?"

"Yes. I'm sure."

She laid a hand on his shoulder, and then left the room, closing the door softly behind her. Dalton touched Laura's cheek and then sat down on the bedside chair, drawing in close. He leaned into her, near enough to breathe her in, folded his hands together between his knees, and began to speak to her, a low baritone whisper, like a father reading a bedtime story to a child on the edge of sleep. He spoke to her for a long, long time while the light slowly changed in the room, while a broad rectangle of sun slowly crawled across the wooden floor until it reached the wall, where it began to climb, changing as it did so from yellow to gold to purple.

There was a brief flaring of orange light as the sun went down, and then it was evening, and during all this time he talked to her, talked and talked to her, pouring his heart into her delicate pearl-colored ear, his breath on her cheek. He talked their whole life through, from Boston to Cortona to Quincy, remembered it all for both of them, remembered every single moment of it.

And through it all she lay there on her side with her small twiglike hands curled under her and her pale withered limbs contorted as if in pain. Feeling nothing. Dreaming nothing. Being nothing.

Finally, after a timeless interval during which he had no more words to speak and he was feeling far more than he could bear, he kissed her lightly on the cheek, stroked her cold damp forehead, reached over to the machine, and flicked it off. The silence that came into the room then was shattering in its intensity and he began to cry.

At some later point during the night—he had no sense of time—he felt a subtle and powerful change in her, a deeper stillness come over her, and he knew that if this was truly where his loving wife had been all these long years, abandoned and unforgiven in this sterile room, she was no longer present, she had gone away from him, and he was now completely alone in the living world.

IN THE MORNING, as he was leaving, after Dr. Cassel had promised to make the necessary arrangements for Laura—she was to be buried where their baby had been laid down years ago, in Laura's family crypt in Boston—he walked down the stairs toward a cool fresh morning, feeling as if he were made of lead and his blood was quicksilver. In a shadowed portico by the open door he saw the figure of a tall man sitting in a wicker peacock chair, legs crossed, hands folded in his lap. It was Porter Naumann.

"Micah," said Porter, "that was well done."

Dalton came into the little portico and looked down at Naumann. He looked very good, for a dead man; he had changed his clothes. Now he was wearing a well-cut dark blue pinstripe suit, gleaming black wingtips, pale pink socks, and a matching pink shirt, open at the neck.

Dalton saw that Naumann had his Chopard back on his wrist.

"You got your watch?"

Naumann looked down at it, smiled up at Dalton. "No. Bought a new one."

"Dante's? Third circle?"

Naumann's smile faded; his expression turned solemn.

"You have company, Micah. Out in the yard."

"I do?"

"Yes. Be careful. See you soon."

Naumann's image wavered, faded. There was nothing in the peacock chair but a faint trace of navy blue mist. A wind blew in from the open window, smelling of oranges, and swept it away. Dalton stepped out into the hard sunlight and saw Jack Stallworth leaning on the hood of a long black limousine.

The engine was idling, rocking the big car gently on its springs. The windows were tinted black and two Agency bulls were standing on either side of the stairs as he came down onto the stones of the courtyard, one blond and one black, both with their suit jackets open, both staring fixedly at him. Jack came forward with his hand out.

"Micah. I'm glad we caught you."

"Where the hell have you been, Jack? You've been out of touch since October fourteen. Today's the twenty-third."

Jack's face hardened up. "Company business, Micah. I don't report to you."

"I was running an investigation. You left Sally flat-footed."

"I hear she did just fine."

"Look. We'll do this later. Have a nice day."

"Micah, don't walk away from this."

"My wife died last night. This is not the time."

"I know. I know. I'm sorry, Micah. I really am. But this can't wait. We need to talk."

"Who's in the hearse?"

"The Vicar."

"I'm not getting in that limo, Jack."

"I wish you would, Micah. It's important."

"Not to me."

"Micah, he's not just going to let you walk. See him now or see him later. You know how it is."

Dalton looked past Stallworth's shoulder at the long black machine, idling gently, sunlight dappling the gleaming body. "I need to know a couple of things."

"Sure. Ask away."

"Was Bob Cole running Fremont's unit."

"Yes."

"Our Bob Cole? The guy who burned himself in Spokane?"

"Yeah."

"He ran Fremont?"

"And two other units. He cocoordinated ops for the entire Mountain Zone."

"You never told me that."

"You're a cleaner, Micah. You didn't need to know."

"You told me Bob was strictly desk. Not a field man."

"And that's the truth. After the Trinidad thing he was never the same. No good in the field."

"He really did commit suicide? Nobody helped him?"

"Not that I'm aware."

Dalton looked at him. Stallworth held the look.

"Who was Cicero?" asked Dalton, watching Stallworth's neck.

"Naumann was Cicero."

Stallworth's throat worked a little.

"Did Bob Cole know who Cicero was?"

"Sure. Bob would have cocoordinated the whole thing."

"Is it possible that Bob leaked Porter's real name?"

Stallworth shrugged. "Not like him. He was a pro. But things go wrong."

"If not Bob, then who? Did you know about Porter?"

"I was responsible for the Echelon end of it in those days, not the field units."

"That's not an answer."

"Fuck you, Micah. I didn't give anybody Porter's name."

"Somebody did."

"It must have been Bob Cole, then."

"Can't ask him, can we? Everybody's dead but you and me."

"Why the fuck would I give out Porter's name?"

"I don't know."

"You really think I did? Even accidentally?"

A silence, eyes locked, and a stillness between them.

"No," said Dalton, finally. "No I don't. I just can't figure it out."

"Real life's messy. Real life is one damn thing after another."

"Yeah. And Consuelo Goliad was one of them?"

"That's what the Vicar wants to talk to you about."

"In a minute. I'm right, though. Porter killed her, didn't he?"

"Yes. He was brought in for that. To make sure."

"Who was in on the job?"

"Fremont drove a Freightways trailer. Milo Tillman and Pete Kearney were in an ambulance. Moot Gibson and Crucio Churriga in blocking cars. And Al Runciman was in a Colorado state police car."

"A lot of innocent people got killed that day, Jack."

"Yes. Too many. It was badly designed. Bob Cole took it hard."

"Why didn't you tell me all this?"

"The Vicar wouldn't let me. He said to turn you loose on it and see what happened. If you needed to know, then we'd tell you."

"Did you know who was killing the guys in Fremont's unit?"

"No. That's the truth. But now we do. Thanks to you."

Dalton stared at Stallworth, the sea wind stirring his hair, his face hard and distant. In his chest there was a heaviness, a numbness, and he figured it was just this numbness that Stallworth had been counting on.

"Why is *he* here?"

Stallworth turned around and looked at the limo. "He thinks we owe it to you."

"Owe it to me?"

"Yes. Will you talk to him?"

"Do I have a choice?"

"Not really."

"All right. Let's go talk to the man."

Stallworth's face relaxed. He smiled briefly, said "Thanks," and walked over to the rear door. Someone inside pressed the locking key and the door slid open. Cool air poured out, along with the scent of new leather. The interior was done in black, with subtle highlights of brass and rosewood.

A frail old man, long and lean, with a cadaverous face and large bony hands, leaned out from the dark interior, showing his teeth, large and yellow, his face wreathed and veined, his watery blue eyes clear and full of intelligence.

He put out a liver-spotted hand, pale as a cod.

"Micah, it's a pleasure."

Dalton took the man's hand, a firm steely grip, released it.

"Mine too, sir."

"Join me for a moment, will you?"

Cather slid over and Dalton got into the car. Stallworth stayed outside, walking away to share a cigarette with Cather's guards. Cather pulled away into the far corner of the limousine, his back up against the other door, his long legs crossed at the knee.

He was wearing a dark blue pinstripe suit, a pale blue shirt, a tie with pale blue stars on a field of deep, rich gold silk. He folded his long hands over his crossed knee and regarded Dalton through heavy-lidded unblinking eyes, radiating immense calm and a complete lack of human feeling of any recognizable kind.

Dalton believed it was quite possible that he would never get out of this car alive, a feeling that Cather was well aware of, and one he liked to encourage.

"You've been very effective, Micah," he said, in his dry croak.

"Thank you, sir."

"I knew Porter well. I regret his loss extremely."

"So do I."

"I read your report. A marvel of concision. If I infer correctly, it appears that someone in our firm was indiscreet concerning Porter's identity. You name no one. Do you have a particular view?"

"Yes."

"Will you share it?"

"Jack thinks it might have been Bob Cole."

"I recall him. A troubled man. Do you find this plausible?"

"I find it convenient."

The lines of Cather's face deepened and his lips grew thinner.

"Are you proposing that one of our people was simply indiscreet, or that one of our people was an accessory to Porter's murder?"

"I don't know. No. Of course not."

"You yourself conducted the postmortem investigation. Did you uncover anything—anything at all—that would lead you believe that someone in the firm had a motive, however tenuous, for exposing Porter Naumann to this murderous Pinto person?"

"No. There was nothing. The only link was through the Goliad operation that afternoon in ninety-seven."

"Nothing else presents itself to your agile, searching mind?"

"No."

"So your sole discomfort here arises from this missing element?"

"Yes."

"Has it been your experience that one's affairs are always in order and that all of life's conundrums will eventually be made clear?"

Dalton smiled, shook his head. Cather bowed, offered a wintry smile in return, and then spoke in a changed tone.

"I understand your wife has just passed away."

"Yes."

"You have my deepest sympathy. My wife died many years ago. Not a day goes by that I do not wish for one more afternoon with her. I would like to make a few broad statements concerning intelligence in general that you may find illuminating, Micah. May I go on?"

"Please."

"Thank you. Firstly, you are aware of the problem of China. The problem of North Korea. The ongoing problems of Iran and Iraq. The general strategic concerns that China—and in a lesser way North Korea and Iran—present. The government of North Korea is very intelligent but effectively insane. To an extent, this is an affectation, a bargaining device, but like all affectations, if allowed to become unnaturally prolonged, as it has, the appearance becomes—may even drive—reality. As for China, her interests will be in direct and possibly violent competition with ours within ten years. Even now she seeks—and has partially acquired—significant strategic nuclear missile capability. North Korea has several sites that would allow her to launch nuclear strikes against many points in the Southeast Asian and Japanese archipelagos. Including Guam, which you may have heard the president refer to recently as 'the next Pearl Harbor.' North Korea and Iran have also demonstrated a willingness—one might say a vulgar willingness—to sell tactical nuclear capability to any and all comers, provided they have ready cash and undertake not to use them against the seller. This is the toxic climate of the new millennium. The new Cold War, we might say. And in this dangerous new world we must use whatever tools we have at hand. You understand that in these matters I offer only a general view, a view that does not necessarily reflect the strategic or even the tactical thinking of the current administration?"

Dalton inclined his head, said nothing.

"Fine. Taking all of this into account, we have learned to greatly value those . . . assets . . . that we have managed to maintain in diverse parts of the world. One of those assets—and in this matter I speak with the utmost faith in your patriotism and your discretion,

Micah, the utmost faith—one of those assets has been for many years and remains to this day a highly placed figure in a company known as FrancoVentus Mondiale. You are familiar with this firm?"

"I have heard of it."

"Yes. You have. Unfortunately, due to a regrettable laxity on the part of some people in a company known as Red Shift Laser Acoustics in Simi Valley, trusted ex-Agency people who had provided an encrypted server that was acting as a blind relay for sensitive communications from this asset in Paris, an employee of Red Shift became convinced that some irregularities had occurred. In a misguided access of patriotic fervor, she attempted to draw some official attention to this matter. An attempt was made to discourage her—in some ways a heavy-handed attempt. I name no names. She made the decision to contact more inappropriate agencies. Steps were taken to minimize this developing problem, but in one of those odd and untimely coincidences in which covert history is rich, her husband was killed in a genuinely accidental—I stress the truth of this—*accidental* crash of a light plane. This event triggered an extremely paranoid reaction and persuaded the individual to illegally acquire evidentiary material with the clearly stated intention of sharing it with a local investigative reporter. This rash decision would have, if exposed in a national forum, led to the slight but real possibility that our asset in Paris might have come under some vague suspicion. Since this asset was in a position to share with us critical information regarding the development of North Korean and Chinese missile-propulsion systems—FrancoVentus has long been illegally sharing this sort of technology with our competition around the world, overtures had already been made to Hussein's regime in Iraq at the time—well, it seemed advisable, although deeply regrettable, that steps be taken to prevent this person from following through on her attempts to destabilize a very important element in our general struggle against the forces of totalitarian extremism around the globe."

Here he reached a natural pause during which he looked at Dalton as if to judge whether his points had been well taken.

"So I lay this before you, out of a sense of grateful obligation for your recent exertions on behalf of your country, and with the greatest regard for your loyalty and your love of freedom. I find it strangely lyrical that such far-reaching and supranational matters should in some way be played out in a field of sweetgrass in southeastern Colorado or in a rather garish double-wide trailer in the suburbs of Simi Valley. Or even here, in this paradisiacal enclave on the shores of the blue Pacific. I'll say good bye to you now, Mr. Dalton, and once again allow me to express our deepest sympathy for the loss of your lovely wife."

17

thursday, october 25
17 wilton row, belgravia
london, england
10 p.m. local time

dalton was lying on his black leather couch in the living room of his stark, inhumanly stark, upstairs flat in Wilton Row, the room lit only by burning candles. Dalton, shirtless, wearing a pair of faded jeans and one white sock, was listening to the torrential rain drumming against his windows and rattling the roof tiles while diligently working his way through a third bottle of Bollinger.

The doorbell chimed in the hall.

He got up, steadied himself with a hand on the back of the couch, and negotiated the long hallway with care—the walls had a tendency to blur and waver and the floor was for some reason not quite level. He keyed the intercom button and said something that he hoped was intelligible into the mike. A disembodied female replied.

"Micah, it's Mandy. I know it's late—"

"Not at all, my dove. I was just—"

"May I come up?"

"Up? Up here? Of course. Here you go—"

He leaned his forehead against the intercom casing and fumbled with the button for a while, his heavy lids closing, then he pushed himself off the wall and maneuvered his meticulous way back into the kitchen, where, after a few minor mischances, he managed to get some coffee brewing; coffee, since Mandy, like all right-thinking people, detested tea—an insipid footwash, she had once called it. The pot was filling nicely and he stood there watching it for a time, idly wondering where the thumping sound was coming from.

"Micah, it's me. Open up."

That voice—it was oddly familiar.

Could it be Mandy Pownall?

At the door?

He decided to look.

It was.

She stood there in the hallway, her arms full of papers and boxes, her face pale in the soft glow of the hallway light. She was wearing a black silk Dragon Lady number and was done up perfectly, hair piled up into a kind of silvery tiara, a pale elegant face, slightly drawn, her lips outlined in black, her eyes shadowy, with a greenish light in them.

"Oh, bloody hell, Micah. You're completely potted."

"Am I?"

She swept past him and went down the hall with her burden of papers and boxes, trailing the scent of frangipani and musk. He watched her as she walked away and reminded himself that, first of all, he was drunk, quite triumphantly drunk, and therefore quite out of the running, and, second, that this was Mandy Pownall, the Virgin Queen of London Sector and old enough to be his . . . his aunt.

He followed her down the hall, using the wall to guide him, and found her behind his granite countertop, searching for coffee cups, straining to reach an upper shelf. The black kimono rode up her thighs and Dalton could see that she was wearing stockings and a garter belt. Seamed stockings at that.

She turned and saw him staring at her legs.

"Oh stow that, boyo. You're no use to anyone right now."

"I have been known to rise to that sort of challenge."

"Not with me, you manky git. Have some coffee."

"I do not desire coffee," he said, with some precision. "I will however have some more Bolly."

He looked around, blinking.

The bottle was nowhere to be seen.

"What have you done with my Bolly?"

Mandy set a cup of black coffee down in front of him. He eyed it as if it were a beaker of bunker sea oil.

"Drink it."

"I would rather set my nose hairs on fire."

She reached for a candle and held it up to his nose. "Here you go, then."

He waved it off, and sat heavily down on one of the bar stools.

"To what do I owe . . . ?"

"Serena Morgenstern told me you've been hiding out up here for two whole days, getting yourself as pissed as a lord."

"Bright girl. Clever. Notices things. I was going to say 'perspicacious,' but I didn't think I could manage it."

"You look like hell."

"You, on the other hand, look like Hedy Lamarr."

"You mean Mata Hari, don't you?"

"Her too."

"Are you coming back to work?"

"In the fullness of time, Mandy. Can't you see I'm in mourning?"

"Laura wouldn't want to see you like this."

"Don't you kid yourself. Laura was a cool hand with the Bolly herself. I recall a New Year's Eve party in Chicago where she was inspired to do a rather memorable striptease on the bar of the Nikko; management was very exercised about it. God she had wonderful legs. And all those present agreed that her breasts were splendid. Both of them, although I tended to prefer the one on the right. Her right, not mine. I named them, you know? Muffin and Scooter. Scooter was the other one. God bless them both. I find it odd that women do not generally make it a practice to name their naughty bits. I mean, consider the possibilities. Not too late for you, dear. Have you ever—"

"No. I haven't."

"Didn't think so. Would you like to know the name of my—"

"No, I would not."

"You're sure? It's quite clever. A play on the Gaelic word for—"

"*Very* sure."

"Well then, as Marcel Proust once remarked, *Où sont les meubles de ma tante?* Here's to the remembrance of things past. Here's to Muffin and Scooter, lost and gone forever. Where's my drink?"

Mandy raised the coffee.

He took it with a sigh. "I see the forces of moral improvement are upon us. How may I assist you to the door, sweetheart? Or would you prefer a window? I have several, all of them offering speedy access to the cobbles that lie beneath."

Mandy, ignoring him, was unpacking what looked to be company files from a battered cardboard box. She set them down in front of Dalton and placed a small stainless-steel laptop computer on top of the files.

He drank some coffee while she did this, staring dully at the files and thinking that they looked familiar. "This stuff is from Porter's desk at Burke and Single."

"Correct," said Mandy, looking at him with her head tilted to one side, her expression unreadable, guarded.

"What are you doing with it? We're not allowed to bring that stuff home."

"Did you love Porter, Micah?"

Dalton blinked at her. Her dark eyes were fixed on his.

"Love Porter? Love's a big word—"

"I did."

"I know, Mandy—it's a damn—"

"We were lovers. You understand? Micah, try to concentrate."

"Lovers? You and Porter?"

"Yes. For years."

Dalton set the coffee cup down and rubbed his face, trying to clear his head. Mandy refilled his cup and watched him in silence.

"Okay. Lovers. Yes, well that's . . . that's fine. I'm glad."

"I'm glad you're glad. That's not the point. All of this stuff is supposed to go to Jack Stallworth by the diplomatic pouch."

"When?"

She looked at the clock on the wall of the kitchen. "About two hours ago."

"You didn't send it?"

"No. Micah, are you functioning yet?"

"I'm getting there."

"So did you love Porter?"

He looked at her carefully for a while. "Yes. I guess I did. He was a fine man—"

"I need your help. I can't send this to Langley until I get it."

"What do you want me to do?"

"You asked me to turn Porter's life upside down. Remember? In the bathroom at Porter's house?"

"Yes. I do."

She handed Dalton a dark blue business envelope. His name was written on the envelope. In the upper left corner were the letters PN.

"It was in my lingerie drawer. In my flat. Taped to the back of the drawer. It's been there for a while, I think."

Dalton held the envelope under the downlight from a halogen, tapped it against his palm. "What's this about, Mandy. You're dead serious, aren't you?"

"I am. Look at this."

She showed him a page of numbers.

He blinked down at it. "Numbers are not my strong suit."

"This is one of the Burke and Single accounts that Porter was handling. Five years ago a lot of funds started to move out of this account. I haven't been able to trace all of it, but nine point seven million dollars went to the purchase of a ship. A cruise ship."

"Nine million dollars?"

"Yes. A French ship, fitted out as a hospital ship—originally *La Celestine,* based in the Philippines. She was reflagged under a Tongan registry and renamed the *Orpheus.*"

"Who owns her?"

"No idea."

"Are you suggesting that Porter has been using Burke and Single funds to pay for a French hospital ship? And why would he, anyway? What would Naumann want with a cruise ship? Mandy, this is just paranoid bullshit. There has to be—"

"Open the envelope, Micah."

"You've already read it, haven't you?"

"Yes."

He peeled the cover back and extracted a satellite photo of two ships, one white and one matte gray, moored very close together, somewhere at sea, and a single pale blue sheet.

—**February 17 2005**—Osama Hassan Nasr—Milan disappeared—
whereabouts unknown

—**February 13 2005** Orpheus moored off Venice

—**March 19 2006**—Hamidullah Kadhr—killed in crash of private
plane off Cagayan de Oro in Mindanao—no wreckage found—

—**March 21 2006** Orpheus docks in Guam

—**September 8 2006**—Aphostikos Sidheros—plane drops off
radar en route to Rhodes

—**September 15 2006** Orpheus off coast of Naxos

—**June 10 2007**—Musaf Ali Mabri—Deputy Chief Pakistani
Intelligence Agency—dies in crash of light plane while vacationing
in Alexandria

—**June 5 2007** Orpheus seen off Cyprus

—photo: NRO Condor Six—Orpheus in International Waters off
coast of Ireland, being refueled by MT Montauk Tanker—

August 11 2007 0923 hours

Dalton looked at the satellite shot again; digitally enhanced, the
shot showed two long ships, surrounded by very heavy seas—one a
white-painted cruise ship and the other a long wide-bodied tanker—
with a boom slung between and some kind of heavy cable, or a fuel
pipe, stretched between them.

"I looked up the MT *Montauk*, Micah. It's leased to Sea Lift
Command. It's a shallow-draft tanker capable of mounting what's
called 'under-way refueling,' operated by the Defense Department.
And here it is linked to a 'private ship' a hundred miles off the coast
of Ireland. What does all this look like to you?"

Dalton rubbed his forehead, fighting a headache. "It looks
like . . . what's the word?"

"Extraordinary rendition."

"Yes. It looks like we're arranging the crash—"

"Or faking the boarding in the first place—"

"—of various light planes in order to cover the kidnapping of
these men. I know the first guy here—"

"Osama Moustaka Hassan Nasr," said Mandy. "He's a terrorist."

"Yeah. He was scooped by one of our ER teams, right off the street in Milan. Some Italian prosecutor has indicted thirteen of our guys for it, or tried to. Hamidullah Kadhr is an al Qaeda computer tech. If we actually have him alive that's a very good thing."

"Especially if al Qaeda thinks he died in a plane crash."

"Aphostikos Sidheros. We know he was funneling money to the Chechens. And this guy Musaf Ali Mabri, second in command of the Pakistani Intelligence Agency. Half of the Pakistani intel units are al Qaeda sympathizers. He's one. Christ, this is a beautiful operation!"

"Yes. I suppose it is," said Mandy, doubt in her tone.

"They're using the *Orpheus* to hold them. Man, a hospital ship. In international waters. Completely secure. No tiresome visits from Amnesty International or the Human Rights Watch. Medical facilities on board. Lots of room for holding cells. Psych wards. They could take these guys apart cell by cell—"

"At sea no one can hear you scream?"

"Yeah . . . Man, forget Gitmo. It's brilliant! Perfect! A textbook black op. Mandy, this is—"

"Micah, listen to me. This is why Porter was killed."

friday, october 26
231 belle haven estates
huntington, virginia
5 p.m. local time

Stallworth's estate took up half a mile of frontage along the Potomac, a rambling Frank Lloyd Wright home composed of red cedar and tinted glass and square beams, hidden from the gate by a stand of old-growth oaks. The setting sun was casting long shadows across the well-groomed lawn, and a fountain jetting up from a formal garden sparkled with golden lights. Dalton walked around the house and found Jack Stallworth in his greenhouse down by the Potomac—a long, glassed-in Japanese-style building with a pressurized double door that hissed when he pushed it open. The interior was easily ninety degrees, the walls ran with mist, and a pale fog hung over the rows and rows of exotic plants that filled the interior. Stallworth called from somewhere deep in a jungle of ferns and vines in a far corner.

"That you, Micah?"

"Yes."

"Back here. Mind the stones. They're a little slick."

Dalton walked down between two low brick tables and pushed aside a stand of sago palm. Stallworth, in jeans and a plaid shirt, was kneeling in front of a large Japanese urn, pushing peat into the rim.

"Nice to see you. Thought you were in London."

Dalton laid the blue envelope on the lip of the urn. Stallworth peered at it over the rim of his glasses, and then looked up at Dalton.

"What's this? You resigning?"

"No. Better read it."

Stallworth wiped his muddy hands on a rag and opened the envelope. He stared down at the satellite shot and then slowly scanned the single page of type. He finished, folded it in three, put it back inside the envelope along with the satellite shot, and handed the envelope back to Dalton. "You best forget you ever saw that, Micah."

"We're running a dark operation, aren't we?"

"Yes. Leave it—"

"The Agency bought the *Orpheus* and we're moving it around the globe. A floating prison. Coordinating with rendition operations. Only we don't have to worry about borrowing Gulfstreams from sports team owners or friends in Wall Street. Because we have our ship right there."

"Damn right."

"Yes. I have no problem with this."

"Then what . . ."

"It's lovely. No FISA court. No ACLU crap about wiretaps or extraordinary rendition or pissing off a prosecutor in Milan."

"Yes. We agree. So what are you so angry about?"

"You gave Porter up to that Comanche, didn't you?"

Stallworth shrugged, straightened up, put a hip on the edge of the urn, and folded his arms across his chest.

"What's this? Revenge?"

"Just curious."

"Porter was *curious* too."

Out of the corner of his eye, Dalton saw a flicker of navy blue. He glanced to his left and saw Naumann's ghost standing by the glass wall, in his blue pinstripe, arms folded, staring at Stallworth, his face set. He inclined his head to Dalton and looked back at Stallworth, who had been watching Dalton's face.

"What are you looking at?"

"Nothing," said Dalton. "You said Porter was curious?"

Stallworth looked away, breathed in, sighed it out. "The *Orpheus* project is critical to our survival."

"I can accept that. I even agree. What I don't get is exactly how Porter was a threat to it."

Naumann's body had become rigid, his face tight. He never took his eyes off Stallworth. Dalton half-expected Stallworth to feel Naumann's glare.

But of course, Naumann wasn't really there at all, was he?

"Porter was a threat."

"How?"

"He was questioning the funding."

"Questioning the funding? What do you mean?"

"He thought far too much money was going out. He disapproved of some of the expenditures. He thought they were ambiguous and might be construed as fraud—in a way, as skimming the funds for personal uses. He wanted to formalize the accountings. He thought that one day there'd be a Senate inquiry—he said that these things will always come out eventually—and he didn't want the cash flow to look . . . irregular. He wanted us to bring in the GAO and take the *Orpheus* project onto the black books of the budget. The rest of us disagreed."

"Who's the rest of us?"

"Reliable men."

"Cather?"

"Of course. The whole thing was his idea."

"Porter would never have compromised the *Orpheus* project."

"No. But he was ready to compromise *us*."

Dalton studied Stallworth's face for a time, a look that Stallworth returned with quiet malice and no trace of unease at all. A kind of half smile played around his hard mouth and his small eyes were cold. Across the little greenhouse space Naumann's figure was still, his expression closed, his eyes dark. Through his body a beam of pale sunlight lay on the broad leaves of a towering fern. Naumann seemed to be wrapped in this warm light, as if it were coming from inside him.

Dalton looked back at Stallworth.

"Who gave Porter's name to Pinto?"

"I really don't know. Someone on Cather's team."

"How did you know that Pinto wanted it?"

"Jesus. The man actually called Personnel pretending to be Gibson. Personnel bounced the call to Bob Cole and Cole pushed it on to me. It wasn't hard to figure out what he was looking for."

"Why not just kill Porter yourself?"

"You."

"Me."

"Yeah. You would never have let it go. We needed somebody for you to hunt. And you did a *fine* job, Micah. We're all extremely—"

"What about his family? Joanne? And the girls?"

"We had no idea Pinto would . . . that was unfortunate."

"Send him to me," said Naumann, speaking softly.

Dalton turned to look at Naumann. "Send him to you?"

Naumann nodded.

Stallworth blinked at Dalton. "Who are you talking to?"

"Porter."

Stallworth's faced went pale, and he raised his hands.

"Porter? Micah, listen . . ."

"Send him, Micah," said Naumann. "Send him now."

Dalton pulled out the Ruger and shot Stallworth three times, two in the forehead, one in the heart.

Then he put the weapon back inside his suit pocket, smiled at Naumann's ghost, took a long ragged breath, and walked away.

19

monday, october 22
colorado highway patrol hq
butte, montana
10 a.m. local time

Captain Bo Cutler was leaning back in his office chair, boots on the desk, staring out at the smoke rising from the slag heap over the crest of Copper Butte when Coy Brutton knocked on the doorjamb.

"What you got there, Coy?"

"Federal Express. For you."

Coy lifted up a package about the size and shape of a beer cooler.

"Who's it from?"

"Don't say, Captain."

"You scanned it?"

"Jesus, no. Should I?"

"Ah hell. Give it here."

Coy walked it over, set the box down on Cutler's desk.

"Gimme a knife there, Coy."

"You think maybe we should call the fire guys?"

"Why? Do I smolder? Am I in flames?"

"Okay, okay. Ease up. Here you go."

He handed Cutler an old Ka-Bar, which Cutler used to slice the white plastic wrap off the package. He slid the wrap down, set it aside, and lifted the box up. It *was* a beer cooler, and it was heavy. He shook it. Something inside it thumped.

Coy backed away from the desk.

Cutler sighed and ran the tip of the blade around the tape sealing the top of the cooler. He put the knife down and lifted the lid off the box. Inside it, covered in melting ice and sealed inside a large Ziploc bag like the ones used to hold cabbages, was a human head. It had been cut off at the collarbones. "Hacked off" was a better description. There was a large star-shaped hole in the forehead, and most of the back of the skull seemed to be missing. The expression on the dark-blue face was one of fear, and the open eyes, though dull and clotted and opaque, still held a look of horror, of mortal dread. Around the severed head was a corona of matted hair, silvery, very long. In the bottom of the box, underneath the head, was a long ivory-handled stiletto. The handle looked as if it had dried blood on it.

"What the *hell* is this?" said Coy, his face green, his mouth dry.

"This," said Bo Cutler, lifting the head up, "is a promise kept."

:REPORT ENDS: PD/GH/OTP/cc NSC
:FILE ARCHIVED AND SEALED.

NOTE: Subject DALTON, Micah, whereabouts currently unknown. All Stations detain subject on sighting. Venice Station covert monitoring VASARI, A., and BRANCATI, A. If subject detained, DO NOT INTERRO-GATE. Quarantine and hold for immediate transfer to DC. All further inquiries related to DALTON, Micah *must be referred to DC/DGI/DNI without exception.*

By Order:
D. Cather, DC/DGI